"... WANT YOU IN MY LIFE."

Garrick's rough velvet voice stroked like passion against her ear. "Stay with me."

Nessa marveled at her husband's words. Only in her dreams could he love one such as she . . . but if 'twas the only way it could be true, then she'd pray to never awaken.

"You are everything I secretly longed for," she confessed. Her words dissolved into throbbing silence as his mouth took the ardent offering of hers with restrained ferocity.

Far beyond rational thought, she tugged at his tunic. She wanted his clothing out of the way, wanted to smooth her fingers down the strength of his body.

Seduced by her glorious abandon, Garrick shuddered and jerked away to quickly divest himself of the last barrier to the melding of flesh to flesh. In silent praise her hands explored his magnificent form, moving up to measure the width of his shoulders with awe. Reveling in this contact with his powerful body, the clean male scent of him, she leaned forward and her small, pointed tongue ventured forward to taste him as he had tasted her . . .

Books by Marylyle Rogers

Dragon's Fire
Wary Hearts

Published by POCKET BOOKS

Wary Hearts

Marylyle Rogers

POCKET BOOKS

New York   London   Toronto   Sydney   Tokyo

This book is a work of historical fiction. Names, characters, places and incidents relating to non-historical figures are either the product of the author's imagination or are used fictitiously. Any resemblance of such non-historical incidents, places or figures to actual events or locales or persons, living or dead, is entirely coincidental.

An *Original* Publication of POCKET BOOKS

POCKET BOOKS, a division of Simon & Schuster Inc.
1230 Avenue of the Americas, New York, NY 10020

Copyright © 1988 by Marylyle Rogers
Cover art copyright © 1988 Sharon Spiak

ISBN: 0-671-65879-4

First Pocket Books printing November 1988

10 9 8 7 6 5 4 3 2 1

POCKET and colophon are trademarks of Simon & Schuster Inc.

Printed in the U.S.A.

◆§ Author's Note ◈◆

Out of the ashes of the Anarchy rose one of England's greatest kings, Henry Fitz Empress. Son of Matilda, who for nineteen long years had struggled with Stephen for the crown, he came to the throne in 1154. By birthright, advantageous marriages for himself and his children, and near constant battles he saw to the birth of the Angevian Empire and reigned as Henry II, King of England, Wales, Scotland, Ireland, Duke of Normandy, Count of Anjou, Maine, Touraine, Aquitaine, Poitou and holder of Brittany and the Vexin. Henry controlled far more land in France than did the French king. With reason, he dreamed of seeing his empire surpass even Charlemagne's. But for his legitimate sons, he might have succeeded.

Louis, King of France when Henry first emerged as a power, was known for his piety and had a wife famed for her exceptional beauty, intelligence and unusually strong sense of independence—Eleanor of Aquitaine. She produced only daughters for Louis and complained that she'd married a monk not a man. The time came when, with her encouragement, he had their marriage dissolved. A bare eight weeks later, young Henry (eleven years her junior) had claimed both the beauty and her important French duchies of Aquitaine and Poitou.

Eleanor gave Henry four sons who survived childhood:

(1) Henry, the young king. He was crowned while his father still lived and reigned. The history of his rebellious battles to replace his father on the throne is probably the reason that, although future heirs to the English throne might serve as regent, they were never crowned before the sovereign died.

(2) Richard Coeur de Lion (the Lionheart). The historical records show him to have been a man devoted to battle from a very early age. Whether fighting on his own lands, against his father, on Crusade or against other kingdoms, sword and lance were seldom far from his hand.

(3) Geoffrey. He was known for treachery and a sly tongue. (Please note that Henry had another son named Geoffrey, an illegitimate son of far more honorable habits.)

(4) John. Unlike the others, he was raised by his father and grew up to be cruel and avaricious as well as sly, weak, and cowardly. In the Treaty of Montmirail, while John was still a small child, Henry divided his empire between his three older sons in theory if not in fact. Because John was not included in that division, he came to be known as John Lackland. Although Henry did provide his youngest with fine titles and some lands, his portion in no way compared with his older brothers'. Spoiled on the one hand and left out on the other, he became an uncommonly greedy person who appropriated whatever he could for himself.

Early on, Henry commissioned a painting on the wall in the Palace of Winchester. It portrayed an eagle standing bold and strong while four eaglets attack him with their sharp beaks and vicious talons. It was a prophecy of what was to come, for all of Henry's legitimate sons repeatedly rose against him or, when not actually engaged in combat with him, intrigued with his enemies.

After his sons' first major rebellion, supported—some say initiated—by the queen (1173), Henry forgave his sons their treason but banished Eleanor to England. She was first consigned to Salisbury Tower (this tower was not located in present day Salisbury but rather at Old Sarum) and though not confined in a dungeon but rather treated with the respect due a queen, she was watched constantly and never allowed freedom to move about as she pleased—a great trial for an independent woman who had traveled extensively. Moreover, for a woman raised in the soft, warm climes of Southern France, England was a cold and lonely exile.

In 1183, while continuing his rebellion against his father the young king fell ill. When he realized death was near, he begged Henry's forgiveness and pleaded leniency for his mother. After his son's burial, Henry began to allow Eleanor occasional travels about England, sometimes for state ceremonies or to attend Christmas/Easter court. In April of 1185, (for political reasons advantageous to him) Henry called Eleanor to France and she spent at least part of the next year in her own duchy of Aquitaine. Then, suddenly, she was returned to closely guarded exile in Salisbury Tower, once again restricted within its walls.

Three years after the young king died, the legitimate Geoffrey was killed in a jousting accident. Only two legitimate sons remained. The eldest surviving and Eleanor's favorite, Richard, was the apparent heir to the crown. However, it was no secret that Henry meant to see his favorite, John, follow him to the throne. The last two years of his life Henry spent fighting Richard and King Phillip of France (Louis' son). As the king lay ill, knowing he was both defeated and dying, a supporter began to read a list of those who had conspired against and driven him to this bleak end. The first name on the list was Prince John.

Betrayed and forsaken by all his legitimate sons, Henry died cradled in the arms of the illegitimate Geoffrey.

At this time in history a monastery or convent was the solution to a problem many families faced—too many younger sons or plentiful daughters. The convent was also the recipient of many wives discarded by husbands either desperate for male heirs or merely desirous of greener pastures. Divorces, more properly dissolutions/annulments, were not as unusual as might be supposed considering the strength of the church. Such conveniences were granted on several grounds, the most common of which were prior commitment (either to one of the opposite sex or the church) or too close a family tie (up to and including sixth cousins). Due to the lack of written marriage records to prove or disprove such distant blood ties and given the relatively small group of nobility which nearly insured intermarriage within the prohibited degrees, it was not difficult to success-fully use this excuse for a dissolution.

To people in this era God and the devil were unquestion-able facts, and the idea of defiling something holy was horrifying. The young king had pillaged the famous shrine of Roc Amadour and when very soon thereafter he was struck down by a sudden illness, his contemporaries felt it was simply God's just punishment for his sacrilege. Men who might kill and maim with impunity trembled at the prospect of thus risking God's wrath.

A postulant nun, to ensure no confusion, is a woman trained to become a member of a religious order but who has not yet made the final decision nor taken vows of celibacy and commitment of her life to God.

Wary Hearts

~§ Chapter 1 §~

Late Spring of 1188

The daylight which had been but a dim rose glow on the eastern horizon when her trip began had nearly fled the west. The woman atop the monotonously plodding donkey was tired. Her beast's awkward gait had left aches in tender places, calling forth sweet visions of the steaming bath likely awaiting her in the fortress. Undistracted by the familiar houses and shops crowded between outer and inner bailey walls, her gaze crossed the moat's placid surface and lifted. Ahead rose a fortress guarded by water and a high stone barricade. Though stark and imposing it drew from her a warmth which eased weariness and lifted the corners of tender lips. To Queen Eleanor, Salisbury Tower meant exile, but for fourteen years it had been the only home she'd known—beyond abbey.

The thought of St. Margaret's, where only prayers and words of devotion broke the solemn hush, brought a prick of guilt. A pang sharp enough to drive from her mind even the overriding question of the purpose behind this summons. She unconsciously smoothed the white skirt of her postulant's habit, berating herself for the failure to regard the abbey as her true home. Although Abbess Berthilde had repeatedly, if gently, stressed the necessity of resigning all

1

temporal ties, she'd yet to find sufficient strength to banish the pleasant memories this place had meant since the day she, as a child, had arrived with her mother and little sister.

Approaching the drawbridge, she let seldom allowed memories of that dark time return like an incoming tide of fouled water. Then only a child, still she'd known it a dangerous deed when her father, a minor baron, had supported the queen and her sons in the princes' rebellion a decade and five years before. He'd been killed in the process, leaving her mother panic-stricken at the prospect of facing King Henry's awesome rage. She lived in terror of a royal proclamation calling her father's fief, Swinton, forfeit for the defiance of its lord—leaving them homeless. When the worst failed to happen, apprehension had slipped into an uneasy assumption that the king dismissed small Swinton as insignificant and no further threat without the baron. No danger even when Eleanor, his queen and the insurrection's agitator, took the three of them into her household. After all, her mother would sigh to soothe lingering misdoubts, what difference could it make with the queen under constant watch and exiled from her base of power in beloved Poitou and Aquitaine. Particularly as Swinton was but a long, thin stretch of land between the holdings of Salisbury Tower and the lands of the Earl of Tarrant, one of the king's strongest supporters.

"Welcome, Sister Agnes." The cheery words rolled from a short, rotund man who seemed squeezed into his tight mail suit. Recalled to her surroundings, she realized her sorry steed had carried her across the wooden drawbridge, and they were poised at the portal into a shadowed passage through the thick bailey wall. Holding wide one side of the massive double doors at the far end of the tunnel stood Harold, the gate guard she'd known for years.

So completely did his words break Agnes free from thoughts of past fears she failed to still the grimace the sound of her much disliked name was apt to bring. The lapse was brief for even as she returned his grin with a smile, she dutifully reminded herself again of the need to put away all such vain and trivial concerns. 'Twas a difficult chore, though assuredly worthy, and one years of earnest trying had not accomplished.

Still she hesitated to urge the donkey from wood planks

2

through stone arch. All too aware of what loomed above, she looked up. Despite twilight's growing gloom, the portcullis bared the dull shine of sharp teeth. Uncomfortable with the threat overhead, she rode under its power. Thankfully, it was lowered only when danger threatened and, though all knew Prince Richard plotted rebellion against his father from the continent and mumbles of dissatisfaction ranged far and wide, none would threaten King Henry's sovereignty in this place.

"Been ever so long since last you was home." Harold stepped forward once Agnes was clear of the tunnel. Guessing her more than ready to leave her uncomfortable seat and stretch cramped legs, he offered her a hand in dismounting. "Mistress Aleria been begging to have you visit ever since they come back."

"And now I'm here." Agnes took Harold's hand and with pleasure quit her bony steed. "My thanks, Harold." Her appreciative smile was warm although weary. Turning to survey the expanse of courtyard between gate and castle entrance, she unobtrusively arched the stiff back she feared likely to never feel natural again. After two years within abbey walls without word, was it possible her little sister's desire for company was the reason behind Queen Eleanor's summons? Though Aleria was a royal favorite, had been since the beginning, Agnes suspected the sharp-witted monarch had a stronger purpose. But what?

Leading her donkey, Agnes carefully picked her way over the courtyard's deep ruts. As if once loosed they'd not be easily restrained, Agnes' thoughts returned to the years following her arrival in this tower. While their mother served as lady-in-waiting to the queen, she and Aleria had run through this courtyard; played hide and seek in guardroom, great hall, and curtain-shielded alcoves cut into thick stone walls; and chosen kitties from a litter in the stable built against bailey wall.

Warmth faded with the unavoidable memory of happy times extinguished by the strange sickness visiting death upon village and tower alike, their mother but one among the many it claimed. She'd felt deserted, alone and responsible for Aleria. Although their mother had loved them both, she had early warned her oldest daughter of the differences between women, particularly those without wealth, and of the disappointments to be found in expecting more than one was due. Plain females such as Agnes, and she herself, were born to fulfill practical concerns while beauties like Aleria were born for laughter and pampering. After their mother's death, Agnes had been terrified of what would befall them. She needn't have feared. The queen had kept them with her as wards. Nevertheless, carefree days had ended and childish gaiety had been smothered beneath the weighty task bequeathed the older daughter by their mother's solemn training. She'd dutifully assumed the burdensome role of smoothing Aleria's path, even when it must be at the cost of her own.

Agnes was so deep in her own thoughts that she barely noticed the stable-serf who took the donkey's reins from her hand and led the tired animal toward the stables.

Yes, the queen had kept them with her, even though all children and widows of men who held fiefs direct from him, no matter how small, were in reality the king's wards. It was his right to find spouses or guardians for them, men who would profit from their inheritances. As she moved carefully forward, through long practice holding her skirt high enough to preserve its pristine whiteness while maintaining a seemly modesty, her eyes hardened with a cynicism she would have denied had she known it there. It looked out of place on a young prospective nun. To her mind there was no greater proof that she and her sister were very small in the scheme of things than the fact that Henry had not taken their future into his own hands. But then, small Swinton was no more than a single blade of grass in the meadow of Henry's vast domain and further reduced when split between the two sisters for dowry.

Agnes started up the steep wooden stairs to the tower's entrance one level above ground, repeating the lesson Harold had taught the curious child she'd once been. Such steps could be burned as a last desperate defense against attack. They may as well be stone for if Eleanor's initial confinement within had failed to draw avenging assault, then after these many years 'twas unlikely to befall them now. Moreover, the resentment of her supporters had mellowed when, after ten years of close supervision in Salisbury Tower, the king had relaxed the queen's restraints and allowed her limited travel about England. A pity it had taken pleadings from his oldest son's deathbed to effect such a change. The joy of freedom, even if only that of a bird transferred to a larger cage, had not diverted Eleanor's attention from her wards nor dampened her affection for them. She'd invited the younger girl to accompany her while Agnes stayed behind with the sisters at the Abbey of St. Margaret. As Agnes had been urged toward the cloistered life from a very early age, it was a logical step. The action, however, had left the dispirited girl with an illogical and silent bruise.

When, for his own political advantage, Henry had loosed Eleanor's tether enough for a return to her beloved French lands, Agnes had remained without complaint in the abbey while Aleria journeyed with the queen. This was Agnes' first visit since their homecoming, and she hoped to learn the reason behind Eleanor's abrupt return not only to England but to close confinement in Salisbury Tower. Had it aught to do with the call for her to return? She paused with hands flat against the rough planks of a heavy, ironbound door.

What difference the motive? The voice of her well-developed and ever vigilant conscience issued a stern caution to simply be glad she was here. She needed time away from the abbey for clear thinking, and to her devotions must add special prayers of thanks for this opportunity, this place free of subtle pressure upon the decision she must make alone.

Under the firm weight of both hands the door slowly opened. Even at this second level the castle wall was thick and its tunnel entrance of length enough for a tall man to lay with arm outstretched at its base and barely reach from one end to the other. But not length enough to still the rush of merry sound from the vast great hall at its end or dissipate appetizing aromas. Unbidden, they brought awareness of the difference between this evening meal and the abbey's plain fare and subdued atmosphere. Agnes's aches and pains faded beneath growing hunger. Suddenly wanting nothing more than to join Aleria and the queen at the high table, she stepped into the room.

"They're awaiting you above."

The voice was soft but caught Agnes's attention immediately. Fondness giving gentle warmth to her smile, she turned to greet Lady Catherine. This woman had replaced their mother as lady-in-waiting and had ostensibly helped in

5

managing the queen's two young wards. Bowed beneath the weight of rapidly advancing years, each time Agnes saw her she seemed to have shrunk more. Her long nose had not. And when under stress, as now, it twitched. A trait which early had earned her the title of Mouse Catherine from Aleria. Having also the timorous nature of that small rodent, it was she who'd been easily managed by the young beauty. Agnes possessed a natural empathy with those less favored by nature and had subtly added strength to the woman's ineffective attempts to restrain Aleria.

"I'd hoped to wash the travel grime away and partake of a light repast." Agnes let the suggestion dwindle away on a note upraised with hope.

Worried frown deepening and nose twitching, Lady Catherine shook her head emphatically. "Oh, no, no. It cannot be. I've been bidden to fetch you up immediately."

Agnes took pity on the other's high-strung nerves and motioned her to lead the way. The unusual request for swiftness, blind to a guest's comfort, pricked her curiosity. 'Twas probably a sinful emotion and unworthy of God's servant. Despite such dutiful reminders, she was hard put to suppress it.

Their progress through the vast room crowded with trestle tables laden with platters half emptied of food and surrounded by men half filled and well-liquored was repeatedly impeded by calls of welcome and questions for her health. Most members of the garrison and the castle-serfs who served them, though firm supporters of Henry and she Eleanor's ward, had known Agnes from the day of her first arrival and bore her a fondness of long standing. The two women finally reached the hall's far side where a stone stairway was built within the width of a courtyard-facing and, therefore, more defensible wall.

From the first time she'd climbed them in childhood, Agnes had borne an unreasonable dread of the curving steps where no natural light penetrated. Portcullis and dark stairways, they were the stuff of her night terrors. She was unsure if such a dislike was shared by her guide or whether the haste with which they ascended was due to the other's need to please. Whichever, in amazingly short time they reached the level of both the queen's apartments and the bedchambers allotted the two sisters.

6

The door to the queen's solar opened silently. The older woman was loathe to interrupt while the queen was speaking.

"What price freedom? What price? Only must I take my beloved duchy, my Aquitaine, from Richard. Take it from him after he has been installed as its duke by both Henry and me."

With the peculiar noiseless, gliding step Aleria had found so annoying when caught by its stealth, Catherine moved to one side, leaving Agnes a clear view of the room. Her eyes went immediately to the two figures full in the fire's revealing light—the first time she had seen them in nearly two years. In the privacy which gave freedom to her boundless energy, Eleanor stood tall and regal while Aleria sat on a stool with hands outstretched to warming flames. The bored expression on the young woman's face proclaimed this a complaint heard oft before.

"He wants to give it to Johnny, his sniveling Johnny!" Eleanor let one arm sweep out in a gesture of contempt. "Only for that will he allow me freedom." Her hands came together in so sharp a clap that although she'd seen it coming Agnes flinched. "I'd rather rot in the darkest dungeon, but that even Henry dare not risk. For my defense and under Richard's banner my people would rise. Then, with such ripe pickings at hand, the young French king would throw not some measly token army but his full force into the fray at Richard's side." Eyes downcast, Eleanor paced a short distance and back again. "Phillip is young but far more wily than his father, my saintly first spouse. Henry cannot risk it. So I am held prisoner, but a queen." Eleanor's chin lifted with assurance of her place of power in the world.

Agnes admired Eleanor above all women. Her famous beauty had not faded one whit with time. Even more estimable, she possessed an exceptional mind and strength enough to stand for herself against any foe, yet was generous and true to those who gave her their loyalty. And most praiseworthy of all, as proven by the love she'd given two motherless waifs of little importance, her heart was soft to those abused by fate. Eleanor's words called Agnes's attention back.

"All this for little Johnny who cried foul once his tiny Countess of Maurienne died and he was no longer assured the title of count. Despite betrothal to the heiress of the largest earldom in England, he is not satisfied—whines that her father will live forever. Wretched boy wants a duchy when he has proven himself unable to manage so much as his own household. He wants more, so his father would see him first duke and then king!''

At least this repudiation of both Henry and John was a refrain familiar to Agnes. It was true that almost from the moment of his birth John had been given over to others while Eleanor moved on to other cities, other responsibilities. Eleanor had kept the older boys well-nigh always with her, but John she'd left to his father, and Henry had kept him ever near.

"Henry thinks that by locking me in this castle he has ended my power." Eleanor's eyes burned with the intensity of her scorn. "He fails to realize that even here I am not stripped of my strength like Samson shorn of his locks. He would see John as king. John, that spineless creature that, though he came from my loins, I have never claimed mine!''

For two years Agnes had been cloistered away where royal intrigues were unimportant and this complaint that Henry meant to see John replace Richard as heir to the throne was new to her ears. Of Prince Geoffrey's death she'd heard and thus knew only two were left from Eleanor's English brood—her favorite, Richard, and Henry's favorite, John. But surely the fact that Richard was the elder and already a man proven warrior made it clear he was heir to the crown.

"What madness and only to spite me by keeping my beloved Richard from what is rightfully his. No, it will not be! I will not allow it! He cannot force Richard to bow to his little brother—not Richard.'' She shook her head and fire-light gleamed over the few strands of silver that dared show in the thick coils of her hair, adding only a rich patina to the whole. "I have already done my part.'' Her smile was satisfied and Agnes was certain that this action, whatever it had been, was the reason for Eleanor's return to the tower. "Now Richard will do his and Henry will lose.''

"I'm here,'' Agnes announced, deeming this the most appropriate moment she was likely to find.

"Nessa!'' The squeal emitted from a small blur of gold

8

and azure which hurled itself into welcoming arms. Agnes smiled into bright hair. Love was a rare and precious gift and she savored each token, from warm embrace to soft sound of the much preferred diminutive of her name created by Aleria and used by family. But castle guard and servants, as well as abbey inhabitants, called her Sister Agnes. For as long as her visit lasted, she decided to allow the name shortened by love to be used, even in her own thoughts. This might well be her last opportunity, for after taking holy vows the pet name would ever be forbidden her.

"Come and eat." Aleria bounced back and impetuously tugged Nessa toward a small table directly in front of the fire but gone unnoticed. "I've been waiting and waiting and waiting."

Nessa settled on a low stool on one side of the table, carefully arranging her simple skirt out of harm's way. The flames threw glowing cinders. Though unlikely to spark a blaze, they would leave unsightly black marks on white cloth—perhaps not a great concern to women with sizable wardrobes but paramount to a cloistered woman who, shunning vanity, was allowed only a practical two. She smiled at Aleria who hovered near, close to dancing with delight as she chattered about all the impressive sights she'd seen and important people she'd met on the continent. Clearly, even traveling far and amongst the great men and women of the world had not dampened her impulsive spirit—nor tamed her tongue.

"Child," Eleanor called to Aleria. "Sit down and let your sister eat in peace."

Aleria looked momentarily rebellious but then shrugged and complied, subsiding onto the stool across the table from her sister. Surprised, Nessa wondered if she'd learned the way of yielding to another's will. A forlorn hope. Nor, Nessa reminded herself, was such a talent necessary for the young beauty.

Eleanor had watched the reunion of sisters with silent interest. They were little alike but shared an honest affection. Although she better understood the transparent Aleria, Eleanor bore a strong fondness for the older sister of far more complicated nature and sharp mind. Bowing to their natural mother's wishes, she had done her best to guide Nessa into the cloistered life despite private questions on

9

the wisdom of such a path. Nessa was not homely nor even plain, unless standing beside her sister's vivid beauty, but her mask of serenity hid a painful certainty of inferiority which cracked only under rare flashes of spirited temper.

As Nessa ate the queen maintained a peaceful atmosphere with idle talk of old friends whom she'd seen while in Aquitaine and of her daughter's visit. Nessa felt sure the visit had been another sore point with Henry. He'd never been fond of Eleanor's children by King Louis of France, half-sisters to his present foe—young King Phillip.

Agnes savored her meal from extravagantly seasoned chicken to the soft wheaten bread she adored but in the abbey had learned to forego as sins both of wasteful gluttony and proud excess. Before she was done, Eleanor had moved on to discuss the rumors of dissatisfaction rumbling through cities and villages, all a result of Henry's law reforms. The nobility resented the clipping of their power and the common folk groaned beneath taxes to fund his continental wars. Nessa admired Eleanor but knew well the enmity between royal spouses and recognized more than a hint of pleasure in the reports of Henry's troubles.

Last bite finished, Nessa forced herself to remain motionless and wait. Idleness provided no distraction from the curiosity she'd tried to deny. She clamped her mouth shut against the irrational demand for answers and clasped fingers tight to still nervous, attention-drawing motions.

When Eleanor realized Nessa was sitting quietly, she wondered what the girl would think of the news? Though, strictly speaking, of import only to the younger sister, she'd chosen not to exclude the elder from a matter so momentous.

Eleanor rose, her grace of movement displaying an elegance attainable to few women no matter their perfection of form. Opening the door, she motioned a waiting servant to carry away the remains of Nessa's meal, leaving the table between the two girls bare. The queen then went to an intricately carved chest standing at one side of the hearth and withdrew a folded parchment from the black-lacquered box resting atop.

As her foster mother returned to the fire, Nessa saw the document had been closed by the king's seal. Practiced at control of her emotions, Nessa allowed no flicker of surprise to show. In all the years of the royal couple's estrangement, letters had never flown between them, and Nessa was uncomfortably aware that this likely contained a matter of import. Shying from deeper reasoning, Nessa sought and found a simple motive for the missive. Surely, she reassured herself, the king had summoned his wife to one state ceremony or another? Nay, cool logic denied, so ordinary a request would merely be mentioned during mealtime conversation. Clearly it portended something more fateful. Something of consequence to her and Aleria. A strange foreboding grew, and slender fingers, clasped together, turned white beneath the strength of Nessa's tightening grip.

"To Eleanor, the queen, residing at Salisbury Tower . . ." Eleanor began reading the formal letter with its stilted salutation which was as a sovereign might write to any vassal. Tension increased Nessa's sensitivity to the older woman's mood, making her immediately aware that beneath Eleanor's pleasant tone lay an effort of will which sharpened its edge. After what seemed an inordinately lengthy passage of meaningless legal rhetoric, Nessa's full attention was seized by the announcement Eleanor next read. "Thus I send my well-esteemed vassal and friend, Garrick Fitz William, Earl of Tarrant, to claim as bride my ward, the beautiful Swinton heiress."

Nessa's eyes flew to Aleria, who had straightened in shock. Although not specifically named, neither sister had any difficulty in identifying the subject of these words. With her golden hair, azure eyes and petite yet lush figure Aleria had even been given the great accolade of being named Eleanor's equal in beauty. Accepting regrettable facts, Nessa viewed herself as but a faded shadow of her sister. Her hair was neither blond nor dark but a nondescript brown, her eyes neither clear brown nor green but some indistinct combination, her height average and curves rather less. Even their names were an example of the difference between them—Agnes, plain and dull; Aleria, light and melodious. Nessa vehemently suppressed a sudden stab of envy! Envy, no matter that it grew not from lack of love, was a deadly sin be she postulant or no. She refused to acknowledge a longing for beauty and not beauty alone but

11

for the advantages it brought—the opportunity for a home of her own, people who cared for her, perhaps even a man who loved her.

"There is no date for his coming." Eleanor disdainfully tossed the parchment to the table between the two girls. "But, knowing my affection for you, clearly Henry chose this way to spite me for my refusal to bow to his demands. He sends a great warrior and his firm supporter to take you from me."

Yes, Eleanor thought with renewed indignation, Henry had selected a strong supporter. One who'd been so busy with his king's battles that although thirty and more he'd not wed. An ailing father had already resigned the title and lands to Garrick; and, as there were no other heirs, it was far past time for him to be about the business of providing them.

Eleanor knew the man very well. "He came as a child to foster with Henry." She paused. The girls knew that all well-born sons were sent to foster with their father's over-lord, there to learn as page and then squire the ways of nobility and knighthood. "Henry could not take the sons of all his many direct vassals into his own home, rather he dispatched them to his various holdings. But Garrick's father was a powerful earl." Eleanor's mouth went hard as she added, "And, just as importantly, because of the friendship between the young lordling and the royal bastard, Geoffrey, Henry kept Garrick with us."

In the early years the two boys had shared a home with her and her elder sons. Unlike most males who came within her sphere, Garrick had disliked her from the first. Initially she'd excused his attitude as a trait inherited from a father famous for his disdain of womankind. She had gone out of her way to be warm and welcoming. Yet, by the time her marriage was shaking under the stress of Henry's liaison with Rosamund, Garrick had turned completely away. He watched her with accusing eyes as he built a bond with Henry and deepened his friendship with her husband's illegitimate son.

While the queen was preoccupied, Nessa's eyes never wavered from Aleria's stricken expression. She rose and moved to kneel beside the younger girl, wrapping a consoling arm about her shoulders. The action called Eleanor's attention.

12

"Don't be distraught—" Eleanor comforted Aleria, certain her pain was born of fear for a stranger chosen by Henry's spite. Emotions ever simple and direct, doubtless Aleria feared her groom old or ugly or cruel or all three and would be reassured by one simple statement of fact. "The earl is little more than a score and ten, lord of a great fiefdom, and—" Eleanor's face went hard. "—as handsome as sin."

Feeling the rigidity ease from her little sister's muscles, Nessa also thought her fearful of a foe's choice as mate and was thankful for Eleanor's understanding.

Eleanor, however, seemed driven to add another and far less encouraging statement. "But just as dangerous and cold as ice."

Both sisters went rigid, apprehensively watching their royal lady, who stared blindly into the flames and saw the past. For the eight years before he came to foster at court, Garrick had lived with a father whose distrust of women and rejection of love as the source of pain was legend. Although the boy had grown into a stunningly handsome man well able to attract any woman, he'd never allowed one of their number past the ice armor about his heart nor shared with one more than a purely physical warmth.

At last Eleanor stirred herself to continue. "Moreover, there's naught I can do to forestall the deed. Henry is king and holds the right to see you wed while I am but a captive queen."

Nessa's brow knit in puzzlement. It was difficult to believe the woman able to stand against a king's demands for a dukedom was unable to refuse a groom for her ward. Nay, most likely Eleanor found the match acceptable. Nessa could even agree with her reasoning. Moreover, she and Aleria owed much to the queen. The least they could offer in payment was submission to a command which, in truth, seemed generous.

Eleanor saw that Nessa's clear logic had divined the truth. When hazel eyes rose and met her own gaze, Eleanor knew the older sister accepted the match as the right course. She was pleased. She'd not have insisted had Nessa disagreed. Although the match was far more illustrious than any Aleria could have hoped to contract elsewhere. Surely there was no wrong in giving Henry the victory in this one small battle—a crumb to distract the ravenous beast while the loaf was carried away by another.

Neither Eleanor nor Nessa were particularly concerned by Aleria's continued sniffles and occasional soft sob. The girl was known for long pouts and copious tears at even the slightest bump in the smooth tenor of her days.

⋑ Chapter 2 ⋐

Nessa released the catch of her headdress and pulled it off. The weather was unseasonably warm and the cloth atop thick hair, brushed but unbound beneath, made the heat oppressive. She smiled as a slight breeze wound cool fingers through the freed mass of curls, lifting the heavy weight from her nape. Then, loosening the drawstring holding her habit tight at the throat, she moved to sit on the welcome coolness of a stone bench placed just beyond a low flowering bush. Here in the center of a complex labyrinth lay its goal, a calm pool filled with water lilies and surrounded by elegantly carved benches. With affection, Nessa took in the loveliness of the garden, nearly a duplicate of Eleanor's own in Poitiers. Tall green hedges formed a maze difficult for any to navigate save those who had played on paths stone-laid before greenery walls grew above a child's head and who were thus familiar with every twist. The high-grown partitions and small alcoves at each false end were designed to provide secret trysting places but provided equally well the privacy she sought.

Dejected and alone with no one to see, she let slender shoulders slump. On Swinton lands before her father's death, the only person who'd had time to spare for her was

Father Cadmaer. Tutor to boys at foster in their keep, the priest had bolstered her painful lack of self-confidence with the notion that a good mind was of more value than a physical beauty vulnerable to the fading of time. Though sensible and comforting, the words had never stifled her hopeless longing for what she lacked. His initial strategy unsuccessful, Father Cadmaer had pointed her toward the cloistered life as the path to greater learning and use for mortal talents unappreciated in a secular woman.

At nineteen, after years of serious training, the time had come. Abbess Berthilde had been patient; but, before the queen's summons arrived, Nessa had felt the subtle pressure growing. Still, the decision put off too long dimmed the sun, blinding her senses to the sweet fragrances and delicate beauty of flowers brushed against her back by a soft breeze. Determined to face the dilemma squarely, she repeated her meager options—take the vows pledging her life to God alone or leave the order. In nearly all other matters she found herself seriously lacking, yet confessed to the sin of pride in one matter—her ability to reason as coolly as any man. Therefore, she should bow to the undeniable voice of reason which declared the choice a simple one to make. She possessed neither wealth nor the great beauty to tempt a man of equal social standing to claim her for wife. She must wed either man or church; and since, unlike her sister, no important lord—young or old, handsome or ugly—would come for her, it must be the church.

Unfortunately, her well-developed conscience held her back. 'Twas wrong to enter the cloistered life for any reason save a sincere desire to devote one's life to God. In an earnest conversation with the abbess, Nessa had admitted she feared a lack of vocation such as her fellow postulant, Sybil, possessed. Nessa's faith was not in question, yet despite earnest seeking after a pure and Christlike nature, she knew herself to be too attuned to earthly matters, too quick to flare at imagined injustices rather than turning the other cheek and accepting them as God's will. The abbess had responded that God had as much need for practical service as for the purely spiritual. Her words had surely been meant as reassurance, but they'd raised the vision of recurring blight in the garden of her future. Having spent her temporal life working to smooth the way for Aleria's happi-

16

ness, not inviting was the idea that here again her role was in performing the practical and mundane to facilitate the spiritual joy of others.

Buried in bleak thought, she plucked a dainty pale pink bloom from its nest of green leaves. One petal at a time she slowly tossed into the soft breeze. Some fell immediately to skitter across the path's rough stones until they found safety in the darkness beneath a towering hedge. Others flew high on shifting winds, curling in graceful loops and whirling beyond tall green spires.

Nessa brought her hands together palm to palm, fingertip to fingertip, and rested their joined edge against her lips as if in prayer, an unconscious habit and a safe escape into private thoughts where others were unlikely to intrude. Life was like the differing paths of those delicate petals. Paths ordained by powers beyond human control. Much as she might wrestle with her destiny, she recognized that she would likely be a petal earthbound and hiding in cheerless safety beneath a towering spire. To others belonged the dizzying dance across sun-gilded heights, dangerous but exhilarating. Unworthy of the first and lacking the necessary requirements for the second, Nessa felt unfitted for either. Knowing only one solace for all questions, thick lashes fell and she prayed fervently for some sign of the right path to follow.

"Welcome."

Still in the shadows of the castle's deep entrance, Garrick Fitz William, Earl of Tarrant, turned toward the speaker. Eleanor was standing at the foot of the corner stairs, regal pride in uptilted chin and challenge in her direct gaze. Though prisoner, she was unquestionably still Queen of England and Lady of Salisbury Tower, demanding and assuredly receiving her due. Along with the briefest bow protocol allowed, Garrick accorded her a slight smile which failed to warm ice-gray eyes. She was queen, his steady gaze acknowledged. Queen above all treacherous women.

"Thank you, Your Highness." Her word had surely been as lacking in sincerity as his response. Unwilling to offer more than did she, he stood his ground. They'd never been cordial, not even while she'd been his foster mother—a time during which he'd watched her plot first with and then

17

against her husband, turning his own sons against him. By those actions had his initial suspicions and poor opinion of the famous beauty been confirmed.

Undaunted, silent minutes passed while Eleanor closely examined her opponent, for opponent he'd ever been. Doubtless he disdained her, now as always, for a manipulative woman. When first she'd met his disapproval, it had been beneath the dignity of a queen to justify herself to a child who condemned without reason. Moreover, how could she explain to a boy prejudiced from birth against all womankind that a woman in her position must either control or be controlled. How could he understand her need to be independent when other women apparently submitted so easily. That they were not queens two times over and mother to the princes and princesses of two realms would more likely earn condemnation than excuse.

Since last she'd seen him, the handsome youth had become a strikingly attractive man. He'd been tall then but now his frame had filled out with well-proportioned muscle. She'd experience enough to judge a man, indeed, prided herself upon the ability. Still lean and light on his feet, doubtless he'd sufficient power beneath his well-controlled exterior to crush a foe with lightning speed. She'd heard as much said in the talk of tower guards who'd returned from Henry's wars and had personally observed the earl in battle. They called him the Ice Warrior. In truth, those charcoal-rimmed, light gray eyes contained ice enough to quell a man or challenge a brave woman. He'd surely been born with an ice barricade about his emotions, for during his adolescent days in her court no female had been able to crack or even chip the tiniest flake from the frozen block he was. And more, the court gossip which never failed to reach her ears said that no matter how beautiful the woman or heated their play even the ladies of Henry's court had been unable to break through his cold shield to the heart of the man beneath.

Garrick stood motionless beneath Eleanor's narrowed gaze until at last her attention turned to his tawny-haired companion.

"How fortunate you are to have had company in your travels." Eleanor made a small graceful motion toward the younger man.

18

"Meet here Conal, Baron of Wryborne." Garrick's introduction referred to neither the woman's name nor title. It was a small insult, one unlikely to be called yet one a proud woman would not miss. "As am I," he continued, "my friend is returning to his lands. Brothers in arms, we've chosen to journey together." By his choice of words, he cautioned Eleanor to leave the younger man, Henry's supporter, free of her schemes.

Eleanor recognized the warning but refused to acknowledge his silent message as she nodded toward her second visitor with a smile full of long-celebrated charm. "Welcome, Lord Conal."

With the openness of a friendly nature, Conal stepped forward to kiss the queen's hand. He shared none of his friend's reticence. This woman might be their foe, but she offered welcome with all courtesy, and with like spirit he would accept it. Besides, this was the first time he'd met the famous woman face to face—and she was uncommonly beautiful no matter her age.

Eleanor's smile warmed. Such open admiration was a pleasant thing and went far to compensate for the other's lack. "I pray pardon but, as I was not forewarned of your coming, a private chamber for you has not been arranged. A fighting man, you'll understand that this fortress was designed for defense and chosen as my abode for its strength, not its comfort. It was little expected that I would be blessed with guests and accommodations are uncomfortably limited. Therefore, though I'll have a mattress brought, I fear you must share the earl's chamber."

"Sleeping on the ground has been our lot for many days." Conal grinned. "Truly, a roof and bed are all I require for happiness." He held his hands palm up in mock humble submission.

"I, on the contrary, require more." Coming to stand behind Conal, Garrick's quiet voice was tight with impatience for time wasted on their pleasantries. "Important matters await my attention elsewhere, thus I must conclude my business here with all possible haste. The first step is to meet my future wife."

Eleanor's eyes went hard as they lifted to the taller man. "Lord Garrick, unhappily I cannot immediately fulfill your—requirement. Having only the vaguest indication of when to expect you, your bride had no reason to remain bound within these walls and is out walking with an old friend." Turning toward Conal she smiled, responding to his amiable nature after a clash with the earl's animosity. "I'm sure you're weary and would appreciate a bath to cleanse away travel grime—and a small repast to tide you over until the evening meal."

Being excuse for the queen's snubbing of Garrick flustered Conal. He was uncomfortable with his new position in the midst of a subtle warfare in which he had no experience. He disliked subterfuge, preferring straightforward battle to political wrangling.

After what he saw as the queen's attempt to use one man against the other, Garrick's lips curved with the closest thing to a smile he'd yet displayed, though cynical. Eleanor never failed to provide further proof of the flaws in feminine nature, demonstrating women ready always to exploit a man's weaknesses.

"But, Garrick," Conal slid down into the wooden tub, immersing even the top of his head in steaming water. "I still don't see how your marrying this woman will aid the king in suppressing rebellion."

Before answering, Garrick, fresh from his bath, pulled a clean tunic over his head, ruffling his thick black strands. "Because, puzzled friend, during my long absence words of discontent and false rumors of planned injuries, like seeds for future harvest, have been sown among my vassals— weeds among the grain." Innate honesty made it hard for Conal to fathom deceitful ploys to turn loyalties. 'Twas a trait Garrick valued but one which made explanations difficult. "Unchecked by my ailing father, these lies, tares of evil, are likely scattered out from Swinton, my bride's dower lands."

As Garrick talked, Conal had lifted a remarkably smooth ball of soap, sniffed its pleasant scent and spared a moment of gratitude to the queen's generosity in providing this luxury, and then wasted no further time in applying it vigorously to gold-streaked hair. Explanation done and despite fingers buried in lather, he sent Garrick a dubious look. "How, pray tell, will wedding its heiress stop a flow of words?"

"They, as nearly everything in life, have a source. Once uncovered it can be halted." Smoothing the crimson tunic over broad chest and narrow hips, Garrick shook his head at the silly picture his friend made with white foam dripping down his cheek.

Conal was unfazed by the other's amusement. "What method do you propose to use in finding this source? It's distinctly unlikely the arrival of Henry's man will coax the perpetrator into confessing." He sank again beneath the warm waters.

Waiting until Conal had rinsed the soap from his hair and risen above the tub's rim, Garrick answered. " 'Struth, and the reason I dispatched two members of my guard to travel as common freemen to Swinton, there to seek answer to my question." He paused, then as if to himself softly added, "Though I'm already near certain of the culprit."

"I fail to see why you need wed the heiress. What has that deed to do with the simple task of defeating a foe?" They were back at the beginning, though much else had been explained. In the merest splinter of a moment Garrick's final words stole Conal's attention. Before his friend could form answer to the first, Conal asked another question. "Who?" He jerked upright creating ominous bathwater waves. "Who is it you think guilty?"

Garrick stepped swiftly back as water sloshed over the tub's rim, striking the bare floor and splashing an amazing distance out. "Without certain proof, I won't call a man's honor into question—so calm yourself."

"But—" Conal began, a shadow of hurt in soft brown eyes.

Garrick lifted a hand to forestall the other's plea. "No, not even to a trusted friend—one of the few I claim. But once I've proof in hand, you I will share the secret with first; perhaps only with you."

Although Garrick shrugged with apparent casualness, through long and close acquaintance Conal saw the anxiety behind the offhand manner. "I understand, even do I admire your insistence on truth first. 'Tis the reason none can ever doubt your honor." He met questioning gray eyes steadily until Garrick's tight lips relaxed into a smile. Grinning, Conal turned the subject. "Now, try again to convince me you must wed the heiress."

21

Garrick groaned in feigned disgust. Taking an exaggerat-edly deep breath, he began. "Swinton is controlled for its heiresses by a castellan loyal to the queen. Until we are wed and the lands taken into my own hands, I cannot banish him and see the growing weeds uprooted and left to dry in the heat of Henry's justice."

"Ah, yes, now I see the political reason for your choice." Wanting to keep the talk light and yet seriously opposed, golden brows rose in question. "But what of the personal?"

The response was an impolite sound from deep within the black-haired man's throat.

Conal shook his head. "You mean to marry for another's advantage, gaining only half of the small Swinton fiefdom."

Garrick laughed at his friend's obvious disgust. Conal had long since made his opinion on the matter known. He could no way understand why Garrick would marry for such small personal gain when a "great earl" should expect so much more from a bride.

Hoping to earn another of Garrick's far too rare laughs, Conal produced a comical leer and again sat up sharply. Happily the first flood had reduced the water level to the point where no further overflow threatened. "I see now. 'Tis the promise of a beauty equal to the queen's you seek!"

As hoped, the teasing comment brought an immediate laugh from the earl, though cynicism lent it a sharp edge. Conal knew him better than to believe such of him. Few in Garrick's acquaintance were unaware of the distrust he bore for women, beautiful women most of all. "Nay, only I have waited too long to do what I know I must. Yet, if a wife I must take, leastways she'll be holder of no great lands of her own." Garrick paused, contempt chilling what next he said. "The wealth of wives brings naught but strife and struggle for power. For proof look only to Henry and his beautiful, wealthy queen."

While Conal finished bathing, Garrick ate a portion of the light repast brought with the heated bathwater. Then, full of energy and anxious to get on with the task at hand, he descended to the great hall. The noises made by servants busy with their chores seemed to echo in the large room as Garrick approached a young lad busy stoking a blaze already roaring in the fireplace dominating one wall.

"Where am I likely to find the queen?" he asked. No use

asking the location of his bride. The queen had said she walked with a friend; and, blessed with remarkably fair weather, he doubted she'd return of her own accord before the next meal.

Startled by the unfamiliar voice, the boy dropped a chunk of wood. That he'd very nearly smashed his foot went unnoticed as he swung around. Face flushed nearly as red as his hair, 'twas impossible to get voice past the constriction in his throat.

Garrick recognized the self-conscious awkwardness of a • boy struggling through the ungainliness of rapidly lengthening bones toward manhood. A rare gentle smile warmed his eyes to smoke.

The boy's adam's apple made two rapid bobs as he swallowed hard. He'd heard the earl was coming; more, he'd heard the men of the garrison speak with respect of this "warrior of ice." Thankful no ice glistened now, he sought to loosen the dry tongue seemingly cloven to the roof of his mouth. Flicking it uselessly over equally dry lips, he answered. "The queen's most like in her solar with her needlework. 'Swhat she does this time most days."

A once gentle smile slid into cynicism. The Eleanor Garrick remembered had no use for such endless undertakings. Mayhap a decade and more of confinement had curbed her creativity into gentle pursuits. Nay, though her fingers wove the needle, he'd never believe her mind occupied with else than schemes.

Gray eyes hardened into ice shards. Under their power the boy unwisely stepped back although the fire flamed directly behind. The earl's hands flew out to restrain him. His hold firm but not harsh, Garrick moved the flustered boy safely aside.

"What are you called?" Garrick hoped to put the lad at ease.

Heart pounding at his folly and the earl's lightning move to prevent its hazardous end, the boy was glad to have so simple a question asked and gave it a one-word answer. "Arnold." Looking up into the powerful lord's reassuring gaze he knew it was not enough and took courage in hand. For the other's unhesitating rescue he was owed more. "And, milord, you've my thanks for a'saving me from so witless a deed." On the last word his voice cracked, rising

23

an octave or more under the pressure of trying to sound adult. His blush deepened to a dark, ruby-glowing hue.

Wisely ignoring the lad's embarrassment, Garrick nodded in solemn acceptance of appreciation difficult for one on the vulnerable path toward maturity to give. " 'Tis safer to stand steady before any threat—real or imagined.'' The caution's seriousness was reinforced by a steady gaze from light gray eyes. "It leaves a man better ready to respond.''

"I'll remember,'' Arnold promised fervently. He appreciated the earl's tact in not teasing him, as other men most oft did, for a thing he couldn't control. And, too, for the earl's giving advice rather than criticism of an ill-done reaction.

"Have you been long in this castle?'' Garrick turned to a subject less sensitive and one that would lead the way to the information he'd come seeking. Likely the lad had been born to service and was bound here for the whole of his life, but 'twas possible he'd been brought from another of the king's holdings.

The boy nodded, pulse calming. Yet, he'd sooner not trust again the voice which had grown unpredictable of late.

"Then tell me, if two friends seek a quiet walk, where would they most likely choose to go?''

"To the queen's garden at the castle back.''

"Within the castle's inner bailey?'' Garrick's dark brows rose in dubious question. The tightly packed town covered every available space between the outer and inner bailey walls. Yet, the hill summit at the center hardly seemed large enough to bear the tower and its outbuildings—surely no room for a garden.

"Oh, aye.'' This was a subject with which the boy was comfortable and he gave a broad, relieved smile. "It don't take so much room, but 'tis near impossible to work. I been trying to get to its center for years, and I never done it yet.''

Get to its center? Brows once raised in surprise now furrowed low over silver eyes.

Seeing the lord's puzzlement, the boy knew he'd been unclear. " 'Tis a maze and, like as I said, don't take so awful much space since the aisles lay one aside the other though they turns every which way.'' He warmed to his subject. "It's got all kinds of little stopping places with benches and the like—just the right sort for a cozy chat

24

'twixt friends." The boy's mouth curled into a shyly suggestive smile.

The comment brought a grin from the earl who saw for what sort of use the boy assumed these "stopping places" were meant, and doubtless rightly so. Hearing his name called prevented Garrick from thanking the boy for his aid, and he turned.

"I beg you, Garrick, let us rest awhile." As if in exhaustion Conal slumped against the arched opening at the stairway's foot. "We've traveled for days, and you've nearly worn me through with the pace you keep."

Garrick shook his head in teasing dissent as Conal crossed the hall with a light speed that denied his claim of fatigue.

"It would behoove a gentle lord to allow his faithful friend to play the sluggard," Conal solemnly advised. "For an hour or two leastways." A gleam in his eyes gave lie to his words.

"Your youth, your lack of experience inclines you toward a faulty course. But, because I am a 'faithful friend' and wise with years and experience, I will lead you true." Garrick folded his hands together and inclined his head in the manner of a teacher preparing to impart the knowledge of the ages. "As a horse ridden hard must be cooled slowly, so too must a man gradually slow his pace."

"Then what, aged one, must we do now?" Conal asked, amusement glowing beneath his feigned expression of earnest pupil at the feet of his mentor.

"Why, like the horse, with a slow, steady pace we walk. My new friend, Arnold," he waved toward the tongue-tied boy who straightened with pride at being named such by an earl, "has pointed me toward the perfect place." He led the way across the vast hall to the outer door, a laughing Conal in tow.

Arnold watched until the men disappeared into the tunnel-gloom of the castle's exit. From the talk of this Ice Warrior, he'd expected a proud, stern lord quick to condemn. Instead, he'd met a man understanding of a young boy's lack and quick to respond in kind to another's teasing. Only that one flash of ice in his eyes had there been but that enough to convince him the man, when he chose, could freeze a foe with ease.

* * *

"Methinks, Old Master of Wisdom," Conal was laughing at the friend he tromped along behind, "we've not only failed to find the center of this delightful maze, but I much doubt we'll succeed in a quest for the path free!" They'd been moving through the green corridors for what seemed to him an age endless—and fruitless.

Garrick glanced back and grinned, the kind of true smile he seldom attained. Conal was but five years his junior yet so direct and lacking in guile he spread about him an open enjoyment Garrick had never been naive enough to know. Seemed he'd been born with eyes unshielded to the world's true nature by scales of innocence. From a father who'd believed women and love the source of pain and a home devoid of either warmth or comfort he'd moved to a court where a mother turned sons against their father and women used beauty to subjugate men and attain selfish goals.

Looking at the path ahead, Garrick responded, "As a battle-tested knight, I'd have thought you wise enough of your own to lift your eyes from the short span to the distant goal." Garrick waved toward a point above and to the side.

Conal's gaze traveled up the crimson covered arm to see the pennants rippling on the breeze from the castle's towers. With mock disgust, Conal shook a still damp tawny head. But, unwilling to see his complaint so easily voided, he argued. "We still have to find our way out through these twisted paths."

Garrick halted and shrugging faced his friend. "We'll cut straight through if other means fail." He gestured at the broadsword ever buckled at his waist—particularly here where his welcome by some was questionable. "I'd hate to see my worthy blade dulled by so paltry a task and am relieved the need is so unlikely. Though only one path leads to the center, of a certainty there are many paths out. I've little doubt we'll leave with more ease than we've solved the riddle."

"Admitting defeat not only by the maze, but by the maid who hides within?" Conal mischievously asked, knowing Garrick would hate the idea of being vanquished by a female at any level.

Garrick frowned in disgust just as a sweet sound floated to him. He instantly moved through twisted paths toward its source.

26

The sun's warmth brought Nessa a peaceful lethargy and momentary calm. Then, of a sudden, the solitude had been broken by the rustling of something moving through the greenery. Hazel eyes gone more green than brown turned toward the noise and found sunlight dancing on glossy leaves that shook. A moment later one member of the castle's newest generation of hunting dogs tumbled into view through a stately hedge. Though stumbling over its own outsized feet, the puppy was clearly practicing the occupation of its destiny by giving chase to prey—a bright butterfly as delicately graceful as its hunter was awkward. With clumsy zest the puppy bounded back and forth in zigzaging pursuit while Nessa's laughter wafted on a gentle breeze with the dainty winged creature. At last the insect settled on a flower just above a wet black nose. The small dog made an earnest if ungainly attempt to pounce but fell to the earth with a thud while his prey sailed higher and higher. Undaunted by failure, the puppy broke back through the hedge to continue the hunt leaving Nessa behind and still laughing softly.

Conal followed his friend's lead, nearly running to keep up. Garrick stopped so suddenly the younger man, guilty again of looking down at his path instead of up at the goal, bumped into the crimson-clad back. As if struck to stone the earl stood motionless. Curious, Conal peeked around a broad shoulder.

Not what I'd expected, Garrick thought, head tilted to one side and eyes narrowed on the profile rising from behind a flowering bush. Here was not the proud beauty he'd expected, yet he'd no doubt that this was his intended bride. The king's informants had overstated her beauty, yet he wasn't disappointed. Her dimpled smile was enchanting. If her hair was light brown touched with sun-gilding but not the spun gold as he'd been told, it was thick and looked as soft as thistle down. And if her eyes were not azure (indeed, he couldn't see what color they were) they sparkled with sunshine and laughter. She looked more real than any of the court beauties who viewed him as the wealthy prize at the end of a cunning game of pursuit. No artifice here, a trait more valuable than rare beauty—that breeder of selfishness and deceit. Perhaps, he cautioned himself, it only appeared so because she was unaware of being observed. But even that wary voice failed to douse the spark of satisfaction.

"Queen Eleanor told me you were walking with another," he said, stepping into the maze's hard found center. "How is it then that there is no other here?"

Shocked by the unfamiliar voice, Nessa jumped up. Headdress clutched in one hand, she looked down to aid a fumbling attempt to close the throat of her habit with the other. Questions collided in her flustered mind. How had a stranger found his way to the center of the maze? Why was he here? Neckline safely fastened, she looked at the speaker and had answer to the second query at least. There could be no doubt as to his identity. With hair as dark as night gleaming in the sunlight and black-lashed silver eyes whose irises were rimmed in charcoal—he was the man Eleanor had named "as handsome as sin." But how came he to Salisbury so soon? His smile had a physical impact that made breath halt in her throat like a bird caught in a snare. She'd meant to be safely away before he arrived. Saint's, he was tall! Her thoughts were a wild disarray of admiring observations and questions too late for their answers to matter.

Hazel-green eyes were wide in the delicate face overwhelmed by masses of brown curls. Still, as shocked as was she, Garrick felt certain she was no more stunned than he to see the woman he'd thought his bride rise a nun, or nearly so.

Nessa valiantly sought to gather her scattered wits. Remember, she told herself, you are the practical one, the one destined to smooth the way for others. A stab of envy sharper than any she'd known struck suddenly. She rushed into speech to deny its coming. "I pray pardon, my lord." Initial words breathless, she exercised considerable will to hold the next steady. "However, I am certain 'tis my sister, Aleria, you seek."

Surprise had wiped away Garrick's smile, and as he nodded acceptance of her explanation his face grew cold, settling into lines that most people saw as arrogant but that were his shield against baring any part of himself to others. Now it hid an unaccustomed disorientation, a desperate attempt to bring things back into perspective and find solid ground beneath the abruptly shifting sands of his emotions. In disgust he asked himself what matter if this woman or another? Even under such stern questioning his usual cynicism failed to erase the unanticipated disappointment that she was not to be his bride. Ridiculing his own response, he swept a slow appraisal over her. 'Twas merely his distrust of beautiful women, he told himself, which bred a preference for this one of more restrained attractions. The observation provided surprisingly little comfort.

"Can you tell me, then, where your sister may be found?" he asked in a low, emotionless voice. "The queen said she was out walking, and I have it on good authority that this is the destination for such pastimes."

Beneath the cold examination of eyes gleaming silver below black brows, Nessa felt as if he were peering deep inside and reading every fault, right down to the response no nun should feel, not even to a stunningly handsome man. Dropping her gaze before his, she put her hands together palm to fingertip and pressed them hard against each other as she forced herself to answer. "I've been here in the garden's center for a very long time and have neither seen nor heard Aleria."

Garrick stood in silence, eyes still intent on the girl, nay, nun whose eyes were lowered and hands pressed together as if in prayer. The white cloth of her headdress dangled from between slender fingers. He was struck with an irrational dislike of the article that would hide a wealth of curls from his sight. A strong urge to touch them and see if they were as soft as they looked brought a downward curl of disgust to his lips. She was a *nun* or as near to as could be. He had only disdain for women of the world, but a nun even he owed respect.

Under the weight of his continuing gaze, Nessa trembled and a strange panic frazzled the edges of her self-control. Clearly he didn't plan to leave her again in solitude. In a voice no longer calm or measured she told him, "I've been here too long." He nodded but his unsettling gaze never wavered. How could he remain so at ease when she was quivering? Never mind, it was true, and his composure only rattled her more. Stumbling over the words as if they were boulders in the path of her escape, she added, "I must go, but if I happen upon my sister, I'll tell her you've come." Nessa dove into the green maze and disappeared as completely as only one well familiar with its mysteries could do.

Though surely not pursued, Nessa dashed through twisting paths with a reckless speed she'd not permitted since childhood. That black-haired stranger was a dangerous man. Beneath those penetrating silver eyes her proudly claimed ability to think rationally had gone into hiding under the mass of confusion deep inside just as a doe before the hunter's arrow quails amidst a thick forest's tangled undergrowth.

⊸§ *Chapter 3* §⊸

Gasping for air and with sides aching from the exertion of her undignified flight, Nessa stopped. Desperately she reassured herself that even if they wanted to, and surely there was no reason why they should, her recent companions would be unable to follow her purposely winding path. She massaged below her ribcage while striving for sane normalcy by compelling ragged breathing into a deep calming pattern. When the discomfort in her side and tightness of her chest eased, her hands flattened together and lifted to press against soft lips as she sought to reorder befuddled wits. Her reaction to him, she rationalized in an attempt to explain it, had been naught but a natural consequence of an unexpected appearance by the man Eleanor had so accurately portrayed. A comforting argument. Unfortunately, her conscience insistently denied its truth. Honesty was demanded of God's servants, and honesty demanded she face the inescapable fact that her heart-pounding, sense-scattering response to the stunning man had as source an awareness born of neither surprise nor alarming description. Barely noticed, another had stood beside him, someone she couldn't begin to describe although she could easily give a detailed verbal portrait of the earl. The disconcerting truth was that the mere memory of the silver-eyed stranger was capable of wreaking havoc on her sound practicality and cool restraint. Was this the first sign of temptations of the flesh? Breath only recently controlled caught in her throat and had to be forcefully expelled. She must pray forgiveness once for her sin and once again for falling to it over a man soon to be brother.

Deeply involved in her own troublesome plight, Nessa failed to hear the intimate murmurs of others approaching. Nor did she realize when a couple rounded the corner and stopped in surprise.

Aleria knew something was wrong the moment she saw Nessa with clasped hands tight against compressed lips and eyes clenched shut in apparently anguished prayer. "Has something gone amiss?" she asked, stepping forward to touch her sister's arm.

Jerked back to reality, Nessa's hands dropped. "Nay—" She instinctively denied her guilty thoughts. Yet, she had to tell of the earl's arrival. "Aye—" But it wasn't something wrong—exactly. "Nay—only—your intended husband is here."

Aleria's amusement at seeing her ever restrained sister so oddly discomposed died under the blow of unexpected and unwelcome news. Azure eyes flew to the castle above even as she stepped back against the shelter of the figure towering behind.

"Nay." Nessa said again. "Not in the castle, but *here*." Her hands sliced down through the air toward garden floor.

"So soon?" Dismayed, Aleria's azure gaze flew to her escort.

Nessa followed the path of Aleria's attention and for the first time noticed the young man comforting her sister—Reynard de Gaise. Not for years had she seen the familiar handsome face, the unruly brown hair. She gave him a warm smile. Then, as now, his unusual height compensated for a narrowness of frame. When a boy, moody and over-defensive, he'd been at foster under their father's tutelage and raised in their keep until the death of its lord put an end to his stay.

From Nessa's expression Aleria realized his presence was a surprise to her. Flustered, she rushed into an explanation. "After father was killed and the rebellion failed, Reynard's family sent him to foster with the Baron of Wycliffe, a supporter of the king. Now a knight, while Eleanor and I were in Aquitaine he was sent here to join the garrison." A less unnerved Nessa would have recognized the innocent smile as evidence of a guilty secret when with overdone sincerity she added, "I've enjoyed the company of one who remembers our childhood."

Preoccupied with her inappropriate reaction to the earl, although Aleria spoke of a past she could have few memories of, Nessa sought no deeper meaning behind the couple's private walk.

"Indeed, Reynard, I too am happy to see you again." Though honestly pleased, her words were rushed as if speedily spoken to leave way for the next. "But now," she looked back to Aleria, "belike we should return to the castle. There you must make ready to meet the earl." And, her disoriented conscience advised, there she could seek solitude to regain her own composure.

Relieved that her sister had neither questioned her desire to remember a past she'd never been interested in before nor sought a more detailed purpose for her solitary walk with a man, old friend or no, Aleria nodded in complete agreement. She linked her arm with Nessa's and turned them all toward the outbound path, anxious to keep her older sister's thoughts from returning to the deed which, at the very least, lacked in discretion.

From her seat at the center of the high table Queen Eleanor presided over the evening meal. On her right sat the earl, Aleria at his other side, while Conal of Wryborne sat on her left, Nessa beside him. With the practice of many years, Eleanor kept the light patter of meaningless talk flowing. A chore aided by few others. Even Aleria, who usually enjoyed such repartee, was surprisingly distracted.

Unable to glance at Aleria without looking in the earl's direction, Nessa failed to note her sister's attention constantly focused on a familiar member of the castle garrison seated at tables lower and amidst a company enlarged by the addition of both the earl and baron's guards. Nessa was mute, hazel gaze firmly on her meal though she could not later have said what the platter contained. Still, she could feel the piercing silver gaze that seemed to probe her soul, and she feared encountering its strength. During the morning, members of the guard, at ease with her near despite her religious training, had talked amongst themselves of their expected visitor, the man known as the Ice Warrior. So cold was he, one stated, he could freeze men with his eyes. Another had laughed and reported that 'twas said, though many women had hunted the prey with passionate fires, none had melted so much as a driplet from his ice heart. Nessa found the last indictment easy to believe.

Garrick labored under an unaccustomed self-digust for finding his attention constantly drawn not to his beautiful intended bride but to the nun sitting quietly at his friend's side. Saint's tears! She was near consecrated to God and his interest shameful. A fool he'd suddenly become with his inability to divert it. This rare lack of total control over his own responses filled him so completely with self-blame he barely heard the queen's words. A fact leaving many gaps in conversation when he failed to answer her repeated queries. Happily, Conal's easy manner spread out to fill resulting voids but the need left him questioning the source of his friend's distraction, never suspecting it a woman, a plain nun least of all.

Despite a beautifully prepared and bountiful meal, none at the high table were sorry to see it end. They adjourned to the queen's private solar above, where shared discomfort would no longer have the whole castle's company as witness.

Eleanor led the way, with Aleria next. While a lord or knight of good station might lead the way in abodes where no royalty dwelt, by custom men armed, ceremonially at least, traveled as protection at the rear. Thus the two men waited for Nessa to proceed them up the stairway.

Nessa would have much preferred to come last with no one behind to watch; but, realizing the futility of her preference, took her white skirt in hand and began the upward journey. Long, winding steps, lit at intervals by oil-fed braziers, were marked night or day by alternating gloom and wavering flame-shadows. When a child, she'd thought the passageway matched too well the priests' description of the road to hell, and never had she overcome the shiver of discomfort it caused. Distracted as she'd been during the meal, now she wished for such inattention. However, rather than occupying her mind to the exclusion of her distasteful surroundings, awareness of the earl climbing after merely intensified her unease. After their earlier encounter he seemed to embody the temptation that drew one onto the downward path, and she felt his warmth like a lure to fall.

Garrick, frustrated by unaccountable reactions, nearly stomped in her wake. Scowling at the grace of the slender figure ahead, his silver eyes slid up to the replaced headdress now hiding the wealth of soft curls. He disliked the white cloth and wanted to pull it off, freeing the bounty beneath. Fists curled to prevent putting desire into action, he crushed the shameful urge and cursed himself for a fool and a sinner.

The higher they climbed the more intensely Nessa felt the presence of the man at her back. Moving from flickering light into gloom a picture flashed into her mind—she standing still, he stepping up and bringing her form into close contact with the full length of his. Her heart thumped so hard it stopped the breath in her throat—surely born of fear, guilt, not—No! Light broke through the entrance to the landing only steps beyond. Nessa nearly threw herself into the haven of candleglow.

Pausing in the upper level's hallway, Nessa steadied her breath and shook her head vehemently, just once, to clear away the lingering remnants of fanciful thoughts. Hearing the men step from stairs to corridor, she hurried into the queen's solar and immediately perched on a small stool set amidst shadows behind the open door. In truth, her legs were shaking so badly she doubted them able to carry her further. Fortunately she'd no desire to move into the warmth and light emanating from the fireplace that was focus of the chamber.

Eleanor had settled into a cushioned chair close to leaping flame and Aleria had curled her legs beneath her on a lush Saracen carpet at the queen's feet. The earl moved beyond Nessa, mouth grim and narrowed eyes pinned to the woman meant to receive his attention. He sat opposite the queen in a chair matching hers. His friend followed, blind to the maid he passed, earning her slight smile. Few men noticed a nun clearly enough to register her presence. He drew a stool close to the earl's side. Talk resumed, enlivened by more concerted attempts at social niceties on the part of both Aleria and her prospective groom.

Garrick had difficulty finding a subject on which both he

35

and the clearly shallow girl could converse. He'd no knowledge of the fashions and gossip that seemed the sum total of her interests, but at last he struck upon a possible opening.

"You recently returned from the Aquitaine?" He'd been there more times than he could count and knew it well.

"A more wonderful place I never dreamed existed," Aleria immediately enthused. "And I met so many interesting people! The Count of Sperry came to visit. He's an old man, but sweet. He said I was the loveliest woman he'd seen since first he met Eleanor. Wasn't that sweet? And . . ."

Garrick realized he'd given Aleria the perfect opening for a lengthy recital of the great men she'd met and the conquests she'd made. He need only offer the occasional nod or smile—and hold his attention from her sister, a nearly impossible task.

At length Aleria turned to the opulent surroundings of Eleanor's native court. "The castle had the most magnificent garden with the sweetest arbors. I walked there with . . ." Unaware of Garrick's boredom, Aleria prattled on and on.

Sweet, obviously a favorite term. Shallow she was, Garrick reaffirmed, but wasn't that the type of woman he sought? Wasn't the only alternative a shrewd schemer like Eleanor? Despite best intentions, his gaze shifted to a quiet postulant nun.

To blank out the others' presence, Nessa concentrated on her surroundings. Affection warmed her lingering study of details which under Eleanor's guiding hand made the chamber beautiful. Rich tapestries and bright paintings applied to plaster covered the walls while soft padded chairs and rare carpets lent a comfort few could claim. Even the room's strong light was a luxury as the multitude of candles creating it were of sweet-scented wax rather than malodorous tallow. The latter were used in the abbey and so few that night was, at best, dimly lit. The comparison smote Nessa's conscience. Her joy in worldly things was surely a sin and further proof of her lack of true calling. No matter. On the morrow she would return to the abbey. Although a cloud of dread darkened, she resolutely denied its presence. She'd not acknowledged a decision made, yet buried deep within lay acceptance of the inescapable circumstances dictating her answer. No amount of heartfelt rebuttals could obliterate the certain fact that, without beauty to tempt a man into choosing her as wife despite her insignificant dowry, she'd no option save church. What difference if the loveliness and comfort of this abode lingered always in her mind like a sweet melody. Worldly delights were not for her but for women such as Aleria.

"Your Highness." The voice was soft and hesitantly called from a door left ajar. All attention turned to a young maidservant who shifted uncomfortably beneath their eyes. "Pray pardon, but a messenger has come and says he cannot put his parchment into any hands save yours."

Giving a reassuring smile to the girl, Eleanor stood. "Thank you, Mildred. I'll come."

The maidservant turned and slipped thankfully away while Eleanor gave excuses to her guests, promising to return directly.

Although he'd finally made some attempt to speak with her, Aleria was uncomfortable at being left nearly alone with the earl and his friend (just like Nessa to have withdrawn to some world of her own when presented with two men so attractive). Accustomed to receiving unstinting admiration from every male who came near, though seldom oversensitive to others' moods, Aleria could hardly fail to notice so startling a thing as her prospective husband's complete lack of interest in her. He'd not once this whole evening remarked on her appearance or even complemented her gown!

"Isn't this color lovely?" she prettily asked, looking down with a coy smile to study her dainty fingers as they smoothed clinging satin over a shapely thigh. "While we were in the Aquitaine, Eleanor had it specially dyed to match my eyes." There. She had given him the perfect opening to repent and atone for his earlier failure. Little as she might want him for mate, the earl was an exceptionally attractive man, and she meant for him to give her his admiration as her due.

Nessa stared at her twined fingers and gave all her energies to suppressing the heat brightening her cheeks, embarrassment born of her sister's boldness. Had she failed to point Aleria in right manners or did the customs of court life allow such actions? Having no answer she mentally retreated to the quiet center of the castle maze.

After the queen's departure Garrick's attention had settled again on the one who sat separate from the flock—a peaceful dove. To him Aleria's words held no more meaning than the incessant squawks from a nest of starlings.

No response was forthcoming. Aleria impatiently looked up to discover that gray eyes, surrounded by the thick black lashes she or nearly any woman of her acquaintance would pay dearly to possess, were not even looking at her! Miffed, she turned her most dazzling smile to Conal. Such punishments seldom failed to raise a satisfying jealousy in male onlookers—and a scramble for her attention. "Pray what do you think of it, gentle sir?"

Suddenly focus of the beauty's considerable charms, Conal lost no time in responding. "I think the queen's been cheated! But could it be else when surely the dye has not been created that could match the incomparable color of your eyes."

Like a much loved cat with a bowl of cream, Aleria lapped up the praise. It soothed the confidence bruised by the man who not only hadn't rushed to duel with Conal for her attention but hadn't even glanced her way. It never occurred to Aleria that another had caught the earl's attention—her sister least of all!

Garrick found himself in the unusual position of having to pull his thoughts from a woman. Never had he found one of their number interesting enough to steal into his mind unbidden—until now. Irritated, he broke into her private world. "Did you live in this castle and on King Henry's bounty for many years?"

The words were polite but bore an icy edge that sliced through Nessa's insulating shield, as easily as a hot knife through butter. Though uncertain of its source, she instinctively responded to the challenge in his tone. "Since nearly the day your king imprisoned his wife in its grasp." Her tilted chin showed no sign of the humility expected of a nun.

The green fire in her eyes brought a satisfaction Garrick would not allow himself to investigate. "What else," he asked, "could Henry do to control a viper who attacks at every turn?"

"He could have put aside his Rosamunds and Alyces to live with Eleanor as the wife he swore to God," she snapped back.

Garrick laughed. "What do you know of such things?" As

a nun how could she understand such relationships as those between men and their mistresses or even wives?

"I know God's commandments—all of them. Do you?" His disdain for her ability to apply logic to things not personally experienced raised Nessa's temper to glowing heat yet her words were as cold as the man spoken to.

A black head shook slowly as if despairing for her naivete.

"Thou shalt not commit adultery is what He wrote on stone tablets. He didn't say woman shall not but men may." She met his gaze steadily, undeniable truth strengthening her statement.

Garrick was not fool enough to continue a line of battle doomed to failure. Clearly, she'd never understand the feminine duplicity that drove men to seek other women. "And what of the commandment also written by God on those stone tablets—the commandment that orders man to honor his father? Your queen stole Henry's sons from him, his heirs. She raised them to disloyalty and dishonor of their father."

Without pause Nessa rebutted his argument. "You left out an important half of that commandment. It says, 'Honor thy father and thy mother.' Eleanor didn't steal Henry's sons. He left them behind while he went off to make war and live with other women."

"Not John, he kept John." Garrick gave the first answer that came to mind, not a wise choice.

"Oh yes, he kept John." Nessa's lips curled in the closest thing to a sneer that had ever touched them. "And what a pitiful excuse for a prince is he."

"Have you met him?" Bound either in abbey walls or the domain of Eleanor's confinement, he was certain she had not.

"Nay, but I know a great many who have." Nessa's fire was not dampened by the cold of his icy contempt.

Garrick automatically repeated oft heard words. "He's young and he'll learn."

"Aye," Nessa mocked. "We hear such 'tis the king's excuse for John's disaster in Ireland, but John has lived a score of years and more. If he's yet to acquire sense so basic, he won't."

Garrick agreed with much of what she'd said, but never would he admit it to her. So long as Henry lived, John was

39

on his tether. After? Great changes would follow no matter the prince who became king. Worry over unforeseeable matters was of no use and a waste of time better spent on problems nearer at hand.

Returning footsteps brought an immediate end to their heated exchange. Throughout Aleria had sat in shock while Conal had nearly burst into laughter at sight of his woman-disdaining friend meeting his match in a verbal battle with a member of the weaker sex, and a nun at that! He viewed the maid who'd battled proud Garrick to a standoff with new respect.

Once Eleanor had settled in the room's center, the enormity of Nessa's loss of good sense swept over her. Standing, she drew Eleanor's attention. "I've a long trip awaiting me on the morrow and feeling in need of rest to face its rigors, I beg leave."

A regal nod dismissed the pale girl who Garrick watched unblinking. He was amazed to have found such fire in a would-be nun. He'd thought her a dove and perhaps she was but one with the talons of a hawk! Yet only did she loyally defend her patroness and no man of honor could denigrate another for that, even be they representatives of opposing factions. Moreover, he was amazed by her lack of guile in hiding her true feelings. The women he knew would have pretended agreement with whatever a man said, the better to hide their schemes beneath. Contemptuous of all mortal women save those who resigned worldly pleasures and devoted themselves to God, here he'd found one who fit into neither the world of the sly and self-absorbed nor the realms of cool and withdrawn piety. His interest in the unusual postulant grew apace with his self-disgust for wrongful thoughts. He was upset with himself and, irrationally, with her for being its cause by refusing to fit neatly into any predesigned category.

⊷§ *Chapter 4* §⊷

Aleria hadn't appeared for the morning meal. Nor was she in her bedchamber. Before departing Nessa wanted to wish her little sister farewell and good fortune with the approaching betrothal, but Aleria was not where she should be. Impatience and irritation grew with alarming speed. To forestall such unworthy emotions, Nessa halted in the midst of the corridor bisecting the upper level of the queen's tower. She pressed palms together and raised them against soft lips in the gesture she deemed an acceptable replacement for other nervous habits. Drawing three deep, steady breaths, she prayed for divine aid in recovering the unhurried, even composure expected of God's servants.

For once Nessa was anxious to return to the abbey. She'd like to have taken her wish for speed as sign of growing ease with her destiny but her depressingly efficient conscience pointed out that her haste sprang more from a desire to escape the alarmingly attractive earl than anticipation for rejoining the endless repetitions of cloistered life. The last phrase—distressing but undeniable—had stealthily crept into her carefully monitored thoughts. Nonetheless, as improper as the idea might be, 'twas an inescapable fact that the cloistered life *was* an endless repetition of the same prayers, the same services, the same duties day after day and year after year—unending, unvarying and inevitably boring for an inquisitive mind. She had hoped to continue her education in the abbey but only a limited number of precious books were available within confining walls. Moreover, questioning the words and thoughts of others was frowned upon, questioning doctrine was heresy. Fervently seeking the simple faith and single-minded devotion of one such as Sybil, her fellow postulant at the abbey, had left Nessa with assurance of her faith in God but ever more certain of her lack of vocation for holy orders.

Weak light of cloudy day barely brightened the corridor's hide-covered window and made no imprint on Nessa's dim view. She'd sought calm and her prayer had been answered, though not as comfortably as she'd expected. Worry over what must be was turned by a shouldn't be then blocked with a no choice which tossed her back to the start. This convoluted path led concerns astray and ended any desire for swift return to St. Margaret's.

Making herself concentrate on the problem at hand, Nessa forced her features into mild lines which hid unworthy fears. Folded hands demurely at her waist, she moved resolutely toward the door of what was Aleria's last possible retreat. The thick oak planks barring the solar's entrance slid soundlessly open to reveal the one Nessa sought. Aleria's fine brows were drawn into what passed for a ferocious frown yet surely brought to the mind of any observer unfamiliar with the maid only the vision of a sulky kitten robbed of her cream. Though delicately flushed cheeks merely increased Aleria's loveliness, Nessa recognized the sign of rising temper in one who always got what she wanted.

"Nessa." Aleria caught sight of her sister and immediately poured out her woe for an injustice done her. "He *is* cold. Cold to the core." She flung a dainty hand toward a point hidden from Nessa's view by the door she'd not yet moved beyond.

Certain who stood there, Nessa struggled to summon her once disdained pride as she stepped inside. For one so lacking in confidence as she, this constant demand for courage was wearying.

Darkly clad and with black hair and deeply sun-bronzed skin, against the dull light from an unshuttered window the earl's silhouette loomed powerful and intimidating. Light gray eyes glistened like ice from the gloom. Ice. Nessa straightened, chin tilting beneath his steady glare as Aleria continued.

"He pays no heed when I say I'll not have him. I clearly stated my intent, with all good courtesy and thanks for the honor of the alliance offered. He scarce acknowledged my words—even when I screamed my refusal to wed one such as he. Make him understand that I'll not do what I don't wish." One dainty foot stamped in temper. The unmoved earl looked more disgusted than penitent. Aleria burst into tears and ran into comforting arms.

Nessa silently rebuked herself for noting how tears, the worst enemy of most women's vanity, merely added silver gilt to the lily Aleria was. She should have foreseen this clash of wills and cautioned her sister against useless demands. Years ago she should have begun teaching Aleria that there always was some will higher than a woman's, be it God's, a king's or a husband's. Now it was too late. She'd long since committed herself to smoothing Aleria's path and couldn't now step aside despite the collision course it meant with that great block of black ice.

"Tear-stung eyes turn red and puff straight away," Nessa whispered in Aleria's ear. She knew the possibility of an unsightly change in Aleria's appearance before any man, and a handsome man most of all, would send her scurrying away.

"Oh," Aleria gasped, falling back. "Your pardon." With a quick glance, Aleria hurriedly offered the earl her excuse. "I must go—" Yet, even under threat of ill-looks, she paused to repeat her appeal to Nessa. "Please make him understand."

The door snapped shut behind Aleria. Nessa stared at its planks for a long moment while firmly telling herself the one waiting was a man as any other, and she had only to hold her pride before her. Mayhap beautiful she was not, but intelligent she was. He might disdain her for her lack of looks; but, she encouraged herself, he would find her able to meet him in a battle of will and words. Unfortunately when she turned toward him her bravery wobbled, and she nearly fell back beneath the force of his gaze. Looking down at the hands again carefully folded at her waist she watched as they

43

turned white under the pressure she exerted though she felt no discomfort. It was her lot to ease Aleria's way and she'd not quail even did it mean standing against the Ice Warrior who was so cold no emotion could touch him. Nessa whipped up her temper to build courage. No matter his lacks, he should have some consideration for others.

"Was it needful to upset her so?" Her words were full of a fine bravado, yet she hadn't the stamina to meet an icy gaze.

His short laugh held no humor. "*She* told *me* she had decided against our betrothal. I was forced to tell her the choice was not hers to make! The king persuaded me to accept her for wife."

Aghast, Nessa's hazel eyes widened in dismay. "You told her that?" Discovering any man had to be persuaded to take her for wife would be a near mortal wound to Aleria's vanity.

"Nay," the reply sounded as if it had been blown off the ice fields of northern lands, "I told her that to me she is no great prize. I have accepted her solely in honor of my king."

Nessa's thick lashes fell to peach-tinted cheeks. It was worse than she'd feared.

Garrick stepped closer, hands clenched with anger. "I have promised my king, and my promises I keep! She asks that you tell me she need not do what she does not wish? Far better you employ your time in telling her that she *will* do what another demands!"

His cold command scraped across Nessa's temper like a rasp across iron. Sparks flared. Under effort of will she kept them safey contained although green flames danced in the eyes which defiantly met silver. "Mayhap," she tightly responded, "the battle for Aleria's compliance would be more easily won by skillful strokes of tact than by your assault of rude demands."

"Tact?" He nearly shouted. "When she tells me what she will do? Best you urge her to go with care and accept as unbending fact that I will not be swayed by any woman— beauty or no." He'd nothing but contempt for men made fools by nurturing a woman's vanity with flattery and bowing to their capricious wishes.

Sparks had won free of Nessa's constraints to smolder in the dry tinder of her anger. Her retort was immediate and fierce. "You could have made a small effort to woo your chosen wife—leastways shown some slight measure of civility."

Dark head tilted back, through narrowed eyes he coldly scrutinized the dove who chided like a twittering jay. With the instinct of a skilled huntsman, he struck at her most vulnerable point. "Where hides the meek attitude, the earnest desire for inner peace which surely a nun should possess?"

Nessa's eyes clenched shut as humiliation swept over her. Clearly he'd seen and condemned her nature. She was unworthy of being a nun. He'd discovered not only those lacks, but his icy examination had doubtless also found her appearance wanting, branding her unworthy as a secular woman. Pulling tattered remnants of pride together she shot back, "I'm not a nun—yet."

The discovery of her lack of inner commitment surprised a smile from Garrick. The idea of her foregoing the cloister brought relief, though he shied away from pondering its source.

The warmth of the earl's sudden smile doused glowing coals of anger and flustered Nessa. Men of ice should not possess such potent charms. Struggling through a tangle of conflicting emotions, with a sharp shake of her head and without considering her words, she continued. "Moreover, 'tis my duty to come to my sister's defense. As my only family she comes first."

Garrick nearly laughed with the added cheer of this further proof of her lack of vocation. "Your belief that a mortal's defense takes priority over the condition of your immortal soul must be of interest to the Holy Sisters whom you seek to join."

Nessa could have stomped her foot as convincingly and as childishly as Aleria. She sought instead to recover her error with an immediate response. "Did Christ not say what you do unto 'one of the least of these my brethren, ye have done unto me?' " Pride in her knowledge and ability to quote scripture brought Nessa's confidence back. "And how much more do I owe my own blood?" In her view 'twas a neatly scored triumph.

Garrick nodded seriously, but laughter glinted silver in his eyes. "And did He not also say that the first and greatest commandment is to 'love the Lord thy God with all thy heart, and with all thy soul, and with all thy mind'?''

Although most men feared and worshipped God, few other than clerics studied His words. Shocked to find him so knowledgeable of scripture that he might quote it for his own purpose, and flustered by the implied rebuke peeling back the cover over her own uncertainties, Nessa's good sense was thrown to the wolves of irrational temper. "As Aleria said,'' she lashed out, "you are cold to the core—as only a man without a soul could be.''

Thick black lashes lowered until naught but a narrow strip of silver revealed the gaze holding Nessa motionless. Many had named him as cold as true ice and never had he found more than amusement in their words. But that this one woman had dared name him the same stung his usually well-controlled emotions so sharply that he took rash action.

"Cold?'' Though a question, he clearly sought no answer.

Alarmed by the sensuous smile that seemed to steam on a face of ice, Nessa would have stepped back were it possible, but like a frightened rabbit she could not move. Not even when, for the first time in her life, the strong arms of a man wrapped her in bonds of flame-forged iron. Someone had once told her that ice could burn, yet never had she believed them—until now.

Unable to give rational thought to his deed, Garrick bent his dark head to the taste of untried innocence. It was sweet like the first berries of summer which leave an unsatisfied hunger of such intensity that for more their seeker is willing to dare the brambles and thorns protecting luscious fruit.

Despite the strong arms about her, Nessa found no harshness in the earl's embrace. Yet gentleness lent a greater fear than cruelty, for it lured her to yield to the fire at the core of his ice, a fire so hot it melted her with its temptation.

Garrick lifted one hand to pull the white cloth from Nessa's head and buried his fingers in the thick curls beneath. They were soft, as soft as they'd been in shameful dreams. He tangled lush tresses about his hand just tightly enough to urge her head back and lay her long elegant throat vulnerable to his lips. Skin like delicate satin. Skin the fragrance of spring.

The fire moved from lips to throat, and Nessa's breath

46

caught with the pleasure. Guilty anguish heightened the ache of desire.

"Sins of the flesh." The words Nessa had not realized she spoke aloud hit Garrick like buckets of water from a glacier-fed spring. His arms fell as his face lifted to the heavens where surely an angry God looked down on him, a sinner.

Suddenly released, Nessa still stood in the thrall of his spell as if the fire of his hold had transferred his ice to her and she was frozen, like Lot's wife, into an unmoving pillar. Nay, she silently argued with her overwhelming sense of guilt. Lot's wife had been punished for disobeying God's directive. Her conscience mocked the sorry attempt at self-excuse. Hadn't she done the same? Wasn't she on the verge of a vow of celibacy, yet standing here yielding to this man of heat, heat which surely rose from the devil's domain? Moreover, his hold over her thoughts and actions assuredly emanated from that selfsame source. With horrified eyes she looked at him—tall, dark, and incredibly handsome like Lucifer before the fall. She ran from the castle as if all the denizens of nether regions were at her heels.

Garrick was no less horrified than Nessa. As to most people he knew, the very idea of profaning something holy was a transgression of the worst magnitude. Finding himself that first day attracted to a nun, even a postulant, had been a shameful thing. He'd passed now beyond looking, even beyond sinful dreaming, to touching. The deed filled him with self-loathing.

"Sister Agnes," the call was repeated more firmly.

Nessa roused herself from where she'd mentally retreated. She was on her knees in the small abbey chapel where she'd been for much of the day, earnestly praying for forgiveness and a sign for what path to follow. She'd been excused from her duties with the sisters' understanding of her need to seek divine guidance on the important decision she must make. Though participating in the normal pattern of worship services, she remained after others left. Refusing to grimace under protest from stiff limbs, she rose and turned to the elderly nun waiting patiently.

"Abbess Berthilde asks that you come to her chamber." With a warm smile and encouraging nod, the older woman slipped away.

Wishing she could attain such peace, Nessa looked down the corridor she must traverse. Little was wasted on such frivolous items as more tapers than strictly necessary, and it was dim. Nessa fought down a traitorous longing for candle-bright rooms and softly padded prie-dieus like those in Salisbury Tower. Without thinking to warn Aleria of the earl's response to her wishes (a lack born of selfish preoccupation with her own trials and sorely repented), she'd escaped its comforts and arrived here during the late hours of the previous night. Every jerking step of her donkey had reinforced another doubt. The earl's arguments had hit too near their mark. She was too involved in mortal deeds, too easy to anger and dispute. But the most important discovery was the one made in his arms. Surely a woman with right character would have stood unmoved or, better, have been repulsed by his embrace. Guilt nearly choked her.

She squared her shoulders and lifted her chin. Doubtless the abbess meant to ask for a decision. She'd spent most of this day on her knees seeking guidance and all she knew at this moment was that she must confess her sin. She strode down the hall determined to cleanse her soul by the doing as soon as possible.

Abbess Berthilde stood waiting in the open door of her chamber, a gentle smile laying creases in plump, apple-bright cheeks. "Come in, come in. Knowing you were in the chapel, I put off calling you earlier."

Nessa forced a smile but it was grim. Anxious to repent before she fell coward and backed out, she began before the abbess could continue. "At the queen's tower I decided to join holy orders, and then fell to the worst sin of my life."

Abbess Berthilde's eyebrows rose but she remained silent, knowing how difficult this was for the girl. She sat on the lone chair in the spartan chamber and nodded for Nessa to continue.

Haltingly at first, Nessa spoke of the earl and her guilty attraction to him. Then, as if the flood gates had broken, she fell to her knees in front of the older woman and confessed her response in his embrace. "You see, Holy Mother," Nessa bent her face to the abbess's knees to hide streaming tears, "how unworthy I am to stand among you, to join your saintly ranks."

"Nay, child," Abbess Berthilde answered, tenderness in

48

her voice and gentleness in the hands that patted the bowed head. "I see a sinner, like as we all are. I see a sinner repentant and forgiven by the Almighty. No one here is without sin. We are not saints, only women seeking service to God to expiate our mortal nature and draw ever nearer to Him."

Nessa felt closer to the abbess than ever before and the life she promised sounded more welcoming. On the other side rose an image with silver ice eyes but a smile of amazing warmth.

The abbess saw the distant look come into the gaze which had lifted in response to her words and she shook her head. Had circumstances been different, the girl would have found happiness in another sort of life, equally worthy but far different. As it was—"Agnes, the man is meant to be your brother, and I fear holy orders and daily prayer are the only hope for cleansing your soul of incestuous desire."

Nessa's head fell forward into her cupped hands. The abbess spoke a truth that brought despair sharper than any pain she'd known before, so hurtful she barely heard the abbess continue.

"None of which is why I called you here. The queen has requested your immediate return for your sister's betrothal."

The prospect of seeing the earl again brought a pleasure that warred in Nessa's heart with shame for its wickedness. Doubtless Aleria had plagued the queen to send for her, but how was she to survive?

ᏸᏕ Chapter 5 ᏸᏕ

A dull roar, occasionally punctuated by laughter or jeering jests, filled Salisbury's great hall. Sitting quietly at the high table, Nessa closed her eyes and savored the familiar, soon to be forsworn sounds of earthy camaraderie. For once her over-active conscience remained silent on the ills of lauding such valueless joys. Again a trip begun at dawn had ended near nightfall with an arrival in good time for the evening meal. But, this time she'd joined the party on the dais—she and her guest.

After learning of the summons to return, she'd beseeched the Reverend Mother to send with her a guard against further transgressions—Sybil, her pious fellow postulant who ever walked the straight and narrow pathway to heaven. Agreeing that Nessa was in need of another's aid in rebuffing unholy desires and that a companion so devout would be worthy example, Abbess Berthilde had allowed that the two should travel together.

Nessa glanced apprehensively to the side. Sybil was seated next to Conal of Wryborne while she'd happily taken the chair beyond, anxious to be as far from the earl as possible. Nessa had thought Sybil immune to masculine charm and was disconcerted to find the woman's pale ivory cheeks gone pink under the baron's obvious admiration. Despite proper intentions, hazel eyes slid past Sybil, past Conal, and past Eleanor—drawn inexorably to the black-haired man near the high table's far end. A waiting silver gaze caught the glance she should never have allowed.

"We'll stop one night, mayhap more, at Swinton Keep," Garrick informed the bride-to-be at his side although his thoughts were on neither his words nor their recipient. The beauty at his side could not hold his attention from the woman his steady gaze had summoned. By Nessa's choice of companions he saw her determination to allow no further lapses into earthly realms. Yet, even as he acknowledged that fact, disappointment ached. Without conscious thought he'd nourished an oddly pleasant notion that the small signs of her discontent foreshadowed a decision to leave abbey behind. Now he berated himself for the folly in such hopes. Long meant for nun, what else was there for her—his sister-in-law? Undeniable reality did not abate his distaste for the deed which forbade easy resignation.

Leaning against the tall, carved back of her chair as if sapped of strength, Aleria barely heard the earl's words. Golden hair still glowed but her cheeks were pale, and azure eyes were as dull as a sky without sunlight. Though her proposed spouse had yet to exhibit the admiration she'd long believed men owed to her, it was not his continuing lack that had stolen her joy. Preoccupied with her woes and forlorn attention focused on a lower table, she failed to note the path of his interest.

The voice of Nessa's conscience, most usually a quiet whisper urging good works and rebuking wrongful thoughts or actions, now fairly screamed warnings, demanding she turn from the Ice Warrior's unwavering gaze. Exercising more strength of will than ever before, Nessa wrenched her eyes from his. A short distance beyond her trencher rested an intricate metal stand with a lit taper atop. Hands palm-joined and raised to her lips, she stared with such unequaled fervor at the candle 'twas near miraculous it did not melt into a lump of useless wax.

Eleanor, aware of each curious current, decided that enough was enough. "It's time we retire to my solar." Putting down the ivory-handled knife used to slice bites from an apple, she stood.

51

Relieved by the uncomfortable meal's end and intending to withdraw into some corner shadowed against prying silver eyes, Nessa nearly jumped to her feet. An action so immediate and lacking in the grace demonstrated by the queen that it drew the attention of all. Nessa's cheeks burned, embarrassment deepened by the knowledge that nothing more clearly revealed a bright blush than the pristine whiteness of the wimple and headdress which provided a close-fitting frame for a postulant's face.

Despite her rush to stand, Nessa held back. Even the earl and his friend departed, thinking she meant not to join them and unwilling to increase her discomfort by insisting she precede them. Thus, she was last to enter the steep, winding staircase. Occupied with her plan to enter last and win the seclusion she sought, she held at bay her childhood distaste for this "stairway to hell." Unfortunately, her plan for retreat was foiled.

"Come sit with me," Aleria invited as her sister appeared in the solar doorway. Sitting on the far end of a bench facing the fire and beside the queen's chair, she patted the tapestry cushion. "Though you were here but days ago, I've missed you. Besides, during your last visit we had no time to talk at all."

Trapped, Nessa complied although it meant taking a seat between her sister and, in a chair at the bench's other end, the man she meant most to avoid. Aleria immediately turned to Eleanor, leaving Nessa desperately seeking distraction. She looked past Aleria and the queen to watch as Conal aided Sybil into a chair some distance beyond. Worry for Sybil rose higher. Conal was talking softly and she was smiling—flirtatiously? Surely not!

"You'll stay longer this time?" Aleria called Nessa back.

"Long enough to witness your betrothal." And, thank the Lord, Nessa silently told herself, that meant only two full days at the most. Turned sideways on the bench and thus her back on the earl, she smiled with forced brightness at her sister. Gaze full on Aleria's face for the first time since her arrival, she was shocked to see how her delicate features were drawn and how her azure eyes clouded at mention of the ceremony. She castigated herself for being so caught in selfish concerns that she'd failed to earlier notice the beauty's unhappiness. Such neglect of her sister was the antithesis of all her mother had instilled in her, of all she'd been taught in the abbey about giving paramount importance to the needs of others. She must talk privately with Aleria, help her understand and accept the path expected of her. Futures had been mapped out for them both nearly since birth. She had grown up knowing the boundaries and expectations of her own, but realized now that she'd failed to see the younger girl mentally prepared for the one chosen to be hers.

" 'Struth we've not visited privately since before your great journey. Come to my chamber tonight, and we'll talk away the deepest hours like we did as children."

As if the words had been some magical incantation, Aleria's bright smile flashed and sparks were relit in her eyes. Nessa had never disappointed her. Nessa had an answer for her every problem. Surely, Nessa would do it again. Confidence in her sister's abilities brought renewed assurance and revived Aleria's natural spirit—flighty yet warm and loving. Although it had all been said before, she chattered of gossip from continental courts. Eventually Eleanor, pleased by Aleria's renewed spirit, picked up the refrain. The two women were soon involved in talk of people and places Nessa knew nothing about.

Though happy that Aleria had relaxed into her usual carefree self (what a change one small promise had made), Nessa's discomfort remained. Azure eyes glowed with a trust that was burdensome. She'd seen it before and on each occasion Aleria had sought her aid in a near impossible feat to smooth her life's way. Nessa had not far to search for a likely hopeless problem—its penetrating gaze was strong on her back.

Beneath the silver weight, Nessa closed her eyes against the small room's intimate, mellow fire-glow. In hopes that the dark man would think her praying, she laid palm-joined hands against her lips and bowed her head. Quiet moments passed.

"Nessa."

Hitherto only two women had used the diminutive of her name but this dark velvet voice belonged neither to her sister nor to the queen. Nay, the voice giving such texture to her shortened name that it felt like a caress belonged to the man

53

who was temptation incarnate. Unwilling to answer the soft call, she weighed her responses carefully.

"Nessa," Garrick quietly called again. Sybil was wrapped in Conal's attentions while the queen and her protégée had become so engrossed in their talk they gave little thought to others.

With no escape, she must acknowledge what she wished to deny. Slowly Nessa raised her eyes to the gray smoke gaze she feared able to lure her far from the path intended for her.

"Your sister told me that as a child she coined the name and that you much prefer it."

Nessa nodded, as if under a spell which had stolen her powers of speech. You must seem a mute fool to him, her good sense berated. Sit up, answer him like the learned woman you are.

"It suits you better."

His comment startled Nessa free of wary reserve; she smiled.

Caught by the sweetness in her response, Garrick tumbled into the fathomless depths of eyes softened to velvet. With a slight shake he sought to clear his mind of subtle enticements before continuing with the purpose of this private speech.

"My action when last we met was ill-done, and I pray you will pardon the lapse of good sense that caused it." His gaze held hers until silver sparks seemed to set flames of green fire within. Irrepressibly drawn from beyond his iron will, more words followed. "I repent of the deed, but not of what I learned—your nature is nowise cold enough to thrive beneath nun's weeds."

His words snapped Nessa out of her trance as effectively as a cold-water dousing wakes the sleeper. "Nay. 'Tis untrue." She automatically and vehemently denied the very thing that had given rise to her own doubts, the thing she most feared. What use a fiery nature when for it there was no earthly use?

"It's a fact as undeniable as the certainty that you sit here beside me." Garrick was unwilling to let her escape reality, unwilling to allow her escape into a life in which she was surely not meant to be trapped.

54

"I tell you no," Nessa gasped, feeling as if his insight were smothering her hard-won submission to what must be.

The ever-changing eyes Garrick recognized as a mysterious mirror revealing her each emotional change were now fear-filled, wide and near all of soft brown.

"Only is it born of unholy temptations that should never have been thrust upon a nun." With the accusation Nessa fanned flames of temper to battle the intended mortal blow to her acceptance of the only future open to one such as she.

Garrick flinched as if struck unprepared by a foe's lance. Yet, even as he fell from the steed of his self-confidence into a mire of guilt, he was hard put to refrain from begging her not to join the order. It came to him as a devastating certainty that he felt envy for Christ's place as her bridegroom, though as wicked and ill-begot as the original sin. As Eve tempted Adam with forbidden fruit, so he had sought to lure a nun from holy vows. Shining steadily through his guilt for such thoughts was a painful fear that he'd found a rare woman of fire and truth only to be forbidden.

"Nessa."

The soft voice from the bedchamber's door summoned the one called from unthinking study of a smudge on white cloth. Preoccupation with her sinful response to the earl, and the ease with which he'd read her true nature, had made it a fruitless investigation, and she'd yet to lift hand to its removal. It could wait. With a gentle smile Nessa turned to the welcome distraction of her little sister hesitating in the doorway.

Aleria stepped inside, closed the door and leaned uneasily against its solid support. Now she was here and, despite her trust in Nessa's unlimited abilities, was unsure how to start.

Looking from golden hair bright against dark planks down the small, curvaceous form to the curled toes of one bare foot rubbing against the other, Nessa remembered the promised talk. Seeing her sister's tension, her earlier apprehensions grew worse. Clearly the younger girl had something to say—or rather something to ask. Fearing her request, Nessa knew she dared not delay a moment longer the task of convincing her sister of the necessity of fulfilling her duties to her king, her queen, and the earl. But before she formed the words to begin, Aleria did.

"You've got to save me from him!" Aleria launched her dainty self headlong across the open space between them. Caught in loving arms, Aleria looked up into a familiar frown of gentle rebuke. "No, truly. You must help me be free of him."

" 'Tis impossible." There was no question but that Aleria spoke of the silver-eyed lord. "He's here by the king's own writ."

Aleria jerked from the other's affectionate hold to stand two steps away. She planted fists on hips and responded with the fire of a tiny termagant. "King be damned and earl, too." Cheeks flushed with both anger and embarrassment for her words, Aleria stamped her foot and boldly added, "I love Reynard and he loves me." She looked to see how her declaration was received.

Nessa's brows arched in surprise, as much for her sister's language as for the claimed love of another. On further thought, she realized she should've suspected as much from their guilty expressions the day they'd stumbled upon her in the maze and from the fervent looks she'd seen exchanged. Her failure to recognize their feelings was one more blame to lay at the earl's door as, without his distractions, surely she would have.

"Afore he arrived we'd reason to believe the queen, even king, would look upon our union with favor. Reynard is a loyal supporter and I but a minor heiress. Now—" Aleria flung herself to her knees beside where Nessa sat, "without your aid we've no hope at all." Nessa appeared distressingly unmoved.

"Surely you see it's impossible for me to wed a man so cold. A man who mislikes me as much as I him!" Small hands clasped Nessa's fingers so tight they'd be numb when released. "He is the Ice Warrior, you ken? Cold and hard as black ice and without even the tiniest flicker of emotion. I'd be miserable with him. Truly I would. You can't mean to abandon me to his freezing hold. You simply can't." Aleria's azure eyes gleamed with crystal tears and silently beseeched her last hope.

Nessa had never been, and was not now, impervious to such poignant pleas. 'Twas her little sister, her only remaining family, who sought compassion and aid. Nessa could no more insist her beloved Aleria bow to this unwanted duty than she had forced her to bow to any unpleasant reality in the past. Again she would smooth the beauty's way. She would find some path around that great block of ice. The knowledge of the molten core within that block of ice mocked her fragile bravado. Nonetheless, it was her duty to aid her sister, and she would.

"I can give you no promise save to do all I can, however little it may be." Nessa gazed unseeing into a far corner's dark shadows. "There must be a way." After a few moments more of silent pondering, Nessa returned her attention to Aleria. She forced a bright reassuring smile as she brushed golden curls back and wiped the moisture from rose cheeks. "Go, seek your rest and leave me to think on the matter." And to pray with unequaled fervor for the answer to this problem which she feared could be won only by divine intervention—a miracle of sorts.

From Aleria's earliest memory she'd trusted Nessa to solve all her problems; and, having never been disappointed, faith in her sister's abilities scattered Aleria's doubts. "Thank you!" Aleria gave Nessa a quick, tight hug, bounced from the bed, and hurried off to her own.

While Aleria slept in confident peace, Nessa sat awake almost all the night alternately considering and discarding possible avenues of hope. In the end, finding her human logic defeated by the realities that bounded their lives, she knelt in prayer and promised to serve any penance, pay any price for the aid she sought.

⋙ *Chapter 6* ⋘

Even without abbey bell to loudly ring the hour and despite a weariness bone-deep, years of training awakened Nessa at first light. From unsuccessful ponderings and troubled prayers she'd slipped into dreams without peace. She had no more found a simple answer to Aleria's problem than she'd earlier found an answer to her own. She sat up and every muscle ached as if the night had been spent in a frantic physical struggle to win the goal.

Her modest bedchamber possessed only a narrow arrow slit to give view of the world beyond and was fortunate to have that. She'd left it unshuttered in the previous evening's preoccupation, first with her uncertain future and then with Aleria's wish to escape the earl's hold. The man and hold she herself had all too recently found wickedly enticing. Dawn light, though weak, sundered the chamber's gloom to lay a path across rush-strewn flooring. Heartsick and near to admitting defeat, she blindly studied the long blade of light until it brightened and grew, stretching to touch a plush rectangle of soft and subtly toned cloth. The queen had given the Saracen carpet to her long ago—to protect bare feet from cold.

The last hope for answer to their dilemma required an

action she'd rather not do. Palm-joined hands pressed against soft lips, holding back a dejected sigh. To save Nessa's toes from cold, Eleanor had gifted her with this rich piece. To save Aleria from the cold of marriage to someone unlikely to ever care for her Eleanor would do more. Nessa was unused to seeking help from others. 'Twas her place to aid, not to ask; but now, for Aleria, she must go to the queen and admit herself unequal to the task.

Resolving to fulfill her sister's wishes no matter the method required, Nessa stepped from the bed. Toes curling against the comforting carpet, she poured water from the ewer into the basin atop a bedside chest. She dashed tepid liquid over face and arms and quickly forced order to tangled curls before donning her habit with the efficiency of long familiarity and a never varying style. It was early yet, and the queen would still be in her chamber. Nessa paused, hand upon the door latch. She knew and humbly accepted that God's response to a prayer, although possibly unexpected, even unwanted, was given by a wisdom never to be questioned. She owed Him thanks for the answer she never doubted came from above and closed her eyes to send upward a quick prayer of gratitude and a plea for a successful outcome.

Nessa stepped from her chamber, glad their male visitors were housed on another level and she need fear no unexpected encounter. The muted sounds of the awakening castle came to her ears as she moved down the corridor to Eleanor's chamber door. Its oaken planks were so thick and tightly constructed that no sound from within could be heard. She rapped firmly for she dare not hesitate or the discomfort in asking another for help might turn her aside from this final chance for a happy conclusion.

Nessa blinked with surprise as the door opened even before her hand had dropped away. Clearly timid Lady Catherine had been on the verge of departing and now stepped aside, allowing Nessa to enter before she went out, pulling the door shut behind.

Giving a warm smile to the girl hovering just within the chamber, Eleanor called, "Nessa, come sit with me."

In response, Nessa moved to perch on a stool near the queen.

Seeing her foster daughter's curious unease, the queen

tried to soothe the girl's poorly hidden anxiety. Turning to stare into a mirror of polished metal, Eleanor arranged a fine linen wimple in graceful folds beneath her chin as she spoke. "It's been years since last you ran to me before the morning meal."

Tension born of an unfamiliar and difficult task made it impossible for Nessa to look directly at the one whose aid she'd come seeking. Instead, hazel eyes fastened on a small jar of blue glass wrapped in delicate threads of white.

Eleanor noted the path of the nervous girl's gaze and tried again to draw her out, hoping to subtly confirm the suspected reason for her unusual strain. "Do you remember the day you came to me with pieces of the crystal flagon my Uncle Raymond of Morocco had given me? You confessed to breaking the precious gift although it was Aleria who'd picked up the pretty object and, unaware of its weight, let it slip into worthless shards. To protect her you confessed, even offered to take her punishment."

Hearing Eleanor laugh indulgently, Nessa began to relax. Here was the friend, the foster mother who had cared for both her and her little sister. Memories of the early days flowed back, burying her anxiety in a flood of trusting affection. Eleanor had comforted and welcomed them in her chamber day or night, became the one to whom they talked and confessed childish misdeeds.

Reflected in the smooth metal surface, Eleanor watched Nessa's tension drain away while she continued reminiscing. Not only had Nessa shielded her little sister, Eleanor reminded her, but she'd settled quarrels between all the children of the castle's inhabitants, even quarrels between men of the guard.

"Nessa, ever the peacemaker. At times I've wondered what my life would have been like had I cultivated more of your talents." Elegantly draped head tilted, Eleanor contemplated the other.

Nessa was startled into looking up. "To be as I am you'd have to fade into the background, and you are far too beautiful to do that." The notion of Eleanor ever being less than the focus of attention was ludicrous. Shaking her head, she added, "I can play peacemaker because I've no niche of my own and no one involved can claim my loyalties belong to only one side."

"Mayhap." Eleanor smiled at the earnest girl. "But you do yourself an injustice. Though not the stunning beauty your sister is, you've a quiet loveliness, a soothing quality harder to find."

Nessa's answering smile was tinged with an odd mixture of wistfulness and cynicism. The description sounded like nothing so much as the image of the perfect nun possessing an inner beauty and a soothing manner beneath her plain exterior. Apparently, even one who knew her as well as Eleanor did failed to recognize the volatile temperament tamped down and hidden but burning within. Yet at near every meeting the earl had roused a fire in her, either anger or passion. The traitorous thought threatened to ignite flames of forbidden longing. She frowned as her ever vigilant conscience commanded that she quickly stamp them out.

Nessa forced her attention back. "Never would you have been satisfied with a life such as mine. You'd have missed seeing the world, missed the fame—and notoriety—of wedding two kings and being mother to children of the royal blood in two lands."

With a wry smile Eleanor nodded agreement. She'd never pretended less than pride in such achievements, even the notoriety. 'Twas better than sitting meekly at home while others stood at the center directing the path of her life and her world. "Aye, although my life would have been more peaceful for it, 'twould have lacked the excitement I craved as a young woman. Perhaps that is the true difference in our natures. It's taken all too many years to learn appreciation for peace and solitude."

For the second time in but a few moments, Nessa wondered at how little the queen understood her. She, too, craved excitement, yet was realistic enough to accept such was not her destiny. Nay, that path was reserved for women like Aleria and Eleanor.

"You want only a quiet life now?" Her quiet disbelief was clear. She knew the older woman who reveled in talk of politics and scandals too well to easily accept such a claim.

"More than you can know, my pet." Eleanor nodded. "Oh, I am not ready for a nunnery, not ready to relinquish the fight for I'll not rest until I see Richard come to the throne in Henry's stead. But see if I don't end my days in peace and solitude."

Meeting Eleanor's pensive gaze, Nessa glimpsed behind the woman's strength and beauty to the reward just beyond her grasp.

Covering her melancholy mood with a bright smile, Eleanor turned their conversation. "This talk of an aging woman's past choices and future goals is not why you are here."

Nessa's attention returned to her mission with a jolt.

"I'm near certain you've come," Eleanor continued, "for the same reason you came that day long ago. What has Aleria done?"

The queen expected the immediate shake of Nessa's white draped head and promptly asked the question that would bring the topic nearer to the suspected purpose. "Then what plea has she sent you to lay before me? It must be of great import else you'd have settled it alone without my aid." Eleanor's brows rose above a knowing smile. Aleria would never bend easily to another's will but neither would she face the rigors of fighting her own battles.

Relief for not having to find words to introduce her cause swept over Nessa. It was useless to wonder how the queen had so easily divined the core of the matter. Nessa could only be glad for her perceptiveness. Hazel eyes fixed on the palm-joined hands in her lap, she began. "As you doubtless know, Reynard de Gaise was at foster in our keep before our father died."

With a cynical smile Eleanor met the searching hazel gaze lifted to her. Aye, she knew the older De Gaise had sent his son to foster with a supporter of her cause, but had switched both his loyalties and the boy's fostering when it was clearly lost.

"Although she was little more than a baby when Reynard first arrived to serve as page," Nessa continued, "Aleria and I knew him well. Now together again, the childhood friendship between Aleria and Reynard has deepened into something more."

Nessa repeated Aleria's tale of love, anticipated approval, and unexpected presentation with another suitor. A suitor who showed no sign of warmth. Indeed, one too cold to provide the careful nurturing fragile Aleria required. At her recital's end, Nessa looked straight into the queen's eyes to close with a simple statement and an appeal. "I spent the whole night long seeking the path to Aleria's freedom. I earnestly prayed for inspiration in my search, and my answer was the conviction that I must lay the problem before you and trust your affection for Aleria to furnish the escape we seek.''

Hiding a smile for this confirmation of the request she'd expected, Eleanor solemnly nodded in acceptance of Nessa's plea for help. She'd summoned Nessa that earlier time to secure her approval of the match proposed by Henry. But when, after Nessa's departure, Aleria had slipped quietly into her chamber and sobbed her unhappiness rather than throwing a temper tantrum as she usually did, Eleanor had realized her opposition to the betrothal ran more deeply than expected. She'd willingly complied with Aleria's plea to have Nessa return. Now knowing the worthy reason behind Aleria's despair, she would see it changed—mayhap, with careful planning, even see the dreams of both sisters come true.

She rose and slowly paced from her soft padded chair before the metal mirror to the window and back. The harsh realities of her life had not smothered the streak of romantic spirit that softened the practical shrewdness of her unflagging vitality. This tale of true love in jeopardy sent her harking back to her days as queen of the chivalric Courts of Love where minstrels sang of love lost and regained. Halting before the window, she stared out unseeing while a downward curve of cynicism marred her previously warm smile. Beyond an opportunity to smooth the course of youth's tender passion, this situation afforded her the chance to return Henry's spite. At least in part to prick her, her long alienated spouse had sent the cold earl to claim a beloved foster daughter. She would take joy in foiling his plan.

Nessa couldn't turn her gaze from the unspeaking queen whose thoughts meant the difference between the success and failure of Aleria's hopes. When Eleanor nodded slowly, defiantly as if to some invisible foe floating beyond the window, light gleamed on the golden circlet which held flowing cloth atop her head. Having no idea what plan the queen had devised, Nessa's breath caught uncomfortably. Too late now for second thoughts. The queen was striding resolutely to the door, calling for servants.

Eleanor met apprehensive hazel eyes with a reassuring

smile, but spoke not a word. During the busy moments that followed, a servant rushed to fetch Aleria while Eleanor gave instructions to others, leaving Nessa in uncomfortable inaction as another did the work of smoothing her sister's path. It left too much time for a fertile mind to imagine fearful deeds. The earl would be angry. Would he call the king's wrath down upon them all?

Behind servants delivering the morning repast that Eleanor had ordered served in her chamber came Aleria, bright hair still sleep-mussed. She glanced curiously between Nessa and the queen.

"Sit down, Aleria. Eat with us. Then, when we've done, I'll tell both you and Nessa what I've arranged." Pleased with her plan, suppressed laughter sparkled in Eleanor's eyes.

A faint gleam of understanding broke through Aleria's confusion, and she cast a questioning look at Nessa, who nodded in silent answer. The tiny frown marring Aleria's brow smoothed away. She sat down and picked up a golden brown crust.

Although her little sister was plainly satisfied, Nessa's anxiety left her looking at the waiting meal as if it were a platter of adders likely to strike but she forced herself to swallow a few bites of bread. Only as she sank her teeth into an apple still crisp after months in the dungeon's chill and heard its juicy snap did she think of the woman she'd begged Abbess Berthilde to send with her. She'd unthinkingly deserted Sybil to take the morning meal alone at the high table with two strange men—one of whom had shown an inordinate interest in the lovely postulant. The little appetite Nessa had mustered vanished, and she put down the apple. What temptation had she placed in the other's path? The answer, not in doubt, chided her conscience. She could not fail to recognize its form for it was very near to the silver-eyed temptation that had fallen into her own.

Both Eleanor and Aleria had long since finished their meal when the distracted Nessa set down her fruit as if its very sight were disgusting. The queen instantly began. "Here is my plan," she announced with the air of a conjuror producing coins from thin air. "We will have a betrothal and a wedding as well."

Neither girl looked particularly pleased, a response

64

Eleanor found amusing. Their apprehensive faces brought a grin.

"Aleria, you will be wed to Reynard before the sun rises on another day."

The pronouncement brightened azure eyes like sunshine across summer skies. But all too quickly clouds of doubt gathered. "How? You claimed yourself unable to alter the king's plan."

"No more will I." Eleanor's answer did nothing to alleviate the sisters' questions, rather it increased their confusion. Without explanation, the queen continued. "Once a marriage is performed, it cannot be undone except by extraordinary means and then only if you are too closely related or have been previously pledged. Neither of which is true of you and Reynard. Moreover, such an action would be an expensive thing which I much doubt Henry would pursue merely to see you wed to the earl."

Aleria was more than willing to accept the simple rationale without questioning the odd wording. But, struggling to bring order out of mental chaos, Nessa focused on the queen's emphasis of Aleria. Likely Eleanor believed a deeper purpose lay behind Henry's action. When that probability was added to the promise of both a betrothal and a wedding and Eleanor's claim that she'd not alter Henry's plan, an ominous pattern began emerging.

"But what of the earl?" Her voice strangled by trepidation, Nessa's question came out a husky whisper.

"Indeed, what of the earl?" Eleanor gave her a teasing smile. "Henry's letter gave no name to the intended bride."

Nessa's suspicion of what was intended crystallized and became all too clear. Her heart pounded but whether with dread or anticipation she dared not explore.

Seeing Nessa's darkened expression and knowing her quick mind had uncovered the plan, Eleanor objected. "Don't claim a desperate need to devote yourself to God. You've long delayed the taking of vows—proof you lack such religious zeal. Yet, had I not read your desire for a secular life in our talk, I wouldn't have engineered this solution to the problem *you* brought to me."

So, there'd been a purpose behind their morning talk. It shouldn't be a surprise, Eleanor did little without purpose.

And the queen was right. She had brought the problem to her—an inspiration she dared not question now. Still—

Without pause for further thought Nessa argued. "But he won't agree." She'd be a poor substitute for the beautiful Aleria and doubtless a great disappointment to the handsome earl.

"If he wants Swinton, and I suspect that purpose lies behind Henry's sending him here, he'll have little choice once your sister is wed to another." Fear and hope mingled equally in the face Eleanor studied with gentle understanding. Long experience in keeping track of subtle shifts in the political leanings of important figures in courts across Europe left Eleanor too knowing to miss the way a silver gaze covertly studied a postulant or to fail in seeing how that gaze proved an irresistible lure to hazel eyes. Garrick would offer a token resistance, but she'd no doubt he would yield, just as Nessa would allow sisterly care to excuse her submitting to an attraction she assuredly feared was sin.

Nessa's cool reasoning fell to disorder beneath the assault of the queen's logic. Confusion once again reigned. She'd been offered what she'd hopelessly longed for—a home of her own. Moreover, she was offered a dream she'd never dared admit even to herself—for husband the man who she'd named temptation in human form. But she didn't deserve these gifts. She was not meant for such bounty. She was neither beautiful nor talented enough to become not only wife but countess! No, this was all wrong—this was a world order tilted askew. She clenched her eyes shut.

"It's true, Nessa, it's true!" Aleria clapped her hands in childish glee. It had taken long moments for Aleria to interpret the strange conversation, but once she understood she was determined to win her sister's cooperation. She had no doubt that Nessa would give her aid, she'd never denied her before. "You can save me from him, give me my Reynard."

"But—" Nessa stumbled, "but it's wrong." She aimlessly lifted her hand palm up. "All wrong. He expects a beauty and I am not one."

"You've got to save me, Nessa." Aleria squeezed Nessa's hands between her own. "Please, please say you will. I can't bear to be that cold man's bride."

Cold— Ice Warrior— Ice but core of flames. Nessa shook

her head in an unsuccessful attempt to clear away the disjointed thoughts plaguing her sensible mind. Despite fingers squeezed by Aleria, Nessa looked to Eleanor, who was smiling complacently.

"Your little sister is pleading for your aid. Would you deny her?" Eleanor knew Nessa could no more reject Aleria's entreaties than she could turn straw into precious gold.

Helpless to simultaneously refuse Aleria, the queen, and her own secret longings, Nessa slowly nodded her agreement. She wished she could excuse her action as only a demonstration of her love for Aleria, her willingness to be martyr for sisterly love. But, too long trained to honesty, she was forced to admit the action not altruistic, rather a falling to selfishness.

" 'Tis settled and so on to more practical matters." The queen turned toward Aleria. "Nothing good comes without price and the cost of your choice of spouse is losing Swinton Keep."

The words surprised Nessa. Small Swinton possessed only one dwelling suitable for those well-born. Although the eldest, she'd been given the fief half without as it had been expected she'd join holy orders and have no use of it. For what reason was it necessary she have it now? What matter a small building on a small fief? Indeed, though the keep was acceptable for those of lesser rank, surely it was too humble for an earl. Unaware, she put thoughts into words. "What difference can it make to him?"

"What difference a small fief to Henry?" Eleanor's gaze returned to Nessa. It should've been plain to one with a mind so sharp. "The same answer in each case. Swinton is a small thorn in the lion's paw and controlled from its keep. His Ice Warrior must have the keep or Henry will roar. Give Garrick the fief with its keep and Henry will likely do no more than snarl once or twice."

Nessa understood and accepted the decree that the earl must have the keep to hold the fief, but still she wondered what use a mighty earl could have for so insignificant a dowry.

"Reynard, too, must pay a price," Eleanor told them. "Henry is unlikely to tamely pay a man who has thwarted his plans, thus Reynard cannot continue in this garrison, for 'tis Henry's."

67

At the prospect of surrendering both her early childhood home on Swinton lands and her place in Eleanor's castle, Aleria's face went white. Noting the reaction, Eleanor was quick to provide a solution to the problem she'd raised.

"I'll send the two of you to one of my supporters in the north with letters urging him to give Reynard a position."

A future among strangers was daunting but Aleria, refusing to let such distant worries dampen the joy in her victory, brightened considerably. "The loss of Swinton Keep is of no import." She shrugged in a gesture meant to show her unconcern. "I'll be happy wherever Reynard takes service."

Nessa feared that the blithe claim of a pampered girl ever allowed her own way was untrue. Too late now for such doubts. Only could she pray that love would compensate. Well acquainted with her sister's immaturity, cool logic mocked the forlorn hope.

Although littered with false pleasantries, the midday meal was amazingly calm. After a morning spent planning the substitution that would see an incredible change in her fortunes, Nessa was sure her guilt must be written on her face. She couldn't meet the silver gaze she felt near constantly upon her. Fearful of what she'd agreed to be part of, she was depressingly certain that, even if he'd failed to see the plot in her, then likely he was wondering how she and the beauty could be sisters.

Nessa entered the conversation not at all, but Eleanor and a suddenly sparkling Aleria, skilled at the social repartee which hides truth, kept the earl busy. Despite shame for her treatment of Garrick, worry of another sort found home in her mind. Beside her, Sybil's quiet laughter sounded often, interspersed with gentle smiles and all in response to Lord Conal's unswerving attentions. She'd sought Sybil's company as protection against the temptation to which she'd now yielded and then shamefully had abandoned her to meet similar lures alone.

Garrick, no stranger to court intrigues, suspected the queen and her beautiful young protégée of some ill deed. Yet, thinking his position unassailable as king's representative in the king's castle, he assured himself that 'twas no more than some petty intrigue and nothing to do with him. Nessa's quiet withdrawal he assumed to be a result of her discomfort in the presence of a man who had laid bare a flaw in her pious commitment.

Nessa rose from the meal with relief. She wished she could retire to her chamber and seek order for her wildly disorganized thoughts, find a logical path to pursue, and build confidence to calmly meet what lay ahead. But, as two sets of white postulant's robes were the sum total of her wardrobe, she'd been directed to spend the afternoon in the queen's apartments where various of Eleanor and Aleria's gowns would be altered to fit her.

Standing, turning, walking on command and feeling like the pin cushion a serf held for the seamstress, Nessa was swept away on a frightening tide of events. She reminded herself time and time again that it was too late to deny the deed but still she was stricken with remorse for the deception about to be played on a man who, apart from the kiss for which he'd asked pardon, was surely undeserving of such trickery.

Most men looked straight through a nun, especially a plain nun. They argued, but the earl at least saw her as an individual. It seemed undeniably wrong to land him with a woman so lacking in the beauty he expected. Her conscience condemned her intended action—and firmly rebuked an irrepressible spot of happiness.

⊷§ *Chapter 7* §⊶

Standing on tiptoe, Nessa peered from the arrow-slit in her chamber. These were the first moments of privacy she'd had the whole day long. The seamstress had freed her barely in time for an evening meal she'd no desire to join, a meal with the man she was destined to deceive. Her dread had proven unnecessary. The earl had gone, she was told, to meet an old friend who held a Salisbury subfief not far distant, and he was not likely to return before the next morn. The queen's pleasure with this unexpected easing of the danger in a plan too soon exposed had been clear. Nessa was thankful, too. Yet, anxiety brought by time growing short for the first step in their subterfuge rose even higher. Although alone, worry over the Ice Warrior's early discovery sent a chill down her spine, as if even now his accusing silver eyes were sending shafts of ice through her guilty soul. It seemed inevitable that just so would he encase her in his freezing hold when the moment of revelation arrived.

The spring days were still short but when, as today, they were blessed with clear skies, twilight seemed to linger, casting its purple haze over all to soften the sharp angles and narrow streets of a village crowded between moat and outer bailey wall. Straining to look as far to the right as she could,

Nessa picked out age-paled walls of a small stone building. St. Stephen's had been built amidst a green meadow before the castle's rising. The noise of town life had steadily crept closer, encroaching upon its peace, but still the chapel stood sturdy and welcoming—proof to Nessa that good survived and outlasted evil. Though it was tightly surrounded by ramshackle shops whose owners lived in upper levels, even an alehouse beset with rowdy patrons, Nessa preferred the simple chapel to the grander place of worship within castle walls.

Aleria and Reynard were likely making their separate ways through the heavy foot traffic of early evening toward the same goal. As the castle's chaplain and clerics were financially supported by Henry and loyal to him, by necessity, the wedding rite was to be conducted in St. Stephen's. Nessa was glad. Eleanor, a captive queen unable to move far without guards, could not attend for fear of revealing all to the king's men, but Nessa would see Aleria wed. After night was well begun, a torchlight gleaming from the chapel's bell tower would summon her.

Gazing at the holy place where as a postulant nun she had prayed, a new misgiving rasped across her tight-strung nerves. Entering sanctified walls in white robes when her decision to put them off had been made would be to stand before God a liar.

Draped across the bed were several gowns hastily altered to fit Nessa. Aleria's had been shortened but Eleanor's lengthened with a panel of cloth at the hem. A soft wool gown caught her attention. It hadn't been particularly flattering to Aleria, its intended wearer. Nessa lifted the misty green cloth and with eyes nearly the same shade admired the delicate stitchery of flowing sleeves and embroidered neckline. They were a contrast to neat but unevenly sewn side seams hurriedly adjusted for less generous curves. This conspicuous reminder of her deficiencies compared to Aleria wounded sensitivities hidden yet tender beneath a flimsy cloak of unconcern. Thick lashes shuttered eyes gone a soft, wounded brown. Her unsuspecting groom would find her lacking in much that he expected. Her conscience rebuked her unhappiness over so unimportant a matter when she possessed a fine mind which was of more value and was longer lasting than beauty. Such virtuous phrases provided no consolation. Despite self-disgust for the pain over a lack she'd admitted long ago, still she couldn't halt the hurt increased by the likelihood of a silver-eyed tempter's disappointment.

To force the problem from her mind, she busied her hands removing headdress and habit. No more time would she waste bemoaning what God had not seen fit that she possess, rather she would thank Him for the gift of a future fervently longed for.

First, she donned a gossamer silk camise whose forest green sleeves, tight to the wrist, would show beneath the gown's wide cuffs. Next she pulled the sea-mist gown over her head and laced it near from under her arms to hip. Thence it widened out in graceful folds to the hem. Having never worn anything so form molding since childhood, she was uncomfortable with its revealing fit and quickly stepped into her voluminous white habit. However, it took time and ingenuity to arrange the gown's sleeves, the back half of which trailed near to the floor, under the habit's less stylish but far more practical length. After long minutes of frowning over the seemingly impossible task, she folded the gown's sleeves back to her shoulders and let them fall beneath the habit's loose sides. By the time she finished arranging the layers of clothing to conceal green beneath white, unmistakable flashes of torchlight were calling.

Saint's Tears! So soon? Nessa cringed at her ill-chosen exclamation. But now she had no time to tame unruly curls into the demure plaits which should be worn by well-born women publicly seen. Too late even to rue the undone task.

Snatching up her headdress and tugging the white cloth into place over thick disarrayed tresses, she hurried to the door. One hand on the cold iron latch, she reminded herself of the need for silence before carefully passing through empty corridors and down the stone stairway. Even the young serf left to tend the great hall's banked fire through the night dozed unaware of the maid who crossed to the exit tunnel and massive door at its end.

Once heavy planks had closed behind her, Nessa leaned back against their strength to look down the flight of wooden steps to the wheel-and-hoof rutted ground beyond. Thus far all was well but the greatest test lay ahead. Her hands came together and rested against her lips while she studied the gate on the courtyard's far side. Torchlight from either side of the door and at intervals down the steep stairs ahead gleamed on her white habit. There was no doubt but that she'd been seen from the moment she'd stepped out. No hiding now and no going back—either in this immediate ceremony or the one on the morrow. Slender shoulders lifted with the deep breath she took for courage. Forcing a serene expression to cover her anxieties, she walked down the steps and across the dusty courtyard, too preoccupied to worry about the dirt which would doubtless cling to her white hem.

From the parapet, a narrow ledge close to the top of the palisade walls' inner side, two guards watched her approach. When near to standing directly below, one called down to her.

"Sister Agnes, why out so late?"

Nessa looked up into a questioning smile. 'Twas Harold, the guard who had welcomed her return to Salisbury Tower the evening she'd first learned of the earl's coming. She concentrated on the insignificant fact to keep from betraying herself with nervousness and responded with a beaming smile of unusual warmth.

"I mean to visit the Chapel of St. Stephen and pray for my sister's wedded happiness." Her words were unfaltering but she quaked inside, fearing these two men who knew her so well would read their untruth. She felt like a liar but reassured herself that 'twas not a falsehood for she'd do just what she'd claimed.

Although she'd never sought such a late visit before, the two men were familiar with Sister Agnes's preference for the village chapel and found nothing suspicious in her leaving. After all, neither had her sister ever been on the verge of marriage afore. They knew her love for Aleria and found it only right that she seek special intercession for the other. Moreover, members of religious orders were known to worship at regular intervals throughout day and night; and, as she was drawing ever nearer to taking vows, mayhap she felt compelled to do so.

Nessa released breath she hadn't realized she was holding as the iron-bound and studded doors swung open. She concentrated on walking calmly into the tunnel. This hour on the morrow the whole trick would be done, and she promised herself she'd *never* again be party to schemes.

Constant lies were so hard to maintain and gnawed huge guilty gaps in her conscience. Moving out of the tunnel's gloom, she started across the drawbridge with Harold's cheerful voice coming from behind to ring shame in her ears.

"Take care, sister, and Godspeed your safe return."

Although Nessa inwardly cringed, Harold's words were only a genial courtesy. Neither guard was concerned for her well-being despite the fact that she traveled alone and possibly through rough company. Without doubt there were men in the streets beyond, men who'd not hesitate to accost any woman foolish enough to walk abroad unaccompanied during late hours. However, even the coarsest would think twice about forcing himself on a nun. Meeting another man's ire for assaulting wife or daughter might not daunt some, but God's retribution was too fearsome to risk.

Aware of the soft white armor she wore, Nessa walked unafraid through dark streets and narrow alleys until very near her goal. Then, at the alehouse's back door, she stepped behind a conveniently stacked barrier of empty barrels and wicker produce baskets to remove her habit and headdress. Taking time to be sure they'd remain presentable for the return trip, she carefully folded and placed them inside the top basket. Then, adjusting the gown's sleeves in natural order and running fingers through thick tresses to loosen headdress-crushed curls, she hurried to the chapel at the short alley's far end.

A meager five candles flickered on the altar where dainty Aleria and her lanky bridegroom stood waiting to begin the rite. The elderly priest's brows climbed nearly atop his shiny bald head at seeing Nessa enter his church garbed in secular clothes. However, his surprise was not as strong as his desire to have the dangerous task done, and he began the ceremony even before Nessa had reached her sister's side. Listening to binding words, Nessa could not still a twinge of uneasiness. How would two so immature make a success of life together? Aleria demanded near constant admiration but seldom offered the same to others while Reynard, lacking in self-confidence, was quick to take offense at even an implied slight. Nessa's misgivings muffled Father Ulfred's words and she prayed earnestly for their happiness throughout the short service. So intent on her supplications was she that she was unprepared for the end which quickly arrived.

"Nessa, thank you, thank you, thank you." Aleria hugged her startled sister tight. "You've given me comfort and help whenever I've asked, but this is the greatest gift of all." Azure eyes lifted to Reynard's proud face, near worship softening their depths. Although still worried for the rightness of her sister's choice, Nessa allowed herself to be reassured by the way Aleria gazed at Reynard with such love and trust that her face seemed to glow brighter than the candles.

"We'll never forget what you've done for us, sister," Reynard added, holding his tiny wife near in one arm and clasping Nessa's fingers with his free hand. "If ever you need us, on my honor, I swear we'll lend whatever aid you ask."

Nessa felt warmed by the sincerity of his oath. She'd always done everything for Aleria without thought of return. Now someone promised a like service to her. The gesture lent a comfort that further calmed her concern for the couple's future.

"Thank you, Reynard," Nessa smiled, "but I fear it unlikely we'll see much of each other in the future." If the earl was coerced into wedding her and she truly took up residence in Tarrant Castle, it was doubtful that these two would be welcomed there.

"Oh, no." Aleria's rose lips formed a round moaning "O." Thoughts occupied by her victory over the cold lord, she'd never paused to consider this step might mean a permanent separation from Nessa, her strength and solace. "You're the one who finds answers for my problems. What will I do without you?" Her voice rose almost to a wail. "I'll need you. You've got to be there."

Aleria's sudden distress bruised Nessa's soft heart but now was the time to be strong, to make the break as clean and painless as possible. Slowly shaking her head, with gentle voice and smile, she admonished her little sister. "From this day on you must go to Reynard with your problems, your joys, your disappointments." Hazel eyes turned to Reynard. "I don't doubt he's far stronger than I, far better able to direct your path."

The young husband straightened with pride while praise of her beloved soothed Aleria's fears. She cuddled closer to

Reynard, smiling with renewed courage as Nessa bade them farewell.

Nessa went out knowing the couple left behind had horses packed and waiting. This first night they'd spend in the celibate priest's cottage, an odd bridal chamber, while Father Ulfred slept in the chapel. At dawn when the outer bailey gate opened for the day's commerce, they would slip free to be far away before the mid-morn hour of betrothal and truth revealed.

Without the protection of her habit, Nessa was apprehensive of the dark alley. Determined to allow no fear, she sent up a quick prayer for strength and rushed deeper into the alley's yawning mouth. Stepping carefully to avoid stumbling over the refuse left at the back door of each shop along the way, she was halfway to the baskets wherein her habit laid waiting when, silhouetted against a patch of open starlit sky, a shadow stepped from the alehouse's rear exit. Nessa stilled in mid-step, breath halted in a fear-constricted throat. The shadow leaned sideways to push through the tavern's door and reach inside. The figure then straightened again with firebrand in hand. Light spilled down the filthy alley, revealing her clearly to the man. Warmth instantly drained from her body leaving her lightheaded and weak. It was neither fear of an unknown assailant nor the stealth-stealing light which froze her. 'Twas the ice in narrowed silver eyes.

Motion arrested by stunned surprise, the pair stood for long moments—this was the last place either expected the other to be.

What in Sweet Mary's name, Garrick silently demanded, *is a neophyte nun doing wandering through the danger of dark alleys in the middle of the night?* With training to parry sudden attacks, he was first to pull his disordered responses into line.

"Why are you here in a place so squalid?" Taking the offensive, he called her to explain before she could do the same of him.

All her worst fears seemed to have taken shape to stand before her—his shape. Thankful that the red tide sweeping up her throat and face would go unnoticed or be attributed to the flame's ruddy glow, she struggled to find her voice and, equally as difficult, believable words to speak with it. "I—I came to St. Stephen's to pray for my sister." She waved in the general direction of the small stone chapel. She used the same excuse she'd given to the guards, it being true—so far as it went. Her conscience, already severely strained, could not bear the uttering of bald-faced lies, to him least of all. She was certain he'd somehow know an untruth the moment he heard it.

Knowing his sudden appearance had shocked her, Garrick laid no special significance on the stutter in her answer. His gaze followed her vague motion. Although unable to see the small stone structure, he knew it was there. As he'd approached the alehouse he'd noticed the chapel so out of place amidst decay. The men he'd sent to Swinton Keep with the task of quietly seeking out the source of rebellion-raising deeds and rumors had returned. Believing they'd least likely be noted by Eleanor's supporters amongst the alehouse's rowdy crowd, he'd met them there.

Gaining courage from the earl's silence when she'd expected him to denounce her, Nessa added, "St. Stephen's is my favorite church—an island of peace in an ocean of wickedness."

"Aye, I saw it earlier." He honestly tried, with limited success, to restrain a cynical smile for her sweeping condemnation. "And I agree it looks as if it should stand in the midst of country fields, ministering to farmers, not hardened townfolk and depraved sinners." His smile deepened with the last two words, but all amusement disappeared as he questioned the wisdom of her visit. "But do you often worship there so late?"

Was he suspicious? Flustered, she found only a weak excuse. "Not often, but I was in need of fresh air for clear thinking." Pray God he'd not ask if a walk in the castle maze wouldn't have provided clean air as well, and with greater safety. Lifting hands palm up at her sides she shrugged. Feeling caught in the act herself, it never occurred to her to question his reason for being not with friends but here and alone.

Garrick's growing suspicion of Eleanor and Aleria's sudden friendliness had aggravated his distrust of women, leaving him ever more wary. Yet, although he mocked the hope, he wanted to believe Nessa truthful and honest; and, despite his distrust, he smiled with a sincere warmth few women had seen. One part of his mind automatically judged possible dangers, but another part found useless hope in his soon to be sister-in-law's talk of a clear mind—possibly to decide against joining holy orders?

"But," one dark brow arched, "now you return to the castle?"

All too aware of the white gown in a basket behind his back, Nessa nodded. She knew what would follow but saw no way free.

"Pray let me escort you." He gallantly offered his arm to her. Though she might trust God to hold her safe as she walked through dangerous surroundings, he would feel better personally seeing her returned to the castle's nearly inviolate defenses.

Nessa risked another quick, hopeless glance at the stacked baskets. Really, there was no choice. She could hardly ask him to wait while she changed back into her habit. Nor could she answer the questions such action would invoke. With a reckless smile Nessa placed slender fingers atop a dark velvet sleeve. Even if doomed to imminent discovery, she would seek to the last to give the newly wedded pair the time needed to escape. Who knew what the earl might do if he found his intended bride claimed by another? Rid himself of his rival? Punish so unworthy a substitute for the insult?

In her experience men raised to do battle, including her father, never hesitated to physically chastise a female. For all his famous disdain for women, the earl had shown no such tendency but she hardly knew him and had yet to see him in adversity—but soon, perhaps very soon, would. Whether he found her out now or later little mattered. In either case the result would likely be the same—rejection, distaste. Mayhap worse if left with no option but to wed her. Once her husband, with right to chastise her as he chose, would he beat her? With a touch of defiance for her fears, she lifted the hem of misty green a short distance above the narrow alley's grimed floor to ease their progress.

Garrick's eye was caught by the motion and he smiled. How like a woman to draw attention to a new gown. He had, of course, noted her change in dress. However, thinking her possibly sensitive about so radical a departure, he'd chosen not to discomfort her by mentioning it. Rather, he silently accepted it as an encouraging indication of a change of intent. It seemed particularly significant that she'd worn worldly garb to the chapel. He refused to explore why it was important to him when she was destined to be his sister, justifying his interest with the excuse that 'twas only right he be concerned for the welfare of one soon to be family.

As they moved out of the dingy alley into wider streets and ever closer to the castle's well-lit drawbridge, Garrick spoke of the weather, the strength of the castle's defenses, and other such matters as demanded no answer. A fine thing that, Nessa admitted. With each step nearer the portal through bailey wall her dread of the light shed by torches set at either end grew stronger. Although she kept her face downcast, as if trance-bound by wavering flames, she couldn't look away but watched through half-lowered lashes. Heart in her throat she desperately prayed the gate guards would not comment on her change of dress.

"My lord, we didn't expect to see you back this night," Harold called out to the earl.

As one side of the massive door was pushed open by the other guard, Garrick looked up to the speaker atop the parapet. "We returned earlier than expected but stopped at the alehouse. My men will likely pass the night there for I very much doubt they could stay upright long enough to walk this far." Garrick was pleased with his smooth excuse both for the absence of the men he'd departed with and for being near the alehouse when Nessa stumbled into his path.

While both guards laughed at the earl's description of his men's condition, relief swept over Nessa—until she looked up and met the smirk of the guard holding the door at the tunnel's far end. Her rotund friend above had apparently chosen to ignore her unusual apparel, but this younger man had failed neither to note nor to place wrong interpretation on a woman who went out as nun but returned worldly garbed and in the earl's company. Nessa clamped her lips together to prevent the moan of protest swelling in her throat. She was well and truly caught. This sighting would ignite a gossip trail as hot and quick moving as wildfire across dry grass. Free hand curled against her lips, she fervently pleaded with all the powers in heaven to see that it not reach the earl's ears before the morrow's betrothal ceremony.

Though he gave no indication to Nessa, Garrick had taken exception to the guard's knowing grin. If this woman meant

79

to leave the order, then she had best learn the principles of conduct that governed well-born females. Never walking into the night unescorted was a rule basic and not to be flouted. And although he found lush unbound curls attractive indeed, it was for that very reason they were never publicly revealed. Someone must speak to her on these matters. Someone, but not he. The idea brought a sardonic smile which downcast hazel eyes failed to see. He was hardly qualified to advise a naive girl. Moreover, were he to attempt even a gentle rebuke, her temper would likely ignite. No, another must tackle the chore, but who? Her fellow postulant was likely as unversed as she, and he could no way approach either the queen or her protégée with the problem.

He postponed the difficult decision, promising himself to think on it again once she was safe inside thick stone walls. Happily he'd been there to assure her safe return, but why had those ill-begot guards allowed her through the gate to wander abroad alone? And what maggot had deranged the younger guard's wits enough to put the wrong construction on their being together? After escorting Nessa inside, he meant to go back and disabuse the grinning toad of his insult to the foolish maid.

Once the bailey gates closed behind them, it seemed to Nessa that a wide and endless expanse of courtyard stretched ahead. She frantically sought conversation to fill the silence which had fallen. Anxiety over her near discovery and its serious threat to the wedded pair's plan brought to the surface of lamentably illogical thoughts the memory of her discussion with this man on her duty to assure Aleria's happiness—and his quick return of Biblical texts. She said the first thing that came to mind.

"You've a knowledge of the Holy Book far beyond most men, save clerics. I was amazed when you quoted scripture so easily."

"Not so unusual for any man fostered by Henry," Garrick answered. "He has a great love of learning and all written knowledge from the scriptures to the wisdom of Greek authors."

Nessa knew the paradox of King Henry, a man so energetic he could never sit still yet a lover of books. He was well educated himself but she found it difficult to believe the claim that their sovereign inspired others to pursue the same knowledge.

"Richard is his son," Nessa ventured, "and I know he writes poetry in the manner of the French minstrels. Eleanor speaks of it often. But I've never heard any man claim him well acquainted with the Bible."

Garrick's smile became a sneer. "No, Richard was raised more by mother than father, and his tastes are much as hers."

Nessa conceded that point for she knew it was true but attacked from a new angle. "John has spent so little time in his mother's company I wonder if she would recognize him in a crowd, yet no one has reported him as a scholar of the scriptures."

Garrick nearly laughed. She was quick with her arguments, never hesitating to point out the gaps in his logic. 'Twas welcome to one who disdained the male flatterers and avaricious women always ready to agree with any comment for purpose of currying favor.

"John is not a scholar of any written word—to his father's despair. We who were Henry's foster sons had more reason to respect his wishes in our education. And, 'twas Geoffrey with whom I shared the love of learning taught us by his father."

"Geoffrey? A student of the Bible?" Honestly astonished, Nessa halted halfway to the castle entrance. The Geoffrey she'd met before his death and knew by his mother's fond reminiscences had never shown such interest.

As the small hand slipped from his arm, Garrick realized she'd stopped. He turned back to the slender figure outlined by the strong light of torches from the gate behind. Her disbelief showed him where her misunderstanding lay, and his gentle laughter was without its usual cold edge of cynicism. "Not Eleanor's Geoffrey, but Henry's."

Of truth, a foolish error. Nessa realized her mistake and pressed her hands against cheeks burning with embarrassment. He'd meant Henry's oldest and illegitimate son.

Garrick reached out to lay Nessa's hand back atop his arm and hold it there as he began walking again. "That Geoffrey is my foster brother and truest friend."

Forced into action by his motion, Nessa's stiff legs carried her forward at his side. She peeked at him from the corner of her eyes. His unthreatening laughter and gentle explanation, without ridicule for her error, allowed Nessa a glimpse of the man she suspected he revealed to few. She much doubted he meant her or any other to see the gentle spirit beneath his ice-hard, ice-cold armor. The intimate if fleeting sight brought with it an awareness of the man she'd tried from the first to deny.

"By virtue of the profession his father meant for him, he was well trained in religious matters," Garrick continued, oblivious of what discerning hazel eyes had seen. "And he shared his knowledge and scripts with me."

Thick curls nodded. Nessa was glad she could show understanding of this at least. His friend had been the Bishop of Lincoln but had questioned his vocation for a profession chosen for him by another, just as she had done. He had resigned his post rather than take holy orders. The king had then made him his chancellor, and that he was still.

"The Bible and Greek scripts, too?"

Glancing down, Garrick was snared by a rare loveliness, like the visions shown only to a privileged few. The firebrands lining entrance steps gilded abundant curls and revealed eyes gone a misty green that matched the fine silk floating about her feet.

"The Latin translations of Greek works," he clarified, hoping the fascination he saw in her face was as much for him as for the books he'd studied.

"Oh, I've dreamed of reading such things." Though her words were sincerely meant, Nessa was horrified by the breathy voice in which they were spoken. She felt caught in the strength of his gaze, wrapped in the warmth of his big body so near.

"I have a small book of Greek tales in my home. If you come to visit Aleria, I'll share it with you." Snared by a temptation he'd sworn to deny, it was fierce fought battle to look away long enough to lead them safely up the stairs to the castle door.

His offer, far from bringing happiness, left Nessa aching with guilty despair. Once he found himself landed with her as wife and she in his castle by trickery, there was little likelihood he'd provide her with such a luxury.

Pausing a few steps within the shadowed passage through the castle's thick wall, Garrick turned toward Nessa and saw her wistfulness. Had the mention of Aleria in his home brought sadness over separation from her sister? Nay, that was bound to happen when Nessa took final vows no matter Aleria's mate. Mayhap she regretted his wedding another? A foolish idea. Yet, despite its improbability, the warmth it brought would not fade.

Still close enough to the door left ajar that light from the torches outside fell full on her escort's face, Nessa looked up. Silver eyes captured hazel in a bond she could not break. Of their own accord, for he'd sworn he'd never again touch this possible nun and certain sister, his fingertips brushed her cheek. Nessa's flesh seemed to melt at his touch and move closer into his hand. Watching thick lashes fall over eyes deepened to brown velvet, Garrick lost the struggle completely. His arms went about the trembling maid whose gentle curves curled against him without thought of denial. Softer even than he'd remembered, luxuriant curls nestled beneath his firm jaw until his fingers trailed fire up her throat to tilt her chin.

Despite closed eyes, Nessa sensed the approaching kiss and yearned toward it, thoughts filled only with the memory of their last embrace, seering, exciting, and temptation beyond measure. His lips merely brushed hers, light and tantalizing. When they withdrew she felt bereft. She rose on tiptoe, seeking. They brushed again. Her sigh came out an aching moan.

The sound was more than Garrick could bear and his mouth closed over sigh-parted lips. Delicious. Freely offered but, like Eve's fruit, forbidden—and too sweet to relinquish.

Nessa was far beyond thought, enveloped by the Ice Warrior's molten core. Now his cold armor was protection for them both against— Bell tones drifted faint but clear through the clouds of passion fogging her mind. St. Stephen's chapel bell called out the hour of matins. At this very moment the nuns at the abbey made their way to worship, the nuns— Abruptly jerking free of arms unprepared for her action, Nessa took a step back, horror in her eyes. Despite her coming marriage, the training of long years whispered words of reproach—yield to temptation of the flesh and endanger your immortal soul.

"Nessa," Garrick reached out to her, pained by the self-condemnation in her eyes. "Passion is natural and not of

83

itself a sin.'' Even as he said the words, he was struck by how little they applied to them. Many, if not most, of his peers would think little of breaking the marriage vow of fidelity, but few men would add the sin of incest with a wife's close kin and none would defile a nun. His beseeching hand dropped as if suddenly turned to stone. "May God forgive my blasphemy."

His assumption of her piety renewed her guilt. As ever under pressure, her hands met in their accustomed palm-joined position. Looking down she saw what she did and was horrified. Feeling more a cheat than before, she twisted them together instead.

Garrick saw the motion as distress for her fall to earthly sin and cursed himself for being its cause. She was a truly honest woman—honest in admitting her errors and in a passion which made the thought of her forever stilling it abhorrent to him. Silver eyes moved from joined hands to pained face and masculine lips curled with disgust for his own blameful deeds. He abruptly strode past her and out of the castle once more.

Standing alone in the empty passage, Nessa listened to the hollow echo of booted feet descending the wooden steps behind her stiff back and felt defeated. Despite his words of comfort, he clearly found her response distasteful. Because of her supposed religious commitment? Or because so plain a woman had no right to such pleasures? Whichever, by this time on the coming day he'd know the truth, and his worst opinions would be hardened into inescapable fact. As she looked over her shoulder and through the empty portal torchlight reflected on silent tear tracks that seemed to burn like liquid trails of fire.

❧ Chapter 8 ❧

The clink of metal against crockery assaulted Nessa's ears, disturbing her dreamless slumber and laying a frown between fine brows. Inside the dark cave of her heavily draped bed, she snuggled deeper into warm covers, hiding from unnamed but troubling realities seeking to force their way into her safe haven. The cloth panel protecting one side of her refuge was pulled aside, allowing daylight to fall harsh against closed lids. Lingering still amidst the muzzy world of half-sleep, her conscience softly scolded that if the sun was strong enough to be so bright, then she had played the sluggard far beyond morning prime. The smell of fresh bread wafted to her and she silently added that at St. Margaret's a morning meal was not brought to those who lazed abed far after dawn and early services had begun. The full recollection of her sister's wedding and her own coming betrothal returned with the unwelcome suddenness of an attack upon a peaceful village. Nessa struggled to sit up while clutching thick bed covers modestly to her chin.

A tray rested atop a low stool. Nessa watched while a serf girl in brown homespun lifted from it a crockery cup full of creamy milk and a platter laden with both soft wheaten bread and an array of fruit. She laid them on a table of modest proportion.

"Her Highness says you are to eat here." Pale blue eyes were full of curiosity. "She directs you to not leave this chamber until she sends for you." The speaker paused, clearly hoping Nessa would share the reason behind this strange command or some juicy tidbit to repeat below, gaining importance by her knowledge.

Nessa was well aware that every word she spoke would be carried to others and pass throughout the castle with remarkable speed. The possibility reminded her of the leering gate guard and the moments with the earl that followed. Her cheeks burned but Nessa restrained the urge to bury them in her hands and instead met the girl's smile with a bland expression and quiet thanks.

Disappointed, the maidservant saw that Nessa intended to hold her own counsel and gave a slight shrug before turning to the haphazard heap of altered clothes on a nearby chest. Pale eyes widened in shock while Nessa mentally cringed. Returning in the midst of night, worried for her sister, and confused by both her response to the earl and his to her, Nessa had scooped them from her bed and recklessly dumped them there.

The girl rummaged through the colorful pile until she found what she was looking for and then delivered another of Eleanor's commands. "The queen says to wear this today." She held up a lovely cranberry red gown that had once been a royal favorite.

Nessa nodded, heart thumping so hard it drove out embarrassment for the servant's interest in odd instructions. Eleanor meant her to wear this to the betrothal—her own betrothal. As had happened so oft in the past few days that it was nearly commonplace, the mere thought of the earl destroyed even the faintest hope for a return to cool logic and calm peace. Her lashes fell to conceal her alarm from the other. As for the choice of garb, she would trust Eleanor. She'd no experience to guide her in what was appropriate for any occasion. Since a child, she'd worn the same everyday and everywhere and had been taught that it was vanity to waste thought on changing styles.

Admitting defeat, the maidservant placed the gown across the bottom of the bed. If the one meant to be nun would not explain, then they must all wait to learn the purpose behind these strange matters, leaving her to report only the secular garments for a postulant—garments carelessly used as Sister Agnes never did. Again the maidservant dug through the stack, pulling out a camise of fine silk and laying it next to the gown. "The queen bade me arrange your hair. I'll leave you to your meal but will return to lace your gown and do as the queen instructed."

Nessa watched the girl slip out before rising from the bed. Her toes curled into the warmth of the carpet beneath while chill morning air on bare skin brought renewed anxiety. The tremor that shook Nessa was born as much from qualms about the coming confrontation as from cold. The girl's curiosity had renewed Nessa's guilt and, rather than blaming the maidservant's curiosity on the queen's directions or her changed style of dress, her sorely strained conscience murmured that the girl had heard gossip begun by the gate guard. Doubtless wending throughout Salisbury were unceasing whispers of her night wandering and return with the earl. Their hiss seemed to shiver over her nerves; yet, though being the subject of shameful rumors was distasteful, it was a matter of small import next to the anxiety in wondering if the nasty words had reached the earl. Had he learned of her change in apparel? Had he discerned the reason behind it? Had the deception turned his disgust into ice-cold hate?

As Garrick fastened the neck of his deep blue tunic, his gray eyes narrowed unseeing on the overcast sky visible from the window of their courtyard-facing chamber. After he'd left the passionate but guilt-ridden girl the previous night, he'd followed through on his plan to talk with the erring gate guard. The man had been left with no doubt of Nessa's innocence—Garrick had taken all doubts for his own. Why had she found it necessary to go out as a nun and then change into secular clothes? Had he erred in thinking her that rare creature, an honest woman free of subterfuge? And why did it hurt to suspect this one woman deceitful when he'd never allowed the truth of feminine nature to pain him before? He'd slept very little. The night was too full of questions, of answers he didn't want to hear, and self-disgust for weaknesses thus revealed.

Seeing Garrick's lips firm into a hard, cold line, Conal deemed it time to interrupt his moody withdrawal. The man was never forthcoming, but this morning he'd reached a new low. When the queen had explained at the morning meal that, due to lengthy preparations, neither of her charges would be joining them, Conal had been too involved with the beautiful Sybil to spare the matter more than a passing thought. He'd found the excuse perfectly understandable; judging by his glower, Garrick had not.

"The beauty will soon be yours, pledged and bound." Conal grinned, seeking a similar response, even if no more than a cynical sneer.

Indeed, Garrick's smile was bitter. The beauty's failure to appear with her sister for the morning meal had seemed a damning confirmation of suspicions raised by the gate guard's report of a postulant's curious actions. Fearing himself neatly caught, he inwardly railed against the bonds. In truth, he didn't want the beauty for wife, didn't want Nessa for sister. Secret thoughts too long repressed broke free to mock his virtuous denials with the irrefutable fact that from the first he'd wanted the two sisters to trade positions in his life. But now with the strong likelihood it would be so, the golden wish had turned to dross for 'twas arranged by the feminine treachery he disdained.

"The whole hinges on my coming," Garrick mused aloud. He could cancel the ceremony, refuse to fulfill the king's plan—and never need face the truth. Yet he was not a man to turn aside from unpleasant realities, to seek safety in lies. He opened the door and marched resolutely down toward the dreaded revelation.

Conal was puzzled by Garrick's strangely worded response. Of course it depended on his coming. How could a betrothal occur without the prospective groom? Shaking sun-streaked locks, Conal realized he'd nearly been left behind and quickly followed.

In the arched entrance of Salisbury's chapel, Garrick paused. Of a certainty it was a beautiful place, the walls hung with rich tapestries and the velvet-draped altar bearing vessels of gold inlaid with precious stones. After a quick survey of the opulence within he understood why Nessa preferred the simple Chapel of St. Stephen. 'Twas the difference between plainspoken truth and eloquently delivered falsehoods.

From where she stood beside the priest at the front of the chapel Eleanor watched Garrick and his friend. Garrick looked more dour than usual. Did he know? No matter, he'd not stopped the first phase of her plan and he was here. If he wanted Swinton he would agree to the other. A faint smile of victory curved her mouth. Surely his preoccupation with Nessa assured that, whether or not he realized it himself, he'd be well-satisfied with the substitution. She gazed toward a serf waiting unobtrusively by the door and gave a slight nod.

Conal watched as Garrick and Eleanor sized each other up from across the length of the chapel. Beneath the queen's steady stare his friend appeared to turn so wholly to ice that Conal thought it near impossible when the frozen statue stepped forward to move toward the two waiting at the altar. Falling into step behind, Conal spared a moment to wonder why Sybil hadn't been invited to attend. At the morning meal she'd told him she wouldn't be here and he hadn't risked offense by questioning why.

"Your Highness." Garrick gave the queen a barely adequate bow before turning to the short, heavyset man at her side. Bending low to kiss the prelate's ring, he murmured, "Your Grace."

So, Garrick silently acknowledged, Eleanor had left nothing undone to see this a binding deed. She'd even summoned the bishop to officiate, the bishop chosen by Henry and loyal to him. There could be no later denial of a thing sworn to before him. Garrick was wryly amused. Clearly Eleanor understood him not nearly so well as she might think. Those close to him knew that once he'd made a promise, he'd never break it and turn his words to lies.

A wall of brown homespun, Nessa's lumbering escort, stepped aside and left her unshielded in the chapel's doorway. Beneath the cranberry gown's skirt her knees shook like willow branches in the breeze. Unable to resist the magnetic power, hazel eyes full of anxiety and hope were drawn to the back of a black head.

Seeing the queen's attention shift to a spot behind him, Garrick realized his prospective bride stood there. He was torn between hoping to see Aleria approaching, thus his suspicions unfounded and Nessa the honest woman he'd believed, or praying to find the one-time postulant taking her sister's place as his bride. He lost either way. Ensnared by bitter reality, he squared broad shoulders and resolutely turned to meet the truth.

Nessa nearly fell back before the handsome face carved of solid ice and eyes that pierced as effectively as silver blades. Features, already cold, hardened before her eyes. She wanted to turn and run but her training to mutely accept even the most difficult tasks stiffened her spine and tilted her chin. He was obviously disappointed, likely disgusted, at being foisted off with so plain a substitute. Now she must fortify herself to withstand his furious demand for an explanation of this poor exchange. Pride might be a sin, but only pride would see her through, and she was determined to neither run from nor cower before this man of ice. She would let his freezing gaze numb her emotions and stand aloof. Unfaltering, she glided down the aisle.

Garrick slowly examined the maid moving even nearer. Here was proof that she was as devious as any other woman, yet he nearly smiled to see her so resolute and brave against something she plainly feared. The gold embroidery at her gown's neck and the edge of long cuffs drew out similar gleams in hair tamed to thick braids and coiled on her head with only a few ringlets escaping to riot about her heart-shaped face. The cranberry shade gave color to cheeks that the white habit had drained. Although she looked frightened, he saw her determination and illogically wanted to protect her—from himself? His emotions were so muddled he felt a stranger to himself. His uncontrollable responses deepened a self-disgust that drew dark brows together in an unmistakable frown which only increased Nessa's alarm.

After what seemed an endless walk beneath his cold scrutiny, Nessa stood at his side before the cleric. Head bowed, she was far too preoccupied with the earl to realize a bishop had replaced the priest she'd expected to preside. In the darkness behind closed lids a silent warning rang and echoed unhappiness. Now it would come. Now the earl would deny her as bride.

The whole chamber seemed to pause in an agony of waiting. Conal's eyes were wide with shock while the puzzled bishop sensed an undercurrent of hostility and glanced between the queen's triumphant smile and the earl's cool cynicism.

No sound disturbed the lengthening silence. At last Eleanor broke the tension. Apparently, Garrick would not ask the reason for this substitution, and she would no longer wait.

"Aleria is wed to her love, a former foster brother and guard in this castle." Her relish in diverting Henry's plan could not be hidden. "The ceremony was conducted in the village chapel last night and the happy pair are far on the path to a new home."

Garrick's expression didn't change but Nessa felt him stiffen imperceptibly at the queen's talk of the village chapel on the previous night. Now he knew the reason for her evening excursion. She felt his eyes upon her and couldn't deny their summons. Quietly she said, "In the chapel I prayed for my sister's happiness." The others would not understand, but with these words to him she argued her innocence of lies at least.

'Twas all she'd said, Garrick mentally conceded. No untruth in words, only in deeds. He gave a slight nod, acknowledging her statement but not forgiving the omissions.

Although curious about their odd exchange, Eleanor continued. "If you wish to claim the dowry of half of Swinton and its keep, you may accept the elder sister as your bride."

Garrick met the queen's direct gaze calmly. Doubtless from her informers in the king's court she knew he'd promised Henry that he'd quiet Swinton's discontent before it spilled further into his own strategic Tarrant lands. He had no choice, even did he want it. Moreover, he silently argued, soothing his conscience by denying any personal choice, the marriages of all well-born were arranged for political purposes. So, what matter which sister he took as wife so long as he claimed the same dowry?

With a cutting smile for his royal hostess, he nodded agreement. Beneath his facade, he refused to acknowledge his irrepressible pleasure with the circumstances allowing him to claim the slim maid standing quietly at his side, eyes downcast.

Nessa's ears strained for some word, to no avail. She prayed fervently, making extravagant promises for the answer she wanted so badly she could never again deny it her heart's desire.

Studying the downbent head with its crown of soft brown braids, Garrick wondered if Nessa's lowered gaze was an indication of fear he would reject her. Nay, he condemned his hope. 'Twas a fool's wishful thinking. More likely she was praying he'd not accept her sacrifice for sisterly love, thus allowing her to return to the abbey where she need never face the hidden truths of a nature she wanted not to know. From her earlier claim that her defense of Aleria came even before God, he could believe her willing to give up personal goals to save her sister unhappiness—even the cloistered life she preferred.

Conal had stood motionless beside his friend as the substitution was accepted, but broke through his shock at the unexpected turn of events as he saw Garrick's cynical expression go positively grim. What silent pain smote him?

To Garrick the idea of Nessa coming to him as an unwilling sacrifice was exceptionally unpleasant. But, was it that? By participating in this scheme had she not proven herself a true daughter of Eve, sent to trick man? No use to ponder. Loyalty to Henry, if naught else, had made the choice. He must see it through.

"Get the deed done, then, and the marriage on the morrow." As soon as possible he wanted free of this place and its currents of treachery. Surely once free, he would again be able to think clearly, to see the way for dealing with whatever came of it.

"Tomorrow?" Eleanor was shocked. "But no bride's clothes have been prepared, no arrangements made, no—"

"You saw her sister wed with equal haste," he coldly pointed out. "I've tasks awaiting me, and can waste no more time."

Nessa was discouraged to find herself classed as a waste of time; but, as her mother had often said, she was not formed for cherishing but for practical matters. God had given her what she'd desperately prayed for. She must not expect more, least of all even mild fondness from the man forced to be her husband.

"But—" Eleanor began anew, seeking balance on the suddenly shifting deck of her plan's ship.

"No." Garrick interrupted again. The notion of wedding

in this place of treachery did not appeal. Nessa preferred the village chapel, and so did he. "In the Chapel of St. Stephen."

Aghast, Eleanor's lips fell open. This was more than she could easily accept. "But it's bound all about with wretched hovels and ministers only to the village dregs."

Garrick's insistence grew stronger under the queen's disgust for his choice. It even brought a smile, though more a sneer. "If we wed, then it will be there and tomorrow."

Wondering if he had chosen the village chapel because of her preference or to prick the queen, Nessa looked up. Feeling her gaze, Garrick's attention turned to her and he smiled.

Nessa's lips parted in an inaudible gasp. How was it that the same motion on the same lips could one moment freeze water with its coldness and the next melt her bones with its warmth?

Chapter 9

"Blessings!" Many voices offered calls of good fortune to the bride each step of the way. They punctuated the cheery din of the crowd of villagers and guardsmen of lower rank, in both the castle's service and the visiting lords', who lined the cleared route from the castle to St. Stephen's. To Nessa, by tradition leading the wedding procession, the route seemed to stretch far longer than she'd ever thought it before.

While, as her attendants, the queen was her usual regal self and Sybil the perfect nun of benign smile and faraway gaze, as the focus of so many curious eyes, what little confidence Nessa had dredged from the depths of her quaking soul wavered dangerously. Reminding herself that a godly woman should have the fortitude to endure trials far more difficult was little comfort when she'd already admitted herself barely equal to this task. Rather than watch the intimidating road ahead, she peeked from the corner of her eyes at the well-wishers on one side.

"Health and happiness!" To amplify her words, a matron had cupped plump hands against cheeks apple-red and apple-firm.

The strapping man at her side laughingly added, "—and

children aplenty!'' As if to emphasize his words, he shifted two young boys, each perched on a wide shoulder.

The suggestive words tinted Nessa's cheeks as warm a pink as the tiny roses twined with ivory lilies in a chaplet atop the thick mane of curls that tumbled about her shoulders and down her back. Winding her way through narrow streets, she forced herself not to slow the pace as she drew nearer the goal earnestly prayed for but now feared. The consequences she'd ignored in letting selfish dreams lead her to this moment now mocked her. Would it not have been preferable to devote her life to the monotony of cloistered walls than to spend it with a man forced to accept second best, a man who'd ever view her as a waste of his time?

"Smile, this is a happy day," a whisper commanded.

Nessa glanced to the side and found Eleanor walking nearly beside her. She complied immediately although the smile trembled.

The queen's purple veil and wimple covered both hair and throat, a perfect frame for her flawless face and piercing gaze. Attention turned to the crowd, she nodded graciously as through smiling lips she spoke quietly to Nessa. "I'd never have made you his bride had I doubted your welcome of the deed."

The queen's forthright statement left Nessa flustered. Of course she'd selfishly welcomed it. *Her* response to the marriage wasn't the problem. But how could she, at this late moment, argue the ethics of an action she'd already accepted? Indeed, what response could she give? Happily fate offered a brief respite. Eleanor paused in her steady walk to accept a gay bouquet of wildflowers from a shy young girl. When the queen turned and gave them to the bride, a cheer went up. Feeling the warmth of a renewed blush, Nessa buried her face amidst blue bells and wild roses. Though she still had no answer, the friendly laughter rolling from spectators in waves of goodwill lent Nessa courage to look again at her royal foster mother.

Eleanor motioned Nessa forward once more, her probing eyes locking with hazel as she softly spoke. "You have an honest soul and I ask that you look inside to find the truth in my words."

As they proceeded Nessa maintained the smile while beneath she struggled with questions raised by the queen's perception. Had her attraction to the earl been so plain? Had others seen as well? Had he? Pray God he had not! His expression when she'd arrived for the betrothal ceremony had made clear his disgust with the substitution and the trickery of the women who'd done it. A belief reinforced by his departure for the village alehouse as soon as the betrothal ceremony was done. She'd not seen him since. What more had she expected? Cloistered she'd been, yet even her limited opportunities to observe human nature had taught that a man's passion was a fleeting and not very discriminating thing. Their few kisses doubtless meant little to him—a fact that made her response a shameful thing indeed. By trickery he'd been compelled to accept her in name, and she'd not resort to deception to oblige him to accept her in truth.

"What ill pricks you?"

Nessa realized her gloomy thoughts had driven the smile from her lips and quickly restored it with a brightness that reassured those lining their way who'd been worried by the bride's bleak demeanor. Its false brilliance did not satisfy the queen.

"Tell me you are unhappy with this match, and I will find a way to prevent it even now."

And to the man already grievously ill-used add the insult of a second bride's rejection, the loss of a fiefdom he'd gone so far to acquire? Never. Through lips aching with their artificial curve, Nessa denied the need. "Nay, you rightly read the hidden dreams I thought were doomed. 'Tis only that he is forced to take me for wife, a thing I doubt he'll ever forget or forgive."

Certain Garrick was capable of such coldness, Eleanor could not reassure the girl she'd no doubt would recognize an untruth the moment it was spoken. Nonetheless, in silver-ice eyes that dwelt on Nessa she'd seen a warmth that had never been there for another. It was reason to hope. "He could have denied you, but did not. And to you as to no other woman he has given a gift."

Smile still pinned to her lips, Nessa cast another quick glance at her companion. Fear of the pain in unjustified hopes failed to prevent the question darkening hazel eyes.

"I feel certain that during one of your talks you told him of your preference for St. Stephen's." They'd turned a corner and the purple-draped head nodded toward the stone building at the lane's end. "For you he insisted that the rite take place here."

For her? Though the likelihood was faint, mayhap it was so. She seized the possibility, allowing the mere chance that it was true to revive her nearly depleted confidence.

Eleanor would happily have let Garrick be wed in an unadorned and shabby chapel, but her affection for Nessa had allowed no less than a monumental effort to see the humble chapel transformed. Knowing Nessa's discomfort with opulence, she'd arranged for masses of cheerful spring flowers to brighten every gloomy corner, enrich every dingy view.

Unable to help herself, Nessa peered anxiously toward the small cluster waiting at the chapel door. What if the earl suffered from second thoughts? What if he had gone, leaving her to stand alone and shamed at the chapel door as just punishment for her part in the trickery? Her heart pounded so loud it ought to have drowned out the boisterous crowd's noise while a tiny frown appeared between delicate brows as hazel eyes studied the goal. Nay, he stood there—no ease for her anxieties in that simple fact for he was clad all in gray and looked so somber it increased her trepidation tenfold. Had he chosen his attire as sign of his distaste for the deed? Was it meant to show that he mourned a dead dream of beautiful Aleria for bride?

The nearer they drew to the chapel, the more difficult it was to take each step. Overwhelmed by a disgusting cowardice, she was unable to meet silver eyes. Fearing to see the handsome face hard with contempt, her gaze fell to the heavy cream silk billowing out with each step. Determined to force her mind from the binding action and the man who was an unwilling participant, she focused on a gown by far the loveliest she'd ever seen, let alone worn, yet of a style too revealing for one used to loose postulant's robes. The mere thought of wearing such a garment before so many, before the dark earl laid a rosy glow on her cheeks. Cut down from one made for Eleanor but never worn, its side lacing made it embarrassingly form-fitting from neck to hips. From thence the luminous cloth flared out to become at her feet a shimmering cloud which trailed behind.

At the chapel's door an impassive Garrick waited beside

the bishop. Standing near, Conal saw gray eyes flash silver at sight of the bride rounding a distant corner and, too, saw them narrow to hide all emotion. After his friend had so meekly accepted the change in brides, Conal had mentally reviewed the exchanges between the two. Had Garrick's interest settled on her? Surely not when the man had coldly rejected great beauties across the Continent and England. With no answer to the puzzle, Conal's gaze settled on the white-clad woman following Nessa and her queen.

Although half-closed lids shielded the nature of Garrick's responses from others, his gaze never wavered from the woman who approached. Nessa's unbound hair, unlike the last time he'd seen it so, was appropriate for this ceremony. Abundant curls left loose ridiculed previous restraints, tumbling down her back in a soft cloud of silky ringlets he could still feel coiled about his fingers. His hands curled against the beguiling memory.

Only to see how much further her weak legs must carry her, Nessa risked a peek just in time to see the earl's fists clench. Warmth drained from her with a suddenness that left her lightheaded. His action was surely a clear indication of his angry frustration with the whole day's work—and its originators.

Garrick saw his bride's quick glance and the way even so fleeting a look had robbed from her all color. Had he stolen an important moment from her with his demand of an immediate rite? Couldn't be. He attempted to ruthlessly quash the fear. After all, the people she knew were present and he'd forced the queen to let it be done here in the chapel she preferred. Moreover, whatever blame he might lay at the queen's door, she'd generously provided for her ward. That was clear in the extravagant gown a once intended nun could not have possessed of her own.

Nay, it was he whose family and friends would not join the wedding party, he who was inappropriately attired. He looked down at the gray velvet of his tunic with its black borders worked in silver. Rich it was but more appropriate for a solemn dirge than a merry wedding day. He'd not chosen it apurpose. When he'd set out for a betrothal arranged by the king, he'd had no plan of immediate marriage and his travel wardrobe sorely lacked proper garb for such an occasion. But then, had it been planned, his father, the king, and friend Geoffrey would have been present. He'd far rather make do with his present clothing than have present those who knew how unsought was the wedded state. And, if formal rites had been planned, they'd have had to host a great many less welcome nobles as well; and, as uncomfortable as his bride appeared to be now, he doubted she'd find such a gathering of jealous, bickering toads any more enjoyable than he. She and her queen had forced him to this deed, and he refused to feel guilty for his haste to see it over. Yet, all his fine and reasonable arguments failed to stifle the twinge of a wrong done.

After that one devastating peek she'd not raised her eyes, yet Nessa knew she'd reached her goal when black boots that clung to muscular calves came into view. She paused unsure what was to happen next while a new fear loomed threatening above. Would he allow the service to go forward but deny himself willing to accept her at the last moment? Horrible thought.

Nessa's hand was ice-cold and trembling. After Garrick laid it on his upheld arm, he left his fingers atop hers. If their chill was any indication, then it was true what they said of his ability to freeze even the warmest heart. Hah! What foolishness to credit a woman capable of this deceit with so rare a treasure. His derisive sound was no more than faintly audible yet Nessa cringed, a motion discerned only by the one standing near and left Garrick with a surely unwarranted sense of guilt.

Feeling as if she were standing before St. Peter, condemned, Nessa fought for pride enough to face even rejection as bravely as the early Christians had met the Romans' lions. Never mind that they had been blameless and undeserving of their punishment while she had participated in the deception that had brought her here. No matter her own culpability, she must meet what came with courage. Soft lips pressed together while her chin lifted.

While the rest of the procession arrived and crowded into the small churchyard, Garrick sensed his bride's struggle for courage. His slight squeeze of her fingers startled hazel gaze to gray. When the face overwhelmed by lush curls tilted up to him, Garrick blessed her with a faint but encouraging smile.

His response, so unexpected, surprised Nessa into returning it with a smile of blinding sweetness, revealing a dimple just below and to one side of her mouth which he'd never seen before.

Fascinated with this new vision, Garrick barely heard as the bishop began the ritual most always completed at chapel door. The choice he'd already made and now he must, quite literally, live with it. Having acknowledged it so, he meant to conceal his wary doubts and seek a comfortable relationship between them. Yet, he wouldn't promise to foreswear all mistrust—'twould be a lie.

A warmth Nessa had thought gone forever returned under his apparent willingness leastways to not punish her. Her eyes stayed bound to silver as, prompted by the bishop, they exchanged vows. She was certain he had little faith in her, but was relieved that he appeared not intent on holding her an outcast in her new home. Letting her lashes fall, she quietly thanked God.

From the forefront of the onlookers, Eleanor watched the two outlined by the flower garland about the doorway. Their dingy surroundings seemed to fade until only golden sunlight and blue sky were real as they spoke the words that bound them forever.

First signing the cross and blessing the newly wedded, the bishop led the party into the chapel for mass. Hands complacently folded atop a generous belly, he took his place at the altar.

Fingers lightly resting on her new husband's forearm, Nessa accompanied him to their place of honor on the bench nearest the front. Behind them, the rest of the company took seats according to rank—the lowliest resting on the cold stone floor.

Although heat from the Ice Warrior's molten core reached out to enfold her, as now he had the right to do, Nessa refused to submit to his likely unintentional call. Anxious not to appear the hopelessly infatuated fool to all, she concentrated on the details of her surroundings. The sanctuary had been dark when Aleria and her choice for mate had stood before its altar. Even now, despite daylight hours and the chapel's small rose window, it would've been dark within but for the masses of candles which lent every corner a golden glow. Moreover, the tapers were waxen. Here no

100

foul-smelling tallow to mask the fragrance of the large bouquets of delicate lilies and wild roses.

All too soon she knew herself able to accurately describe the chapel's every tiny detail, yet the bishop still droned on in a voice so monotonous that even one such as she, well-versed in Latin, could not follow. Against every sane intention, every cautious protest of good sense, hazel eyes peeked at the stunning stranger into whose hands she'd only just committed her life.

Again she thought of that day in the garden when she'd begged God to show her the right path, and the wickedly handsome earl had soon appeared. Her husband had not chosen her, but she recognized him as God's answer to her prayer. Still, as her conscience disallowed a lack of complete honesty, she admitted to participating in the trickery that had brought her to this rite but argued that the scriptures said, "all things work together for good to them that love God." She found both a measure of peace and a reaffirmation of her faith in the certainty that the Lord had taken her sinful deceit and turned it to good—for her at least, and she would do her best to see it work to his good as well. She'd strive always to be worthy of God's merciful love, of the blessing of home and husband of her own, and would do all to smooth the earl's path and thank Him unceasingly.

Nessa gazed at the statue of St. Stephen glowing in sunlight falling through a rose window high on the opposite wall. In a prayer of gratitude, she sublimated both her trepidation for a relationship she'd no practical knowledge of and discomfort with the man who surely did not see a blessing in this joining.

Garrick had felt the weight of eyes more brown than green upon him and knew when they moved to the statue of St. Stephen. He saw lashes fall and a golden brown head bow over palm-joined hands. Did she pray for a good marriage or for fortitude to survive the wedded state she'd never meant to be part of? His customary impassive mask kept the downward curl of unease from his lips, but a moody storm deepened the gray of his eyes.

When the mass was done, flowers pelted the couple as they left the chapel to lead the party's return to Salisbury Castle. Once there, Nessa knew she'd only have time to exchange her extravagant gown for more serviceable garb of

101

deep green wool. The earl insisted they depart immediately, allowing no time even for the usual feast. With the aid of the curious maidservant who'd helped her prepare for the betrothal ceremony, Nessa was soon changed and her hair demurely coiled atop her head.

Nessa insisted on personally folding the cream silk gown, and as she did so told herself not to expect unmerited considerations from the ill-used earl. Her husband, she reminded herself, breath catching at the reality behind that unbelievable truth. He'd warned them he'd waste no more time on traditional celebrations of a marriage he'd been tricked into accepting. Anxious not to be the cause of delay, she snatched up the bundle and without time for fanciful fears sped down dark winding stairs one last time.

The courtyard was a mass of people, each busy with tasks of their own. Metal rang and horses whinnied as members of the earl's guard examined their steeds, checked saddles and bridles, and called gruff greetings to one another. They were impatient to depart from a place that housed their enemy, but no more so than their lord. Nessa watched as the earl, already changed into dark wool traveling clothes and a crimson-lined cape, answered questions and gave orders, clearly anxious to be gone. Gone.

She looked back to the castle—her home. Aye, she'd been away more than here in recent times but still it was a wrench to know it would never be home again. Home was an unfamiliar castle in unknown lands. Her knees shook at the thought. Though thankful, she feared her ability to adjust to so many new things at one time. New home, new servants, new companions—new husband. The soft bundle clutched against a suddenly tight chest, she prayed for strength to bid farewell and move into the future bravely.

Garrick had seen to the stowing of a basket filled with Nessa's pitifully few possessions and a prie dieu, unadorned but of finely crafted wood, which a servant had insisted belonged to "Sister—ah—Lady Agnes." His new wife plainly lacked the acquisitive nature he much disdained. Although her one piece of furniture inferred the lack borne of religious training, still it pleased him—but then too much about the maid did that. He caught sight of her waiting demurely beside a wagon in the midst of a column of men and horses near ready to depart, undemanding of his time or attention as few women would be. Moving to her side, he took the square of neatly folded cloth from her.

"Are these all you wish to take?" With the bundle in his hands he gestured to the items already loaded.

"Aye, they are all I own other than the few things left in the abbey for which I've no further need." She stared at the hard-packed courtyard floor, failing to see Garrick frown at her mention of foregoing even the smallest item for the sake of their marriage. He'd as soon think himself the one wronged, bolstering the idea that the marriage was none of his choice and restraining the oddly hurtful thought that the exceptional maid had rather spend her life within cloistered walls than at his side.

Sunlight glinted on his dark head as he curtly nodded before moving to the vehicle's rear. He deposited the bundle carefully beneath the stout cloth cover that as they talked had been rolled out over the wagon to protect its contents.

"My lord," a voice called out as Garrick straightened. "I and Baron Wryborne's knight have a question for you to settle."

The earl turned to find Conal's trustworthy Sir Jasper standing calm against the belligerence of Sir Erdel. After his last visit home, as favor to Sir Rufus, Castle Tarrant's aging guard captain as well as his friend and supporter, Garrick had accepted the man's grandson, Sir Erdel, into his service. He'd taken him to Henry's court and battles and given the young knight a chance to prove himself capable of some small part of the older man's good sense and ability. He'd never be so foolish again. A guard captain's task was to provide leadership and organization to those who served below, a responsibility more than adequately fulfilled for him by Sir Rufus and for Conal by Sir Jasper. Sir Erdel's pretentious manner, twice as annoying in one so young and inexperienced, had alienated not only the guardsmen who served beneath him but also his fellow knights. Rather than smoothing their way, his argumentative nature had caused problems at every turn. Squaring his shoulders, Garrick excused himself to Nessa with a slight smile and turned to the arrogant knight.

As soon as the earl was close enough to clearly hear, Sir Erdel overrode the elder Sir Jasper's quiet words to present his own reasoning. "I say, as the day is half gone, it's only sensible that we take the longer path around the forest edge. No need to tempt the brigands who lay concealed in wooded glades to snare their prey. Then in the morrow's full daylight we can march straight through the forest to reach our goal in the same length of time offered by the shorter but more dangerous route."

The plan was so clearly a foolish one that Garrick nearly laughed his scorn but, in fairness, he turned to Sir Jasper. "What say you to this 'new' route?"

"I say it is many times more treacherous than the known and well-traveled path." Dark blond hair already tucked beneath the coif of his chain mail, Sir Jasper was ready to depart. Nearly of an age with the earl, his blue eyes met silver-gray steadily as he gave his reasoning. "In the dark what difference to brigands if we sleep at forest edge or forest center? Moreover, finding a new route through the forest is not so simple and quick a chore as Sir Erdel implies. One wrong turn, and likely there'd be several, would insure that it take many hours longer and surely mean a night spent in unfamiliar woodlands, a far more dangerous repose than the one the shorter path entails."

Sir Erdel had heard Sir Jasper's argument before and allowed his attention to move to the earl's bride—plain and surely too timid to offer a man worthy heat, like tepid water next to the fire of ale or silky string of rich wine.

Nessa, with nothing to do but wait, watched as he listened to the knights. The elder one stood respectfully while the second, dark and insolent, spoke. When the other began to respond, the dark one's brazen stare moved over her from head to toe. She was shocked by the contemptuous assessment in his eyes. So long had she been in nun's habit that she'd never been subjected to such insulting gazes. When he turned away with a smirk she was certain he'd found her sadly lacking. Her cheeks burned.

"Your bridegroom means to soon be gone, my lamb, so wish me farewell now." Once the cold earl had moved away, Eleanor had begun wending her way through the milling crowd, noisy with the excitement of imminent departure, and now stood beside Nessa.

After the example of how little welcome she was likely to find on Tarrant lands, the sound of her foster mother's voice sent a surge of melancholy for all things loved and familiar over Nessa. She threw her arms around the queen. They'd said good-bye many times before, but this threatened to be more permanent.

Eleanor was surprised by the reserved girl's fervent display. Revealing how deep Nessa's fears ran, it touched her heart. She squeezed the girl and then, still holding her arms, leaned back to offer advice. "No matter the circumstances that brought it about, your marriage is as real and true as any other."

Nessa could only nod, determined to restrain the flood of tears which threatened to overflow the banks of her eyes. Expose her feelings through quavering voice she would not.

"I pray you make a better match of it than I." Eleanor added, meeting unnaturally bright hazel eyes. Concerned, she hesitated yet her desire to protect the girl from possible harm renewed her determination. "Let me give you a warning. Beware of Sir Gilfrey's spite. Finding himself ousted from Swinton Keep by your marriage, he'll surely seek redress."

Nessa was surprised. She'd thought her distrust, nay, dislike of the man unshared by any other. The queen hugged Nessa again before stepping back, although she still held the girl's fingers in a firm clasp.

"Remember, if you are in need of help, send me a message and I'll give all within my power." Eleanor's smile was reassuring.

Discomfited by the private conversation between the devious Eleanor and his new wife, Garrick had quietly moved to stand within earshot on the wagon's far side just in time to catch the last promise. It sounded innocent enough, but his distrust of the queen made it difficult for him to accept any word she spoke for what it appeared to mean. The royal viper was capable of hatching some plot to use Nessa as the worm in the center of his apple, of giving his wife the role of spy or even originator of trouble. Yes, he could easily believe it of Eleanor, but the idea of Nessa as true traitor left a bitter taste—had the fruit Eve shared with Adam borne the same acrid flavor? All he could do, must do for his own peace of mind, was to watch closely for any communication between them. Open and easy would go unquestioned, for they were bound by affection, but secretive would mean his suspicions confirmed again.

"Nessa, your good sense in beginning your leavetaking immediately is appreciated. It's time for us to depart."

On the point of denying it her good sense, of telling him it was the queen's work, Nessa hesitated when Eleanor squeezed her fingers and imperceptibly shook her head. Before she could weigh the wisdom of not explaining, the earl spoke again.

"We've already lost far more than half the hours of daylight and can afford to lose no more." Garrick had seen the silent communication between the two women. He didn't know or care what its purpose was but feared, as a bad omen, Nessa's capitulation to the other's direction. His mood was not improved and although he courteously helped Nessa mount, he barked orders to his men.

Ahorse, he and Conal with their knights led the procession. Guardsmen brought up the rear while Nessa and the cart rode protected in the center. Only as they neared the gate did Nessa realize that in submitting to the earl's haste she'd lost the opportunity to both bid Mouse Catherine farewell and apologize to Sybil both for bringing her here for no purpose and for sending news of the unexpected wedding back to the abbey with her.

"God go with you, Agnes. We'll be missing you."

Nessa's eyes flew up at the sound of her disliked name but smiled when she saw Harold again standing atop the gate, his wide girth shaking from the energy of two arms waving good-bye.

"And God be with you," she called out, waving in return just before they passed into the tunnel through the wall. One hand on her new little palfrey's broad back and one hand holding the reins, she looked behind for a last glimpse of friends and home.

After years of enduring jostling journeys atop angular mules, Nessa found the small mare amazingly comfortable. This wedding gift from the queen was much appreciated yet she was weary of steady motion by the time dusk had settled its ever-deepening cloak of soft darkness about them. They'd left rolling meadows and fields behind to travel into a dense forest. Whereas Nessa was frightened by the castle's dark winding stairway, man-made and to her ever threatening, in the solitude of spreading oaks and towering elms she found peace. Surely here, among the living things He'd created, was God's true sanctuary. As yet there was no moon, but light filtered down from the sky and Nessa occasionally caught the shimmer of white petals against a shadowy wall of greenery. Knowing her mount would follow the other horses, Nessa let her eyes drift shut and listened to night sounds. Insects chirped among lush grasses, birds called to their mates, and forest creatures rustled through the dense undergrowth bordering both sides of the path as they moved about their own natural business. Peaceful, so peaceful.

Garrick had dropped back to be at Nessa's side when he called halt to the day's travels and was intrigued by her gentle smile and closed eyes. Did she weave pleasant dreams? Was he a part of them? Expecting her to be full of complaints and demands, as had the women circumstances had earlier forced him to travel with, once again she'd pleasantly surprised him.

Lost in the magic of woodland mysteries, Nessa drifted from night sounds to scents. She knew flowers bloomed along their path although even were she to open her eyes, it was surely too dark to see them there. Yet, after the heat of day their fragrance seemed to intensify when borne on air evening-cooled, and she sought to identify each. Lily, wild rose, lavender, and—

"We'll rest here tonight."

The voice unexpectedly near broke Nessa's pleasant dream state. Her eyes flew open and she found the earl's shadowy form all too close. He was a commanding figure on his own but atop his massive black destrier, he towered. The moon just rising above treetops sparked silver in his eyes. She caught her breath and hastily looked away. They were bearing down on a fair-sized stream, and in an open spot on its bank lay the cold ashes of past fires, demonstrating it a spot frequented by travelers.

Garrick swung down with the graceful ease of one well-used to hours ahorse. After handing the reins to a guardsman with directions to lead his steed to the water's edge, he turned to aid his assuredly horse-weary bride's return to her own feet.

"Doubtless you've found the journey tiring, so let me help you down." His words were not an offer but an announcement of intent and Nessa recognized them as such. Anxious to be quit of her palfrey, she'd not have demurred even had she been given the opportunity. Rather, she gave him a wan smile of agreement.

Although accustomed to being given aid in dismounting, as a postulant nun she had merely been offered a hand or arm to steady her descent. Therefore, when two strong hands wrapped about her waist and effortlessly lifted her above the saddle, she gasped and reached out to clasp broad shoulders as the only firm anchor in a suddenly tilting world. Though seeking no more than simple stability, the feel of iron-hard muscle rippling beneath her touch presented danger of another kind. Breath oddly caught somewhere between lungs and tight throat, she'd have jerked her hands from a contact that burned if she could have.

She was light as a dream, Garrick thought, still holding the soft form above him, much aware of gentle curves—as if an example of her tastes not for the ostentatious but for the elegant simplicity of graceful lines.

Through night shadows a wide hazel gaze fell to silver, remaining bonded all through her slow descent to earth. Even after her feet touched the ground, and she had perforce to look up rather than down, still she could not break his visual hold.

"Garrick." Coming to stand behind his friend, Conal offered a quiet warning. "You've a much interested audience, a thing I doubt either you or your bride will appreciate."

Ears of a sudden opened to the earthy speculations murmured amongst his men, Garrick's hands fell away and he turned to the surreptitiously watching men, stern caution in ice-cold eyes. Silence fell over their audience with a telling speed.

Although the words had not been directed to her, Nessa felt as if they and the watching eyes had condemned her for a sinner, for the fallen women she could easily believe her response to the earl made her. Fingers caught in the deep green wool of her gown, she stared blindly at the turf her feet were surely attached to for all time for she could not move.

Garrick glanced behind and saw Nessa's shame. His anger at his men's action increased. How could they not know what insult it was to a once intended nun? Nay, he reproached himself for the injustice. It was not their wrong but his. He should never have put her in such a position, and he would not again. Accepting the fault did nothing to lighten his mood.

He returned to stand in front of her, shield her against still watching eyes. "They," he jerked his head back, "intended no insult to you. 'Tis only the sort of banter ever given new-wedded couples. In truth, you should consider yourself fortunate that by dragging you away direct from the ceremony I saved you from far cruder treatment at the hands of your own. Locked away from earthly matters, you've no understanding of the ribald customs in which most people take pleasure."

Unable to look higher than his boots, Nessa still found some measure of comfort in his explanation that his men meant her no more ill than other brides—except for the dark knight who'd earlier found her lacking. Him she believed incapable of aught but contempt. When strong fingers covered the small hand clutching green cloth, she let the earl lead her toward the fire now gaining heat beneath the care of men mere shadows against colorless moonlight. Chilled, she welcomed the blaze's warmth.

Garrick left his bride, arms outstretched toward the fire, to scout for a location affording at least an illusion of privacy. On journeys he normally spent the night wrapped in his cloak on any patch of ground somewhat free of stones, but he'd not allow Nessa to sleep amongst his men without a measure of seclusion. The willow whose weeping branches trailed to the ground on one side and into gently flowing waters on the other offered more than he'd hoped to find. For Nessa's comfort he gathered armfuls of tall grasses and laid them in the green cavern. Atop this soft mattress, he laid a folded bedfur so she could sleep both atop and beneath its protection from night damp and chill.

Conal didn't know where Garrick had gone but was certain he'd not meant his wife to go hungry. "Your evening meal is served, milady." Atop both palms he held out a cloth square on which rested a chunk of bread and generous slice of roast venison.

Alone amidst a large group of men, all strangers, Nessa was terribly self-conscious. Turning, she was relieved to find a friendly smile. "Thank you, kind sir." She accepted the offered meal and gave him her warmest smile, baring her unexpected dimple.

Saints! Under the power of her charmingly unaffected smile, Conal could understand his friend's fascination with this damsel. "If the minstrels are to be believed," he responded, showing her to a fallen log a respectable distance from the rest of the party, "then 'tis the duty of all good knights to lend aid and offer protection to fair damsels."

Settling on the rough bark, Nessa failed to prevent an answer not well thought out. "But I am not a 'fair damsel.' "

"You are lovely. I've only just realized it myself." Conal answered with his usual honesty. "I've been too blinded by the stunning beauty of both the queen and your sister to see you clearly. Same as after looking direct into the sun, one cannot see anything well." He didn't mention that the great beauties, who like the sun could burn, hadn't kept him from appreciating serene Sybil with her cool loveliness of the moon. "Moreover, Garrick finds you the fairest of them all. For years I've known him and have never seen him respond to a woman as he has to you."

Meeting clear blue eyes, Nessa shook her head sadly. " 'Tis only that you've never seen him in close contact with a nun. He, like all men, treats one meant to be God's bride differently."

Conal gave her a gently teasing smile. "If he responded to you only as God's bride, he'd never have wed you himself."

Embarrassed, Nessa's gaze dropped to the yet untouched bread and meat in her lap. "He didn't choose to wed me. That you know, for you were there when the trick was revealed. I fear he will never forgive me for my part in that wicked deed."

Conal was too well acquainted with Garrick's stubborn and unbending nature to dispute the last but he would argue with the first. "You are very wrong if you think Garrick could ever be forced to a deed truly against his wishes." Willing her to believe his words, he studied the down-bent head gilded by firelight. "I know the political reason for the match, and I also know he could have refused to comply without blame from the king."

Nessa looked up to meet the baron's level gaze. Was it true? Had even some tiny part of the earl wanted the marriage? The possibility, no matter how remote, added a

110

small spark to the hope whose fire hadn't been completely doused in her soul.

"That he wed you, means he wanted it so." Even Conal had more tact than to add that the earl's choice could as well have been made because he deemed the political necessity too important to deny as because of a desire to claim her for herself.

"I see you've taken care of my wife." Garrick approached from the back and startled them into looking over their shoulders.

"You can tell he's a good hunter," Conal said with a look of mock disgust. "He creeps silently upon unsuspecting prey."

Nessa gazed at the coldly staring man looming above and prayed he'd not heard any part of their conversation.

Conal rose. "As you've returned, I'll leave her in your care."

"See you remember that she is now and always in my care." Garrick hadn't heard their words but didn't like the way Conal gazed into his bride's eyes.

Garrick's voice was cold and to Conal the slightly stressed "my" was an indication of jealousy or at least possessiveness. He found this emotion, which his friend had never shown before, an encouraging sign boding well for the couple's future. First bowing in teasing assent, a grinning Conal departed.

Nessa was left alone again while the earl went to fetch his own supper. In helpless admiration she watched as the man who had claimed her in his care approached the fire. His powerful form, silhouetted against leaping orange and yellow flames, moved with a grace that demonstrated agile strength controlled but waiting to be loosed against foe. Never could she doubt his protection less than a tangible force to be reckoned with.

As he returned, Nessa's eyes fell to her still untasted meal; and when he took his seat at her side, she found it near impossible to eat. Although each bite faced a battle in descending her tight throat, she persisted in nibbling at a golden crust. He'd been right when in their first disagreement he'd said she knew nothing of relationships outside abbey walls. Her only experience with wedded couples came from the few years she'd spent in Swinton Keep with her parents whose relationship had been one formed by her father's intimidation and her mother's submission beneath oft dealt blows. From the keep she'd come to a castle where lived a queen exiled by her spouse. Some of the knights in the castle guard were wed, but as she'd moved to the abbey before she was old enough to note their ways, she was lamentably uninformed on life within the bonds of marriage.

What did he expect of her? Her knowledge of such matters was limited, but she'd seen more than one tipsy guardsman engaged in a passionate embrace with a serving girl. Embraces like as she had shared with the earl. With the thought came a tingling curiosity. Surreptitiously she watched as his strong hands divided his bread. She could near feel them caressing her back, drawing her closer for a kiss that melted resolve as if she were the one made of ice which his fire melted to steaming water.

Forcing herself to look away, she watched as one guardsman rose to stride a short distance from the fire, wrap himself in his own long cloak, and lie down. The sight brought tension of another sort, one unpleasant. Beyond their violent exchanges, the only fact she clearly remembered about her parents was that they'd shared a common bed. From the corner of her eyes she peeked up at her new husband. Would he expect to share her bed, such as it was, this night? After the embarrassment of the descent from her palfrey, the shame in possible further public embraces flooded her cheeks with a color she was relieved would go unnoticed in the firelight's ruddy glow.

Staring with distaste at the bread still in her hand, she knew she'd eaten as much as she could without being weighted down by food which surely turned to stone once swallowed.

Garrick felt the maid's tension growing. Did she think him so crass as to subject her to a near public deflowering? He put an end to her foolish fears.

"I've a need to talk with my men but if you are tired from our day's journey, I'll lead you to your bower to find rest."

Nessa gave him the same sweet, dimpled smile she'd given Conal for an earlier rescue. Fearing her voice would waver, she wordlessly nodded and stood. He'd offered her a bed and at the same time reassured her he'd not soon join her there.

112

Rising, Garrick held out his arm. She placed her hand atop it and let him lead her over uneven ground patterned by shadow and moonlight. At the willow's edge, he swept trailing branches aside to reveal her waiting bed, soft and secure in sheltered privacy. Without hesitation she settled on the soft mound.

"Thank you for such luxurious accommodations." Nessa's dimple peeked so deliciously it seemed an invitation to seduction. Abruptly flooded by an unexpected tide of burning desire, Garrick used every scrap of his famous frozen control to restrain a nearly ungovernable compulsion to join her in the cavern's questionable seclusion. He desperately wanted to loose the bounty of her hair and learn at last if her flesh was as warm, as soft, as willing to curl about him as the ringlets that had clung about his fingers as if they'd a will of their own. Impossible folly but if he remained a moment longer, he'd truly give his companions something to snicker about. With a curt nod, he let the curtain of willow branches drop to cut off the all too tempting view of the woman now his wife.

The earl's long stare had summoned from Nessa's depths a heart-stopping, breath-stealing warmth which his following cold reaction to her sincere appreciation made all the more hurtful. For long moments she sat, staring into the darkness where the overwhelming man had stood. Finally she forced her hands to move, pulling pins from her hair to let her braids fall over her shoulders. She was unused to having her curls so tightly restrained and the style had grown more uncomfortable with each passing hour. But freeing the braids coiled atop her head was not relief enough. She loosened the plaits to comb fingers through tumbled locks, finding a few crushed petals remaining from the flower chaplet she'd worn for the ceremony. It seemed so long ago. Thinking of the morning, of the chapel, of the flowers, and of the people's good wishes, she lay back on the soft cushion so considerately provided. Exhausted by the busy day, she relaxed into a light slumber.

Garrick had returned to his men and begun a discussion he drew out until, one by one, the others drifted away or dropped to sleep where they were. He'd no further excuses for delay. Knowing they must rise again in but a few short hours, he finally slipped quietly into the willow cave and

113

frowned. Nessa had fallen asleep on top of the bedfur rather than inside its folded warmth. It was chilly now and before morn it would be truly cold yet he deemed it too dangerous to awaken her. Asleep she was an enticement he could withstand. Awake and close in the dark, he was not so certain of his own restraints. Still, the grass mattress looked inviting and the maid was safely sleeping. He carefully stretched out at her side, arranging his cloak atop them both.

To Nessa's drowsy mind it seemed as if someone had provided the luxury of fire-heated, cloth-wrapped stone to warm her bed. She instinctively snuggled against it.

Feeling gentle curves yield pliantly along his full length, Garrick experienced an immediate but unwanted response. He was adamant in his decision to allow no closer embrace in this nearly public place but realized that she unconsciously sought warmth. Surely, he rationalized, it was his duty to provide it. Feeling justified he laid his arm about her shoulders and eased her near. A delicious scent of crushed petals rose from the soft cloud of curls brushing his cheek. Yielding to an innocent lure, he gently nuzzled into its silky abundance, inhaling the heady fragrance.

In Nessa's dreams warmed stone became the enticing, forbidden heat of the silver-eyed tempter, the one whose kisses burned with a sinful sweetness she could not refuse. Even in sleep feeling those lips against her ear, she turned her mouth to meet them.

Under the unexpected but passionate fire of untutored lips, Garrick's proud control fell to ashes. The arm once gently urging delicate curves near now crushed her closer to the power of his long body, but no closer than she wanted to be, for suddenly the woman in his hold seemed striving against all barriers to be closer and closer still. One arm slid beneath to hold her even tighter while the other hand moved to seek the gentle curves whose softness he'd earlier longed to caress.

As seering lips trailed fire from mouth to cheek to throat, Nessa felt the tantalizing approach of an intimate caress unknown. Face buried between masculine throat and shoulder, the first brush across a soft peak sent a tremor to her core. When its inflaming touch returned, she bit the flesh beneath her lips. The hand returned to firmly caress straining

114

flesh while his mouth again took possession of hers, demanding and receiving.

Their kiss deepened as never before and Nessa's dark world spun with fiery sensations as his tongue initiated a dance of advance and withdrawal that their fully clothed bodies imitated without design. His hands slid down her back to cup her derriere and pull her tight against his desperate need. The groan which welled up in his throat came from hers filled with aching desire. His hands had begun carelessly jerking the cloth barrier of her gown from his goal when the erotic trance was broken by the faintest of snickers from men only a few feet beyond the willow wall whom he'd thought long ago at rest. He froze for long, painful moments, striving for control.

Suddenly bereft of welcome fire, Nessa moved, seeking its return but instead encountered an iron-strong clasp which held her away. Garrick rolled to his back and stared into the darkness above. This was no place for the consummation of their marriage. Neither would he seduce a sleeping virgin into a desperate passion lacking in gentleness, nor would he initiate an embrace she'd likely wake to regret as sin. The thought increased his self-disgust for he'd no doubt she'd wake ashamed of even this incomplete deed.

Dream had blended into reality, and either the painful ache of unfulfilled desire or the restraint of a bruising hold had brought Nessa to full wakefulness. But, although Nessa had no doubt of what had happened, she'd not heard the sound which put an end to it. All she knew was that the earl had stopped as suddenly as if truly turned to ice. She should be relieved, yet that righteous thought offered no ease for an aching void. Nor was there aught but pain in his apparent ability to so easily freeze his response, to turn from her when she was clearly incapable of a similar deed. Her oversized lack of confidence lent a new twist to her fears. Had he been sleeping too? Had he dreamed he held in his arms Aleria, the beautiful bride he'd expected, only to awaken and find Agnes?

115

❧ *Chapter 10* ❧

Not even the pleasure of riding her palfrey rather than the donkey she was more accustomed to could lift Nessa's spirits from the abysmal depths to which they'd fallen. As if divine powers were showing their displeasure, sometime during the night a heavy overcast had spread above. Clouds hung so low that in places as the company journeyed the path was obscured by trailing tendrils of mist. Nessa settled the thick wool of her green cloak closer to thwart invading fingers of cold. At least the threatening rain hadn't yet fallen to turn dusty track to a mud-bogged mire.

The earl had been gone when she awoke to gray-shrouded dawn. And if his absence had not been proof enough of his distaste for her and her night passion, then 'twas made clear when he'd sent Conal to deliver her morning meal. She unsuccessfully comforted herself that it was all for the best. Even given the chance, she couldn't have met silver eyes although for most of the day she'd been unable to turn her attention from the broad back ahead, crimson-lined cloak blown back from wide shoulders to reveal gray-clad thighs and black booted calves. She'd memorized the path of thick, dark hair from crown to nape where ends brushed cloak collar. It was much shorter than most men wore. Likely a choice providing less toil for one whose life was spent traveling or fighting on the king's behalf. The vague memory of biting him in the vulnerable expanse between neck and shoulder returned. She cringed. Truly some wicked imp had found in her a hitherto undiscovered weakness to sins of the flesh and played upon it as skillfully as did a master musician his instrument.

She tore her eyes from the embodiment of temptation and resolutely turned her attention to the passing scenery. In surprise she realized they were very near Swinton Keep. Its palisade wall of upended and sharpened logs placed tight together could be seen through rapidly thinning trees. With the discovery came an echo of the queen's final warning and the assault of a new anxiety. The earl's ability to disturb her was borne of fascination but her response to the man inside the structure they fast approached sprang from revulsion.

Since the days of Nessa's childhood when Sir Gilfrey had served her father as guard captain, he'd repelled her. Too young to hide her feelings, he'd recognized her instinctive aversion and found it amusing, never letting an opportunity pass to stand near, to touch, to whisper nauseating words. Even now she shivered with distaste at the memory. In hopes of stilling her apprehension, Nessa sternly reminded herself this time she came with a man who claimed to be her protector. Moreover, a powerful man whom Sir Gilfrey dare not offend. Fear the earl's rejection she might, but his pride alone would disallow injury to any he'd named his own, and her faith in his strength was firm enough to lend her courage as they neared the towering wall.

"Who comes?" The loud call echoed from the far side of the palisade's wooden gate.

"Garrick Fitz William, Earl of Tarrant and Lord of Swinton by right of my wife, Lady Agnes of Swinton Keep." At the head of the line, Garrick stood in his stirrups to give the response.

From the narrow walkway near the top of the wall's far side a man peered through the gap between two logs' pointed ends. Lacking helm, a few locks of thinning hair fell in a tangle that clearly hadn't seen a comb in long days. The man turned to speak in the courtyard behind. "Here's a man what calls himself Lord of Swinton, Cyril." The words were

117

a jeer. "I fancy as I hadn't ought to let him in without our lord's command. What says you?"

A bleary mumble and crude, indistinct laughter could be heard from the courtyard beyond. The gate guard looked down at the earl again and sneered. "We already has a Lord of Swinton and him you are not." Greasy strands brushed angular shoulders as he shook his head and mocked, "Wed to holy Sister Agnes. Hah! Thinks you we are so witless as to be easily fooled?"

Nessa recognized the speaker as one of Sir Gilfrey's lackeys. She didn't doubt the two lords who accompanied her, with their joined forces, could force entrance with little trouble and less time, but bloodshed was unnecessary. Besides, despite the price of a later penance, she'd enjoy dislodging the scorn from the gate guard's dirty face.

"I fear, Alfred, 'tis true you've been made the fool if you believe Sir Gilfrey is lord of my lands." Nessa's voice carried with the pure clarity of a bell tone as she urged her small mare into position beside the earl's massive steed.

Garrick glanced toward a smile of sweet serenity. The woman had ridden to the fore of a force met with hostility, and he admired her daring though near certain it was simply the action of one bred to compassion and intent on preventing the painful lesson he'd have been constrained to wreak upon his opposers. But the bright green gleam of amusement which crept into her tranquil gaze at sight of the guard's craven reaction gave him pause.

Nessa watched with the anticipated enjoyment as Alfred's mockery faded into cowed apprehension before he dropped from view.

"I—I beg mercy, milord," he gushed through the gate his shaking hands hurried to unbar and swing wide. "So many robbers afoot that we've grown chary. Who can know but what some devil-blessed robbers might a' stole your banner and ridden here to claim they was you and yours."

It was a feeble excuse, not worth Garrick's time to acknowledge. No robber could be so successful as to possess steeds or armor and command men such as his. Nay, more likely this structure sheltered more than a few of the forest "brigands" Sir Erdel had so feared. As they rode through the gates his attention locked on the two-story wooden building in the courtyard's center. A man, doubtless the

118

previously unseen Cyril, ran toward it and disappeared inside.

Within moments a commotion at the doorway heralded the emergence of an armed group. Lank brown hair resting on meaty shoulders, Sir Gilfrey stood in their lead with naked broadsword held threateningly across barrel chest. It gleamed wickedly even in the weak light of a cloudy and rapidly aging day.

Garrick motioned Nessa to fall back behind the protection of his armed force, but she prodded her horse into a canter to keep up with his steed's longer pace. Silver gaze already flashing his response to the other man's challenge turned on Nessa with wordless command. His only answer was a small chin tilted defiantly and eyes sparkling with green fire.

She was aware of the irony in her reaction with the earl standing as both source and recipient of her courage. Drawing a deep breath, she turned her attention to the man standing at keep door. You stood up to the earl, she admonished herself, so don't falter now before this, this thing of slime and dung. With the origin of her bravery so near, she was pleased to find herself able for the first time to meet belittling eyes unflinching.

So, the waiting castellan silently derided, the pious little nun had found herself both a man and a measure of bravado. When first he'd come to Swinton Keep and met the thin girl-child, he'd been amused by her aversion to him. Slyly taunting and sending her skittering away had given him his first taste of power—and addictive emotion. He'd once meant to claim the girl for his pleasure and her inheritance for his own. Only hearing the queen had sent her to become nun had diverted his original plan. Then, when her beautiful sister had traveled to the continent with the queen, he'd been certain she'd be claimed there by some great noble with no interest in a small English dowry. Aleria's future bound on the continent and believing Sister Agnes would have no need for Swinton, he'd felt safe in his position, safe in claiming the land at least. Now came the wretched girl to deny him both. Resentment burned in narrowed eyes.

Garrick examined his foe, noted the venomous gaze, and instinctively placed a possessive hand on Nessa's shoulder. "By our marriage, Sir Gilfrey, I am now Lord of Swinton as

119

well as Earl of Tarrant." Silver eyes met and defeated Gilfrey's glare.

Bowing his head with ill-grace, Gilfrey responded. "As you bear the proof at your side and have a small army to back the claim, I've little option but to cede you the fief and its keep."

"Being warrior with experience enough to know you would fight the claim if you could, I command that you and yours depart immediately." Garrick motioned to the score of men standing belligerently near the keep door.

Sir Gilfrey sneered but merely shrugged as if the demand was of small import and turned toward the door. Although he intended to pack and be quit of this foe-tainted place with all possible haste, his mind was busy devising a later retaliation to punish these lords and the nun for summarily expelling him from a position which long years in possession had surely made his.

"Sir Gilfrey," the earl spoke again, "I've had reliable reports of pilferings both small and large, as well as fraudulent acquisition of rights—all since nearly the day you became castellan here and all laid at your door. Too, I know of the unmerciful taxes you've squeezed from the people while blaming the king's greed for what fell into your own pocket."

Nessa gasped. She'd never heard of these wrongdoings and was appalled at the ill-use of her people. Her people—a curiously pleasant concept. As a nun humbled to God and serving all humanity, she'd named none her own before.

With a tight smile Garrick glanced at the woman clearly dismayed by the deed he'd accused her castellan, the queen's supporter, of committing. "Sir Gilfrey and his men," he flatly informed her, "have done more to spread discontent through the common people than Henry's just laws ever earned."

"And claim you to never tax the people for your own use?" Scorn coated the words of the unrepentant knight.

"No more than my rightful share as their lord and protector." Garrick's response was immediate and the ice that gleamed in his gaze froze further words in his opponent's throat. "While you've taken to yourself that and a great deal more, so now I bid you and yours be gone with no more than your steeds and what clothes can be packed on their

120

backs. What remains I will see divided amongst those of this fief whom you beggared."

Trembling with fury at the command which returned him to poverty but unable to stand against it, Sir Gilfrey whirled, stormed into the keep, and up to the lord's chamber that for years had been his own. Garrick swung from his huge destrier to follow the angry knight, motioning members of his guard to provide similar escorts for each of the departing men.

When Sir Gilfrey's men and their vigilant companions had disappeared into the keep, Conal dismounted and moved to the frowning maid's side. "Mayhap you would prefer to test your legs for strength without a large audience?"

The voice drew Nessa's gaze from the empty doorway to the friendly face below. She wished she could as easily turn her mind from the confrontation just past. Sir Gilfrey's hostility toward Garrick alarmed her. Hadn't Eleanor warned of the man's vengeful nature, a fact she'd long known but that seemed all the more dangerous with confirmation by a queen.

"As often as I am called to do it, I've never been able to end a day's ride with less than relief." Conal chatted lightly, intent on distracting the maid from obviously unpleasant thoughts.

He proffered his hand, and Nessa was relieved to accept this more familiar method of descent. She'd not forgotten the previous night's startling, if exciting, flight through the air or its embarrassing end. Conal led her into relative privacy at one side of a door open to the clatter and rude comments of men forced to depart with uncommon speed. The glow of firelight drew her to a hide-covered window not yet shuttered against soon coming night.

"You knew Sir Gilfrey from before?" Conal's question was more an intended interruption of her apparent anxiety than request for answer to something unknown.

Nessa nodded and window light glowed on coiled braids, laying a golden halo around her head. "He was my father's guard captain when I was a child in this place." Her response was automatic and expected, but to Conal's surprise she added a heartfelt denunciation. "And of a more cruel and vengeful man I've never heard tell. He neither forgets nor forgives."

121

On the upper level, under the earl's steady gaze, Sir Gilfrey crushed every piece of clothing he could into a roll of awkward size and proportion. Beneath such close observation it was impossible to slip even one of his jeweled belts or gold goblets into the pack. His anger simmered and by the time his task was done had heated to a dangerous boil. Pack slung over his shoulder, he stomped down the stairs, bellowing for his men.

At the sound of Sir Gilfrey summoning his men the woman on the outside of a hide-covered window turned, trying to peer into the room beyond. Nessa could hear every word but see no more than hazy forms—the earl all in gray was taller than the others while the ousted castellan who wore a gaudy combination of colors was a bright splotch. Her hands twisted together. Their figures she could see but not their faces and her distrust of Sir Gilfrey made her anxious not to miss so much as one expression.

Unaware of the small figure on the window's far side, once his men had gathered about, a fuming Sir Gilfrey met Garrick's gaze again. "I swear I'll see you dead for this taking of all I've worked years to hold." His voice dripped with the acid of animosity. "See you dead and take that shrinking little nun for my own. She'll pay endlessly for the evils you've done me."

Garrick froze, silver eyes glinting with such icy power that Sir Gilfrey fell back. The threat against his own person Garrick dismissed as simply the last resort of a defeated foe struggling to save face. However, his first impulse was to destroy the one who dared speak menacingly of his wife. Only the powers of cold reasoning kept his fury contained. Such words were merely the harmless verbal assault of a desperate and near powerless man.

Sir Gilfrey's threat against the earl had fallen on Nessa's ears like a blow; and, unable to see the speaker quail before the cold force of the man he'd sought to alarm, she was terrified. Her fear increased under the certainty that so strong a lord as Tarrant would dismiss it without serious thought and not guard his back where the hand of cowardice, of treachery would strike.

Through dusk's growing gloom, Conal watched anxiety grow in the maid's wide eyes. An emotion so strong that she stared at the dull glow of a cloudy day fading on the horizon and appeared not to notice as the troop of exiled men marched past to claim stabled horses and ride out through a palisade gate which closed behind.

Shortly after the departure of Sir Gilfrey and his men the storm that had threatened all day broke its restraints to wreak a wild vengeance on the land. Thunder rolled and lightning flashed while rain pelted the earth with drenching force. Garrick had little pity for the men he'd sent into the storm's fury, but he could not, would not expect his own guardsmen to spend the night in its discomfort. Thus the small keep would be crowded with men sleeping side by side, sleeping even in the corridor outside the keep's only private chamber, the lord's chamber which he'd meant his bride to occupy alone while he avoided temptations yielded to the last time she'd slept at his side. After their passion was cut short of its goal, Garrick had spent the night past in unfulfilled discomfort. He was no more willing this night than the last to subject his wife to a near public embrace, but the storm forced him into an unintended proximity while the nearness of his guardsmen reinforced the need to restrain his desires. Determined that this night be different from the last, immediately after the vicious knight's departure he sent Nessa to the lord's chamber, no more than a walled loft above one corner of the great hall. So anxious was Garrick to avoid the untimely enticements of a naive woman who failed even to know what she invited, he dispatched Conal with her evening meal while he ate with their guardsmen below. Conal, the friend he'd cautioned against too much interest in what was his.

After the tawny-haired baron had delivered her meal and departed, Nessa climbed into the high bed and pulled the edges of its shabby drapes together. She closed all four sides, attempting to form a haven against the chill of a chamber whose only warmth rose from the fire in the great hall below. Sitting cross-legged in the middle of the bed her parents had once shared, she plucked at the clean bedclothes a shy serf had provided. When the earl had requested she retire to the privacy of this room, her mental search for the means to ease his danger from Sir Gilfrey's threat had so fully occupied her mind that she hadn't noticed the frost left in his tone from his recent clash with the castellan.

Now Nessa's fears for his safety lay temporarily buried beneath a more imminent concern. As her husband, would the silver-eyed tempter expect to share this bed? And if he did, would he turn to her as he had the night past, reveal his molten core? Her heart pounded but again she shied from questioning whether with fear or anticipation. Hah! Her conscience mocked. Surely after yestereve the answer was no longer in doubt. Nessa forced the truth from her mind. Fear of her inadequacies and the memory of him holding her away when she sought a return of his fire made facing the certainty of her own desires humiliating.

As the hours crept by and the dull roar of men's voices from below faded into silence, Nessa found herself foolishly near tears. He hadn't come, and that he stayed apart from her seemed an obvious demonstration that his previous night's heat had been nothing more than an animal response to a faceless feminine form. Or, more likely, a desire for the dream of Aleria which had turned to disgust when he awoke to find Agnes in his arms. Despair rose in a tide too high for the sea wall of Nessa's proud control and a flood of tears overflowed the banks of her eyes while a sob blocked her throat. She threw herself face down to muffle the sound against a lumpy pillow.

Amidst a stone ringed pit in the center of the great hall a blazing fire had earlier roared but now had fallen to coals. Conal had bedded down in a dark corner shortly after the end of their meal and their guardsmen, save those standing watch on the palisade wall, had long since drifted to sleep. Only a drowsy Sir Jasper remained awake at his side. Conal's reliable knight clearly felt it his duty to remain with the earl until he sought his rest above. The hour was very late— or early, depending on your view. And the morrow would be another long and tiring day. Despite his best efforts the knight fell into a light doze, and Garrick realized that, for the other man's sake, he could no longer postpone his retreat. Surely it was safe, he reassured himself. As exhausted as he was he could lie beside the maid and never know her there. He rose and Sir Jasper jerked awake to meet his departing nod with an odd mixture of guilt and relief.

Garrick carefully picked his way through slumbering men. At the bottom of the steep wooden stairway, he lifted the burned-low stub of a single tallow candle from the midst of its extinguished brothers before climbing rickety and deeply shadowed steps. On the landing at the top he found a man precariously near the edge and with his booted toe nudged until the body rolled safely away to flatten face down, cheek cushioned on a curled arm. Stepping over him and then another, Garrick reached the chamber door.

Closing the door softly behind him, Garrick moved to the curtained bed as quietly as booted feet on bare plank floors allowed. Gently pushing one panel of cloth aside, he looked down at the maid sleeping with one hand curled to a fist against her lips. The candle's puny flame burned brighter on abundant curls and gilded the tear stains still visible on flushed cheeks. They smote him as sharply as an invisible lance thrust. Was she unhappy that he'd not joined her here? Nay, he mocked the hope, more likely she struggled still with the revelation of her passionate nature, blamed him for forcing it upon her.

No matter the pain Nessa's unhappiness gave him, he could not look away from the pure lines of her delicate face, the soft glory of her hair, or the gentle lines of her form. He wanted nothing so much as to lie at her side, cradle her in his arms, and comfort her sadness with the warmth of his love. Love? He'd never allowed that dangerous word to mean aught to him but amusement for other men's folly. And he would not now. Not for this woman who meant either cold piety or painful treachery. Not now. Not ever. Irritated with himself for allowing a close study of the alluring maid, he broke the spell by blowing out the candle and laying them in darkness. He stripped and cautiously slid under the bedcover, careful to touch her at no point. It was all to no avail. He could no longer see her, but he could feel her near, hear her soft breathing. Not until weak predawn light glowed against the dense mists of a foggy morn did the exhaustion of the previous sleepless night and two days of travel overwhelm his awareness of her closeness and bury him in the depths of sleep.

❧ Chapter 11 ❧

"Bloody oaf!"

The heartfelt exclamation woke Nessa with a start. Holding utterly still she listened as the voice fell to an indistinct whisper, joining the dull murmur of men waking beyond the closed chamber door. With the sounds came memory of her unhappiness over her new husband's absence but a few hours past. Before her mind could formulate the question, the warmth of another nearby gave answer to the earl's whereabouts. Afraid to open her eyes, she waited thinking the man at her side would soon rise and join his supporters. In the room's lengthening silence, she heard the steady rhythm of his breathing. That the guardsmen were waking proved the hour of dawn had come and likely passed, yet he was deep in sleep. Certain herself unequal to facing a man— any man, but particularly this one—in the intimacy of a draped bed, Nessa exercised great caution in sliding first one leg and then the other through drapes closed on her side and ease from the bed.

It was customary to sleep nude, yet with the possibility that the earl might join her and unable to overcome her lack of confidence, Nessa had chosen to sleep in her forest-hued camise. Having awakened with the man in her bed, though

126

of a certainty now his right, she was thankful for even the thin, nearly useless silk shielding her distinctly inadequate form. As she ran nervous palms down sleek cloth to tug at the hem brushing against her thighs, her timid gaze was inexorably drawn through the curtains' narrow opening to the bed's occupant. Eyes gone green widened.

Clearly he suffered from no undue modesty—he was near all revealed. But, with such perfection of form why should he? 'Tis wrong to even glance upon him, rebuked the prim and unrelenting conscience she'd begun to resent. After all, they were wed—and by a bishop! Still, years of strict training could not be easily overcome and a distinct feeling of forbidden sin remained although, as with every enticing misdeed offered by this lordly tempter, her better self lost the struggle which she couldn't summon the will to win. No more able was she of pulling her gaze from the smooth plains of his body than she was able to stop breathing and yet live. This was the first time she had seen a man even partially unclad— and he was beautiful. Not the soft, tender beauty of a woman, but strong. Even scars from battles fought long past, faint white lines crossing sun-bronzed shoulders and traveling down to disappear in the black curls on his chest, only emphasized the perfection of his powerfully muscled form. A near overwhelming urge to trace them with her fingertips rose and lured her with the possibility of following their path to his core of fire. But with it grew shame for her need to claim his physical beauty in even this small way when she could offer none in return, when in the past two nights he'd proven himself without similar desire for her.

Even as weary as the hard days and near sleepless nights of the journey had left him, Garrick's warrior training insistently warned him that he was watched. One moment he was asleep and the next moment fully conscious and sitting up to meet his foe—foe? Before him stood a slender nymph cloaked in a wealth of soft brown curls and clad only in a short, silk camise which ended tantalizingly at the top of shapely thighs. From that stunning view, his gaze moved up to a piquant face and wide eyes nearly as deep a green as her enticingly thin garment. Once again, although assuredly not by design, she tempted him at the worst of times. He could hear the increasing noise of the men below who were doubtless impatiently waiting for him to give direction to their day. With difficulty he summoned his armor of cold control.

Under the close examination of a dark gray gaze Nessa was sure she'd been found wanting. The wickedly handsome man's face revealed no more emotion than a mummer's mask, and she felt certain that the rejection she'd feared had become a reality. His only use for her was the claiming of Swinton for some political purpose of his king. What else could one as plain as she expect? Truly the few kisses they'd shared, for her own self-respect she dared not acknowledge more, had been borne of nothing more than proximity and the momentary madness of moonlight which flatters any woman. She'd already fallen so far from grace that adding the sin of pride could mean little, and again pride alone would carry her through. To preserve her flagging self-esteem, if naught else, she would convince him she no more wanted him than he her.

"If it would ease your way," she began, chin tilted, "I am willing to remain here at Swinton while you go on to your lands."

Black brows snapped together. What nonsense did this woman speak? Despite her half-nude state she stood before him suddenly prim and remote, and her quiet announcement that she preferred to have none of him roused his temper.

Even had she not seen his anger, she'd have felt its waves pounding on the shore of her self-confidence. Why, if he couldn't bear to claim her as wife in truth, was he so furious? Her talent for logical thinking quickly offered an explanation. Stay she behind he would be made a fool before his men. Hastily she offered an alternative. "Or, I will live in your castle without sharing your chamber. Thus, you need not force yourself to sins of the flesh on my account."

Garrick's face went as still as if frozen into immobility. Thick black lashes fell, cutting off the inflammatory sight of the one who was wife, yet, only by his control and wish not to see her subjected to other's crude jests, a maiden still. Not trusting himself to speak, Garrick stiffly rose from his side of the bed and pulled on the first thing that came to uncaring hands—the same gray he'd worn the past day. Her talk of sin was proof to him of her pious nature and distaste

128

of him for forcing her to face the passionate side of her nature. A thing which did nothing to ease his ill humor.

Embarrassed, Nessa had stepped back from the opening in the draperies with its view of the man dressing but she watched as he strode to the door. Hand laid on the latch, he turned to speak.

"The error in allowing this marriage is mine. I accept the blame. However, no matter our personal inclinations, I must have a legitimate heir and only my lawful wife can give him to me."

The door shut behind him with a quiet more ominous than a loud slam. Left in privacy, legs that had supported Nessa only through effort of will lost strength and she crumpled to the bed. His talk of having made a mistake in wedding her and, even more, of the need to put aside personal inclinations for the sake of begetting an heir made clear both his regret for tying himself to her and that he viewed bedding her as an unpleasant though necessary duty. She sat up with both arms wrapped about her midriff and head bowed nearly to her knees and acknowledged that his plain speaking made her desire for him a truly shameful thing.

A droplet of moisture splashed on her bare leg. She'd done more weeping in the last day than in the previous ten years. Her self-control was in need of emergency repairs. Summoning every crumb of fortitude she possessed, she pushed unruly emotions back into the sensible channels laid down for them years gone by. She was a plain woman, Nessa staunchly reminded herself, only a plain woman. God had given her this opportunity for a life beyond the abbey. She must be thankful and put aside the greed which demanded more. Her life task was to work diligently in fulfilling the practical tasks given her without bemoaning her lot. Despite the best of intentions, even such rigorous self-discipline failed to fill the aching void in her heart. She instinctively knew that examining that voice would only increase the pain.

"The taxes you've been called to pay were not levied by King Henry's command."

Garrick paused and let his gaze travel over the odd assortment of village leaders and freeborn farmers who filled the keep's hall. They waited to hear what difference it be whether taken by king, earl, or castellan if taken the fruits of their hard work were. They'd shown no emotion when he'd announced the change in overlordship, not even surprise at the marriage of their lady, a once intended nun. By the lack he realized too much had happened to leave them surprised by any deed or able to easily believe a lord's words. Garrick understood their doubts. Sir Gilfrey's every action had assuredly meant another burden inflicted upon them. It would take time and patience to prove he was a man of a far different mold and worthy of the trust they'd learned by hard experience to give no man with power over their lives. Already in possession of extensive holdings in need of his attention, he could not personally oversee this small fiefdom. Thus, only by careful choice and supervision of a new castellan could he demonstrate his intent for justice.

The morn was half gone when an increasing hum of activity from below roused Nessa from her bleak thoughts. Certain she'd soon be called to join the others and too aware of her lack of readiness, she quickly rose and stripped off the forest green camise that the earl had stared at so long before coldly speaking of their marital relationship. She paused, thin silk crumpled in pain-closed fists, until the sound of a door repeatedly opened and closed struck her with an illogical fear. Had Sir Gilfrey and his men returned to do battle? Her clear reasoning fell mute, failing to point out the obvious fact that rather than a door quietly opened, a vengeful force's mere approach would have been met with battle cries from the palisade wall.

Nessa snatched up the first item of clothing she found and, sparing no time to first don a fresh camise, pulled on the cranberry gown. Only as she rushed to the landing beyond chamber door did she realize just how immodest was her garb's unfastened back lacing. Happily, her arrival went unobserved. The attention of an audience comprised of both guardsmen and commoners dressed in much patched homespun was held by the speaking earl. The sight, so far from the battle she'd feared, raised a strong curiosity. Silently folding her legs under, she perched in partial concealment on the stairway's highest step and peered through the rough columns of its dilapidated railing.

Clearly these strangers clothed in little more than rags

130

were the people of her dower lands. Between the poverty of their dress and gauntness of their forms Nessa saw the truth of their ill treatment at Sir Gilfrey's hands. She felt guilty for all the years she'd turned her mind from a castellan in whom she'd seen only threat to herself, never thinking of his likely abuse of the people who'd even then been her responsibility. Shifting her eyes to the commanding figure of the man she'd wed who stood tall and squarely met the measuring gaze of those he addressed, she listened as he announced a much reduced and more reasonable tax.

By smiles, though strained and tinged with skepticism, the people showed a hesitant approval and whispered amongst themselves, their murmur a breeze of cautious relief. The sum was reasonable, one they could meet and still have a measure left over. Yet they were leery of unjustified hope. Great lords were not known for holding to a single course. Although today this earl said it was so, tomorrow he might face a costly conflict and demand more to support his battles. They knew him not at all and wondered if his word were an honorable thing. Even given a willingness to part with life's blood in holding an oath to fellow noble, would he hold his word to common men as dear? Only could they wait to see the truth of the man.

"I called you here this morn to announce this reduction." Garrick concluded his speech, tucking flattened hands into the wide leather belt at his waist as if to emphasize that he wore no sword in demonstration of his intent to deal with them in justice rather than brute force. "And also to tell you that though I and your lady travel on to Castle Tarrant, I leave behind an able representative who will see to your needs and protection." Gray eyes moved over the group whose attention was fully his. Their wariness vibrated as clear as warning bells. "Him have I chosen for my absolute faith in his honor. You may bring your problems and disputes to him with assurance of a fair response."

Each man of Swinton began to scrutinize the earl's guardsmen one by one, assuming their new castellan was one of their number.

"Unfortunately he can remain only a short time as duties on his own fiefdom await the coming of Lord Conal, Baron of Wryborne."

In the gloom behind the earl, Conal rose from his seat on

a bench pushed against the wall, and as he moved forward to stand at his friend's side light from the central fire glinted on the sun streaks in his hair. Nessa was amazed that so important a man had agreed to bide his time here in so negligible a holding. Surely he, like the earl, had more important matters calling him. Had she needed it, here was proof of his affection for the earl and of the importance his friend plainly placed on the task of putting Swinton to rights. She mentally cringed, laying her forehead against the rough wood of the railing and letting the thick mass of her soft curls fall forward over slender shoulders. That the chore was necessary emphasized her failure in allowing the lands of her dowry to fall so far into disrepair.

"Before he must leave I'll bring another to be castellan here—under my close watch. One selected with care to ensure both honesty and justice for Swinton." A penetrating silver gaze moved from one man to another, ensuring his words and their meaning understood by each. "Go then and spread this news." Garrick waved toward the door, standing motionless while men gone quiet under the full import of his words filed out.

With the attention of the two lords below trained on the backs of departing men, Nessa deemed it safe to rise and straighten legs aching from long moments of crouching.

Some instinct, like a homing pigeon freed from afar, turned Garrick's eyes to the slender maid hovering at the top of wooden steps. She wore the cranberry red gown he'd first seen when a substitute bride arrived for betrothal to a man all too willing to accept the trick. Without camise, the gown's rounded neckline revealed an expanse of skin not meant for others to see and the rich disarray of curls flowing past her waist reminded him of his failure to see her instructed in the rules governing well-born women. The enticing vision was sweet enough to make him nearly content with the lack, were he but its sole recipient. Awareness of Conal at his side and, worse, a hall full of milling guardsmen brought a distinct stab of jealousy—no!—anger at both her and them. Nessa was his and his alone.

Unexpectedly caught, Nessa's weak legs nearly gave out under the force of an intent silver gaze. Not so naive that she didn't know herself ill-prepared for public display, she'd intended to return to the chamber as unobstrusively as she'd come. Her bare toes curled against the use-smoothed plank beneath, and the fingers of one hand tangled in unbound hair to push it back from blush-tinted cheek and the vulnerable curve of a graceful neck.

Conal followed his friend's gaze to the one above. A seductive sight was the red-garbed woman framed in a glory of gilded curls—and a revelation as startling as the dimpled smile he'd earlier discovered. Truly here was a secret delight any man would desire to possess as a private joy. His friend's good fortune was exceptional. Wed for another's benefit, foully deceived, yet at the end left with a prize. 'Twas a windfall only uncommonly blessed men could dream of attaining.

"Beauty awakes to warm the day." Conal's grin accompanied the quote from a popular minstrel's song which he called out. Striding past his friend's black frown, he quickly climbed the stairs but paused one step below the object of his words and blocked the view of the curious men whose attention he'd drawn.

Garrick followed with a tread considerably heavier. The other man's foolery was irritating, more so when he saw the shy smile it won from the bride who only a short time past had made clear her distaste for him.

"Conal, how can you stay here when worries from your own lands call you home?" Nessa tried very hard to keep her thoughts as well as her eyes from the embodiment of dark disapproval beside the laughing baron.

Conal! Garrick fumed. She called him by his given name when she had never done the same for him, although it was he whom she'd wed. He coldly answered the question addressed to another. "He was hesitant until I pointed out that the Abbey of St. Margaret is perched on the border between this keep and the queen's lands—less than a day's ride away." He'd spoken without first considering his words but even the unplanned reference to Conal's interest in another woman could not make him consciously admit himself jealous. He'd never been jealous, never in his life. And, after thirty plus years, he refused to fall to that trap.

"But Sybil is truly meant to be a nun." Nessa's distress drove from her thoughts even the embarrassment of being seen so improperly clad and the earl's clear displeasure.

"Her vocation is pure and deep." The possibility of virtuous Sybil falling as result of her useless call for protective company was horrifying.

"Don't fret." Conal reassured the obviously troubled girl. "I would no more force Sybil to give up a sincere devotion to the cloistered life than Garrick forced you."

His words effectively halted Nessa's protests but not her anxiety. Apparently Conal thought her willingness to replace her sister as bride born solely of a decision to leave the order. Nessa was too aware that she'd never shared Sybil's devotion to abbey life, too aware of the role her fall to sinful temptations had played in making her choice to see the matter clearly. She feared that Sybil, despite a far stronger commitment, would be led astray by temptations that would never have crossed her path without the plea for a companion at Salisbury Tower.

Garrick had raised the subject to drive a wedge between his bride and Conal, but Nessa's distress plainly sprang from an emotion deeper than mere envy for admiration given another. It was equally plain that she was alarmed by the possibility of another pious woman forced to accept a descent into worldly transgressions. During the time between leaving her in the chamber above and the arrival of his audience, he'd analyzed each of their passionate embraces and became certain that, although she could not deny her desire, her response to him awoke only guilt and resentment for causing her fall to sins of the flesh.

"Pray pardon, I must prepare for our leavetaking." Nessa deemed her words appallingly breathless. All too aware of the gown open down her spine, she offered a smile brave, despite its slight wobble and backed her way to the chamber door. Once safely inside, she quickly dressed with all the modesty she could manage. Her cream linen camise she tied close at the throat and, with an unexpected wish for a return of her voluminous habit or leastways something of similar style, she chose a deep brown gown she could lace up the front loosely so as to avoid form-fitting tightness. She barely had time to coil hastily braided plaits atop her head before a servant came with a summons to the midday repast.

At the high table, which in this keep was on the same level as all others and had only the distinction of being placed center front, Nessa was too conscious of the cold earl at her side. With him she shared a trencher heaped with food her tension-churning stomach found repulsive. Apparently oblivious to her presence, he gave the baron directions for the fief's reorganization and dealings with serf and freeman alike while consuming a healthy portion as she sat silent and ate nothing.

The keep was too small to comfortably house a group as large as the combined force of the two lords' guardsmen, and its hall rang with the noise of the many sharing a simple meal. Laughter echoed and the words of those at crowded tables created a low rumble. Still, Garrick felt the tension of the chamber's only woman. She'd taken not one bite nor lifted wine to drooping lips.

Garrick shrugged in a subconscious effort to dislodge the weight of a seldom experienced guilt. His anger with her had been unfair. This morning she'd merely spoken the truth of her feelings. What more had he wanted? He who claimed always to seek plain facts rather than pretty lies. Still he, too, had spoken truth. They were wed—a fact he doubted he'd change if he could despite his words to her—and it was necessary for her to accept it so. The vision of her submitting to him out of duty was distasteful when he longed for more. Mayhap her comment after he'd offended her sister by his cold treatment that he should have tried a gentle wooing was the answer to the problem. Though he shrank from the foolish excesses to which he'd seen men go to please a woman, he could leastways deal gently with Nessa.

When the meal was done the travelers, reduced nearly by half as they'd leave the baron and his men behind, were soon ready to depart. In a courtyard mud-slimed by the previous night's pouring rains, Conal helped Nessa mount with careful courtesy and a teasing twinkle in light blue eyes taunting the glowering leader.

"I only ask that you watch over my friend as closely as he's proven he means to watch over you." Conal whispered as he bent to kiss her fingers with such exaggerated fervor that a tide of rosy color warmed her face—a tendency threatening to become habit.

"I will watch for his safety," Nessa answered his foolery with a serious bargain, "if you promise to warn of any hint of spiteful revenge from Sir Gilfrey."

135

"Done," Conal said, squeezing her fingers before loosing them. Pleased by her concern for Garrick, he met her anxious gaze steadily.

Nodding acknowledgment, she took her place in the procession behind the irritated earl and his mocking knight, Sir Erdel. Although glad the journey was near its end, as they passed through the open palisade gate cloudy hazel eyes gazed back at Swinton's unimposing keep. This departure saw the consignment of a final familiar abode to the lost past. Ahead lay an unknown castle filled with strangers. Never before had she traveled to a place where no friends awaited—a place where she was destined to spend all her remaining days. The prospect was daunting. But, she resolutely reminded herself, for this she had prayed and for this she must strive to be worthy—no matter what stumble holes or stones littered the path to contentment.

Garrick saw her wistful gaze back, and his eyes narrowed. He assumed she found friendly Conal's easy warmth more attractive than his cold control. Never had he been concerned if a woman found him attractive. By relentless pursuit many had demonstrated they did. Truth to tell, he'd happily trade the insincere fawning of all the others for the honest admiration of just this one.

As the afternoon wore on, the initial banter of guardsmen anxious to return to a home not seen in months or years faded, replaced by the monotony of plodding hooves. Their anticipation had reinforced Nessa's trepidation for the unknown every stride brought nearer. Welcoming any distraction, she'd allowed herself to ponder a subject elsewise forbidden—the hidden personality of the man she'd wed. The Ice Warrior they'd named him, this man more concerned with returning justice to her people than with enriching himself at their expense as Sir Gilfrey and even her own father had done. He had studied the scriptures and beneath his ice armor dwelled the gentle spirit she'd once glimpsed. An extraordinary man—powerful and strong, gentle and just.

Suddenly she realized what a foolish smile she wore while her thoughts were focused on the man who regretted her company and would never see her as other than the poor substitute foisted upon him by deceit. Her attention turned to the passing scenery with a gaze so fierce it was a miracle no fires were lit.

Though she was tense and disheartened, the view's magical beauty first soothed and then lifted her spirits. Sunlight had defeated morning mists and brushed the fresh spring countryside with splendor. Lush meadows carpeted with verdant grass supported a gay assortment of flowers—tiny white daisies, bluebells, and shy buttercups. And the forests, where only occasional slanting shafts from the sun broke deep green privacy, were alive with a melody of their own—birdsong accompanied by rustling leaves and the low hum of a stream's steady flow.

When dusk stole both color and detail from the world, the mare's gently rocking pace lulled Nessa's ragged worries and wounded thoughts. It grew nearly impossible to keep heavy lids open. As before, the mare would follow the other horses whether or not she tugged the reins. So, her sluggish mind assured, if she braced herself carefully and kept her back rigid, then simply letting her eyes close for a few moments would bring no harm. She slipped into a floating state between wakefulness and deep slumber, aware of sounds but unseeing and too dazed to quickly respond.

Under the mysterious trick sleep plays on time, it seemed no more than a moment had passed but it could have been hours later when a touch roused Nessa. Jerked awake, her shift in weight sent her small mare dancing to the side where with surprising force it bumped a massive stallion and its rider who loomed near.

"God's Teeth!" Sir Erdel growled, forced to calm both his steed and hers. "The earl's waiting for you to join him."

Looking into features even darker seen through night gloom, Nessa wondered what wickedness had brought this penance upon her? Or, more precisely, which? She'd been piling them up faster than penance could be performed. Leastways the irritated words had driven the last remnants of misty sleep from her mind. The company had come to a stop below the crest of a hill where the earl waited, a powerful black silhouette against the sky's deep blue velvet. Even with little sleep and after hours of riding, no weariness marred the perfect symmetry of his strong form. He seemed to command the placement of moon and stars as easily as he

137

disturbed her rational thinking and commanded her responses.

Why had they stopped? Her heart thumped with uncomfortable vigor. More importantly, why had he called for her now? Had her surrender to sleep been so serious a misdeed?

❦ Chapter 12 ❧

Castle Tarrant." Unashamed pride in his hereditary home filled Garrick's voice as he waved across a shallow valley to the structure atop the next rise. "The Earls of Tarrant have held this land since before the memory of man."

Nessa's gaze followed the line of his outstretched arm to where, outlined by a low risen moon, an impressive fortress towered over the flickering homefire lights of a small village nestled below. Its darkness was unwelcoming yet she refused to cringe. "How can that be when surely you are descended from the Norman who conquered it little more than a century past?"

"Aye, but descended too from the only child of the last Saxon earl, a woman who was wife to its first Norman lord." Garrick's hungry eyes traced every bold line of the structure which seemed as much a part of him as muscle and bone no matter how seldom he'd rested within.

Nessa nodded but her attention never wavered from Castle Tarrant. Its four towers reached boldly toward the stars, their crenellated tops like teeth-edged mouths open to bite chunks from the heavens. A fitting place for men famous for their repudiation of the gentle side of life. The unpleasant thought sent a shiver down her spine. Ridiculous! she scolded herself. Ridiculous to be alarmed by so sweeping and unfair a characterization. Particularly as she knew it untrue of the earl who had merely built a near inviolate armor of ice about his sensitive spirit. As for his father, well, she'd no right to condemn a man unmet.

"It's been nearly three years since last I was here." Vexed with himself for the hint of sorrow in his statement, Garrick straightened his shoulders and in a tone devoid of emotion added, "I'd as lief have this journey done."

He glanced toward the maid at his side and found her chin bravely tilted despite anxiety-widened eyes. As she'd approached in answer to his summons, she'd looked so apprehensive that he'd wondered what frightening thing his fool knight, Sir Erdel, had said after calming their steeds. But seeing her dismay increased by the sight of his home, he knew her fearful of what awaited within. Years absent himself, he had no words of reassurance. There was only one certain answer, and it was unlikely to give her ease—Earl William. His father had long ago resigned the title to him, his heir, but to both he and all the people of these lands the man would ever be titled earl—although styled the "old earl" to differentiate between father and son. The older man did not know his son had agreed to a betrothal, even less that he'd taken a wife. Garrick's lips firmed to a grim line. No help for it. Unable to give her comfort, it was useless to linger here berating himself for the message not sent. Motioning her to remain at his side, he spurred his steed forward.

Forced on toward the intimidating fortress, Nessa resolutely turned her attention to a lower view. It was a more reassuring sight, for doubtless daylight would reveal the wide valley's flat lands fertile and green-furred with crops newly sprouted. She found it necessary to constantly urge her weary mare to keep up with the faster pace of the earl's much stronger steed.

In a short time they reached the outermost bailey wall. The earl rode directly to the midpoint between firebrands set one on each side of the gate and turned his face up to guards invisible in the gloom above.

"My lord," a surprised voice called, "we'd no word of your intended return!"

"But you are heartily welcome," another dark shadow

quickly amended, leaning down to lift a firebrand from its ring and by its orange light show himself and his fellow guard to their lord.

Nessa knew the moment their attention moved from the earl to her. She'd have known even without the stunned silence that surely proved to all waiting that they'd discovered a shocking addition to their lord's party. Although they were not foolhardy enough to question the presence of the woman-despising man's feminine companion, she felt their examination as strongly as if they'd lifted her to the ground and critically studied every detail of face and form. Moreover, she knew their eyes remained on her as the party moved through the portal and beyond. If the weight of their curiosity had in truth been as heavy as it felt, she'd have been sorely bruised before she escaped their view.

To think neither of the castle ahead nor the gate guards behind, Nessa concentrated on the moon-bleached countryside on either hand as they rode down a lane between gently sloping fields. Tilled furrows laid patterns of light and shadow in seemingly endless repetitions, a soothing sight. Yet all too soon they arrived at the village clustered near the moat surrounding castle wall. The hour was late and it was eerily quiet with only an odd gleam of firelight shining through a crack in closed shutters. Between the humble structures and moat's edge lay a cleared space maintained as additional defense against a hostile attack.

Drawing ever closer a faint noise caught Nessa's attention. Purposely ignoring a glow all too near, Nessa let her lashes fall and listened intently. The soft ripple must be moving water, proving the moat had a diverted river as its source. Flowing water was much sought after since stagnant moats were likely to turn fetid in summer heat. Concentrating on such details aided her valiant effort to keep her mind from the structure looming overhead, filled with strangers certain to be disappointed in their lord's choice for wife. Before long, torchlight defeated Nessa's fragile defenses and demanded she meet its origin.

Firebrands set close together cast a yellow glare over the rough planks of a lowered drawbridge but left in gloom the arched pathway through curtain wall at its far end. Between the bright light and hollow clatter of their progress over wood, Nessa was forced to face a reality she could no longer avoid—they had arrived. Find your courage, hold it before you, and bravely meet whatever comes, she silently commanded. Find her courage? With the question came an absurd idea. She peeked at the man who rode beside her, and a dimple-revealing grin tugged at her lips. To the baron he'd adamantly declared her in his care. If that were true, then he should rightfully be the source of her courage, yet she doubted he'd appreciate her clutching him before her.

Too soon came the sound of horse hooves striking a rock-laid floor, a sound that echoed in the close confines of the entrance tunnel. Nessa discovered that she was no fonder of this dark passage, lit only by eerily flickering flames from oil-fed sconces wide-spaced and of very little use, than she'd been of Salisbury's stairway. Likely, she reassured herself, it was merely a result of heightened nerves. The encouragement was of small immediate comfort. Striving to maintain what flimsy scraps of bravado she'd pieced together with the tenuous thread of silly thoughts, she was relieved when they rode free of the gloom.

Ahead lay the square courtyard's broad expanse. Each corner bore a tower, the whole joined by crenellated curtain walls of formidable width. A movement caught Nessa's eye. She turned to see a young serf scramble toward the tower on the right and disappear within. The same tower toward which the earl led men revived to bantering life by this end of a long absence. It seemed that just as one of Sir Gilfrey's men had run to warn him of their coming at Swinton Keep, here too they would be announced.

Garrick dismounted at the bottom of steps leading to the portal where their herald had entered. Thick walls guarded its silence, but he'd no doubt of the pandemonium his unexpected coming had raised within. Knowing curious eyes were watching, with a wry smile he turned to his waiting bride.

Moments from presentation to a horde of critical eyes, Nessa's anxiety threatened to demolish teetering bravado. When strong hands wrapped about her waist, far from the shock lent by her first such descent, she almost clung to broad shoulders.

As Garrick lifted the maid from the mare's back, he looked into the small face lit by flickering torchlight. Her lips were compressed in a concentrated struggle for courage and there was panic in the doe-soft eyes trained on the entrance as if expecting it to take monstrous form and devour her. He set her gently on her feet but did not release her from his steadying hold.

"My people have near given up on me to bring them a countess." He understood her apprehension of the intimidating fortress's unknown inhabitants and meant to assure her of some measure of welcome—and to compensate for an undoubtedly less pleasant reception by the old earl.

Glancing up, Nessa was enveloped by a rare gentle mist in gray eyes.

"I swear they'll welcome you." The solemn words were so low that even if excited men went suddenly still, they'd not hear.

"I see." A wobbling smile stole tension from soft lips. "They'd welcome even the Greek Gorgon so long as you name her countess?"

Garrick threw back his head, laughing with a freedom few had heard before. The unusual sound surprised not only the men of his guard but those fortunate few able to peek from shadowy entrance and cracks in shuttered windows.

Still smiling with unaccustomed warmth, Garrick lifted Nessa's hand and laid it formally atop his upraised forearm to lead her in grand manner up sweeping stone stairs and into his home. The scurrying of many feet proved his belief of unseen observers. It only deepened his amusement. Their curiosity for a sight never seen afore was justified. So let them stare.

Moving in measured steps they cleared the arched entrance and found sufficient time had been given. The men of the garrison stood in orderly rows, waiting for their captain to speak to the earl first. Castle serfs hovered at the edges of the vast great hall, making not even the slightest attempt to look busy.

Unable to maintain her poise and meet curious eyes simultaneously, Nessa kept her gaze trained to the floor, seeing only booted feet as a man of wildly disordered white hair and much lined face stepped forward.

"My lord." With the easy movement of one much younger, he sank to one knee and kissed Garrick's fingers in formal honor of his earl. "Castle Tarrant welcomes you home."

"Thank you, Sir Rufus." Garrick's response was equally formal. "I'm pleased to be here after many detours on behalf of the king." As the knight rose to his feet, Garrick could feel the curiosity growing like swells of steam from water heating. But for the tension which must be growing as fierce within Nessa he'd have let them dangle awhile. For her sake it was best to have it done. "My delays had purpose and an ending you've all waited long to hear." Gray eyes looked around the room and took in every curious face. "Let me present Lady Nessa," he lifted the arm still bearing a small hand, "Countess of Tarrant."

As water left to grow too hot boils over, the room broke into a roar blended from whispers and shouted congratulations.

His introduction surprised Nessa into glancing up. He'd not mentioned her true name—an appreciated deed. A gray gaze still more mist than frost met her surprised eyes. He smiled and winked so fast only she could see. The action shocked a bubble of laughter from Nessa's tight throat and left a dimple-peeking grin.

In that moment Garrick was happier with and more certain of the rightness in his marriage than at any time before. Mayhap his bride was as innocent as he'd first believed, guilty only of being used by others. Although such reasoning meant she'd truly been forced from the cloistered life, surely her response to him justified the hope that, despite her cold words at the start of the day, with the slow and careful wooing he'd been contemptuous of in other men he'd lead her to content with their bond.

"Welcome, my lady." Sir Rufus's grave voice broke the wordless communion between new husband and wife.

Nessa's attention turned to the speaker clad in scarlet and gray, the colors of Tarrant, and made a startling discovery. The man who stood with proud dignity was as apprehensive of her reaction to him as she was of his. But why? Despite his age, that he spoke for all the others proved he was in their lead and this assuredly by the earl's appointment. If the earl approved, of what possible import was her opinion? Nonetheless, his back was stiff with pride but his eyes wary of her possible disdain. Wary of her, as the earl and his father were reputed to be of all women. Was it some peculiar ailment bred by these walls?

"Thank you." Her answer was simple and soft but accompanied by a warm smile.

Her sincerity and shy smile earned Sir Rufus's immediate liking. She weren't a haughty lady too fine for the likes of him. But perhaps she didn't know the truth of his heritage. He'd watch her close to see if her opinion changed once it became clear. He looked toward his lord and was amazed to catch a momentary gleam of pride in the gray eyes watching the woman.

"Your return is well-timed. We're in sore need of your direction." Knowing and appreciating his lord's preference for plain spoken truth, the aging knight did not hesitate to speak without further ado what he felt should be known.

Sir Rufus had earned Garrick's full attention, and the gaze that he turned on his guard captain had gone abruptly silver ice, penetrating and demanding explanation.

"Rumors of rebellion what you wrote that I should watch for have begun. And stop as rumors they don't. Hear I that word's been sent for farmers and villagers, young and old, to gather weapons and prepare for a fight." Gnarled hands folded together and then separated as fists in unthinking demonstration of his words. "They's been told a wave of common men, even armed only with picks and hoes, by sheer numbers will—more like than not—defeat troops trained to war, win against an aging king who can't so much as keep the loyalty of his own sons." Hands now flat with lifted palms seemed to beseech an explanation of how anyone could succumb to such obviously faulty reasoning.

Garrick was surprised that his knight, painfully honest but also discreet, had so quickly and publicly come to the point. It made all too clear how serious matters had become. By expelling Sir Gilfrey from Swinton, he was certain he'd banished the sower of rebellion's seeds but clearly could not stop there. Nor had he expected less. His mouth flattened with self-condemnation. By his preference he'd been gone too long, had failed to give his own the strength of their earl's justice and leadership. But early on the morrow he'd begin the careful, time-consuming task of uprooting the weeds in men's minds, of providing the reviving water of attention to encourage the sprouting of a lush growth of healthy loyalty. Loyalty to their earl and their king.

Accustomed to the queen's political diatribes, Nessa gave

little notice to Sir Rufus's, hearing instead the word patterns of one of peasant stock. An interesting fact, for seldom was such a one made knight, even less guard captain. Moreover, he was plainly proud of the distinction else in all the years he must have spent in Tarrant Castle surely he'd have adopted the speech style of his fellow knights, near certainly all well-born. She admired his ability to accept, indeed, be proud of himself for what he was. Firelight gilded the soft brown curls that escaped from the tight confines of braids coiled against her nape as she tilted her head to one side and studied the aging knight, unaware of the slight smile of approval curling her lips.

"Rise and end taxes for the benefit of another." Sir Rufus's disgust for men's gullibility was heavy in his voice, thickening his peasant accent. "The fools didn't ought but believe they that who comes after will free them and end hated tariffs." Embarrassed by his own vehemence, he glanced to the new countess. Although she'd apparently paid little mind to his words, she looked at him with approval. His earlier hesitation washed away. She was, in truth, a lady like no other, and her he liked.

The earl thanked the gathered company for their welcome and bade them return to their evening's ease before he turned again to his guard captain. While the two men softly discussed the actions to be taken, Nessa had her first opportunity to look about her new home. The hall was the largest she'd ever seen but seemed to be filled with only men—save the few female servants, slovenly but shyly smiling, who huddled near the huge fireplace on one wall. A closer look at the room's condition revealed it poorly cared for. Obviously no gently bred woman with attention to comfort, beauty, or even common household arts had been at work for some time. The walls were bare stone when even the simple abbey, which disallowed vain adornments, had large tapestries with instructive pictures from the lives of Christ and the saints to provide some aid in maintaining warmth. The floor rushes she'd hardly noticed in her tension as they first entered were old, musty, and harbored a disgusting array of filth.

Garrick looked down and caught the slight frown between delicate brows. His gaze followed the path of hers, and the frown born of his discussion with Sir Rufus grew considera-

146

bly grimmer as gray eyes lifted and narrowed to survey all that she had seen. When his attention returned to his bride, hazel eyes met his steadily. If he'd seen the slightest censure for the lack of luxury or irritation with him that it was so, he'd have dismissed it as a greedy woman's demand for what was lacking. But there was no blame in her, only recognition of an honest appraisal, and he realized for the first time that this place was devoid of far more than luxury. Castle Tarrant was his hereditary home and for its strength and importance he was proud of it but a thing of beauty it was not, nor ever in his memory had been. His father's holding and his father still living, he'd never considered changing its appearance or criticizing its care.

His father. The thought brought back the need to face their reunion. A meeting he anticipated no more than Nessa likely did. As a child he hadn't known the cold, forbidding man who'd sired him and when as men they came together for the sake of the land and title that bound them both, they came nearly as strangers.

"My father still keeps to the tower?" Garrick's voice was flat.

Nessa's hands were now folded demurely at her waist, and they no longer touched at any point, yet she could feel the strong man's tension as if it were a living thing within her hold.

"Hasn't left it above three times since another bout of that cursed ailment hit him during the last harvest season. It don't never leave loose of him." Sir Rufus's words were bitter with helpless frustration.

Listening quietly, Nessa heard the knight's affection for the man he spoke of—perhaps the reason he retained his position of honor despite advancing years? Nay, that decision rested with the man at her side. Suddenly the meaning of Sir Rufus's words broke through her preoccupation with the emotion behind them, and her nervous strain increased tenfold. It was true then? The strange rumors that for years had spread through Salisbury castle and lands. Rumors of more than his woman-disdaining ways. 'Twas said he was a virtual recluse suffering with an illness that never truly healed but returned again and again. Stricken, some believed, by God as punishment for his harsh ways.

"But he knows I've come?" Garrick asked, face closed into its usual cold, emotionless mask.

"Don't doubt but what the whole countryside knows by now." A wry smile accompanied the allusion to an active gossip trail.

"Then best we waste no time in joining him there." Garrick motioned toward a door in the far wall revealed as the guard captain stepped aside.

Walking across the wide distance of the hall, too aware of the many who watched, Nessa's tension clouded her eyes. They went to meet the father of the man at her side who was intimidating enough without another like him to double her need for courage. As they approached the door a movement caught her attention. A girl of nearly her own age, clearly a castle serf, had moved to open the door and met Nessa's gaze with a cheery smile and admiration in her eyes. Nessa blinked at the sight. Ever used to living in the shadow of famous beauties, this was the first time a stranger had looked at her with flattering approval, and it went far in reviving her valor. Lightened spirit echoed in a gaze shining green, she gave a warm smile to the girl before stepping through the door with the earl at her back.

Nessa stopped. She'd a choice of three directions in which to go—up the steep stone stairway at whose foot they stood, or in down narrow corridors branching out on each side.

Garrick glanced toward the corridor on the right. It was the most direct route to the West Tower and his father. Yet, he'd sensed Nessa's discomfort with dark, narrow passages and didn't wish to increase her stress over this unavoidable meeting. Moreover, he felt in need of a few private moments to prepare her and though he'd not willingly admit to it, himself for what was to follow. He turned toward the stairs.

After climbing a great many broad steps and past portals opening to two higher levels, Nessa began to wonder if ever they'd reach their destination. At last they came to the small landing at the top of the stairs. With an ease which was surely deceptive the earl shoved open the massive iron-bound door on its far side. In the wavering pattern of light and shadow cast by the tower guard's lone torch, she saw that they stood at an entrance to the walkway near the top of the curtain wall connecting all towers. As protocol demanded, the earl indicated that she should stay close beside the wall on one side while he walked next to the sheer drop between parapet edge and courtyard floor.

Curious onlookers left behind, in the soothing dark beyond the guard's station, Nessa's taut muscles eased. A momentary respite for awareness of the handsome man she walked beside was impossible to ignore now that all distractions were past. Peeking at his powerful form from the corners of her eyes a new tension awoke and grew ever stronger until it seemed to throb in the silence between them. The night was not as black as his hair for its shadows made only a misty background for him. A man aloof, cold—but with a secret core of soul-melting flame.

Folly! Think of something else. Think of the man waiting for you to come—frightening but preferable to showing herself caught by the unintended lures of one who had no use for her beyond brood mare of legitimate heirs. With that bitter fact she commanded her thoughts into other veins and averted her face. She was so intent on her need to ignore his presence that when he moved in front to halt her, she stepped straight into his broad chest. The unexpected contact felt like a jolt of lightning. She looked up into silver eyes that flared as bright and jumped back.

Simpleton! She denounced herself. Such a reaction so near a sheer drop to the ground far, far below was dangerous! One no sane person would take. *I seem ever to show myself a fool to the one I want most to impress*. The unplanned admission of a desire for his approval increased her self-disgust. The earl had reached out to steady her, hands clasping her shoulders. His touch burned, ice could burn—she'd learned it true before now.

Seeing her frown, he nearly smiled but held it at bay for fear she'd think it meant in ridicule of her embarrassment.

"You were trying so hard to see what lies out there," he waved toward the darkness beyond curtain wall, "I thought it best to stop and let you have an unobstructed view." With the hand still resting on one shoulder, he turned her toward the wall's nearest notch. It was as good an excuse as any to stop, and he'd find the way to begin while her attention was turned elsewhere.

Unwilling to directly meet the power of gray eyes whether passion-dark or silver-blazed, Nessa looked blindly through the downward dip in the wall from which defenders could fire arrows and then duck back behind the protection of the high merlon beside. She was thankful for the moon that bleached color from her cheeks and the light breeze that would hopefully cool them before they reached their destination. Realizing they were beyond easy hearing range of the guards at each tower and wondering for his true reason in stopping here, still she appreciated the moment to reorder her scattered wits. Slowly the mists of distress dissipated and the view came into focus—the hill from which she'd first seen this castle such a short time past outlined against a velvet sky. With peace came renewed spirit to face whatever lay ahead. She had come this far and survived half the process of meeting strangers. At least soon the last would be over and she need never fear it again.

"I must warn you," Garrick began, "my father is unlikely to welcome you—or any woman." Garrick feared this a complete understatement of his father's almost certain resentment of them both. Though they'd never talked on the subject, or nearly any other, Garrick had always assumed the old earl wanted grandsons to carry on the family name and honor. Such would be only natural, but on closer thought Garrick was forced to admit that his father's emotions were far less than natural on any subject.

In the growing silence, Nessa wondered if he were awaiting an answer and tentatively offered, "I'd heard that would be his reaction." Actually what she'd heard was far more daunting but no way could she repeat to him such sinister accounts.

"No doubt." He smiled at her tactful reference to dark rumors but the sardonic curl to firm lips chilled. "Both I and my father are famous for it. How did you find the daring to wed the Ice Warrior?" A ridiculous question when he'd seen passionate fire in both her anger and desire—she possessed courage enough and more. "Never mind. That you did proves you brave enough to face my father and never flinch." He offered her his arm as he added, "To blunt his jabs of disapproval, I chose not to warn him of either my impending betrothal or hasty marriage, forestalling a build-up in his arsenal of vicious words."

Nessa was not encouraged to discover that the man they'd soon face was to be abruptly landed with her. She doubted he needed much time to snap back with spite. They came to the West Tower's door in a disgustingly short time although it had seemed her feet were leaden and dragged every step of the way. They entered, descended to the level below, and stepped from stairwell arch into a single corridor bisecting the whole floor into two equal parts. As they moved down the aisle, she realized only one door opened on each side. This castle's design was different than any in her experience which, her conscience demanded she admit, was severely limited. Garrick rapped on the door to the left, but Nessa glanced apprehensively at the one opposite. 'Twas sealed closed with chains and locks which by their layer of dust alone looked to have remained undisturbed for decades. What fearful secret lay hidden there? She turned her attention back to the door they faced berating herself for idle curiosity but aware that whatever waited in the chamber ahead seemed suddenly a lesser threat than the unknown behind.

The door creaked open, but only wide enough for a sharp face atop scrawny neck to poke out. Dim light from beyond shown on a nearly bald pate adorned only by sparse clusters of hair grown long and dangling on stooped shoulders. Nessa tried to suppress the shock that had loosed a gasp, while suspicious eyes glowing with malevolence examined her closely. How could such a wizened, homely creature have sired so magnificent a man as her husband?

The small man backed away, pulling the door open. To Nessa's surprise, Garrick stepped past the man at the door as if he weren't there. Caught looking over her shoulder at the one so slighted while moving forward at the earl's side, Nessa was unprepared for what followed.

"Father, I've brought Tarrant a countess."

Nessa's head snapped around to see a man rising from a padded chair before the fire. Once on his feet he stood as tall as his son with a mane of thick iron-gray hair and lines carved by pain on either side of a firm mouth. Having earlier believed the person she'd heard guardsmen refer to as the old earl was the unsuitable creature who'd opened the door, her mouth fell open in a soft "O" at the sight of this overwhelming man. Before her eyes he swayed, but whether due to her lightheaded confusion or his infirmity, she was not certain.

Garrick dropped her hand and reached out for the older man, helping him settle safely again into the padded chair.

"While the leeches grow fat, I grow weaker." With an arm whose sleeve was rolled down but cuff unfastened Lord William waved toward a bowl beside his chair. "Derward promises me returned health if I lay my flesh bare to them thrice each day but I only grow weaker." The words were full of bitterness.

As he spoke Nessa looked closer. The first impression of a strength equal to the younger man's faded; and, despite a pride-raised chin and the scorn in his fierce examination of her, she saw his extreme thinness and limbs that trembled.

"So, my son, you have wed." A derisive laugh rumbled from deep in his chest. "I hope leastways you got great lands in exchange for this sorry prize."

Nessa glanced up to see Garrick's response. His face was so cold it had surely turned to an ice unable to move in answer.

"He refuses to answer, thus clearly did not." A stare full of contempt returned to the female in question. "So, girl, you tell me what dowry prize you brought."

Had he been disappointed for a beloved son, as she'd once expected, Nessa would have crumpled with shame. But his scorn was as much punishment on his heir as truly felt disdain for her, and she refused to quail beneath it. Her pride rose as she met his gaze full on and calmly answered. "I am prize neither in beauty nor wealth, my lord." She paused hoping her words would convince him she also lacked fear while in truth she rallied courage for the announcement bound to draw disgust if not wrath. "My dowry is but one-half of Swinton and its keep."

"Hah!" His one word response held all the energy he'd failed to physically demonstrate, and his eyes flashed at the younger man. "You're a fool."

Apparently unmoved, Garrick steadily watched the man who had sired him but never given a moment's affection or approving word for any action. He'd long ago learned to bury the pain of rejection beneath the ice barrier he was famous for and turn to a carefully selected few for honest friendship—Geoffrey, Conal, Henry.

"You should have demanded both beauty and wealth for the pain a woman delivers to even men wary of her lures.

152

With great subtlety she'll steal the heart from a man and once in her hands will squeeze it dry of love and joy."

Nessa wanted to shout a denial at the old man, tell him there was no possibility of the earl loving her and less of her causing him pain, even were it within her ability. But she was not brave enough to break the wordless communication passing between the impassive Garrick and belligerent Lord William.

Beneath his frozen exterior, Garrick was shocked. Although they were nearly strangers who, in the past decade and more, had exchanged words necessary for the fief's management and little else, he and all the country knew Lord William's dislike of women. His whole life long he'd assumed they two shared the same cynical distrust as source for their attitude. By these words Garrick had discovered it untrue else his father would have understood his preference for an unassuming woman with no great dowry to lend false pride and encourage schemes.

"I am weary, weary of you and weary of this world, so go away and let me end my days here in solitude." Lord William languidly waved them back and with closed eyes let his head fall heavily against the cushion behind.

Nessa blindly departed at Garrick's side and passed the chained door, her thoughts lingering on the bitter man left alone with only a leech-bearing toad. Not until the cool air on the open parapet stung her cheeks with color did she rouse herself to the present and her companion.

Again, half across the walkway between towers Garrick halted. "Once more, I beg pardon for my sire's rude reception."

Irritation with his father had hardened his tone but Nessa questioned the cold's underlying source. Could be he was upset with himself for wedding her rather than following Lord William's advice. Certainly a powerful earl could've had his pick from the great beauties and important families across the land. The discomforting proof of her fear lay in the sudden realization that he'd begged pardon for his father's gruff attitude but not the man's condemning words.

"Though we are bonded by blood, we are as alien to each other as two men who meet by happenstance on foreign soil. Less common ground than even I had supposed. Now the land is all that binds us." Without another word he turned to continue on.

Knowing it expected, Nessa hurried to keep up with his longer stride. Rather than descending to the great hall where they'd first arrived, here too Garrick led the way only one level down. At the chamber twin to Lord William's in the other tower, Garrick threw open the door.

Nessa's gaze was immediately caught by a welcome sight. Before a blazing hearth stood a large tub. As if it were a magnet and she formed of soft ore, it drew her to trail fingertips in bathwaters sweet-scented and surely meant for her. She was more than anxious to slip into the steaming liquid after days of travel when quick rinses with cloth dipped in cold streams had sufficed. The tub formed of tight fitted planks and padded for comfort was all of luxury to her.

The sound of a closing door pulled her attention from the anticipated bath yet she did not turn. Doubtless the earl had shut the door, but with him on which side of it? She was afraid to look. They were wed in God's sight, as well as man's, and he had the right to stay within. Nonetheless, she felt she'd likely die of mortification if forced to disrobe before him and reveal her lacks so brazenly. She remained perfectly still, ears straining for even the sound of another's breathing. Quietness reigned, giving her the courage to glance about the empty chamber.

There were closed wooden shutters nearby. Curiosity carried her to them. Lifting their bar she peeked behind and a grin of satisfaction glowed. They protected not a narrow arrow slit but a window, a real square open to sky and view below, one which would allow bright sunlight to warm the whole room. She shut and barred them again before turning to lean against their sturdy planks and survey the rest of the room. A tall wardrobe stood on one side of the door, pegs driven on outer edge to hold cloaks and hoods, and on the other side rested a chest with padded seat and carved panels to hold personal treasures. This window was on one side of the fireplace and on the other, far enough for safety, near enough for warmth, was the bed. A large, wide bed so high above the floor Nessa would truly have to climb into it. Clearly the lord's bed. A sobering thought. Best she thank God, and the earl, for the privacy afforded her now to get

154

her bathing done and be out and abed before he returned. She ought to feel frightened at the thought, or feel the need to summon courage to meet the demands he would make. But the only emotion evoked was guilt for their lack and for the anticipation she could not deny.

Garrick had gone from Nessa to order that a bath, unscented, be poured for him in the unused chamber across from his own. Within the warm waters, while easing away the stiffness of travel and irritation raised by fault-finding words, he decided to spend the night in this room. There was a bed, smaller than his own but adequate and infinitely more comfortable than the ground he'd nearly grown used to in past years. He'd never forced a woman, either physically or emotionally, and would not start with the one he had wed. He'd decided to woo his bride and so he would.

As he rose from cooling water, even with a nature as suspicious of women as his, he was forced to admit she appeared to be as unlike the selfish females he knew as ever one could be. Although traveling at his punishing pace, she'd not complained. Even faced with his stark, barren castle she hadn't demanded from him the luxuries she must know he could provide. Moreover, despite her initial alarm, she had faced his father's hostility with admirable strength. Stepping from warm bath to cold floor he also admitted that her unusual nature was likely born of her piety. A depressing thought. No, he would not force her to further abandon her principles—at least not tonight.

Across the corridor, feeling lost in the bed's vast width, Nessa huddled beneath covers growing colder and colder. Never mind the claim of willingness to live apart which she'd spoken first, he'd said he would have an heir. But the fire was burning low and the bath water had lost its heat, and he hadn't come. Seemed only further proof that he could not bring himself to bed with one so plain, proof of his father's just repudiation of the marriage. Despite the numbing coldness growing in her heart, hot tears welled behind closed lids.

No! She would not allow them to scald her cheeks. She would not. 'Twas no worse than she had always known secular life would be for her. Indeed, far better. She was wed and had a home of her own. Not a beautiful woman meant for pampering, she must concentrate on the practical

155

responsibilities that came with her new position. The castle's condition was lamentable, and it was her duty to restore it to order.

Though her thoughts had been too full of tension to remark it at the time, now she wondered for the reason behind the castle's lack of well-born women. Surely some of the knights necessary in so large a garrison must be wed—where were their wives? No matter, she sublimated the pain of knowing herself unattractive to the man she'd wed in plans for castle improvements and the heartening warmth in the memory of a girl's admiration.

❧ Chapter 13 ❧

From the concealment of shadowed archway between stair-well and great hall, Nessa surveyed the large room's occu-pants. Though come for that purpose, she hesitated to join the men finished with their meal but lingering about tables both on the dais and below.

After a restless night haunted by visions of the tempter whose silver-ice eyes melted the soul and whose touch burned with wickedly sweet fire, she'd overslept the morning meal's start. She'd not awakened until a firm knock came at the door. Then, huddled in the privacy of the heavily draped bed, covers tight to her chin, she'd peeked through cloth edges as an elderly and none too clean woman delivered a tray of food. Unwilling to set either an example of sloth for castle serfs or for the men of the garrison a picture of idle nobility living off the toil of others, as soon as the woman departed, Nessa had jumped up. The sum total of her meager wardrobe had been deposited in the lord's chamber during the hours of yestereve while she and her husband met with the old earl. As she hastily chose and donned a gown she wondered what the castle inhabitants thought of a bride who arrived so poorly outfitted. For that matter, what they thought of a plain bride so clearly less than their earl deserved.

She'd eaten only the few bites she could swallow amidst her preparations. Now, even as she clasped her hands together and started forward, behind the high table the earl rose to his feet. The signal for a general exodus. In the doorway itself Nessa paused. The hall had suddenly become a tangled mass of men, each moving with the steady purpose and assured path she lacked.

"Sir Rufus—"

At the sound of the earl's voice, Nessa's gaze traversed the rapidly emptying room to find him near the outgoing door. He'd be easy to find even were it crowded still. By his height alone he rose above others. He was clad all in the charcoal gray he clearly favored and buckling his broadsword about his waist before bending to lift a waiting bundle. When his attention returned to his guard captain, Nessa looked to the aging man as well.

Standing before the massive hearth which surely shared its chimney with the one in the lord's chamber, Sir Rufus turned from testing the sharpness of his sword's honed blade in flamelight.

"I'll be away most of the day and even for the night— visiting my vassals, as you so wisely suggested." Garrick shook out bundled cloth and swirled his black, scarlet-lined cloak about broad shoulders. "Prithee apprise my sleeping wife of my absence." He kept his oaths. Even silent promises made to one who did not hear. He'd decided to leave the maid a maid until he'd wooed her into willing surrender—a deed which had gifted him with a sleepless night and the likely prospect of more to come. He dare not risk waking the tender damsel himself for fear he'd fall again to her unknowing enticements and be forsworn.

Nessa's attention again on the earl, her breath caught in renewed appreciation of his breadth of shoulders and power of form—something one of her previous training should not notice, but did. He was her husband and there was no sin in finding him fascinating, she soothed her conscience. In answer it mocked: her husband but a man who found no attraction in her. Surely a fact that made her reaction to him shameful. 'Twas a lost cause for he was tempter, indeed. She'd been unable to reform her wrongful responses for the

158

sake of religious commitment, and doubted herself better able to now end them for the sake of pride, though doubtless lost for the strength of will it proved she lacked.

That Sir Rufus lifted an arm in acknowledgment Nessa did not see for her eyes remained melded to the handsome earl until he disappeared through the courtyard door.

Once her mind was her own to control again, she silently conceded that the earl's intended absence perfectly suited her plans. She immediately bore down on Sir Rufus. He was of such venerable age he must have inhabited this castle since time began and so possessed all the knowledge she needed but lacked.

"Sir Rufus." She called softly from behind his narrow back.

The guard captain was unused to the sound of a gentle-born woman's voice. Momentarily surprised, he whirled to face the speaker. The new countess patiently awaited his response without reproach for his brief lapse of memory.

"Good morrow, countess." He bowed politely with the words. "The earl bade me tell you he'll be gone the day and likely night too." Suddenly realizing that she'd almost assuredly heard the earl's instructions herself and yet had sought him out, he immediately added, "But what would you have of me?"

During the knight's repetition of a fact already heard, Nessa gracefully covered the tension his formal recognition of her status brought. Best she become accustomed to the title as for the next many years 'twould be hers. "Because you are the head of military matters in this fortress, I deemed it best to ask you to whom I should speak regarding household concerns."

The blank look on his face was not promising.

"Is there not a woman responsible for the castle's care?" Nessa carefully held her tone even, anxious that he not infer disapproval of its present state.

"They's not been a well-born woman here for many a year."

Nessa's brows rose. "None?" She didn't expect an answer to the question born of surprise. "Are all the knights unwed?"

Sir Rufus grinned, revealing a gap of several teeth missing

on one side. "Nay, there's several as are, but their wives prefers the village for home."

Preferred a small village cottage to a castle's amenities and protection? Nessa had never heard tell of such a thing and didn't know how to ask this man for the true purpose behind it. Instead, she returned to her original line of questioning. "Surely, at some point there was one charged with its upkeep?"

"Aye, Maud there was, but she weren't well-born and left of her own choosing." He wasn't certain what the lady's purpose was, but he didn't like anyone probing into matters done and best forgot. "Seems you ought be more concerned with what lies afore us than what's past." The words were far ruder than should ever be offered a true lady but by virtue of his age and length of service he'd some rights too. Ending nosy ways was one.

Nessa nearly bit her tongue clean through. She'd no wish to irritate even one person within these unfamiliar walls, this proud man least of all. She reached out to gently touch his arm. "Please pardon if I have offended, for I've need of friends in a place where I am stranger. Only did I seek aid from a woman knowledgeable of this place and its care so that I may acquit myself well in the lady's responsibility to put things in order."

The last lady Rufus remembered had done naught but demand with no thought of service herself. This woman claimed willingness to fulfill responsibilities of her own, and he could but admire her for the intent.

"Aye, well, I aught not have said as what I did, but I got loyalties. No ill done, we'll start afresh and I'll tell you true 'twould be a fine thing to see this castle returned to what it once were—but long, oh, so long ago."

"I don't know what once it was, but I mean to see it shiny clean and very soon." She smiled, nodding with firm resolve.

Although she wanted very much to know what he meant by what it once was, she held her tongue for fear of offending again. She did risk asking one more question, easy to answer and unlikely to affront. "Amongst the serfs here meant for castle labor, can you tell me if there is a woman whom I can instruct in helping me lead the tasks we must do?" She'd have liked to ask for the girl of cheery smile and admiring eyes from the previous night but was unsure how to go about it without possible insult to his judgment.

"There's Old Enid, the one what brought you a tray this morn, and there's Merta whose got more energy than most." With furrowed brow he paused and scratched his head, which only did further damage to thick white hair that would stand in strange angles like an alarmed cat's fur.

"Was it Merta who held the stairwell door for us last night?" Nessa quickly asked to ease his obvious difficulty in calling more names to mind.

"Oh, aye, that were Merta." He'd brightened with the relief of no longer needing to work a memory excellent at recalling the past but too often failing in remembering present facts and faces.

"How then can I find Merta?" she asked with a sweet smile.

"You've finally askt a question I got answer for just this quick." He snapped his fingers and strode toward a door behind the dais which surely led to the kitchens, calling the girl.

"What you want, Rufus?" Merta came to the door and, arms akimbo, lit into the poor messenger. "I gots my duties, too, you ken?" It was apparent by the wet splotches from neck to knees, that Merta had been left with either the morning wash up or the cleaning and cutting of stew ingredients. "And if you don't let me get back to them I promises you a wicked pixy'll curse your next meal with a plentitude of salt what'll leave your eyes watering for a twelvemonth or more." The affection underlying the threat stole its sting.

"Now I'm sorry I commended you to the countess." Sir Rufus folded his arms, waiting with certain satisfaction.

"Commended—" Merta stopped, wiping her hands on the cloth tied about her waist and anxiously looking past the aging knight. Had she ruined any chance by her foolery? Despite her sweet smile, was the countess a haughty lady to be offended by her teasing? Relief swept over Merta when she saw the dimple-bearing grin of the woman approaching. A little of her tension oozed away yet, flustered at being summoned by one so fine, but some remained.

For Nessa, amidst a dark fortress full of men and tension, Merta's humor shown like a beacon of saving light. That fact, not hindered by the admiration in mud-brown eyes that met hazel, decided the matter. The girl might lack skills, but she was the one to appoint as personal maid and to aid in her castle plans.

"I don't want to tempt the wicked salt 'pixy,' " Nessa said in mock seriousness, "but if you could spare a few moments, I've a task for you."

"Milady, if that wicked creature threatened aught of yours, I'd splat him for certain sure and never heed the dreadful things as they say will happen if you harms one of their number."

"Then, come talk with me in the lord's chamber." Nessa waited for the girl to pull the stained cloth from her waist and hand it to the grinning knight. Together they walked up the stairs. Raised to humbleness, Nessa had never been comfortable with servants walking behind her like lesser beings. She preferred those she knew to walk with her as friend—and she hoped this girl would become a much-needed friend.

Once inside, Nessa went to sit in a chair on one side of the small table placed where the tub had been the night before. Merta hovered near the door unsure of what her action should be.

"We can talk easier if you'll sit across from me," Nessa invited, waving to the empty chair. "You're but the third person I've met inside these walls, and I'd truly appreciate a friendly face." Nessa mentally cringed. She sounded critical of her reception, a thing she'd not meant to do. Choose your words with care, she silently reprimanded herself.

"Well, they all says as I've got that," Merta answered with more boldness than she felt as she moved to the offered seat. More than almost anything in the whole of her life she wanted to please this lovely countess, but feared her clumsy, unrefined manner and teasing tongue too crude for one gentle-bred.

"Merta," Nessa began, feeling her way and hoping to avoid pitfalls such as she'd stumbled into with the guard captain, "I tried to talk with Sir Rufus but he was unwilling to speak of the past." It suddenly occurred to Nessa that this sounded a nosy search for juicy gossip which would bring disdain on any wife. "Not that I want to know past

162

deeds, for I do not. Only do I seek to learn who last was responsible for castle household duties."

Merta grinned. Plainly the lady had got herself bit by the testy knight. "Sir Rufus won't talk about the past nowise and women even less."

Nessa was relieved to see the girl's amusement but was worried by her talk of the guard captain's common refusal to speak of the very things she'd asked. She looked down to hands palm-joined by nervous habit. No wonder he'd been affronted.

" 'Tain't been living long enough to know the whole story nor be there many hereabouts what does, save Sir Rufus and Lord Williams, and Maud—the one you was seeking."

The calm offer of the name she sought brought Nessa's gaze up.

Merta solemnly nodded. "She were maid to the old earl's wife. The woman what died aborning your man. Even did she serve the heir as wet nurse for a time—and stood chatelaine of this castle for that little while. Don't know what happened, nobody don't, save she and the one who done it, but there was a day when Lord William sent her right away. Never has she come back, though she bides in a little cottage on the village's edge."

"Who took up the household duties after she'd departed?" Nessa's thoughts were whirling with the strange tale so succinctly given and asked the one question clear in the morass.

"Her gone, we serfs was left and none trained to run an abode like as gentle-born folk do, Castle Tarrant least of all."

Nessa sat quiet after Merta's voice died away, processing what she'd learned. During the early years of her husband's life there had been no gentle-bred ladies, only a woman despising-father. She understood the source of his prejudice against women a little better for her knowledge. Shaking away thoughts of little use in her present course, Nessa looked back to the other girl. "Then Maud still lives in the village?"

"Oh, aye, that she is. Nor she ain't alone, though both her husband and only child got carried away by a plague what fell long years past."

Though likely unintended, the statement brought questions. Did it mean the woman had been reduced to selling her favors to castle soldiery? Surely her age, if naught else, would forestall that possibility. Merta didn't keep her in suspense for long.

"She overcome her sorrows by taking in children left orphans by the same illness what took hers. They's always talk as to where the money comes from. Inheritance from husband or her own people up north? Or is it that the old earl paid her to leave? No matter, she's taken in the homeless young all these many years."

Nessa realized the illness that had taken Maud's family was probably the same culprit that had taken her own mother. After a moment she said, "Can you lead me to her cottage?"

"Aye. But, had you rather go alone, I can give you directions for 'tis hard to miss." Merta wanted to accompany the countess desperately but felt it only right to give her the opportunity to be without another.

Nessa studied the solemn face before her. She had no desire to force Merta to an unwilling journey. But her support would be appreciated. Nessa knew she'd be the focus of many curious eyes and longed for the company of another. The flicker of hope in mud-brown eyes was confusing. Could be born of either wish. As the girl would not state a preference, Nessa took a chance.

"As stranger to most, walking alone is an uncomfortable task. But I've done more difficult things; and, although I'd deem your company a boon, you need not go if you had rather not."

Merta's wide smile gave her answer even without a breathless "Oh, nay, I want to go. Only did I think it fit that you should know the simplest directions will take you there so you needn't cumber yourself with me for the sake of the path." She started to rise but the lady's quickly raised hand stilled the motion.

"One more question and then we'll begin." Nessa drew a deep breath. This question was more nearly the nosy one she'd not wanted to ask before, yet one she felt impelled to have answered. "Why do the wives of castle knights live elsewhere? Truly why?"

"What they says is that they's used to finer places, ones what are better kept. 'Tain't true. They're well-born right enough but of only lesser gentry and never lived nowhere as mighty as Castle Tarrant, mayhap better kept but not finer. In truth it comes to the old earl's snarling at them 'til they trembles and the young earl's cold eyes what freezes them if ever they draws near. Afore long they begs their menfolk to take them away." Merta suddenly realized she'd spoken ill of this lady's husband and went beet red. "I—I—" She gulped, unable to say more.

"Thank you for your honesty." Nessa rushed to relieve the girl's embarrassment. "I understand their reasons very well. The earl terrifies my sister, and I've had my moments too." Not wanting to discuss the matter further and anxious to forestall thoughts all too easily drawn into dwelling upon the man, Nessa rose gracefully. "Now let's away and be about our chore."

The two women were soon descending the broad steps of the stone stairway within the width of tower wall. At the bottom Nessa started to move into the great hall intending to leave by its door and from there walk across the courtyard to the gate and drawbridge beyond but Merta put out a restraining hand. Tower as corner, thick stone walls moved out at right angles from the stairway end. Nessa had noticed the unusual design the night past, and even she knew enough of warfare to realize that the narrow interior corridors must, for the sake of keeping any weakness in structure far from the battering power of siege weapons, tunnel through very near the protected courtyard side. She assumed that by turning to the right she would reach the old earl's West Tower, but it was the left path Merta motioned toward. Nessa's dread of narrow, ill-lit passages roared to life, but she swallowed her reluctance and followed Merta's rapid steps only to have her heart kick up an erratic thumping when her leader abruptly halted. The weak light of a single oil-fed lamp weaved dim patterns in the shadows against an unexpected wall.

Merta opened a door unnoticed in its center and led the way through. Nessa found herself amidst the castle curtain's tunnel entrance through which they'd ridden on arrival. Looking to its outside end, she saw the drawbridge bathed in the blinding light of day and blinked rapidly against its sudden assault on dark adjusted eyes. The two girls paused, allowing their eyes to grow accustomed to the change—until a shadow blocked the light.

"Well, if it isn't the little pig-girl all grown up." The voice was derisive.

"All grown up and still far too good for the likes of you." Merta snapped back.

"Since when did a serf count for anything next to a free-born man and less to a knight?" She'd obviously cut Sir Erdel and his response was meant to be as hurtful. The arrogant knight thought so much of himself there was only disdain left for others.

"Since," Nessa stepped from behind the taller girl and gave the answer her new friend could not, "she became maid and companion to a countess."

"Huh." The knight dared say no more but his snort of contempt said it all—both serf girl and countess meant little in a castle without welcome for women at any level.

The two women watched him stride away with equal dislike.

"Thinks as what he's so much better'n me. Hah!" Merta muttered to herself, forgetful of her companion. "Wouldn't be free-born, even less a knight, weren't it for his grandfather. Leastways the old knight don't put on airs and pretend to be gentle-bred." As she spoke, Merta stepped out on the day-lowered drawbridge and began to stride briskly across uneven wood planks.

Startled by her words, Nessa had nearly to run to catch up. "Wait," she called.

Merta turned, shamefaced for her unthinking words and irritated haste. "My ma always says as my tongue clacks faster'n my mind can work and I says the wrongest things. I fears you'll rue the day you took me on."

"Nay, I prefer honesty to pretty words without sincerity. Your long legs are my only complaint." Her gaze swept down the tall girl's form. "Isn't easy for me to keep pace with you."

Merta's wide grin flashed with relief. "Then I swears I'll dawdle so as you can walk natural like."

Nessa laughed. "I'll hold you to that oath, see if I don't." Together they moved over the hard-packed roadway across the open space between castle and village. Occasional carts bound for Tarrant passed them, their drivers joining field laborers to surreptitiously eye the ill-matched pair, one fine-dressed lady and one homespun-clad serf.

As they arrived at the village outskirts, Nessa found courage to ask the meaning behind Merta's muttered rebuke of Sir Erdel.

Merta shrugged, yet felt she owed the lady an explanation. "Simply that his grandfather was serf bound to these lands, like as I. Only was he freed after saving the old earl's father from an arrow in the back."

"How?" Nessa's curiosity, held under tight restraints for long years, once loosed no longer accepted easy control.

"Spied a sly foe hiding in bushes and dived in to knock his deadly aim askew. Rufus was made free man and, in recognition of his bravery, trained to knighthood."

Surprised, Nessa halted mid-step, oblivious of the many watching in the distance. "Sir Rufus?" Although it seemed certain, she could barely believe the aging guard captain and a knight so young and rude as Sir Erdel were closely tied by blood.

Merta turned to face her lady. "Aye, the man who commended me to you and still serves as guard captain—an honor he won not by his first deed but by valor in battle. He and I gets along well for all I love to banter with him. He don't put on airs."

Nessa recognized the last statement as further proof of Merta's dislike of the younger knight, yet would not pry by questioning the reason for it. She had, in any case, no time for they'd arrived at the small village's outer edge and a meticulously kept but humble cottage. Merta led the way through a small garden of green herbs interspersed with cheery blue and yellow flowers to rap on the door. Although nearly accustomed to being watched, while waiting for an answer to their knock, Nessa felt the touch of unseen eyes. Doubtless 'twas the orphans Merta had told her were here and like all children curious. She turned her head to encounter a dark and solemn gaze peeking around the cottage's edge. High-pitched giggles proved others once there had scurried away while the owner of the deep brown gaze steadily returned her attention without sign of fear, even defiantly.

The creaking sound of a door swinging wide drew Nessa's gaze to a short woman of comfortable proportions. Framed in the opening she paused only a moment before waving them inside.

"I am honored, my lady." Maud's voice was soft but her words well-bred and evidence of a very efficient gossip trail.

"And I am pleased to meet you for I've had a time finding you." Standing just within the small structure, though not obviously looking about, Nessa saw its clean, homey condition.

Maud met hazel eyes, her friendly smile an acknowledgment of the difficulty in learning of her from almost any of Tarrant's own. "Glad I am that you've come, as I have few visitors," she added, motioning her guests to a simple bench near the home's central firepit. "But what brings you to me?"

"I have a boon to ask of you." Believing the woman would appreciate a direct answer, Nessa went right to the point.

"Of me?" Astonishment lifted brows nearly to the edge of the clean white veil she wore over neatly confined gray hair.

Watching her hostess ease herself down onto a matching bench on the fire circle's far side, Nessa chose her words cautiously. "You were the last lady to have care of the castle, a duty now mine." In unplanned emphasis of her next words, her hands came together palm-joined. "I've been trained to the religious life and am unsure of my tasks although one look reveals the need."

"I've not seen the inside for a great many years but by all accounts 'tis true." Maud nodded, leaning forward to ask, "But of what aid can I be to you?"

Praying she'd not offend, Nessa spoke tentatively, "I don't know what sent you away, but hoped to persuade you to return."

Maud straightened her spine, a motion that effectively drew her away. "I'll be glad to give you what little help I can, tell you what you seek to know, but return to the castle I cannot do." The downward droop to her lips came not from anger but regret.

Nessa looked about the small abode and understood the woman's reluctance to leave such warmth for the austere castle.

"Nay." Maud's normal cheery spirit reasserted itself and

168

she laughed, shaking with the merry sound that laid deep creases in her plump cheeks. "I like my home well enough but 'tis not that which I cannot leave. Doubtless 'tis good-hearted Merta who has told you about my past duties and likely of my responsibilities here." She turned and called out to the row of heads peering around a still-open cottage door. Three young children obediently clustered about the motherly woman, the youngest crawling into her capacious lap to hide her face shyly against a generous bosom.

"This is Carl. He's eight." Maud told Nessa, pointing to the oldest boy. "This is Meg who's almost six." She gestured to the girl on her right. "And this one is my little Beata." She hugged the toddling on her lap, tickling her to bring a charming giggle.

Nessa smiled at each in turn. She could see a close family resemblance between these three with their light brown locks and eyes nearly the same shade, but where was the one who'd stood steady when she caught him staring?

"And one more I have." Maud lifted her chin and called, a little louder this time. "Will, you come too."

The boy Nessa had wondered about came to stand in the open door. His chin was tilted up with clearly false bravado and he watched the lady visitor warily while hanging back, as though staying as near the escape route as possible and still obeying.

"Here you see my four reasons for not returning. The old earl would never allow them inside. Can't bear children, he can't, not even his own."

Nessa had always heard Earl William was a cold, uncaring man but only since arriving here had she begun to understand that his attitude extended to his son, perhaps his son most of all. An example an impressionable youngster had surely been doomed to imitate. Thinking of Garrick's unhappy childhood pained Nessa so deeply she failed to realize she'd thought of him by name rather than title. Fearful of a new and tender ache, an urge to comfort a man so hard and cold, she returned her mind to those before her.

She was touched by Maud's generosity in caring for those in need as even the church seldom did. She'd given up the religious life, but here was a way to offer practical service to God. After all, Abbess Berthilde had said He welcomed the

169

practical too. With courage born of a righteous chore, Nessa spoke.

"No longer is it up to the old earl who comes to Castle Tarrant." She smiled at Maud with all the assurance she didn't feel—and it weakened by Merta's gasp. Clearly the other girl felt the old earl would dispute her claim. She heartened herself with the weak hope that, as he seldom left his tower, mayhap he'd not even know them there. Remembering the days of their childhood and Aleria's laughter echoing in Salisbury Tower it seemed depressingly unlikely, but God was on her side and that was an end to the matter.

Maud beamed through the tears washing her face, and her voice trembled. "An answer to prayer, that's what you are. An answer to all my desperate prayers. Gladly will we come, come today." She lifted the littlest from her lap, rising to shoo them out to play.

Her words had given Nessa's resolve the strength of iron and nothing would now deflect her from seeing them comfortably installed in the huge fortress.

Will was the last child to leave the cottage and before he did his eyes, full of mingled hope and apprehension, locked with Maud's. When the three women were alone, Maud slowly sat down again, the light gone from her face. "There is more I must tell you. Something which may change your decision."

"Nothing can do that."

Maud smiled at her certainty. "Pray heed and know that yours was a decision none would blame you for voiding as 'twas made without understanding of what you do." She shook her head, holding back the new countess's denial. "The three younger ones are from one family and have no relations to take them in. The oldest, Will, he's special in a way that may make you change your mind."

Nessa knew there was nothing that would make her change her mind, but also knew Maud would not come until she'd heard it all. She gave the speaker her full attention.

"When my lady died bearing your husband, the old earl drank something awful and in a stupor raped one of the castle serfs. He'd no memory of it the next morn, and when she claimed to have born his daughter, he'd not believe her speaking true. She left the castle in shame.

"That little girl grew up a beauty with a happy nature that

170

sought no more than the plain life she led with her man, a woodcutter. One morn while she carried a midday meal to her husband working in the forest nearby, leaving their little son asleep in the loft,'' Maud motioned to the one above their heads, ''a fire engulfed their hut. Returning, she saw the blaze and ran home to climb up the ladder through the thick smoke of burning thatch and save her boy. Somehow she broke through the wall and dropped him to safety before collapsing to perish in the flames.''

Nessa crossed herself at the woman's sad fate and let her hands fall to her lap palm-joined.

''Without his lovely wife, the lad's father lost interest in life. He took dangerous risks until, within the year, he too was dead. The boy then lived with grandma but old age took her last year, and only I would take in the old earl's rejected grandson.''

''Will?'' Nessa asked. Maud nodded. ''His parentage is of no matter to my invitation. Indeed, I feel I right an injustice by taking him where he ought to be.''

Maud beamed again. She admired this woman's courage, no fine lady too good for the likes of bastard children or too important to bother with low-born orphans. ''Must tell you, my small hoard of money is gone, and I can't provide what we can't grow for ourselves. The neighbors are generous but they've got families of their own.''

''All I ask of you, is your help in returning Castle Tarrant to order, in making it a pleasant place to abide.''

Suppressing her skepticism for the possibility of attaining such an atmosphere, Maud offered, ''Then I hope you'll allow me to oversee the cooking—it's a task I've learned to love, and I believe that a good meal goes far to improve a man's spirit.''

''I think your talents will be deeply appreciated, Maud.'' Nessa hesitated to elaborate, fearful of offending Merta, who'd been involved in preparing the poor meals she'd seen thus far.

The prospect of a wider variety of ingredients to work with, which surely were available to the castle, was exciting yet the possibilities brought to mind a new fear. ''After years of making plain, nourishing meals for my children, I may need inspiration and wish I'd recipes for the fine foods meant for castle fare.''

"That I can provide." Nessa was pleased. Things were going well with her plan. "I'll write the queen and ask that a scribe be sent to her cook, a very fine cook, to write out a few for us."

Plans made for a move that afternoon, with promise given to send a wagon to collect them and their belongings, on uplifted spirits Nessa departed with Merta.

◄§ *Chapter 14* §►

T hank you."

Nessa's soft words startled the young serf who'd earned them. In Davy's experience the noble-bred did not express appreciation for tasks done by those born to do them. Turning, he fell willing slave to a sweetly dimpled smile. The Ice Warrior had done himself and them all amazing well in choosing this lady for wife—despite her sudden appearance and distinctly odd style of dress. The sturdy adolescent moved away to join the growing ranks of castle serfs summoned to the great hall who milled about and grumbled at the interruption of their daily routine while waiting for explanation.

Nervous and at a loss for words now that the time had come to speak, Nessa busied herself forcing her mass of curls into submission beneath the protection of a sturdy coif borrowed from Maud. No beauty was she, but she'd not shame her husband by dressing for meals or occasions of import in garb less than his lady ought wear. To insure the success of that pride-saving goal, she dare not risk her few gowns remade from the queen's and Aleria's wardrobes in the menial work she meant to undertake. Her alternatives were limited. When donned, tall Merta's skirts dragged on the ground while those belonging to Maud, even shorter than she, at least fell to the right length. She'd only just come from changing into one of the older woman's voluminous gowns and, as she looked down into the great vat of white-wash awaiting, checked the security of the belt wrapped three times about her waist to hold an overabundance of cloth out of her way.

Anxious to prove herself no lazy slugabed, she'd risen and set serfs to brewing this concoction before the guardsmen had arrived for the morning meal. On her return the previous day, without hint of condemnation for its present state, she'd directed that floors be swept clean of old, musty rushes. With garrison men gone about their business and all in readiness, she was anxious to begin brightening interior walls and had just gathered her courage when a childish voice piped up at her side.

"I wants to help." A small hand tugged at Nessa's skirts.

Nessa glanced down to find Beata, expression caught between hopefulness and a pout. "And so you shall, sweet lamb." Nessa pretended a serious examination of brushes spread out beside the vat, each formed of dried grasses bound to a stick. She chose the littlest to put into fingers too tiny to wield any handily. Looking up, she smiled at the three children clustered near Maud.

"You may all help for 'tis a big task and calls for an army of workers." Her attention shifted to include the crowd doubtfully watching and listening.

"Such work is for serfs."

The hall went still, as if even its stones had sprouted ears straining to hear the new lady's response to a defiant boy.

Hazel eyes flew to Will's diffident face, his expression a youthful imitation of the earl's cold impassivity. Her heart bled for the boy caught between pride of unacknowledged heritage and shame for a tainted parentage not of his choosing. Caught in sympathy, she forgot the crowd of interested onlookers.

"Will, 'tis not—" Maud broke the silence, horrified, but the lady's upheld hand stopped her words.

"I am not a serf, Will." Nessa's gentle voice was calm and patient. "But even as Countess of Tarrant I have duties and find no shame in honest toil. 'Tis my responsibility to

174

see this castle well-kept in manner befitting its noble importance.''

The boy nodded, abashed and confused by the lack of rebuke for his plainly wrongful words.

To ease Will's embarrassment, Nessa immediately issued an invitation. ''The task is large, and I would appreciate your aid.'' She selected a worthy brush and offered it with a reassuring smile. ''Besides, 'tis a chore that can be fun. When my sister and I were young, we pretended that each stroke was a bright sword strike against dark opponents.''

The listening children giggled and Will grinned as he took the proffered ''weapon'' and made a mock stab at an imaginary foe.

A rush of whispers and soft laughter blew away the hall's quiet. Even the most reticent, the most ill-tempered were won by the lady's understanding and willingness to join them in their toil. The waiting crowd surged forward to take up brushes and set to work with an enthusiasm seldom shown. Very soon the huge room was filled with an infectious warmth shared equally by each member of the whole, none of whom had noticed the tall, dark man half shielded by shadows in the entrance tunnel.

Garrick had returned from a journey to check the condition of distant tenants and farms. The deterioration he'd found was disheartening, yet he accepted the blame as his own. Too long he'd stayed away and only much time and labor would repair the harm. While the men who'd accompanied him took up duties in stable or armory, he'd arrived in the archway in time to hear both his wife's response to an unknown toddler and the lack of disapproval in her calm answer to the defiance of a vaguely familiar boy.

Nessa's warmth soothed his ill temper and brought a vision of her as mother to his child—a mother generous in affection and understanding, a mother such as he had never known. The thought reminded him of the crude way he'd spoken to her of his need for an heir. He rued both his anger and words, regretted leaving the unique woman to believe he desired her only for the sake of an heir. A son was important but never would he seek the yielding of her sweet self only to fulfill a duty—either his or hers. Nay, although since their meeting his own emotions had become strangers, he knew there'd be neither pleasure nor true satisfaction in an embrace grown from aught but free will and mutual desire. He'd earlier restrained his passions and would again until he'd won the surrender of this provider of a warmth he'd never known before.

Even amidst the large group of merry workers near done with the first wall, Nessa felt an invisible touch, as if someone were repeatedly stroking her back. She turned. Hazel eyes unerringly found the dark man half hidden in gloom and leaning with masculine grace against the entrance arch. He was staring directly at her and her heart thundered so loud she felt certain it must overwhelm even the laughter of many. When his attention moved pointedly to small strangers, she recalled all too clearly what had kept her wakeful most of the previous night. While Maud, even Merta feared Lord William's rejection of the castle's new inhabitants, she had worried about Garrick's reaction to her claim of a right his and not hers.

Garrick watched Nessa's dainty chin tilt as she pulled the shabby cloth from her head, shook freed curls to tumble down her slender back in splendid disarray, and moved to stand before him. Truly, he must speak to her about keeping the soft cloud modestly confined, and he would—as soon as he found the spirit to add coils of suppression to one already overburdened with restraint.

"My lord," Nessa began.

Garrick laid a finger against soft lips, letting it linger in a gentle caress. "Garrick."

Stilled breath blocked Nessa's throat, and thick lashes fell. Only when his touch withdrew was she able to begin again. "Garrick, I invited your one-time nurse, Maud, to return and help me put your mighty fortress to rights." There was no response. To further justify her action, Nessa added, "She's a fine cook whose talents can only be useful."

Forced by continuing silence to look up, Nessa found gray eyes, too close and darkened to smoke, studying her lips intently. They felt suddenly dry but when a pink tongue-tip moistened them his eyes flashed with dangerous silver sparks. Her gaze dropped to study bare floor planks as if they were the most precious of scripts. It was not distance enough and, hands behind and twisted tight together, she stepped back to continue.

"Maud is responsible for these children. They've no one

and would be left to play beggar or thief were it not for her."
Once begun and certain of the importance in her oath to see
the orphans provided for, the words came unwavering and
fast. "The castle is so very large and so many chambers go
unused, that I felt justified in bringing them here. They'll
earn their keep."

Again Garrick stood silent until hazel eyes full of false
bravado but with both pleading hope and wariness beneath
rose to meet his. He excused his nod as merely the next
move in a campaign to win Nessa to his intent. Even to
himself he did not admit that the children's laughter lightened the dark hall near as much as the whitewash, and their
happiness lent warmth to a place long given over to cold—
or was Nessa the source of it all?

After her husband had gone to resume his duties, with
heart lightened by his easily won approval and more by the
touch offering hope for warmer relations between them,
Nessa returned to tasks yet undone. Two of the castle's
towers, she'd learned, were used only for storage of supplies
and armaments and thus needed no immediate attention.
Old rushes had been swept from all the chambers in this
tower. That left only the West Tower with its recluse—and
she'd seen for herself how badly in need of care it was.
Reluctant to command that another be subjected to Lord
William's spiteful tongue, Nessa accepted the duty for her
own.

From the alcove cut into thick stone wall devoted to
storage of such utensils, she collected a strong bristled
broom and a large square of folded homespun. Determined
to hold misgivings at bay, rather than retracing the parapet's
path with its curious guardsmen, she turned into the corridor
branching off to the right from stairwell edge. She refused to
surrender to unreasoning fear of the gloomy path and
marched briskly into its shadowy length, resolutely turning
her thoughts to the man at its end.

Before meeting Lord William she'd expected to find him
intimidating, and so she had. But in the time since they'd
met her thoughts had returned again and again to the man
shut into a tower, alone and suffering. That his isolation was
by choice did not lessen her pity for the one confined not
only by stone walls but locked by cold habits within his own
thoughts and regrets, and surely he must have them. Was

his bitter disposition the result of his self-imposed solitude, like wine which left too long unopened goes to vinegar?

Within the narrow passage, deep in her thoughts and accustomed to the soft echo of her own footsteps, of a sudden a noise not of her making shivered up Nessa's spine. *Calm yourself, witling,* she berated herself. *Even a sound so small as a needle dropping would echo in the tight confines of these stone walls.* It was no comfort, particularly not when the next sound was considerably louder than the ting of a falling needle. Beyond cool reason and despite arms already burdened, she lifted her skirts and dashed down the hallway as if all the imps of hell were at her heels and nearly convinced they were.

Her terrified flight seemed endless. When finally she reached the West Tower's stairwell, gasping for breath, she collapsed on its lowest step. She told herself in no uncertain terms that even if 'twere littered with sneering guardsmen she'd return by the parapet path and never venture here alone again. Anxious to be far from this place as quickly as possible, she rested only long enough for the worst trembles to be gone and strength enough to hold herself upright before rising and gathering her cleaning materials together.

The old earl's level was reached without further mishap, yet as she approached his chamber her attention was again caught by the heavily barricaded door opposite. Neither she nor any other would be allowed to clean whatever horror lay hidden within, but leastways the dust could be swept from long untouched chains. Folded homespun fell into a heap on corridor's floor and her broom attacked the chore with zeal.

"What are you doing?"

Thundered words were so unexpected Nessa nearly dropped the broom as she whirled to face the furious man looming in his chamber's open doorway.

"I've come to sweep the old rushes from your chamber." Her response was little more than a squeak, but she compensated for its uncertainty with a brave smile.

"Then you lack for wits as well as wealth and beauty if you think what you were sweeping are rushes." Lord William's anger had given him a strength he'd not had in years, but it faded with the speed of his rage's receding fervor.

"Not rushes, only dust left too long and a shame to me

178

who am responsible for seeing the castle restored to order."
Nessa was on firmer ground and proudly straightened.

Sagging against the doorframe, Earl William watched the girl gain in strength while his departed. To his own surprise he found himself amused by the spirit of this unpretentious female as by nothing in years, although he refused to show it. "Your responsibility?" His thick brows rose with the sarcastic words.

"Aye, and I never take a responsibility lightly." Pride lent Nessa's answer a calm she was far from feeling. "Your chamber is part of my lord's castle, and it will be cleaned."

"Your lord's castle? Hah!" From a height superior even though he was not standing tall he looked down his nose at the girl. "By that you mean my heir who is stranger to his lands."

Nessa's chin went up as she instinctively defended her husband. "When have you made him welcome here?"

For the second time in one day, Garrick stood as unseen observer of his wife's surprising actions. Her instant rebuttal of words belittling him was surely further proof of a loyal nature unlikely to play him traitor and offered one bright spot of ease amongst the darkness of the many ills and lacks on his fiefdom, all waiting to be cleared. Nonetheless, before his sire attacked again, it was time for them to know he was here.

"You sent Derward to fetch me."

Stunned, both Nessa and Earl William looked to the powerful man standing with arms folded across broad chest and legs planted wide. Nessa felt she would wither and die beneath ice-glinting eyes albeit they were trained on his father.

"Aye, I sent for you." Earl William had planned a private talk wherein many things were possible, but this woman had put paid to his hope. And if not her, then 'twould have been another for never did his tentative attempts to reach his son go well. By habit he'd scorned his heir's care of their lands and by it hardened the target's heart. Yet, he'd summoned Garrick for a purpose, and one he could not postpone. "Although I leave my chamber never, I hear of most deeds hereabouts—falling rocks and treacherously threatened death."

It was Garrick's turn to be startled. The speed of his

179

father's informants was amazing for they'd returned but a short time past. He wished not to speak on the matter at all, with Nessa near even less. As he looked down at the woman standing brave between two stubborn men, the silver ice in his eyes melted to the steaming gray of a mountain hot spring on a cloudy day.

"I thought I saw you a short distance ahead when I entered the corridor, but I must have been wrong else you sped here on feet winged like Mercury's."

His amusement made it plain that he knew she'd run in terror, yet the heat in eyes so recently frozen burned insult to gentle ashes. Unfortunately her embarrassment was un-affected and a blush stained her cheeks peach pink.

With interest, and concern, Earl William watched his usually fierce son's gentle handling of the bride he had to admit possessed a subtle loveliness. Were Garrick to love the maid, pain would follow. He claimed a father's right to worry even though his son had grown too far from him to heed any warning. Combing fingers through thick gray hair, he forced his mind to more immediate dangers and made a less oblique demand for answer.

"As you returned from your night's journey, did or did not a rock fall so near 'tis only chance that saved your life?"

Black brows lowered. "A nasty accident and past."

Refusing to be put off with casual excuses, father pressed son. "I was told it was not one of many nor part of a natural slide but seemed rather to take deadly aim."

Garrick glanced at Nessa's white face and shrugged. "Your spies saw intended danger where there was none." He'd not discuss or to another admit his belief that it had been done apurpose—but not meant to kill. An unsuspecting target so close was unlikely to be missed. Thus, he was certain the accident had been meant to frighten him into abandoning his suppression of rebellion.

The news of Garrick's near deadly accident, if accident it had been, horrified Nessa and immediately brought to mind the wild threats Sir Gilfrey had made only days past. Had that strange vengeful man dared accost the earl on his own lands?

"If danger to you is of no import," Earl William continued undaunted by the other's apparent unconcern, "then may-hap you'll find more interest in danger to your heritage."

Black head tilted to one side, Garrick studied the other through narrowed eyes. Baiting words had earned his attention.

"My 'spies' report a meeting last night between men of Tarrant and Swinton's castellan." The old lord's dark gaze challenged another dismissal.

Although his impassive expression revealed nothing, Garrick was discouraged to learn that his people had met with the one he'd thought a danger past, and met with him while he was so near. He said only, "Conal of Wryborne is Swinton's temporary castellan—the other has been banished."

"Banished from Swinton?" A mocking smile accompanied the question. "Only to skulk about in Tarrant's forest lands."

Garrick merely shrugged although inwardly he accepted the words as reinforcement of the need for immediate action to end Sir Gilfrey's influence. He turned his attention to the woman so upset that palm-joined hands rested against her lips.

"Come, Nessa," Garrick softly invited, "I'll see you safely through the nether regions."

Nessa looked up into eyes, again warm smoke, and ignored the amusement tugging at his firm mouth. Caught in his warm gaze, she laid her hand atop his proffered arm and departed unmindful of tasks undone and materials left behind.

As they approached the corridor through "nether regions" Nessa hoped he'd not chide her for the earlier unseemly flight down its length. She was relieved when he merely asked if Sir Rufus had told her of his overnight task.

"Aye, but I entered the hall just as you charged him with it, so there was no danger of my going uninformed."

Garrick wondered what had held her from stepping forward to acknowledge the words herself and wish him godspeed, but merely nodded and spoke again. "I feared he would forget to pass the message to you as his memory grows ever less reliable."

"Likely a sign of his many years," Nessa ventured. "He's uncommonly aged for a guard captain." Too aware of the man forced to near intimate closeness by the narrow passage, she kept her eyes safely lowered to the faint glow of light brightening their gloomy path as they neared the next oil-fed sconce.

"Indeed?" Garrick's eyes narrowed with displeasure for her disparagement of a worthy man victim of an inevitable change.

Nessa, never looking up, didn't see his reaction. "Your choice to let him live out his time with honors retained is admirable."

A rueful smile curled Garrick's lips. Again he'd unfairly condemned this undeserving woman. "The honor remains his but his eventual replacement, Sir James, bears most of the burden and in the unlikely event of an attack would assume full command."

"Sir James?" Nessa asked, peeking up. "Not Sir Erdel?" She'd believed the young knight's arrogance born of some unspoken logic, likely the certainty of replacing his grandfather in a position of honor.

"The position is not hereditary." Garrick smiled down at his hesitant questioner. "Sir Erdel is too full of groundless pride and possesses too little skill at either arms or tact. Until he learns to humble himself enough to respect even a foe's strength, he will be a last choice."

As the two stepped from corridor to stairwell, they failed to see the figure ducking into shadows beyond.

❧ Chapter 15 ❧

Delicate brows rose in surprise when Nessa saw the forgotten broom leaning beside the old earl's chamber door, homespun cloth neatly folded and left beside. She'd returned this following day determined to allow neither fears nor allurements to turn her aside from the chore yet undone. Refusing to hesitate while misgivings grew, she knocked briskly on ironbound planks.

A muffled roar from the far side was disconcerting but she stood firm until the door opened a crack. Narrowed in suspicion, beady eyes glared at her from the same weasely face that had first peeked at her from this portal. The door slammed shut so quickly she blinked and recoiled a step. Bracing herself against further rebuffs, she lifted her fist again. Before it could make contact, the door was flung wide and Derward scurried into the shadows.

"Hah! Thought you'd return—responsibilities, you ken." The rough words seemed to take with them the last of the old earl's energy. His head fell limply against his chair's high padded back, ruffling dark gray hair and tilting face so that its deep creases of pain were more clearly revealed. "Come then and be done." The demand was no more than a whisper.

183

Holding the broom before her as if it were a sword, Nessa stepped into the chamber with a boldness she was far from feeling.

Heavy lids struggled to rise, intent on a long examination of the visitor. The new countess looked as if she were armed and advancing against a dangerous foe—he who possessed barely strength enough to keep eyes open and none to lift head.

Nessa's gaze fell to the weakened lord half lying with bowl resting near an outstretched arm bearing several repulsive slugs.

Lord William saw the direction of her disgusted gaze and had he sufficient energy would have laughed. "Aye, I'm taking another treatment and pray it will soon see my health returned."

Not pausing to consider its wisdom, Nessa questioned, "How is it that men capable of forming great strategies for war can believe that a thing that steals vigor is remedy capable of restoring strength?" To her way of thinking it should be clear to the simplest mind that such actions as bloodletting and leeches were unable to build what they took, 'twas only logical.

The impertinent maid, for though beyond the age of most newly wed William couldn't see her as a woman full-grown, was incapable of man's advanced reasoning. Yet her question seemed sincere and he smiled slightly as Derward crept forward to enlighten her.

Nessa swung around at the touch of a scaly hand on her arm.

"Nay, lady." Derward looked at her with a condescension that immediately pricked Nessa's pride. "You do not see the true source of such healing." He continued with carefully chosen words as if explaining to a feeble-wit. "The evils that sap strength hide in the warm blood flowing fast through one's veins and only these creatures bred in slow-moving streams and still water marshes are capable of seeking them out and sucking them away."

"A simple blood letting would not do?" Nessa willfully held her tone neutral, free of the agitation simmering beneath.

"Not do at all. Only would it take good with bad while

these leeches, applied thrice daily, will soon see our lord restored."

"For how many days have you applied your cure?" The question was softly asked.

"A fortnight today." Ever suspicious, Derward looked at her belligerently.

Wasting neither more time nor breath on the wizened man, she spun to meet her father-in-law's near closed eyes. "I challenge you to leave off this practice for the fortnight next. Then, as honorable man, compare truly which leaves more strength in you."

Silence stretched while Lord William stared into Nessa's steady gaze. When his response finally came, it was noncommittal. "I'll consider it on the morrow." The words were a faint sigh, and he rested a moment before rasping again. "Get on with your task and leave me soon, for I'm in need of my bed."

Beneath the oppressive weight of Derward's animosity, Nessa set to work. Leastways these matters had for a time driven other worries from her mind. After his gentle words and warm touches the previous day, she'd expected Garrick to join her in the lord's chamber, his chamber. He'd not come. Though he'd claimed to need, nay, require an heir of her, he seemed unable to bring himself to her bed. She railed against the lack of experience in the ways of men and women that left her unable to understand. The best course, she told herself, was to keep her mind from matters with no answers. She'd almost succeeded when she realized that again in her thoughts he'd become Garrick. A dangerously intimate way to think of a man who did not seek her closeness.

Yielding to suddenly vigorous strokes, the old rushes were soon swept out onto the homespun square she'd laid open beyond the door. As she bent to roll the cloth over soiled rushes and secure the bundle, she was relieved to see the leeches were being removed. Rising to stand in the chamber doorway, she spoke.

"I will leave this bundle beyond your door and send someone to carry it away. Then, I'll not intrude on your rest again until the morrow when I come back to oversee the spreading of new rushes. Good rest to you." She nodded and withdrew.

* * *

Sitting demurely before the private solar's hearth, Nessa realized she'd only to stretch out folded fingers to touch the firm muscled thigh of her lord. So near and yet he had as well been on foreign soil. Still, had it not been for a haunting fear for his safety under Sir Gilfrey's threats she'd have found a contentment never dreamt of before. That fear and one further cloud on her horizon—it overshadowing the whole. Though he took pains to include her in conversations at table and as oft as not joined her before this very hearth in early evening to bestow warm smiles and share calm words, he came never to her bed.

Reminding herself not to moan for what she couldn't have but to be thankful for what she'd been given, with days of practice she turned her thoughts to her duties, a methodical and hopefully distracting review of the previous week's achievements. Old rushes had been replaced by fresh ones sprinkled with sweet-scented herbs and the castle brightened with whitewash inside and out. With Merta's encouragement, the castle inhabitants had worked together on the tasks, even off-duty guardsmen, one setting example until an army pitched in to see each done with much bantering and good will. Their aid, Nessa had jested, was a result of energy lent by plentiful meals. Since Maud had set to her chore, repasts had been tasty if plainly prepared, and daily she asked if Nessa had yet sent for the promised recipes.

Searching for some further diversion from awareness of the strong man who seemed content to quietly relax, dark head heavy against his chair's high back and lids drooping over gray eyes, Nessa thought of the progress she'd made in the West Tower. She'd returned to the old earl's chamber the day after she'd swept it clean. He'd been alone. Glowering, but without a word, he'd motioned her and her helpers inside. While others bestrewed the room with fresh rushes, she'd closely examined the chamber's poor condition. Seemed unlikely it had been recipient of more than cursory cleaning for long years and was surely a task destined to require many days' work. Before leaving, she'd calmly informed her father-in-law of her intention to be there the next day and again as often as need be to see his apartments in proper repair. His response had been a disgusted shrug yet she'd found it encouraging that leastways he'd not vigorously refused.

186

During the days that followed she'd held to her words and returned to clean cobwebs from dark corners, reorder cluttered chests and see to the restoration of a magnificent wardrobe years since abandoned to moths and mildew. His dark resentment had repeatedly burst forth in bitter dialogues, but she'd stood steady beneath battering words, answering only when questions were asked. His caustic remarks no longer had power to sting for she saw beyond his gruff exterior to the lonely old man who'd lost his path to the rest of the world, a stranger even to his son. What she did not see and dared not ask was if he'd accepted her challenge and contented herself that never again had she seen sign either of sly Derward or his loathsome leeches.

"I'm told you visit almost daily with my father. Is his health improving?"

Garrick's question, so near the subject of her thoughts, startled Nessa, and she hastened to correct the image of a social visit that he implied. "I go to see his chamber cleared and cleaned as it's fallen into shameful disrepair." Hearing her unconsidered words, she worried that they sounded a criticism and quickly moved on to the subject of Earl William's health. "The first day when I returned to sweep the old rushes out, Derward had his vile slugs preying upon the patient."

Garrick heard Nessa's disdain, the usual response of women to slimy creatures. "You find Derward's cures disgusting?"

Nessa nodded, but though she still gazed into twining orange and yellow flames, she heard his patronizing amusement—as if she were capable of thinking no deeper than outward appearances. "I do not understand how anyone can believe that that which steals strength is able to restore strength." Glancing sideways to see how he received her argument, she saw silver laughter in his eyes and her long absent temper simmered. He appeared unable to take her logic seriously and that she could not meekly accept.

"Derward said he'd been applying leeches to Lord William thrice daily for a fortnight. I challenged your father to leave off their use for a like time and test if strength were not restored by disuse rather than use." Her chin went up and she met his gaze with a confidence given by complete faith in her cause.

Garrick studied his bride from half-shielded eyes. Her logic was sound but he deemed it likely born more of religious faith than cool reasoning. Had St. Benedict not instructed his followers to make no use of medicinal cures as man's health was in God's hands and it was wrong to interfere with His decisions? Fresh from a Benedictine Abbey, doubtless Nessa, as too many of the people on Tarrant, believed his father's ailments a just punishment for his sins.

"I don't know if he has accepted my challenge but since its issue I've not seen them in use." Nessa calmly expanded her challenge to include this second apparently skeptical person. "I believe his strength is returning for rather than languishing in a chair or his bed while I work in his chamber, he paces from one side to the other like a caged animal, and his words are no longer faint whispers but loud and vehement."

Loud and vehement—sounded as if his father had truly been restored. Garrick's mouth curled in a wry smile. But whether from use of leeches or disuse neither he nor his bride could say.

In the lengthening silence, rising to overshadow Nessa's firm belief in the reasoning, came a fear that he was disgusted with her meddling in family matters. What difference be she right or wrong if Garrick resented her attempt to control his father's healing. Did he see it as another example of women's schemes to control men's lives? She was deeply relieved when a small giggle interrupted.

Both seated before the fire turned toward solar door. Opened a crack, Will's glower showed above. Below, apparently jabbed to halt her poorly timed merriment, Beata held chubby fingers flattened against a tight-closed mouth. Nessa had made it her custom to gather the children about her for a story while Merta aided Maud in seeing to the kitchen's night closing. Never before had the earl lingered so long as to be here when they came, and they were uncertain if they should enter or retreat.

"I wondered what kept you." Shooting a quick glance toward the man at her side, Nessa was relieved to find him smiling. A small and somewhat cynical smile but not the frown for their unexpected arrival she'd half expected. "Come, sit by the fire while I think of a new story for you."

The children trooped in. Nessa scooped Beata into her lap

188

and the small girl cuddled comfortably near. Her brother and sister shared a bench nearby, but Will held diffidently apart from the rest, settling cross-legged on the prickly rush-covered floor. Nessa gave a particularly bright and reassuring smile to the boy surreptitiously studying the powerful lord.

"I've told you of David and Goliath and of Daniel and the lion's den—" Nessa's words trailed off as she considered which Bible story would best satisfy them this night.

"They've heard of Daniel and the lion's den, but have they heard of the lion rescued by a mouse?" Garrick's words drew a round of startled eyes. Having spoken without previous intent, Garrick was nearly as surprised as they.

For his tolerance of the children Nessa was thankful. She'd have asked no more, and thus was shocked by his willingness to participate in this ritual.

"Thought not. Few have heard of a Greek slave named Aesop, fewer yet those who know his tales." Silver eyes held hazel for a long moment before he went on, leaving Nessa tingling from the intensity of the fleeting visual bond. "This story speaks of a mighty lion brought low in a trap formed of heavy netting."

"A fish net?" ventured Beata, sitting up straight.

"Aye, like a fish net, but made of stout rope and much stronger to hold a fearsome beast." Forearms resting on muscular thighs, linked fingers between his knees, and eyes more nearly on a level with the children's, he held his audience spellbound while he told how a tiny mouse had, with patience and unending toil, done what the lion could not and set the great creature free.

Nessa enjoyed his story every bit as much as the children until she realized it must be a part of the Greek book translated to Latin which he'd once promised to share with her. That he hadn't shared it reinforced her certainty that he saw her presence here as the result of disgusting trickery. Moreover, she'd never belong no matter how hard she worked or if the people of Tarrant accepted her. By the time his tale was done she'd nearly lost hope for their marriage and had to rouse herself from descending gloom to shoo the children off to their beds. The younger three left obediently but, again, Will held back. With false bravado he met the earl's questioning silver gaze.

189

"King Henry is the lion of England. Are you his mouse sent to free him from nets of treachery?"

Garrick was startled by the lad's clear perception of a political problem but immediately answered. "Nay, I am no mouse at Henry's feet. As a noble-blooded man I am more a member of his pride. You, young sir, could fill the position of mouse to his lion and aid him free of entangling nets."

Nessa nearly cringed as Will, under the unintended insult, jerked straight, chin up and shoulders back.

"I share the same noble heritage," Will boldly claimed before whirling to run from the room as shameful tears fell.

Brows lowered in puzzlement, Garrick stared after the boy. What meaning lay behind his words? He'd have thought them born of need to impress, even with untruths, had his proud face not been tearstained. How could it be that he was of noble blood? How when he was orphan raised by servant and dressed as serf?

Nessa saw her husband's frown and feared him angered by the boy's claim which he was sure to deem a lie. A baby when the boy's mother was conceived and rarely since childhood residing near, it was little likely that Garrick knew the existence of this unacknowledged nephew. Would he send Will away? To divert his attention she quickly spoke. "My thanks for sharing your tale with us. I fear mine limited and apt to be oft repeated."

Willing to dismiss the perplexing child from his thoughts, Garrick turned toward his wife. Her hands were twisted tight together. Discomforted by his frown? Wanting to ease her tension, he smiled and quietly asked, "You know of Aesop and his tales?"

"Nay." Nessa was reassured by the tempter's smile but, as always when gleaming eyes were so near, her breathing became embarrassingly unsteady. "In the abbey we learned stories from the scriptures—" she rushed to say. "—Or saints' lives. No more." The last trailed into silence. She'd already forgotten both his words and hers under the paralyzing power of his gaze.

Garrick's smile deepened, pleased by this evidence of her response to him. Pray mercy, his plan to earn her willing surrender was nearing its goal.

Caught in a gray whirlpool shot through with blazing silver, Nessa felt drawn into the Ice Warrior's molten core, its flames transferring their heat to her. Deeply submerged, when he rose and broke the bond she felt bereft. Did he mean to leave her now?

The warm glow of cheeks brushed by soft curls escaped from demure coronet of braids gave Garrick joy as he went to a chest at one side of the bed. Nessa watched curiously as he knelt before its carved panels, opened the top and rummaged inside. When he stood and turned toward her again, he held a cloth-wrapped square.

"I owe you my gratitude for all you've done to make this castle so welcoming."

Pleased, Nessa couldn't suppress a dimple-revealing smile.

"You're beautiful when you smile." His words were faint, as if no more than spoken thought.

She shook a head down bent to hide her face, pleasure-warmed and deepened to near the same hue as her cranberry gown. Several more ringlets broke free to snuggle against graceful nape. Fool to be warmed by flattery. She was no beauty and knew it. In payment for her toil did he feel it necessary to produce pretty lies?

Garrick was surprised to realize that she didn't believe him. He didn't lie and she should know it true. He willed her to look up and read the sincerity in his eyes.

As from when first they'd met, she felt his unspoken summons but refused its call, even clenching lashes tight in determined denial. No longer could she continue meeting the power of his gaze. One moment more and she'd throw herself into his arms and beg him to have done with his torment, with subjecting her to enticements he meant not to fulfill.

Garrick moved to the seated woman's side, impelled to prove the truth of his statement for both his sake and hers. "Have you never looked into a mirror or even the smooth surface of a pond?"

Startled by the rough velvet voice all too near, Nessa shook her head more firmly. "Reflections of self encourage the sin of vanity." The words were the instinctive repetition of those she'd often heard in the priests' strictures to others. Yet, beyond an unintended glimpse while fetching water, it was true that she'd looked upon her own reflection as seldom as possible. Not, to her shame, for the sake of avoiding the sin of vanity—an unlikely failing for one such as she—but because she had no wish to be reminded of her lack. Which was probably a sin in itself.

By Garrick's reasoning she'd not only effectively prevented him from pursuing his argument but had again taken the opportunity to remind him of her pious devotion. He studied her crown of soft brown plaits, tresses tightly bound, hidden from firelight that would strike golden sparks in each curl, just as the heat of her natural passions was restrained by religious training. He'd not let it be so. He had roused the fire and tasted the passion in her before and would again—tonight.

"This betrothal gift is belated but one I believe you'll enjoy the more for my knowing your preferences."

Surprised into looking up, Nessa's gaze fell on a book in his outstretched hand. As if in a trance, she reached out to accept and hold it close. Books, painstakingly transcribed, were of great value. She had hoped he'd allow her to read his precious hoard but never had she thought he'd give her one to be her own.

Garrick watched her tenderly smooth the small tome and wished she'd as warmly caress him. He'd surely waited long enough—and to little purpose. Ever busy with her tasks, with caring for his father and the children, she seemed rarely to notice him.

"It contains Aesop's tales, new stories for the children." He hoped in this small way to temper her religious fervor.

Remembering her earlier certainty that she'd never be forgiven, she accepted the gift as token of his pardon for her part in the trickery behind their marriage, and more of his accepting her as integral part of his castle. "I'll cherish every word." Her serious gaze rose to the strong man towering above.

Garrick tumbled into eyes now brown velvet pools and as welcoming as he'd ever seen them. They were wed, and it was time that she accept it. Waiting had only led her to believe he expected no more. He'd not force her to his will, and this inviting vision surely meant there'd be no need. Letting one hand cup her nape, delicate curls clinging to his fingers, he bent toward petal soft lips that parted on a trembling breath.

Fearing some wicked imp would steal the precious moment, she yearned up toward the caress she'd longed for. The first brush of his lips was so light that it was torment. A faint whimper called them back. He fit his mouth to hers with exquisite care, nibbling, teasing until a small hand tangled into thick black strands, pulling him nearer while the book softly fell to the floor.

Garrick came down on his knees beside Nessa's stool and wrapped his arms about her, urging her gentle curves near. Nessa felt as if she'd been stripped of bones as well as rational thought and clung to broad shoulders, wanting the sweet, heady closeness to go on and on while the kiss deepened to a hungry ferocity that grew hotter each moment. A knock broke the aching silence.

Garrick's low growl ended with a foul word he'd never thought to use in a lady's presence. A word Nessa had never thought to hear knowingly spoken in hers, and even less thought to have a hearty wish to echo it.

Face closed into grim lines, Garrick rose and turned to call, "Enter."

Although Sir Rufus let the door swing open, he stopped respectfully one short pace within the private solar. A man of many years, he had no doubt that his arrival had been poorly timed. What with them being newly wed and all.

"The men await your instructions for the morrow."

Garrick nodded, and the white-haired knight withdrew. He was disgusted with himself for forgetting a chore so basic in a haze of desire. The hour for its doing was long past and doubtless men anxious to seek their beds had grown impatient. He looked down at the woman outlined by the fire behind—tempting, so tempting. He desperately wanted their coming together but feared this untimely interruption would see her slipping again behind her shield of piety.

In a frustration of body and spirit, he helplessly shrugged. "I must go and see the matter done."

Nessa nodded, but the dark man had already turned away. Watching him stride from the chamber with a masculine grace near sinful in its beauty, Nessa felt rejected. As so oft before, while she ached with unsatisfied longings, again he'd easily turned away with no sign of like distress. Beyond that one fierce word, he'd gone to ice. It must prove her hopelessly inadequate, unable to arouse in him the depth of passion she felt.

193

First bending to retrieve the precious book, she rose to leave the solar and climb one flight of stairs to the lord's chamber. There, hoping to halt the pain, she busied herself preparing for the night. She undressed, neatly folded her soft gray gown, laid it in the chest on one side of the bed, and placed the volume of Greek tales atop. After washing with water gone tepid and brushing thick curls until they glowed, she stretched out beneath heavy bedcovers. The bed was massive, never meant to hold only one, leastways not one as small as she. She felt lost and more alone than ever before.

In the quiet her thoughts returned to the unexpected gift. Through drapes open on one side to the heat of a still blazing fire she studied the collection of tales lying atop the chest. A betrothal gift. She hadn't even known such traditions existed and berated herself for the lack. If only she had something to give him in return. But what had she of value to him? Many years in an abbey had left her with few possessions and none worthy to be present for a wealthy earl. Nothing was there that he wanted of her—save an heir. That morning in Swinton Keep he'd said it was one thing he needed of her. 'Twas one thing he could not procure by himself. An heir was the only gift she could give him and if he could not find passion enough for her to complete the intimate embrace, then she must initiate the deed.

Taking her responsibilities as lady of the castle seriously, she'd examined its every chamber, save the chained room across from Lord William's. And she knew that the supposedly empty chamber across from this one had been occupied every night. Too embarrassed to let speculation rise, she'd seen to its cleaning herself and never had the deed been mentioned between them.

Before she could fall faint-hearted from the task, Nessa slipped from the bed high above the floor and pulled a coverlet free to wrap about her nude form. She carefully crossed the rush strewn floor and its pricks for bare feet. Easing the chamber door open a crack, she peered up and down the hall dimly lit by oil-fed wall sconces. It was empty. Only faint sounds from the great hall below could be heard. Determined to go now before her courage gave out, tugging the coverlet tight and holding it above the floor, she dashed across the narrow corridor.

The opposite door fell open beneath her touch. She stepped quickly inside. Leaning against its firm planks, she drew a deep breath and struggled to calm her thumping heart. The chamber was empty, and near a cold hearth lay an unmade bed. The servants thought the room unused, and she made it up only on days when she had time and opportunity, and when certain he'd not interrupt her chore. The room was chilly without a fire. She crossed the room and bent to stir coals near gone to dead embers until weak flames licked at the small chunks of wood she tempted them with. Only did she pray she could as easily find the method of stirring his passion to flame. Surely here, in a supposedly empty chamber and in the depths of night, nothing and no one would there be to bring another frustrating end aforetime.

In response to a crude jest by one of his men, a jest about returning to his bride, Garrick laughed as if it were an accepted certainty. But as he began to mount the broad stairway his face went still. He was determined that this night see an end to their mating dance. If she was not ready to welcome him now, she never would be, and he could bear the wait no longer.

He paused at the chamber door seeking inspiration for words to cajole or caresses to seduce a chaste wife. None were forthcoming. Gifts? To earn their last embrace he'd given her the book, the only thing he possessed that he knew she'd treasure. She'd shown no longing for pretty clothes or precious jewels. He grimaced. Never before had he been willing to offer a woman so much as a pin and still they'd pursued him. How was it that the one woman he sought wanted nothing from him? In the end it was him she must take, and he'd just as soon she took him for himself or not at all.

He quietly eased the door open, stepped inside and shut it behind him again. The bed was empty. He turned toward the prie dieu he found so off-putting. It would seem a near sacrilege to make love in the same room—particularly to a former postulant. But she wasn't there. She wasn't in the chamber at all! He slumped against the unmoving planks behind. Here he'd worked himself up to the deed and some protecting spirit (an angel?) had saved her. Likely she'd gone to the chapel to spend the night on her knees in atonement for her fall into earthly realms. It was a bitter thought. Biting his lip, he pulled himself up, opened the door, and resolutely stepped from the room of disappointment.

Disgusted with the pain welling up inside, he named himself fool same as others he'd disdained for allowing a woman such power in their lives. The chamber where he slept would be cold, as cold as his soul and a just retreat for a man of ice. His cynicism was no comfort as he opened its door. Unexpected warmth rushed toward him even as his attention was caught by the leaping dance of flames glowing against soot-blackened hearth. But not even the beauty of the welcome fire could turn his stunned gaze from the profile of a figure revealed by its light. Sitting on a low stool, wrapped only in dark coverlet and soft clouds of gilded curls, was the one he'd thought beyond his reach. Draped cloth had slipped down slender arms to reveal the long line of an elegant throat and frame shoulders of transclucent pearl. That she hadn't heard his entry over the sound of a crackling blaze was clear. He studied her beauty, all the more precious for its subtlety, a treasure not shared with the masses but his alone.

With a knight's training to silent approach, Garrick came to stand beside Nessa. Though she heard no sound, she felt his presence and, as if beyond being surprised by him, she slowly looked up to meet a gaze gone flashing silver. Those bright gleams were a warning of danger but instead she fell victim to their sweet assault, feeling their touch as fully as the brush of the fingers that reached out to caress her cheek. Again his ice armor opened to tempt her into its molten core. A temptation calling for her reckless submission and one she'd no will to deny.

Trembling sweetness rested on the lips Garrick brushed with flame. His curved when he felt the tremor spread to shake her from head to toe. Wrapping his big hands about her waist he pulled her up against his long form, leaving the concealing coverlet behind in a disconsolate heap. He wanted to feel those delicious reactions, know himself their source. Never before with a virgin, never before had he been the first, the one to initiate untutored responses—a heady thought that lit fires in his blood.

Only the strength of masculine arms held Nessa upright on legs afflicted with weakness. She'd come to give herself into his embrace but was amazed at her own audacity in walking into the tempter's power, overwhelmed by his ability to play on her senses like a master minstrel the strings of his lute. She feared herself only able to fall far short of his needs, to disappoint him in every way, and she hid her face in the curve of his throat.

Burning with awareness of each warm brush of enticing curves, Garrick exercised every shred of control he possessed to handle her with the tenderness she deserved, determined to carry her past her own restraints to the wild sweetness beyond. He wound his fingers in thick curls, lifting them to bare her vulnerable nape. "Your skin's hot," he whispered, nibbling the smooth expanse.

Beyond rational thought Nessa spoke her thoughts aloud. "Ice burns."

A low laugh rumbled as his lips moved to nuzzle into the silky mass of soft, soft curls atop the head which embarrassment had buried against his chest. If he was ice, then she was the sun that thawed it, like a warm spring day melts a winter-frozen pond.

Forehead resting against the source of the sound, the reverberations were a magical call and without conscious decision she fell to temptation. Her face lifted and lips touched the firm skin of a sun-bronzed throat with insatiable curiosity, an addictive pleasure that led her to explore.

Garrick went still beneath the tentative brush of gentle lips over his throat and down to skin bared by laces loosened at the neck of his tunic. He struggled to remember the importance of moving slow and not frightening her with the strength of his desire, but in the end a sound far different than laughter rumbled free. His groan startled Nessa, and she jerked back.

"Nay, sweeting." His voice was deep and darkly textured. "Your caresses are a luxury I'd likely die for." Suddenly he withdrew his arms and pulled the offensive cloth barrier between his flesh and hers over his head and flung it carelessly aside.

Nessa's breath caught painfully in her throat at the stunning sight of a hard male chest, all strong muscle with a wedge of black curls tapering in a vee from below broad shoulders to disappear beneath the chausses tied at narrow hips. He was truly an incredible temptation in human form. In that moment she wanted nothing more of life than to feel its heat. Her hands curled to prevent the shameful deed.

Her brown gaze, so intense it felt like a phantom touch, licked teasing flames across Garrick's control and seared him with need for the reality of a caress only a breath beyond reach. He lifted her hands and lay them against his chest. "I watched you caress that fool book and ached to have your fingers on me."

The feel of firm muscle and smooth skin beneath her curled hands raised an excitement so strong Nessa bit her lip. Here was the opportunity to fulfill wicked longings, yet, restrained by the invisible chains of inhibition, she couldn't move until he flattened her fingers against burning flesh and tangled them in wiry curls. Suddenly nothing existed but the feel of him, all heat and iron-thews beneath, and the devastating sensations that surged into being with this freedom to touch where she would. Beneath ever more daring caresses across the tempting plains of the massive chest rising and falling heavily, she could feel a potent hunger growing, spreading its raging need to her.

Garrick's low growl broke a tension stretched so taut it must bring action. She looked up into silver ice eyes melted to smoke as he let his hands sweep down from fragile shoulders to the small of her back and from thence up her spine, pulling her into the curve of his long, hard body.

The shocking pleasure of her bare skin crushed to the heat of his broad chest sent a wild shudder through her and heavy lashes drifted down on a soft moan. She'd have fallen had he not caught her in strong arms to carry her toward the waiting bed. The covers were rumpled from his near sleepless night past, and looked welcoming, as if they'd already played within disarranged folds. Shoving them aside, he laid her there but held back to possessively study the delicate perfection of her elegant curves, alabaster and coral amidst a frame of luxurious fire-gilded curls.

Nessa felt cool sheets against her back as strong arms drew away. Gazing up in fear that even now he would leave her, she tumbled into eyes gone near all charcoal and just as hot. Snared by their power, she couldn't look away as he came down to sit down beside her and let his fingertips lightly trace from the base of her throat through the shallow valley between her breasts to explore the tiny indentation of her navel. They started a tantalizing return journey over the same path. Her head arched back and eyes closed as a strangled gasp escaped her tight throat.

Her helpless reaction to his touch fascinated Garrick. Up from the satin texture of her tiny waist slowly, slowly he let his now outspread hand glide over sensitive skin that trembled.

Nessa felt the maddening caress climb the first gentle swell and approach the summit only to hesitate a breath from its tip. Her breath caught in an agony of waiting. As the seconds stretched into an aching eternity heavy-weighted lashes rose to find his near black eyes intense on her small breasts. From her lips came a whimper born of fear for his disappointment in her limited endowments which near choked her—until his palm moved up in a warm, slightly abrasive caress that drove all thought before it.

Filled with a hunger undreamt of and mindlessly wanting to return the same shattering excitement, she reached out to rub her palms over him in imitation of his caresses. But the touch of firm flesh was not enough. She twined her arms about him, recklessly arching up to brush her curves across the sweet rasp of wiry curls.

Through a fog of desire, Garrick fought to remember that where this one woman was concerned there were limits to his control. Anxious not to allow surrender to a passion so fierce it would render more pain than unavoidable for a virgin, he put his hands to her shoulders and, through effort of iron will, did not pull her closer but rather held back an embrace too inflaming. Moving his palms up to cup her face for a tender kiss, he eased her down and stretched out at her side.

Despite Garrick's best intentions, their kiss burst into hungry flames. Nessa felt she'd been turned to molten liquid and flowed toward Garrick like a river downhill. The feel of her melded to his every angle and plane was more than Garrick could resist. He wrapped her tightly in his arms, crushing her close while savoring lips sweeter than mulled wine and hotter than fire.

Beneath the clinging silk of Nessa's curls Garrick's hands swept down to cup her derriere and pull her tight against his raging need. Instinctively she twisted nearer, inciting him to rock her hips intimately against his in primitive rhythm with the plundering of his tongue in the warm cavern of her mouth. Only the barrier of his linen chausses saved her from a taking too violent. The knowledge was a shame to Garrick and, fighting to temper the heat of his blood, he rolled to his back, rigid and gritting his teeth in an effort to force control on fiery passion.

The rush of cold air over skin turned to flame by his wickedly exciting caresses brought Nessa only far enough from the haze of the tempter's fires to convince her that he meant to leave her—now when she could not bear the loss. He would close his ice armor safely about himself and leave her here shuddering in the purgatory of unfulfilled desire.

"No!" The cry of denial came out half plea for surcease, half moan of pain for certain loss.

Garrick lifted up on one elbow to lean over the rare beauty in his bed. Firelight turned to liquid gold the silent tears streaming from the corner of her eyes to their destiny among the curls spread in disarray across rumpled bedcovers. They smote him with guilt such as he'd never before known.

"Sweeting, is it so hard for you to give yourself to me? Would you have me leave?"

Nessa wildly shook her head, eyes clenched shut.

"Then why do you cry?"

Pain, pain to admit her passion when he could turn so easily from her that even now he offered to go. "I thought you *were* leaving."

"Nay," he bent to tenderly kiss the tears from flushed cheeks. A gentle touch that flamed and fed the blaze of her consuming need. "Only do I rid myself of the last impediment to our joining." And restore enough sanity to make the deed a pleasure to you, he added silently. What relief that she'd not wanted him to depart for 'twas doubtful he could have found the strength.

Nessa peeked up and fell helpless to the heat in his near black gaze. Sinful as it might be, she couldn't turn her eyes from him as he rose to strip off chausses. Muscles sun-bronzed and glowing in firelight rippled with the action. When he stood before her nude, she was stunned anew by his masculine perfection. Unbelievable to think that he was hers. Filled with breathless anticipation and aching hungers, when he came down to her, nothing could hold her from him. And this time Garrick did not try.

He gloried in the certainty that she'd found his form as exciting as he did hers and welcomed her silken flesh against his, letting her experience his powerful contours, without crushing her to his strength. Nessa wrapped her arms around his neck, tangled fingers into cool strands of black and savored the texture of the hard plains of his back while he played again the fiery beauty of the tempter's song across the desire-tight nerves of her willing body.

When once more she helplessly writhed against him, Garrick felt the end of his control slip away. He couldn't hold himself from moving against her in a rhythm as old as life. One hand speared into the wealth of curls behind her head as he rolled her to her back and rose above.

"I've dreamed of your soft body clinging to me as willingly as your curls cling to my fingers." He slid one leg between hers and shifted to lie full atop her slender length. Nessa cried out with pleasure under his full weight, as hot and strong as iron fresh from forgers' fire. And as he lifted her hips to aid their slow joining, she instinctively twined silken legs about him. A moment of pain was lost in the inferno their joined bodies created. She was certain the desperate pleasure could not increase nor the fire burn fiercer—until he resumed his wicked rhythm, rocking them deeper into the flames. The tempter's song grew wilder and wilder. At last, accompanied by his deep growl and her soft cry, it shattered on a piercingly sweet note.

In the afterglow, she snuggled into Garrick's embrace, damp with a passion previously unknown. He felt blessed. In all the years with all the women, never before had his partners in passion been inexperienced and never before could he truly believe himself source of their desire. They who'd known many knew the way to please, the way to simulate desire, and he'd never been certain he was the source of their response. Nessa was different, special, real. Too honest to hide her reactions to his every caress, too inexperienced to pretend a feeling untrue.

❧§ Chapter 16 §❧

A long blade of dawnlight falling through the chamber's arrow slit pierced sweet gray mists of contented slumber to rouse a reluctant sleeper. Eyes shuttered by thick lashes, Nessa slowly came aware of the firm pillow beneath her cheek—firm, warm, and furred. In short, a broad masculine chest. Tender lips curled with hazy memories of warm loveplay and she snuggled closer against Garrick's whole long form. Even deep in slumber his arm bound her close. Ice? Not the night past. Nay, then had he been tempter to wicked pleasures and source of welcome fires.

Something nibbled at the edge of her content and a frown puckered delicate brows. No matter her wish elsewise, the persistent annoyance wouldn't abate, disturbing her peaceful drift on the gentle haze between dreams and reality. She forced one lid to lift and squinted into a light too bright to fall from their chamber's west facing window. Both eyes snapped open. In their chamber they were not, although soon Merta would be there to rouse her for the day's duties. 'Twas an awkward position. She'd pay near any price to remain at Garrick's side until he roused, perhaps to renew their passionate games as he had so oft during dark hours. Yet, she lacked sophistication to easily deal with the questions that would be raised once her bed in the chamber across was seen to be unused. Particularly as she had worked so hard to ensure others unaware that her husband slept elsewhere.

Carefully sliding from Garrick's hold, Nessa eased from his side. Once standing, she moved to retrieve the discarded bedcover from where it had fallen before the now dead fire. She wrapped its softness tight about her bare form while studying a magnificent male body. Aye, she confirmed anew, temptation incarnate. But the thrills the sight sent through her were not born of fear. His tempter's spell still held strong sway and she nearly drifted back to his side but abruptly stopped, reminding herself of the necessity for an immediate departure. She forced her gaze away from his enticements and lifted trailing cloth to ease the path of leavetaking from her lover's chamber as well as his bed.

Back in the lord's true chamber, which henceforth she hoped they would share, Nessa loosed and threw the coverlet over its intended repose. Studying its effect carefully, she bent to twitch it askew on one side and then nodded. Now the disarray was appropriate for a night spent within. She washed with tepid water before slipping on a plain linen camise and bent to lift from a chest the first gown which came to hand. Deep green folds of wool slid easily over a cream toned underblouse. She'd have to wait for Merta to close the back laces. But, having met her goal to prevent embarrassing discoveries, she let tense muscles relax.

The beautifully carved and polished prie-dieu she'd brought from Salisbury Tower had been settled into a shadowed corner. Falling to her knees on its low, padded bench, she began her morning devotions, silently thanking God for gifting her with this home and this husband. To her thanks she added a prayer that their coming together would result in the heir Garrick sought and another prayer for herself. A prayer that her husband would be able to accept her as true wife from this day onward.

Chilled by the loss of a mutual heat, Garrick came awake to find Nessa gone. Had she risen, as he'd feared, ashamed of their heated play? Had her disgust of the man who'd drawn her down into earthly realms been increased by his taking of her offered duty and turning it into more than she wanted to give, forcing her to feel the pleasures of humanity rather than sublime martyrdom for her sister?

A man of action unwilling to leave questions unanswered, he abruptly sat up. The room was empty. He reached for his chausses and jerked them on. Without bothering to don a shirt, he flung open his chamber door and moved to the one opposite. Pausing, hands clenched, he forced his responses under the icy control built of years. Only then did he silently ease the iron bound planks wide. He took one step into the room and halted at the sight of his wife on her knees in prayer. The answer he'd sought now seemed clear. No doubt she begged forgiveness for yielding to temptations of the flesh. The certainty that she found their loving a shameful deed hit him with the force of a giant's lance thrust, sundering even the shield of his suspicions and driving deep into his heart. He fell back, quietly drawing the door closed, and returned to a chamber grown cold after their night of shared fires.

Nessa remained in prayer until a light rapping broke her concentration. Calling entry to Merta, she rose. Merta was startled by the radiance of her lady's smile, but relieved to see the countess happy. She'd a boon to ask and though she never doubted her lady willing to help, it was easier speaking to a woman clearly content.

Never one to waste time in idle chat when important realities were pending, Merta went to the subject immediately. "Milady, a matter there is for which I begs your aid."

Her maidservant's request surprised Nessa. 'Twas the first time she'd asked a thing for herself. "Tell me what you seek, and I'll do whatever I can."

Nervous now that she'd begun, Merta moved behind Nessa and began pulling back laces together before continuing. "Recall you the serf who brung ladders for aid in whitening tops of walls?"

Nessa vaguely recalled a husky young man of pleasant manner and laughing eyes. Holding her yet unbrushed mass of tangled curls above Merta's busy hands, Nessa nodded.

"This day," Merta gave a final tug, tied the laces, and stepped back, "he goes to the earl's court in the great hall."

The silence lengthened while Merta drew a deep breath before plunging on. "He'll be after permission for us to wed."

Nessa whirled. "What wonderful news! I am so very pleased for you." Laughing with delight for another's entering the ranks of the happy wed, she took the other woman's hands in hers and squeezed. The fingers she held were ice cold and Merta looked anything but joyful. Had she completely misunderstood? "Is it a match you would forestall?" Still holding chilled hands, she leaned forward to look direct into serious mud-brown eyes. "Is it that you wish me to intercede to see the deed denied?"

Cheeks gone deep red, Merta vehemently shook her head. "Oh, nay. Oram is all I desire and 'tis the opposite boon I asks."

"Gladly I would stand for you before my lord and tell him your pleasure in the choice, but I doubt 'tis necessary." Nessa was puzzled. Such matters were dealt with quickly in every lord's domain. Only if parents refused or claims were made by those free and, therefore, of more weight would such requests be denied.

Merta's eyes glistened as with a wavering voice she explained. " 'Tis Sir Erdel, that snake, who seeks to foil our happiness."

Nessa, fond of the cheerful girl ever willing to lend hand and merry banter to any task, hated to see her so low. She released Merta's hands to put an arm around her waist, leading her to a chair before the hearth. Untended through the night, only a few coals glowed weakly among gray ashes. When the taller girl was seated, face hidden by shaking fingers, Nessa knelt in front and waited to learn what mischief the unsavory knight intended.

Struggling to gather together the shreds of her composure, Merta scrubbed damp cheeks and spoke again. "When I were little more'n a child, but early grown, and Erdel an arrogant squire, he caught me alone behind the stable where I were slopping the pigs." A sob tore free from Merta's tight throat, but she resolutely continued, tears drenching pale cheeks. "He ripped my gown and meant to use me for he said 'twas the right of free man to take a serf at his pleasure. Oram come to drive the cows to pasture and saved me for he was bigger and stronger than Erdel then as now.

"He's been my friend and protector ever since. We loves one another, but Erdel hates Oram—and me—and says as he'll have me first. He can't win in physical combat against

Oram, and for a knight to bring broadsword to unarmed serf would be to shame his blade and himself. Yet, to avenge himself on us, as free man he can claim me today and keep us apart. Then I knows Oram will be driven to an action what'll see him punished harsh for his attack on a free knight.'' Her voice crescendoed in a wail of despair.

Nessa moved from Merta's side to the three-legged metal stand that held a basin within the iron circle at its top. She emptied its contents on dwindling coals and into it poured what water remained in the ewer on the shelf above. When she'd earlier used the first the once warm liquid had been tepid. What was now left had gone cold. Lifting a clean cloth square from the stack beside, Nessa dipped it into the cool water, wrung the excess out, and folded it while returning to a sniffling Merta.

"When you feel prepared,'' Nessa quietly said as she gently applied the cloth to red puffed eyes, "I'll accompany you to the great hall and stand for you against Sir Erdel.''

Below the damp square a radiant smile bloomed. As their last hope, Merta put her trust in the countess. Soon she'd regained composure, and followed Nessa down the steep stairs, only traces of a pink flush about her eyes and nose hinting earlier distress.

One hand against the cold stone arch, Nessa paused in the great hall's entrance. It was filled with an odd assortment of folk, yet amazingly quiet for so large a gathering. In deference to the lord's court, those awaiting their turn before his judgment risked no more noise than occasionally shuffled feet or a murmur in undertones to fellow petitioners.

The high table was cleared of white cloth and burdened only with parchment and inkwell, utensils of the scribe seated beside the earl ready to record each judgment. Standing erect, white hair spiked upward with pride equal to the coxcomb of a strutting cock, Sir Rufus stood in the open space below the dais to summon each petitioner in order of arrival. Garrick sat in his high-backed chair at the table's center, eyes narrowed as he listened impassively but with complete attention to a ragged serf.

"A piglet born to me only sow was stole and roasted by that rotter.'' Cheeks purpled with renewed rage, he flung a condemning and none too clean hand toward a stout man waiting at Sir Rufus's side.

The damning gesture was too great a provocation for the accused, who bounded forward, overfed belly shaking, to vehemently deny the other's claim. "Can't steal a thing what's mine!" His belligerent words were directed at the first man but when he turned to his lord an ingratiating smile sat uncomfortably on anger-stiff lips. "The piglet were born of his sow but sired by me boar after he promised me a quarter of the litter for the deed. He give me none, and so's I took what was mine."

"Hah! He admits his crime." The first man nearly crowed.

"Weren't a crime. 'Twas mine by pact and I gots two who heard your oath." He motioned the others forward and each supported his claim.

"Were your sickly boar the sire, I'd a given 'em to you. But me sow would be left barren if I'd not got Clyde's boar to see the deed done proper. And when the piglets come, I give those promised to the sire's owner, Clyde." He put his hands on bony hips and met the stout man's glare.

Sir Rufus waved yet another man to stand between the foes. The unfortunate Clyde looked fearfully from one man to the other and was near trembling when his gaze rose to the earl. "Me boar is the sire, hence I gots the three piglets in me sty."

The right to make judgments on one's own domain was a right jealously guarded by all nobles, and Garrick took seriously his duty to make just decisions. After questioning them all, he determined that either boar could equally as well have been the sire and ordered the sow's owner to see that each boar's owner receive three piglets. When the man protested that then after he'd given the lord's portion into castle keeping he'd be left with but a quarter of the litter, Garrick suggested it would make a fine lesson to be certain in the future that the first attempt was a failure and the contract accepted null by the one before committing to another.

Nessa listened intently and was again pleased to find her husband a man of justice. It gave her courage for the dispute likely approaching as Rufus next motioned Oram to step forward.

Cap crushed nervously between large hands and unruly brown hair combed into an unnatural tidiness, Oram stood before his lord with an appropriate deference but no servility

207

on his rugged face. "I come to ask approval of a marriage betwixt Merta and me."

Garrick found his straightforward words a pleasant change from the ingratiating compliments that too oft preceded such requests. He'd smiled and opened his mouth to give his approval when another stepped in front of Oram.

"I claimed the maidservant long past." Sir Erdel spoke loud and looked behind to Oram with a smirk of arrogant triumph. "A free knight comes afore a serf."

Nessa saw a dangerous flush rise to Oram's broad cheeks and knew her moment had come. Speak now, elsewise watch the attack that would see Oram consigned to the harsh judgment mandated by laws prohibiting a serf's attack on a free man.

"Sir Erdel's claim is of wicked intent and wicked attempt." Nessa had the attention of every person in the crowded hall as she calmly walked from the stairwell archway to stand below her husband on the dais. "Moreover, your knight means to claim my maidservant not for God-blessed union but sinful adultery."

Garrick had been stunned by his wife's sudden appearance, but silver ire flashed as he studied the palm-joined hands at her waist and looked past uptilted chin to meet a steady hazel gaze. By her argument, once again, she proved her devotion to righteous ways, for no one living with the queen and bred on tales of the king's passing liaisons could possibly believe all unions were first church-blessed. Yet, even without her speaking he would have declared against Sir Erdel who intended no good to a loyal servant. Ever determined to mete out justice, he spoke.

"Sir Erdel, your designs are ill-meant and will find no support in Castle Tarrant." A gaze of ice shards cut to the heart of the knight's overbearing conceit.

Sir Erdel fell back two paces beneath the fierce assault while Oram's jaw dropped. The furious loser whirled and for a long moment turned a poisonous gaze upon Nessa.

Nessa cringed beneath Sir Erdel's unexpected glare and turned to gaze after him as he stomped from the hall. As if a pall had been lifted by his exit, from the hindmost fringes of the crowd Merta dashed forward to enthusiastically hug her.

"My blessings for your wedding day." The earl nodded toward Oram, then turned silver eyes upon Merta who stood

208

between the countess and her soon-to-be husband. "And to you as well."

Though relieved by the departure of Sir Erdel and his spite, even her happiness for the couple was diluted by the cold emanating from the earl. Had her appearance in his court been such a wicked thing? Had she broken some unknown law against intercession? Or did he simply find her action too strong a comparison to Eleanor's independent ways and interference in royal matters? While Oram swept Merta into a joyous embrace, Nessa's gaze went to Garrick. She felt frozen by the impact, unable to move until he turned to Sir Rufus with request to lay the next matter before him.

To leave the space before the lord bare, Nessa had begun to follow the happy couple from the hall when Sir Rufus's words caught her attention. Stepping behind a cluster of men, she listened.

"Lord Conal's man is here asking to speak private with you."

"Sir Jasper?" Garrick asked in surprise.

"Aye, my lord."

Certain that only an important purpose would bring the knight here, Garrick stood immediately, gray eyes looking over the faces of the crowd. "Stay. I'll soon return." With his unblinking gaze he silently assured them that he'd not unfairly end their day for grievances and justice, but would come back to listen until they'd all been heard. Attention again on his white-haired knight, he directed, "Bring Sir Jasper to me in the solar above."

"That I will do, but he asks also that Lady Nessa be present." Knowing his lord would be displeased by the request, Sir Rufus held his voice as rigidly composed as his features.

Already impassive, Garrick's face now seemed coated by frost. What possessed either friend Conal or Sir Jasper to make a public demand most men would take for insult? Though Swinton was both dowry and part of Nessa's dower, so long as he lived the land and its chattels were his to use as he willed. He forced a cold smile and answered with deceptive mildness.

"Aye, Baron Wryborne knows her interest in her child-hood home and is ever one to see to a woman's happiness." His cynical words reduced the apparent insult to an affectionate jest about Conal's desire to emulate the chivalrous manners of the minstrel's legendary knights such as Gawain and Lancelot.

Breath caught in her throat by the request came out with a gasp when Garrick stepped down from the dais. She whirled and scurried up the steps before he could reach the first. Throwing the bedchamber door open, she dashed across the room to collapse on the small stool at the table before the hearth. That Conal had insisted she be present proved he'd remembered his promise to send her word of any danger to his friend—and that a message had been sent meant there was a threat. Palm-joined hands pressed to her lips, she sought to steady her breathing and force control on scattered thoughts, achieving only minor success before a tall dark figure filled the yet open doorway.

"Pray join me in the solar. We've been summoned to hear a message from Lord Conal." By long practice Garrick's low tone was devoid of emotion. He more than half believed his own excuse for Conal's action. Surely the only culprit was his lack of guile.

Nessa studied her husband's emotionless features for a long moment but couldn't tell if he'd seen her wild flight only steps ahead of him. She nodded and rose with as much grace as still-shaking knees allowed. Preceding him from the chamber, she wondered whether his irritation grew from anger at her interference or Conal's ill-thought action. Mayhap neither was the real source and his dark mood was born of disappointment with their past night's play—a heart-crushing possibility. But, though she'd thought it a pleasure beyond belief, she hadn't the experience to judge against that he surely possessed.

Sir Rufus waited at the solar door, Conal's man at his side. At their approach he pushed ironbound planks open and moved aside for them to enter. Garrick waved Nessa to a chair. She settled upon it with relief. 'Twas a miracle she'd made the near endless journey without either faltering or weaving like a sotted fool.

Garrick chose not to sit but rather took a stance before the hearth, hands clasped behind his back and legs planted wide. His chin rose as Sir Jasper moved into the room while Sir Rufus closed the door as he departed.

Nessa recognized the importance of the visit not alone by

the tactless demand for her presence but also by the fact that the knight had come to them straight from his steed, travel-grimed and mail clad.

"Lord Garrick." Sir Jasper bowed low to his host. "I've been sent to bring news from the court."

Black brows rose. "From the court? Have you not, then, been at Swinton Keep?" And, Garrick silently wondered, if not news of Swinton, why was Nessa's presence required?

"Aye, we've remained within Swinton's boundaries, save for Lord Conal's pilgrimages to St. Margaret's. This is news had of a traveling minstrel fresh from the king's company; news Lord Conal believes you should know." Sir Jasper paused, hand on sword hilt, waiting for the earl to acknowledge the source.

"What had the minstrel to say of such import it needs send you here and with such urgency that you've not taken the time to refresh yourself before delivering it to me?" He refused to mention the slight in the demand for Nessa's presence. With eyes narrowed to silver slits, Garrick awaited the answer.

"Only danger to you would force such haste." Aware that the earl would doubt the truth of his message, Sir Jasper's tension increased. He forced further words through nerve-gritted teeth. "He claimed to have been present when Prince John pestered his father for greater possessions, like as his brothers have had."

Garrick's short, derisive laugh interrupted the other. "No news in that. 'Tis the spoiled princeling's vocation. The only one for which he shows true talent."

Sir Jasper cleared his throat and began anew. "The news is the king's response. Under the prince's constant whining, King Henry promised—Lord Conal says rashly and doubtless in unthinking frustration to see his son quiet—"

"What? What did he promise?" Garrick demanded. 'Twas unlike the sturdy knight to dither and hedge his words with another's.

Anxious to have done with the unpleasant message, Sir Jasper immediately answered. "He promised Prince John would have the lands and title of the next earl who died without heir." Lord Conal was young and apt to action without proper planning, yet Sir Jasper would never dispute an order directly given, least of all a duty entrusted to him

211

in honor of his loyalty. Thus, he'd come and done all as directed.

"The prince is betrothed to the heiress of the greatest earldom in all England." Firelight gleamed against night-dark hair as Garrick shook his head, speaking more to himself than the other. "What need has he of mine?"

"Betrothed for a decade, but not wed, not earl, and in control of neither the land nor its wealth." Sir Jasper rationally pointed out. He didn't agree with the way the message had been sent, but believe in the danger he did.

Garrick doubted that the minstrel had ever been to Henry's court. If he had, why would he be traveling as far afield as Swinton? Nay, more probable, he'd been sent from Eleanor—known patroness of minstrels. Sent, moreover, to the young and gullible Conal. Certainly Sir Gilfrey had gone to his liege lady and told her that young Lord Conal had taken temporary custody of Swinton Keep. During their time in Salisbury the treacherous queen had likely recognized the young man as one easily fooled. Yet, despite renewed irritation that Nessa had been brought to hear the whole, he'd not insult his friend by openly disputing the story's origin. Rather, he'd wait to see what followed.

"I thank you for making the journey," Garrick told the knight. "And I trust you'll tarry the night. Knowing, as I do, the limited meals of travels even leisurely embarked, I'm sure you'll appreciate a few morsels to tide you until the evening meal. Seek out Maud, our new cook." Vexation aside, he was amused when Sir Jasper brightened. The knight had visited here often enough to remember meals poorly prepared and poorly served. "You'll be provided with an abundance of fine-tasting foods."

Certain the prince was avaricious enough to wreak any villainy, Nessa recognized a clear danger to Garrick in the warning Conal had sent. This new menace, when added to Sir Gilfrey's threats and the knowledge of a near-fatal rock missile, buried her beneath a great weight of dread. Only could she thank God most earnestly that Sir Gilfrey, supporter of the queen, was unlikely ever to meet Prince John, his father's son all through. Their efforts joined into one would be horrifying indeed.

As Sir Jasper turned to go out in search of the castle cook, his eyes met the countess's and both recognized in the other

212

a sincere concern for the earl's safety. Once the door had closed upon the knight's back, although apprehensive of his dark mood, Nessa's fear for Garrick drove words of caution from her lips.

"For the sake of his greed, I worry the prince will do you harm." Her voice was soft but seemed to echo loud in her ears.

Garrick examined Nessa coldly. Her alarm sounded sincere, yet his long-ingrained distrust of women rose like a wall between them. By this apparent distress was she subtly reinforcing the queen's attempt to drive a wedge of doubt between him and his king? One so great he would give up his efforts on Henry's behalf, even break with his liege lord to support further rebellion?

Seated beneath his emotionless study and fighting against its uncomfortable weight, Nessa rose to meet him on a more equal footing—to little purpose as he was so tall he still towered above. He seemed certain to deny this impending threat as he had others before, and her anxiety for him overcame even her sense of helplessness in the face of his closed ice armor. She moved to his side and laid a small hand on his powerful arm.

"Only would I beg you to take great care as you go, guard against unsuspected foes." She felt his muscles tighten beneath her touch and looked up into eyes gone to silver ice.

After one night in his arms did she believe her powers over him strong enough to sway his intent? Yet, how could it be true of a woman who so oft in one day's time had shown him her sorrow for the loss of religious life? His thoughts were in turmoil as if a melee had commenced within his mind. Fears for her treacherous guilt on one side strove against the near conviction of her basic piety on the other. And in the midst all the while he longed for assurance of her innocence in either deed.

Garrick inclined his dark head and then, as if her touch pained him, abruptly pulled away to march from the chamber. Falling into a well of despair, Nessa stumbled back to the lord's chamber, where fear-given strength deserted her. She stumbled to the bed and collapsed across its wide surface. First by interference and then by spoken concern she'd driven her husband from her. A deed that would thwart her only weapon in his defense, the bearing of an heir—

unless, and she prayed it be so, one already nestled within. Arms wrapped protectively about her flat stomach, she curled up like a wounded child and let her anxieties pour forth in a torrent of tears.

As the flood eased, she forced herself to calmly review the warning, to seek some method of ensuring the earl's continued health. In very little time she accepted the wretched truth that beyond waiting and worrying there was nothing she could do alone. Garrick had proven himself bound to deny the warnings of others and to distrust any word she spoke. Alone she couldn't see him safe. She needed the help of another, another such as the baron who'd been a true friend, truer than Garrick knew. If only she'd had the opportunity to speak privately with Sir Jasper. The possibility was remote—or was it? While the earl had returned to the people waiting, the knight had gone to seek a meal. Could she slip down and, shielded by the crowd, pass unnoticed into the kitchen?

Nessa jumped up to splash cool water on flushed cheeks, scrub them dry, and hurry down winding stairs. Peeking around an edge of the arched entrance she found the hall yet filled with a mass of people all grouped about the dais, and she easily moved unseen along its outer boundaries.

A short step within the kitchen Nessa paused. On one wall the large room housed two massive hearths with bake ovens between. On the other wall were shelves for tidy storage of pots and platters and hooks to keep a variety of utensils close to hand. Down the center ran a line of work tables. Sir Jasper sat at the one nearest. As they were midway between meals, other than he, inside were only two young boys turning spitted pigs over the fires and a third hauling in loads of wood to feed hungry flames.

Feeling like a stuffed partridge ready for table himself, Sir Jasper rose from the "few morsels" provided to tide him over 'til evening repast. The new cook, Maud, had bustled in to prepare something more like a feast before rushing off to see to the selection of proper greens for a salad. She had fears for the freshness of both the purslayne and rosemary if they were gathered from the kitchen garden by any but herself. He turned to find the earl's quiet bride in the doorway. Despite suspiciously rosy face and shiny nose, she was pretty, and he smiled gently.

Nessa appreciated the knight's tactful lack of comment on, or even visible acknowledgment of, the signs of her distress. She waited no longer but came forward to speak immediately in a tone so low the others would not hear.

"Warn your lord that his friend will surely fail to take heed of his words." Nessa's tightly laced fingers turned white beneath the pressure exerted. "Pray give the baron my plea for his continued vigilance against growing threats."

Sir Jasper nodded. "The warning already would I have given." Warm was his smile for the woman so honestly concerned for her wary husband. "Once for him and twice for you. Yet, you must know that, with or without our request, the baron would guard over his friend's safety."

᪥ Chapter 17 ᪥

Our lady's a beauty right enough, a beauty as much within as without.''

Merta's words brought their unseen subject to a halt inside the stairwell's shadows. How could she enter the great hall close upon a comment so warm? As Nessa hovered betwixt retreat and advance, from beyond the corner's edge another voice sounded.

"A beauty?" The man's tone dripped with scorn. "Nay, so plain she fades into nothing aside her sister, Aleria—the one meant to wed the earl."

Nessa's hands came together and twisted painfully, a pale imitation of the hurt Sir Erdel's disparaging remark sent lancing through the fledgling self-confidence already lacerated and left in tatters by a fortnight of her husband's withdrawal. The loud hum of murmurs that followed proved the hall was crowded and each person there had heard the damning words.

"Another was meant for our lord?" A voice Nessa recognized as that of a young squire asked the question she dreaded. "How then came this lady to us?"

"By the same feminine deceit disdained by our Ice Warrior. The Lady Aleria stole away to marry the simple knight

216

she loved while a supposedly pious postulant, Sister Agnes, connived with the scheming queen to wed Earl Garrick.''

The cold fingers Nessa pressed against shame-scorched cheeks could not restrain their heat. Now all would know her part in an ill-done and disgraceful deed. Those who heard it not firsthand would hear it from another, and the news would spread with the fierce fervor of wind-fanned flames. Mortified, she was certain the people of Tarrant would condemn the plain and wicked Agnes who'd conspired in such foul trickery. A strange ringing sound, like a bell tolling within her head, drowned out the steady drone of voices beyond the wall. As the ringing grew louder and louder, in an effort to halt the sudden spinning of her world, she flattened herself against the surely unmoving stone wall.

"What were that?" Merta, closest to the stairwell opening, had heard an odd rustling sound followed by a sharp crack. Fearing prying tattle overheard by their lord, she backed several steps, leaned around the corner of the doorframe, and gasped. Like a useful cloth discarded once the task was complete, Lady Nessa lay in a crumpled heap.

"Fools." The single scathing word cut through the great hall's chatter to silence.

Angered by both the speaker of thoughtless words and his curious audience, Merta hurried to kneel at the lady's side. Others came but those without useful hands to lend she glared into retreat.

"I'll carry her above," offered a penitent Oram. No matter her manner of arrival, she'd brought to Castle Tarrant a warmth and peace not found for many a year. 'Twas a disgrace to him that he'd quietly listened when he should've defended the gentle lady.

Merta hovered near as Oram's strong arms lifted her friend, but before following him above she directed young Will to fetch Maud as quick as might be.

Sir Erdel remained just beyond the stairwell opening while others slipped away, too shamefaced for their part in the scene to meet his gaze directly. Clearly, despite its truth, the tale they'd found fascinating had discredited him in their eyes. But, he reassured himself, their opinion was of no import. The thought was quickly followed by apprehension of the earl's reaction should he learn the source from whence news of his duping spread.

From the conversation he'd overheard between the earl and his countess the night of their arrival, Erdel knew how poorly his lord regarded him. This action, he realized, might well see him not merely disdained for higher duties but banished from Tarrant and his wrongdoings reported to possible future lords. Under the threat of such stigma, Sir Gilfrey's arguments sounded even better. The night after the unintentional eavesdropping by which he'd learned the earl's true opinion of him, he'd attended a secret meeting between the former castellan of Swinton and disgruntled tenant farmers. Were the earl removed from the scene surely, as Gilfrey claimed, a new order would arise. And why not he as one of the men at its forefront? Were he responsible for the deed, mayhap even its leader. Pondering the matter, a scowl darkened his face as he strode from hall and castle.

Maud waited only long enough to hear Will's disjointed but blessedly short account of the incident before rushing above with all the haste allowed by her considerable bulk. She found Oram awkwardly waiting near the door, plainly uneasy in his lord's private chambers. Bending over the countess, Merta anxiously wiped a damp cloth across smooth forehead and pale cheeks.

"Fie, what unhappiness that black-hearted knight ever leaves strewn about him." Maud shook her head in disgust as she rolled to the younger woman's side. " 'Tis a wicked thing he's done—for which I pray God will mete out just punishment—and soon." She began chafing Nessa's chilled fingers while softly crooning the same senseless words of comfort she used with the children.

Nessa had returned to the world of unwelcome reality just as she was laid upon the down mattress but chose to stay in the safe cocoon of the dark world behind closed eyelids. Even as she'd realized that only a love with roots deep in her soul could render such painful fears, Garrick had shut himself away from her—and others. Since the morn following her night in his arms, nothing more than a cynical smile had marred his frozen face, and before its bitter cold she'd retreated ever further into herself. Neither busy hands nor long hours of toil could numb an aching heart or quiet a worried mind. Only the concern exchanged between Merta and Maud lent motivation sufficient to lift heavy lashes. No matter her own problems, she wouldn't add trouble to their day.

"Ah, ladybird, awake now?" Maud's soft words were warm and she patted the fingers still in her hands.

Nessa attempted to force a smile on lips which refused the command, resulting in a trembling grimace.

Near everyone on the earl's demesne was aware of the chill that had settled between their lord and lady. Clearly Lady Nessa found her husband's manner a weighty burden, for she spent hours praying and the rest of her time faithfully meeting each responsibility. Although grown pale and quiet, she personally saw to every detail of the castle's care and inhabitants' comfort, as if seeking escape from dreary worries. A woman of uncommon understanding, Maud deemed it time for the young countess to learn more of the background which had built a wall of cold reserve about the man she'd wed. But needs be she first clear the path by removing the boulder of the recent unpleasant scene.

"Never you mind what that nasty knight says. Be it that the people tattle and gossip, and enjoy it too, still 'tisn't nary a soul on Tarrant what will believe ill of you."

" 'Struth she speaks." Oram, big hands nervously knotted together, agreed from the doorway.

Nessa gave the penitent man a reassuring smile. His broad face glowed with sincerity, and she'd no doubt he regretted his small part in the belittling of the woman who'd stood against a free-born knight on behalf of him and his betrothed.

"Aye." Back from cool cheeks Merta brushed the soft brown curls that in the fall had escaped from their constraints. "Already have you proven yourself to we all."

Appreciative of their friendship and encouragements, no matter how little she believed, Nessa smiled more naturally. Only as she struggled to sit up did she realize her front laces had been loosened and gaped alarmingly. Embarrassed with Oram at the door she fell back again, hands clutching edges together.

Maud shook her head at the lady's renewed anxiety and turned immediately to Merta. "I expect others are concerned about their lady's well-being. Mayhap you and your man could go below to assure them she is recovered."

Merta moved to Oram's side and led him from the chamber, quietly closing the door as they left.

Maud returned her attention to the fragile woman seemingly lost in the expanse of the huge bed.

"Things are seldom as bleak or dreary as they appear." Determined to give Lady Nessa insight on the nature of her lord and the reasoning behind it, she began talking of deeds she'd spoken of to no other. "After Lady Odlyn died bearing an heir for Earl William, I took the babe and nursed him with my own newborn."

Nessa had learned this fact before, yet gave her full attention to the cheerful woman gone serious. As Maud spoke of her long-dead family, surely painful memories, Nessa met concerned eyes unflinching and stilled her nervous fingers. When the older woman went on to talk of rejection, Nessa wasted no time wondering why she spoke now of a deed she must prefer forgotten. Rather she gave the words respect by listening quietly.

"For four years I stayed and cared for the shy boy whose father never spared him so much as a moment nor even a glance. Then came the time that man, Earl William, heard the toddling call me what he'd learned from my own son— mama. Irrationally determined to protect his heir from the pain of any woman's love, the earl sent me from his castle that very day."

Fine brows puckered and Nessa ventured a query. "Pain of a woman's love? Your love?"

"Aye," Maud's smile was sad. "I argued but he was adamant, although to salve his conscience for a deed he knew unjust he sent wealth enough to see me and mine through many a long year. From then until you arrived no woman has braved his ire."

"But why?" Nessa couldn't understand how a maidservant's motherly affection could be a threat. "It makes no sense."

"You've the right of it. 'Twas a foolish action, but men obsessed have lost the power of rational thinking."

"Obsessed? Did he hate his wife so much that he must bar all other women from his son's life as well as his own?"

"Hate?" Maud's mouth dropped open. "I've failed to speak aright. 'Twas not hate that did the deed but a love so powerful, a loss so hurtful, he could not bear the chance of further pain."

All the pieces fell together, like shards of colored glass

that when put together made an awesome picture. Her taciturn father-in-law had loved too much, not too little.

"Lady Odlyn was a beauty inside and out," Maud continued. "And the earl's love for her was so great that when she died he wailed his pain 'til it must surely have shaken the heavens. When his voice fell to silence, seemed like as if his heart had been drained of all softening love and warm emotion had turned to hard, cold stone. In one night of drunken anger he vented his fury on an unwilling woman—Will's grandmother—who he could no more accept than he could allow love to grow for the son whose silver eyes and black hair were too strong a reminder of his lost love."

Maud's voice faded into silence, and Nessa stared sightlessly through her. Now she understood her father-in-law better, and her compassionate heart cried for the man whose painful love-lost had been distilled into sour loneliness—a terrible waste of life. Even more, she better understood the man she'd wed. Early deprived of his only source of love and bound in a castle with only a bitter man 'twas more a miracle that he'd grown to be so just and honest than that he found trust and love hard to give.

"Fie!" Maud's eyes had risen to the unshuttered window. "The sun is losing its strength and the day's late gone. I trust Merta to keep the others at their tasks, but best I be there to see the meal rightly prepared." She patted slender fingers and rose.

Nessa captured Maud's plump hand, restraining her departure. "My thanks." In emphasis of her simple words of gratitude, she gave a light squeeze before releasing the older woman.

With a return to her normal cheery manner Maud grinned before bustling out to get on with her chores.

Pondering all that Maud had told her, Nessa lingered abed. Inevitably her thoughts turned to Garrick and the dangers grown more threatening under his refusal to admit they existed. It was some time later when she forced fearful questions without answer from her mind. The fire was burning low, and the room had grown dim. Her eyes flew to the window and found that light of day was no more than a faint rose glimmer on the horizon. She jerked upright. There was no time to waste. Hastily shoving escaped curls between the coils of thick braids and smoothing anxious hands over

221

rumpled skirts, she rushed from the chamber and down broad stairs toward the evening meal near begun.

In the stairwell archway she froze. Indeed, as feared, she was late in coming. The trestle tables extending in long lines at right angles from either end of the dais were filled with boisterous guardsmen impatient for their food to be served. And she must walk the hall's full length to reach her seat at the earl's right. Certain every eye would follow the progress of the deceitful woman amongst them by trickery, she wanted badly to turn and flee. Hands instinctively palm-joined and pressed against rose lips that seemed the brighter for the pallor of her face, she besought the Almighty's power for courage to do what she must. Taking a deep breath and allowing hazel eyes to rise no higher than the path immediately before them, she quietly moved toward her destination.

Nessa slipped into the high-backed chair at Garrick's side, positive that the tale of the shameful scheme that had made her their countess had passed throughout Tarrant. Expecting to be the focus of curiosity for all in the hall, she studiously examined the table's smooth white cloth and the manchet bread platter placed between her and the earl. As young pages in training began serving a savory-smelling meal, she was ominously aware of the unnatural quiet that had descended on a place normally reverberating with banter and loud conversation.

Garrick also felt the odd atmosphere. He was all too aware that the strain between him and his wife was common fodder for gossip and that the people's sympathy lay with her. He assumed their discomfort born of disapproval for him and his actions and suffered an unaccustomed guilt for the possibility, nay, likelihood that he'd unjustly accused a woman of duplicity. Accuse women of such deeds had he done again and again, but with reason. This time he feared he'd seen danger where there was none. What wrong was there in a wife's care for a husband's well-being? What excuse had he in punishing her for that care? With his demand for truth and justice in others, the prospect of his having fallen so far short of his ideal darkened his temper.

Keeping her head bent, Nessa peeked at those seated at the closest tables below. They were carefully looking anywhere but at her. Surprised, she looked up to glance about and found the same true all around. Could it be they felt

222

unable to look upon so treacherous a woman? A weak supposition when in truth they appeared too sheepish to directly meet her eyes. Only the young squire who'd asked the dreaded question at length found courage enough to meet her gaze. Closed fist laid against heart he bowed his head low in a gesture of honor to her—clearly his plea for forgiveness. Warmth flooded Nessa and bloomed in a dimple-baring smile for the youth struggling toward manhood.

Seeing the squire's action and Nessa's response, Garrick's dark brows snapped together. She smiled at the boy when in recent days she'd given him only pain-filled stares from wide brown eyes that looked like bruises and smote him with guilt. So oft on her knees was she that he feared he'd truly driven her away after at last he'd begun to win her to him. He cursed his habit of doubt, and frustration with his own actions did nothing to alleviate a mood blackened by these strange doings in his hall. He turned to Nessa with a cold smile and ice glinting eyes.

"What matter is afoot that so deranges my garrison?"

In the silence his words carried to every ear and elicited a communal gasp. Likely the earl would be enraged by their knowledge of his fall to women's ploys, and his ice cold anger was a fearsome thing that no man among them would willingly meet.

Knowing herself the center of attention, Nessa realized they feared she would tell the lord of their regretted slight to her.

Wanting to sooth their anxiety, Nessa immediately answered in a voice loud enough for all to hear. "No matter of import, save a lump from a clumsy fall that was no one's fault but mine."

A wave of approval warmed the hall and a burst of talk broke the uneasy silence. Within moments it settled down, and the meal proceeded with normality save for the occasional broad smile or glass lifted in silent toast to their countess.

A clumsy fall? By the woman who, though she flaunted her charms not at all, was more graceful than any he'd seen before? Garrick wanted the truth of the deed but doubted he'd win it from men so clearly hers. It irritated him no end that his people were her allies and that some secret deed lay between them. The suspicious nature he'd damned but moments past rose anew and whispered distrust. At a time when he was struggling so hard to win loyalty and avert rebellion, had she won their support for Eleanor's plot? Did she and they conspire? Nay, it could not be! He must get control of his wildly fluctuating emotions, think with the cold precision he was famous for. Yet, how could he when presented with a woman who refused to fit into either of the molds designed for females. She must be either pious or wicked schemer. She must, but the distaste each possibility brought was so sour he couldn't bring himself to believe.

Fighting to remain calm beneath the weight of a steady silver examination, Nessa was relieved when the meal had done and rose as soon as the platter of cheese, nuts, and fruit was removed.

"I beg leave to take Lord William his evening repast." The words were disgustingly weak. She stepped down from the dais before her husband could speak and escaped to the kitchens through the doorway behind the high table. By habit, she lifted one of the wooden trays which pages, just finished with their serving duties and scurrying away, had left leaning in orderly rows against the outer wall. Placing it atop a broad cutting table, she moved to fetch a loaf of day-old bread from a shelf beside bake ovens and turned, nearly bumping into Merta.

With hands on shoulders, the taller girl steadied her lady. She was happy to have this opportunity to apologize again for the incident she blamed herself for. "So sorry I be for that insolent knight's disrespect." Sincerity darkened mud-brown eyes.

Stepping back, hands upheld to forestall the words, Nessa answered. "Pray speak no more of the deed for 'twill grow worse if the earl learns of it. Let it rest that Sir Erdel bears as little love for me as I for him and no further damage can he do me." She wished she believed her own claim for she feared Sir Erdel capable of a spite willing to wait even years for release.

"Speak of it no more will I, saves to apologize for drawing you into his web of hate by my seeking of your aid against his hurt of me." Merta's merry spirit lay beneath a layer of regret.

This reminder of her defense of Merta only reinforced Nessa's apprehension of the arrogant knight's long-held

224

grudges. He'd waited years to spite the girl for her rejection. To ease her friend's remorse, Nessa hid her worries behind a bright smile.

"They're all deeds past and best forgot. Let's be on with present tasks and think only of happy plans for the future— your future with Oram." She gave the bride-to-be a teasing grin and stepped around her to select a loaf perfect to halve for platter to hold the old earl's evening meal.

As Nessa placed bread on the tray, Merta laid a hand atop two smaller and stilled their movement. "Aye, but let me take on this chore while you seek your rest." The delicate woman looked as if a good wind would blow her away, and the afternoon's faint surely meant all good care should be taken. Moreover, after Lady Nessa's distressing experience, Merta felt the last thing she needed was to face the old earl's reviling tongue.

Nessa turned hands palm up beneath Merta's hold and closed her fingers over the other's to gently put them aside. "I feel as well as ever I have, and I enjoy my visits with Earl William." Merta's snort of disbelief brought a grin to peach lips as Nessa returned to her task, slicing the loaf in one stroke and ladling savory stew over the two halves before topping them with slices of roast pork. Recognizing defeat, Merta added fruit, a portion of cheese and a handful of nuts while Nessa poured still warm mulled wine into a crockery mug.

Now that the castle was in good care, Nessa had made Earl William's meals her excuse for visiting him. And after hearing the story of the painful beginning to his bitterness, she was even more determined to see he was not allowed to withdraw further into loneliness.

Through sheer determination she'd made near every trip to the West Tower by way of the dark and narrow interior corridor and could almost convince herself she'd overcome childish fears. Nonetheless when, a few steps from the end of the corridor's gloom, she heard a firm tread threatening to overtake her, her heart kicked up a furious pounding and her hands began to shake. Berating herself for the reaction, she risked a glance over her shoulder. Garrick was not far behind, dark brows scowling above eyes glinting silver ice. She couldn't pretend his disapproval meant for any but her, and its impact increased her tremors.

225

When the bottom of the stairway was come to, instead of feeling relieved she contemplated each step as if it were her foe and likely to snap at trespassing toes. Caught between the ominous flight of stairs and the displeasure of the man at her back, Nessa clamped her lips together and began to climb slowly and with deliberately placed steps. Ears attuned to the steady footfalls behind and sensitive to the man's impatience, surely a result of her necessarily cautious progress, memories of her long-dead father returned with such realism she could almost believe he were the one following. Thusly had her father prowled when things did not go his way. And her father's irritation had only ever increased until he'd vented his anger with casual blows which, though slight taps of his might, had been painful and well able to drop the child she'd been to the floor.

At last the upper level was gained, and with relief she moved toward the chamber. Garrick reached around her to throw open the door while Nessa, too aware of her companion's bad temper and caught in threatening memories, held so tight to her burden that her fingertips went white. Although from experience she knew extreme care oft ended in clumsiness, as she stepped into the chamber of her destination she leaned away from the strong arm still holding door wide. The tray's far corner unexpectedly banged against the doorframe. Smooth wood slid from her fingers, falling sideways to catapult its load into the room while it hit the floor and bounced aside. Before Nessa's horrified eyes, with incredible slowness the crockery mug slammed against hard planks and shattered, flinging shards out in a wide arc like a barrage of sharp arrows attacking the floor's rush cover. An attack quickly followed by the spreading stain of blood red wine.

Garrick let out a sharp expletive. Almost before the overturned bread could splatter the thick drops of its burden across the floor, in instinctive defense Nessa cringed against the doorframe, arms lifted protectively over her head. Huddled against cold wood, she waited but heard only the sharp rasp of her own breath. The waiting was surely worse than the pain of a blow and she'd rather have done with it. She turned, back flat against the welcome support of uncomfortable frame. Garrick's expression was black as thunder while silver bolts of lightning flashed from his eyes. Through harsh

226

experience and years of being taught that such was the duty of women, Nessa restrained a momentary rebellion and sank to her knees, crossing herself and praying for strength to meekly accept and submit to his anger.

"Hah! Such piety must make for a cold bed."

Until the words were spoke, Nessa had forgotten the second witness to her clumsiness. She understood the bitterness that lay behind the older man's words but still they hurt.

From long habit Lord William had criticized without thought of the reaction it might bring. His daughter-in-law looked as if she'd been hit by the physical assault clearly expected, and when she rose to run from the room, he was heartily sorry for the taunt. She'd never been else than pleasant, patiently putting up with his sharp tongue and listening to his long reminiscences with apparent interest. She hadn't deserved such treatment.

"I'll send someone to clean the mess." Garrick's words were curt and the glare he gave his father fierce before he whirled to stomp away.

William's dark eyes narrowed on the empty doorway and saw the incident replayed. Nessa's reaction both to the spilled tray and to his criticism revealed the marriage not so strong as he'd previously believed. Hidden in his solitude, he'd seen no signs of distress and hadn't thought to question his informants on the health of their relationship. Now, in great surprise, he found himself fearful not alone for his son's pain at woman's hand but for that tender creature's happiness at Garrick's. As he slowly closed the door, he heard the echoed footfalls of a man fast descending tower stairs. Was Garrick in haste to make peace or render the punishment she'd feared? Not for the first time of late, William wished he had built a closer relationship with the son unlikely to seek his advice or accept it if offered.

Garrick's long stride ate up the corridor's length and still he didn't overtake his wife. Her cringing fear of him had drained away a sennight of irritated suspicion to leave him angry—with himself. He damned his failure to earlier make her sure of his intent to use her only gently. Despite his low opinion of women as a whole and unlike many others, he'd never hit a female. It seemed to him that such actions proved

227

a man incapable of winning by aught but physical force, and were thus an admission of defeat.

From the main tower's stairwell archway, Garrick glanced into the great hall. A group of guardsmen had gathered about the vast hearth to swap highly colored stories and drink ale while over the one trestle table still assembled another group bent in a spirited game of dice. He hadn't expected Nessa to return there but had wanted to be certain. No moment to waste, he acknowledged that as he'd not caught up to her despite his superior speed it meant she'd crossed the parapet walkway and by that shorter route was likely already ensconced in her chamber's stronghold. No matter, 'twas the lord's chamber, his chamber, and she cound not deny him entrance. He took the steps two at a time and soon reached the chamber door.

At the sound of a door swung wide and bouncing against the wall beside, Nessa buried her flushed face even deeper into the pillow beneath. Curled up in the midst of the bed, trying to disappear into its barren width, she froze as a large hand wrapped about her shoulder. With great gentleness the hold rolled her to her back, but she clutched the pillow's soft barrier before head and shoulders as if it were a warrior's shield.

"Nessa." Garrick's voice was deep velvet and enticing.

Nessa was ashamed of having given way to fear in the first instance and more of cringing before him rather than standing proud beneath his punishment. But, having already revealed her basic cowardice, she couldn't bear to meet the power of silver eyes.

Garrick saw her distress. Rather than insisting she yield, he carefully lifted her, pillow and all. With one hand he bent into the crook of his neck a head soft with the abundant curls escaped in her hasty flight while the other reached between to tug the pillow from her hold. At last he had tear-damp cheeks bare against his throat and her delicate curves close against his chest. He leaned back against the pillow remaining at the top of the bed. The draperies were closed on three sides, and he reached out to release the cord holding the fourth. Heavy tapestried cloth fell, shutting them into a dark and intimate cave.

"Where did you learn to accept another's blows?" The question was soft, slow, and unthreatening.

Feeling as if the tempter had mysteriously transported her to some private world safe from the intrusion of reality, Nessa answered with an oft repeated phrase learned long ago. "Woman caused man to sin, thus 'tis woman's lot to accept his punishment."

Garrick slowly shook his head. He, too, was familiar with the excuse but had no use for it. "Who taught you such drivel?"

Drivel? 'Twas a word Nessa would willingly assign to it but not a description she'd ever thought a man would use. Leaning a breath away and tilting chin up, she struggled to see his expression through the gloom but saw only the gleam of a white smile. It was reassurance enough to earn her response.

"Father Cadmaer."

Dark brows rose. "I didn't know there were priests in the Abbey of St. Margaret's."

Having once turned her gaze to his face, Nessa couldn't look away and with her response came a tremulous smile. "Priests come to administer the sacraments, but Father Cadmaer was not among them. He was the tutor-priest at Swinton Keep when I was a child."

"Ah," Garrick nodded, "and what else did he teach you?"

"To read and write and pray for a nature worthy of Christ's bride."

He'd that man, then, to thank for her pious aspirations. Pulling her close again, Garrick rested his chin atop her crown of braids to keep her from seeing the grimace her answer brought. Thinking of how near she'd come to fulfilling Father Cadmaer's training, he hardly noticed when her head bent lower.

"I failed at most." A sob blocked Nessa's throat, and she paused to swallow. "I took my father's blows, but with defiance; and I've recent proof of a nature totally unsuited for the church." By speaking the words, she released her guilt for failing the expectations of both her mother and the priest and floated on a comfortable awareness that she no longer felt remorse.

Holding her while she snuggled into his embrace, Garrick would willingly have believed her free of pious aspirations but, like an opposing knight on a tiltyard delivering a fierce strike, her words of guilt for their passion landed a resounding blow.

So filled with relief was Nessa that she didn't notice that he'd gone still as frost-layered stone. Pulling far enough away to look into his face with eyes now accustomed to the gloom she was pleased to find herself protected from the power of silver gaze by his lowered lashes. She doubted herself equal to the deed she meant to do while meeting it full on. For the first time in days they were truly together and, anxious that this harmony continue, she bravely reached out to caress his cheek.

Fearing her touch given as consolation, he peered from half lowered lids. The smile on her face was reassuring but her study of his mouth spoke volumes. He needed no further invitation and, refusing to heed the fear that she'd again regret it in light of day, leaned forward to join his lips to hers.

She'd come seeking yet the tempter's fierce fire was more that she'd expected but no more than she desired. Slipping silken arms about his strong neck, she tangled her fingers into thick black hair, urging him nearer. The kiss immediately went so deep and hot that she moaned beneath its sensuous demand.

Worried that he'd hurt the delicate creature already wounded, Garrick pulled his mouth away. A difficult task. With dark head thrust back and eyes clenched shut, he struggled for restraint. A restraint driven beyond his ability to regain by tender lips that brushed sweet torment over his throat to the laces of his tunic. And when small fingers released their hold of his hair, moving down to tug at the ties, he sat up and ruthlessly ripped the cloth barrier away.

Fascinated, Nessa watched as with his action powerful muscles flexed beneath their mat of curling hair. Even before he'd flung the offending garment away, she reached out to smooth her hands across the hard contours. Shuddering beneath the caress, Garrick pulled her up into his arms and his mouth opened on hers, devouring her eager lips until she melted against him, seeking more, trying to get closer and closer still. With a passion-stiff smile he moved his kiss to her cheeks and throat while freeing her gown's side laces with haste-clumsy fingers.

"I want to feel you against me again, all of you." The

sound was a low growl and sent a shiver of desire through Nessa. An impatient hand slid through loosened laces to cup a small breast.

"It burns," Nessa gasped yet arched into his hold.

The whimpered words and ardent response stunned Garrick. He was shaken by the feel of curves so soft they were like warm rose petals in his hand, hard tips branding his palm. His mouth laid a trail of fire across passion-flushed cheek to reclaim hers again in a devastating kiss.

Nessa thought she would faint for a second time that day when the warm, callused hand contracted on her throbbing flesh but did not miss a beat of the tempter's song strummed again in desire over her taut nerves. When he slipped his hand free, an anguished protest escaped her tight throat, and she pressed aching curves against his strong torso.

Pleased by her uncontrollable need, Garrick crushed her nearer as he whispered, "I cannot sleep for want of you, and now I will have you as hungry as I." Taking hold of her gown's hem, he slowly pulled it up, his hand gliding lightly over silken skin every inch of the path from ankles to throat before suddenly pulling it over her head and tossing it to the end of the bed. Hands on her shoulders, he sank back and desire glittered in the eyes that blazed over the sweet flesh above and visible through her nearly translucent camise. Holding her immobile, he leaned forward and with his tongue stroked fire over a deep coral tip beneath gossamer cloth. Head twisted to one side and trembling with unbelievable pleasure, she sagged in his grasp. Who but the tempter she'd named him could be source of such delicious torment?

After pulling the delicate cloth from her body, Garrick lowered her to the bed and let silver flames burn over the reality behind his tantalizing dreams while he efficiently divested himself of the last cloth to come between. Her eyes were closed but Nessa felt the heat of his gaze as if it were a physical touch and could not prevent the helpless response surely visible to him. All-consuming need left no room for embarrassment so when he stretched out at her side making no move to continue their pleasure, she tossed pride away and rose on one elbow to slowly caress the muscle-ridged planes of his chest. But the feel and touch of him only deepened the hunger. Desperately seeking to tempt the tempter in demand for surcease, she twisted sensuously against his powerful form, twined fingers through the wiry curls on his chest, and tried to meld her mouth to his once more.

Garrick kissed the corners of peach sweet lips, the satin of her cheeks but avoided her open mouth until she groaned with frustrated desire. Only when she plainly wanted him as badly as he wanted her did he take her face between his hands, holding her motionless until eyes burning with hungry green flames opened.

Lost in the blinding silver at the center of near black eyes, Nessa fell into his fiery core, helplessly surging against his unyielding strength. Visual bond unbroken, at last he joined his lips to hers, taking her tongue into his mouth as he clasped the gentle curve of her hips between his palms and lifted her slender form above him until with a mighty upward thrust he blended her wanting flesh with his own. Hands curled over her round derriere, he held her bound tight to him and with the wicked, primitive rhythm of the tempter's tune rocked them deeper and deeper into the hungry blaze. At last the near unbearable tension burst in a passionate shower of glittering sparks. As they drifted on clouds of satisfaction, strong arms tenderly held Nessa close, and she clung to the tempter whose torment was a welcome pleasure.

❧ Chapter 18 ❧

Wrapped in gentle folds of sleep, still Nessa moaned softly as her heat source withdrew. Her arm went out in search of firm muscles and warm responses but found only quickly cooling cloth. Forcing lashes to lift, she found an unexpected brightness and groaned in earnest—not for its discomfort to eyes, as a direct assault was blocked by the broad shouldered man sitting on the edge of the bed with back turned to her, but for the end it meant to the pleasures of dark hours. Falling to temptation, she ran her fingers down his spine, and a strong tremor shook him.

Garrick glanced behind with a mock frown. "No more of that, sweeting, else I'll never see my responsibilities met."

In light of day Nessa was amazed at her own boldness and pressed against her lips a hand seemingly burned by the touch of his flesh.

Seeing her uncertainty and fear of offense in so welcome a caress, Garrick shook night-ruffled hair and twisted about to lean across her slender form. "Never hesitate to touch me. I welcome your caresses. Surely I've proven it well. Only must I take up my duties, which I do happily with the assurance we will share our private haven again only daylight hours hence." He lifted the fingers still curled against her lips and teasingly kissed each one, then leaned over their joined hands to brush tempting kisses across the tip of her nose and each corner of her mouth before settling to drink its nectar in earnest.

Nessa had twined her free hand into thick strands of black and did not release him when he withdrew his lips from hers to pull a breath away.

Studying petal soft lips, he murmured, "Until the night is ours again."

His intent silver gaze was as potent as a kiss, and Nessa sighed her protest when he eased free of the fingers in his hair. With admiring eyes she watched light bronze his powerful torso as he turned to pull on his chausses.

"You'd think with summer begun the floors would not be so cold," he commented as he stood, fastening ties at his waist. "But I suppose 'tis nature's way of seeing us fully awakened."

Sliding across the bed and letting her body curl into the dent in the feather mattress left by his, she smiled. Having already decided that the gift she'd thought to give the evening of their first coming together had been no gift at all but rather an excuse for taking what she wanted, even in the days of their estrangement she'd begun pondering what to give instead. Now she knew just what he would appreciate— the small Saracen carpet which had lain beside her bed in Eleanor's castle. Pleased, she laid back content to study the welcome tempter, all masculine grace and power, as he gathered up his hastily discarded clothes and made ready to cross the hall to don fresh attire.

"Garrick," she called, very much aware that this was the first time she'd spoken aloud his given name.

At the sweet sound, Garrick turned. One hand on the cold iron door latch, he gazed into an enticing face overwhelmed by the thick disarray of soft curls he'd released after the past night's initial desperation had found fulfillment. An even stronger call were lips bright as sun-kissed peaches and just as sweet, as witness their slightly swollen curve. He nearly threw all responsibilities aside and returned to taste them once again.

"Mayhap your days would be speeded and our time lengthened if your belongings resided in this chamber?" Her voice was nearly breathless with fear that her suggestion was too bold and worry that she'd overstepped her rights.

As he nodded, his warm smile and the heat of the dark smoke clouding his eyes were reassurance enough. "Tonight." His single word promised both return and rekindled fire.

After the door closed on his retreating form, Nessa cuddled against the bedclothes and pillow that so recently had held the man she loved. She dwelled on delicious memories of hot play and tender interludes within the intimate cave of this shrouded bed. From thoughts of longings satisfied she drifted into pleasant dreams. Waking some time later she was horrified to find strong light slanting near full across the chamber from a sun half done with the path to its summit. She sat up abruptly. The morning meal was long over and likely the preparations for the next well underway. For the first time since she'd taken the duty herself she'd failed to deliver a meal to the West Tower.

With this reminder of the old earl came memory of the past evening's scene, and Lord William's bitter words returned to haunt her. Yet, the pain they'd initially rendered had been worth the comfort they brought. She owed the lonely man gratitude, not the censure he must surely believe intended by her failure to appear. Leaving the bed determined to be at his chamber door with the midday repast, she went to kneel at her prie-dieu for morning devotions. Rising, she remembered, too, the old earl's comment on piety making for a cold bed. This very day while her lord's clothes were being returned to where they belonged, she'd have her prie-dieu moved to an unused chamber one level below.

Hoping Garrick would return for the noontide meal, she studied her meager wardrobe and carefully selected the cranberry gown she'd worn for their betrothal. To emphasize its golden embroidery at rounded neck and sleeve she donned the creamy camise of fine linen. After brushing soft brown curls to gleaming health, she plaited crimson ribbons into their wealth and wound the braids into an intricate coil at the base of her neck. Only after stepping into the soft wool gown did she realize the foolishness of her choice. It laced in back, a task she could not complete alone. As if in answer to her problem, a soft rapping sounded.

"Enter," Nessa called, certain it was Merta although she'd come considerably later than usual.

Brown eyes peeked around the edge of a barely opened door as if fearful of intrusion.

"I'm relieved to see you for I cannot close this gown alone." With a mock grimace but laughter shining green in her eyes, Nessa twisted to show the gap left between unlaced edges.

Grinning, Merta stepped into the room. She was pleased to see her lady so clearly happy. It was time and past for the noble couple to find peace betwixt themselves. " 'Tis welcome to know one is needed yet." At Nessa's inquiring glance she shrugged and mournfully explained. "Your man said as you wasn't to be disturbed and that instead of aiding you here I was to take the morning meal to the West Tower in your place—mayhap ever more." Her tone gently teased for the obvious reason behind the command.

"Nay, unless I sprout another pair of hands upon my back, your aid will I always need." Nessa's joyous spirit spilled out in silly words such as were disallowed in the serious realm of abbey life. But even as she spoke she recognized how embarrassed they'd each have been had the girl arrived as early this morn as had become their habit. Moreover, had she risen in time to deliver Lord William's morning repast, she'd have had to leave her love yet abed and lost precious moments in his company. She was responsible for castle duties, but first and above all came her lord. Surely 'twould be only right for her to assign another the task of taking the old earl's first meal to the West Tower.

Though standing behind, gently tugging laces together, Merta was tall enough to see faint signs of worry on Nessa's smooth face.

"Mayhap, in future, best I waits 'til after the earl appears below?" Merta tentatively suggested, anxious to spare her too beleaguered lady further concern.

The haste with which Nessa agreed proved her relief at the offer. Yet, she would assign to someone other than Merta the task of delivering the old earl's morning meal, for soon she, too, would have husband and temptation to linger long abed.

"When is your wedding planned?" She asked, realizing

that she'd been so consumed with her own troubles that they'd talked little since winning the earl's approval.

"Wednesday week." Merta gave the tied laces a final pat and stepped back before qualifying her response. "Leastwise, we hopes the priest Tarrant village shares with Burling and Offaden can then be here." Merta's cheeks glowed pink with anticipation.

The village chapel was little more than a windowless hut. Remembering the candle-bright and flower-filled location in which she'd pledged her life to Garrick, she found distaste in the idea of her friend taking such a serious step in surroundings so dingy.

"Father Simon is always here." Referring to the castle's priest, Nessa tentatively approached the matter. "If you are willing, the ceremony could be performed in the castle's chapel." She'd hoped her offer would be a welcome alternative but was surprised by the delighted sparkle in wide brown eyes.

"Be you certain you wishes it so?" Tamping down her excitement, Merta sought reassurance that such an action was possible. "The earl, canst he bear the sight of mere serfs come to the chapel of his mighty castle for so simple a deed?"

In truth it hadn't occurred to Nessa that Garrick might find distaste in her suggestion although 'twas true serfs were commonly bound by local priests or itinerant friars in simple village churches, even humble huts. Yet, she'd risk it for the sake of her plainly thrilled maidservant.

"Wednesday week it will be." She smiled confidently.

Merta stuttered profuse gratitude. Then, as Nessa had already bound her own hair, she left to share the good tidings with Oram.

Nessa wasted no time in following. To insure a return in time to join the man she hoped would be at the high table for the noontide meal, she quickly loaded a tray. With fresh memory of shattered crockery and spreading stains, she filled a plain metal pitcher to accompany plentiful food. This with a matching goblet she placed on the smooth wood plank beside thick slices of fine wheaten bread, slabs of cold roast pork from the previous night's repast, a new baked mince pie, and fresh picked berries.

The radiance of her happiness seemed to light the whole

route through narrow corridor and up wide steps to Lord William's chamber. Carefully balancing the burden on an out-thrust hip, she freed a hand to firmly rap on the closed door.

As if she'd returned to an earlier time, the door cracked open and beady eyes peered out.

"I've brought Lord William's meal." She firmly announced, carefully taking the tray in both hands and holding it before her.

"Nessa?" The question boomed out as a large hand wrapped about the door's edge above the weasely face which fell to danger as the planks were jerked wide to allow a better view.

Though startled by the action, Nessa held tight to her burden and calmly answered. "I've returned." Her eyes bravely met the older man's deep brown gaze.

"So you have, so you have." A broad smile flashed across normally taciturn features, and he leaned forward to relieve her of the burden. "I feared you never would again. But, come in." He backed away to allow her easy entry.

Nessa hesitated, torn between the wish to reassure this man that she held no grudge for his words and her desire to make as speedy a return to the great hall as could be managed. During the moments she paused, in his peculiar scurrying way Derward moved from behind the door to glare at her from around the old earl's broad back. She'd not seen the strange little man since last they'd crossed verbal swords and she'd issued her challenge. She feared for the purpose of his visit, and her gaze went from his venomous stare first to the empty table beside padded chair and then to their host's cuffs, drawn tight and tied at wrist.

"Hah!" Lord William's booming laugh echoed against stone walls as he placed the tray she'd brought on the empty table where she'd feared to find a bowl of unsavory slugs. "You've no reason to worry. Only am I reporting the results of your test to friend Derward. Come in and let me share them with you, too."

Curiosity drew Nessa into the midst of the chamber. If he had truly accepted her challenge, then its results were clear, for he stood robust before her. Yet, Derward's malicious presence scraped across her nerves like fur rubbed the wrong direction. Her hands were tightly palm-joined but she allowed no other sign of the tension quaking inside to outwardly appear.

"With each day since I banished leeches from my arm, I've grown in strength and health. 'Tis you who saw the secret, and I will ever praise you for the deed."

"Nay, my lord." Derward's voice rasped through the good cheer as effectively as the jagged teeth of a saw through wood. "She's a witch who has put you under her spell. Who but a wicked enchantress could bend you to her will?"

Nessa's mouth dropped open in horror. Would either man ever understand that 'twas merely the result of a logical mind and the care given a lonely, deserted heart? Only one argument had she. Only one, but backed with truth's power.

"On the bones of St. Margaret whose abbey was my home for a decade and more, I swear no such evil practices could ever be mine."

"Derward!" Lord William's one word was as effective as the lash of a whip, and its object cowered beneath the blow. "I have said you may remain as Tarrant's physician, dependent upon your promise never to speak such slander again. Now be gone from my sight before I change my mind."

Blabbering apologies and servile praise of the lord's generous forgiveness, Derward backed quickly from the room.

"The Abbey of St. Margaret?" Iron-gray head cocked to one side, Lord William studied her carefully. Having spent so much time within sanctified walls 'twas small wonder she'd fallen so naturally to her knees before an apparently threatening danger.

Without considering the wisdom of her explanation, she said, "I was meant to become nun in their order and spend all my days amongst them—until the matter of your son's marriage arose."

"The king sent my son to take Christ's bride from Him?" Disbelief for his king's willingness to so offend religious powers after his humbling experience with Thomas à Becket was obvious in raised brows and questioning voice.

She'd set a trap for herself, Nessa realized, and had no choice but tell him how she'd come to be wedded with his son. Choosing words carefully, she told him of her father's support in rebellion and his death, of Eleanor's care of the three females left behind, and of her beautiful sister and the man she loved.

"I had to choose between seeing my sister happy in her marriage or myself secure within abbey walls."

"And you take your responsibilities seriously. That you've proven. So, you turned your back on holy orders to take your sister's place as wife to my heir?" William could only admire her strength of character, but 'twas cold comfort for the pain he felt for his son, a man unable to claim the heart of the woman he'd wed.

"As you say," Nessa slowly nodded but couldn't let the matter rest on half-truth, nor allow this man to believe her action an undesired sacrifice and his son tied to a woman unable to love a human male. Staring at hands twisted together, she added, "But also because I'd come to know my nature unsuited to the life—too attuned to worldly beauty and comfort, too prone to pride, too easily driven to anger—and too able to fall to one man's fiery temptations."

Hazel eyes bravely rose to meet the relieved satisfaction in Lord William's slowly growing smile.

"Blessings on your union," Nessa whispered into Merta's ear before giving the beaming bride a quick hug and stepping back to make way for others crowding around.

Her maidservant's inordinate pride in the wedding site had encouraged Nessa's creative energies and, following Eleanor's example, she'd seen the once gloomy chapel not merely scrubbed to a shiny cleanliness but brightened by armfuls of flowers and masses of candles. Its unexpected beauty had held the audience in hushed awe throughout the ceremony. Only now as they poured into the great hall for the waiting feast did boisterous spirits break into the usual crude bantering and shouted good wishes.

"Your first attempt at organizing a formal gathering is clearly a success and bodes well for future needs—the marriages of our daughters mayhap?" Garrick wrapped an arm about Nessa's middle and with the other motioned toward the merry crowd, an odd assortment of serfs and noble knights.

The embrace was welcome and Nessa leaned against her love's powerful form as she looked up to meet his smile. "Their happiness makes it worth the toil." She nodded at the beaming bride on the arm of a bashful groom plainly struggling to appear manfully unimpressed by all the fuss made of their joining. Not only had Garrick allowed the wedding in his castle's chapel, but he'd suggested that she arrange this feast to celebrate after.

"Moreover, it seems the whole of Tarrant is intent on enjoying the celebration," she added.

"Aye, though I've yet to see the disappointed Sir Erdel." Garrick's wry laugh for the man's poor spirit melted into a hum that joined the merry song off-key voices had just begun.

Nessa felt his deep voice gently reverberate in the chest she rested against and smiled. During their past fortnight of happiness she'd tried to push aside all thoughts of threatening matters. Garrick's mornings were always full of tasks for the demesne's care, and he'd spent many days away calling upon his far-flung vassals, but a few afternoons and every evening had been hers. He'd taught her the moves in games of chess and even, in response to her pleas, how to play dice. Together they'd walked across the green fields beyond the castle wall, ridden through the forest nearby, and talked of such simple matters as household tasks, vassals' needs and even of books—but never of their political differences. Garrick had even begun teaching the two orphan boys how to ride, giving particular attention to Will although she knew he had no understanding of the boy's claim.

All this he had done and then filled her nights with pleasures undreamt. Nonetheless, while he was away, no amount of work could protect her from the assault of fears for his safety. Too many of them there were—all with names: Sir Erdel, the spiteful man, was likely anxious to see her pay for interfering with his plan, but danger to her was the least of her concerns. She feared he'd seek retribution on the lord who'd slighted his puffed conceits. More danger lay with Sir Gilfrey who she was certain would seek revenge for the loss of what he'd long claimed his. Worst of all, Prince John who wanted her love's title and lands. Though a cowardly creature, she didn't doubt his greed well able to fill any lack left by craven fears.

"Sweeting, what pains you?" Garrick felt the growing tension of Nessa's slender form. Was she offended by the bawdy jests that here, as at every such gathering, were bandied about?

Called from the darkness of overshadowing anxieties,

Nessa looked up into smoke-gray concern and smiled. "All my toil has caught up with me now the deed is done, and I am weary."

"Then best be that you retire early." The advice was half in serious concern and half in suggestive purr. "I doubt the new wedded pair will notice our departure once the feast is past."

Surely, Nessa justified a probably selfish decision, by her labor she'd earned a long evening with her love. She gave Garrick a soul-melting smile.

The hour was early, yet none disputed the earl's right to call the crowd to their seats behind tables groaning beneath the weight of a plentiful repast. Wine and ale flowed and the already raucous party grew steadily more so. When timbrels, lutes, and pipes set up a tune for dancing, Garrick motioned the groom and his bride to take the honor of opening the floor where few would be steady enough to perform the intricate patterns, and the heavy step of those who tried would make it a dangerous undertaking.

"Milady, milady." The call was repeated several times before it pulled Nessa's interest from spritely tune and amusing antics of the tipsy dancers creating strange patterns of their own. She looked down to see the shiny bald pate of an itinerant peddler who stood below the raised dais. He'd arrived the day past and been invited to tarry and enjoy the wedding feast.

Once the man saw he had her attention, he spoke. "I soon leave for Salisbury."

"You travel at night?" Nessa was shocked by the notion of anyone willing to journey through the dark.

"I must for I promised I'd be there by day beyond the morrow and lingering here for this fine fete," he waved around tables now lightened of their abundant dishes, "makes it necessary for me to begin my travels now. So, if you'll give me the missive you asked that I deliver to the the queen, I'll be on my way."

With a sidelong glance at her husband, Nessa nodded and rose. "I'll fetch it from above and meet you at the outer door."

Garrick frowned as he'd not for precious days, and she gave him her brightest smile. Determined to reveal no hint of the surprise gift she'd written to request, she offered what she hoped was a casual and believable excuse, one that was in part the truth. "Maud believes a variety of special dishes are necessary in a place as important as Castle Tarrant and mourns her limited talents. Thus, I promised to write and request recipes of Eleanor's fine cook." Before Garrick could question her, Nessa stepped down from the dais and followed the wall to the stairway.

With the clarity of a warning bell the decision Garrick had made on their wedding day returned to mind—watch closely for any communication between her and the treacherous queen. Nessa's excuse was weak and rankled his suspicions. Why only now, some time after they'd settled in Tarrant Castle, had Nessa sent for the recipes? From talks with his vassals and common farmers he'd grown certain Eleanor, working through the treacherous Sir Gilfrey, was behind the transparent scheme to create disharmony on their lands and weaken the king's bulwark against rebellion. He didn't want to believe his honest wife a part of the plot and had near convinced himself that it could not be so, but Nessa's obvious subterfuge in hiding the content of her message to Eleanor watered the unwelcome seeds of doubt sown so long ago.

The peddler lingered below the high table, waiting for a safe path to open amidst lurching dancers and was about to risk a dash through their number when his noble host spoke.

"You go from here to the queen?"

"Aye." The man's plump hands came together, and he nodded obsequiously. "To Salisbury Tower where I will request to see the queen and lay your lady's missive direct in her royal hands and no other's, just as the gracious countess directs me do."

"In the queen's hands only." Garrick's words were not a question but a cold restatement of fact.

Nonetheless, the listener nodded vigorously to the man he could now see others were justified in naming Ice Warrior. Realizing the earl no longer required him, nor even knew him still there, with deep relief the peddler made his escape.

Garrick's suspicions were black and threatened to smother the warm happiness of recent days. His relief in finding his wife no longer pining for the religious life had blinded him to other doubts. Now they'd broken free of passion's restraints, and he feared himself a fool to trust and—love?

Nessa was waiting in the castle's exit corridor when the peddler arrived. She handed him a parchment whose materials she'd begged from the cleric sitting always at Garrick's side when judgments were rendered. Having no seal of her own, she'd closed it with her thumb imprint and now studied the blot of wax as she entrusted it to a man she prayed would fulfill his promise.

"Into Queen Eleanor's hands and no others." She repeated her plea before releasing the missive.

"I swear it on the Holy Cross," he promised, tucking the folded square into the layers of cloth across his beefy chest.

His words reassured Nessa for surely whatever other oaths a man might break, none would risk offending the Almighty by sundering one made on sacred relics. She nodded solemnly.

The man started to turn but paused, hesitantly looking back to offer a warning. "Be you a supporter of the queen and your lord of the king, likely one of you will be interested in the gossip that a man of my itinerant habits hears. Says they that men wearing Prince John's colors have been seen skulking about the area, never coming forward like honest men but rather hiding in bushes and slipping away from would-be questioners."

Nessa felt as if she'd just been doused with a bucket of water drawn from the frozen North Sea. Prince John on Tarrant land? For what purpose? What purpose to hide and "skulk" in bushes? What purpose but the one she'd feared from the first.

She made her way back to the table and took her place at Garrick's side but neither of them had the heart to rejoin the jubilation. Unable to shake off her preoccupation with the news she'd learned, Nessa unthinkingly twirled the wine dregs in her goblet with ever increasing speed. How could she bring it to Garrick's attention, make him take the danger seriously?

The cold armor Garrick had dwelled within for years but had put off these past many days now seemed to hover over him as he watched his wife lift goblet to sweet lips and drink the remnants it contained without notice of their assuredly sour flavor. He could only assume 'twas schemes shared with the queen that held her attention so completely he was excluded.

Nessa felt a growing chill but felt certain it was born only of her own worries. Deciding there was nothing to be gained by prolonging inaction, she turned to Garrick.

"The feast is truly done." She motioned toward platters holding bare bones and little more. "Can we not escape to our chamber?" Her smile was a curious mixture of longing and anxiety.

Though fervently hoping his suspicions were unfounded, the unwanted icy wall of wariness was forming again between them. Yet, he hoped to see the still thin barrier melt beneath their joined fire and stood to offer his arm to her.

Certain of the importance of its outcome, Nessa braced her courage for the scene to come and placed her fingers atop a hard-muscled arm as she rose.

Seeing their lord and his lady ready to depart, music faded into the same silence as laughter and merry chatter. The center of attention, Garrick lifted his free hand and reassured the group fearful of an early end to their enjoyments.

"Continue as long as you will, for we leave you in Sir Rufus's capable hands." The words were encouragement enough, although a tipsy Sir Rufus looked little able to attend to his own needs let alone another's. The crowd's boisterous noise quickly returned to its previous rowdy level.

Climbing the steps to their chamber at Garrick's side, Nessa mentally rehearsed and then discarded one beginning to what she must say after another. All too soon the door had not only swung open but shut behind and his arms were closing about her. She'd no time left to strive for well-thought words and laid her palms against his broad chest to hold him back.

Startled at this first repulse of his advances, Garrick's brows drew into a puzzled frown. Seemed she'd not truly meant what her haste to reach this chamber had appeared to promise.

"As he departed the tradesman told me 'tis said that men wearing Prince John's colors have been observed hereabouts. 'Skulking' he said, as if they'd no wish to be seen."

Garrick's frown deepened as he stepped away. Men in John's colors "skulking" but not wanting to be seen? Someone had little respect for his intelligence, trying to pass off so patently false a tale. If they wanted not to be noted, then would they wear a prince's colors? Not likely true.

245

"Don't you see?" Hands palm up were extended toward him in supplication. "John seeks your title and lands and has sent men to secure them for him."

"John is a bumbling child." To Nessa, Garrick's statement held more than contempt for the prince. It scorned her argument.

"A child of more than a score and two?" Her response was derisive of the prince but, already filled with cold anger, Garrick heard it as derision of his rebuttal.

He immediately answered, "Likely he'll be a child at two score and more."

She was desperate to make him acknowledge the threat. "His age excuses him of black intent not at all, for his brothers each mounted dangerous rebellions against their father while younger. Nay, he is part of the 'devil's brood' and born sly."

Garrick could only shake his head in disgust. She knew well how Henry's sons had incited costly deeds—her own father's life a part of their price.

Seeing his negative motion as rejection of her logic she snapped back. "Are you also blinded by the father's love and unable to see the truth of John's nature?"

"I see John for what he is—weak and cowardly. Far too cowardly to stand against me. But by your arguments I see you have small faith in my abilities as warrior."

"Nay!" The response was driven from her throat by his hurtful assumption that she lacked confidence in his valor.

Garrick was beyond listening to her explanations. "You think I would fail to defeat so inept a foe as John, even be he pursuing the path you fear."

"That you would defeat him one to one there is no doubt. But I, too, doubt a 'child' so sly would personally stand against you—'tis the reason he sent others to do the deed, to carry out the wicked plot I've no doubt he is capable of devising."

"Who can touch me in the midst of Tarrant, my own domain?" Certain the inept "accidents" had not been meant to succeed, the bitter curl of Garrick's firm mouth made his disbelief clear, and the barrier between them grew with quick-forming layers of frost. Her warning seemed too plainly meant to cause a rift between him and his king, advancing some plot of Eleanor's to blacken John and further her beloved Richard's pursuit of the throne.

The icy disapproval flowing from silver eyes nearly froze Nessa where she stood, but she couldn't easily accept the renewed separation threatened by his irritation with her talk of danger from one of the king's own. She fought her way through the chilled air betwixt them to wrap her arms around his broad chest. He stood unmoving beneath her embrace for heart-stopping moments. She had nearly given up when suddenly he bound her fast against him with a hold tight as bands of iron. Surrendering to the welcome crush, she turned her face up for a fiery kiss and felt as if she'd been taken into the blaze at his core. She was ready to be consumed and reborn from the ashes like the phoenix of Greek legend. Yet, a cold ball of fear for his safety survived, and when Garrick broke the kiss and bent his lips to caress her throat while loosing her side lacings, she was driven to beg caution.

"If naught else, I pray you go with care as I fear for your life."

Her words effectively killed Garrick's desire. His arms fell like lead-weighted cloth, and he stepped back to study her dispassionately. Had she, even in love play, sought to sow discontent, turn him from his path? Was she naught but another Eve come to tempt man with the sweet fruit of her passion?

Garrick turned and left the chamber, closing the door with an ominous gentleness that left Nessa gasping under the pain of his soul-wounding blow.

ᴈ§ *Chapter 19* §ᴈ

Milady, strangers have arrived, and I was sent to call you, but couldn't find you anywhere.''

Turning from the soothing view of peaceful countryside seen through a window at the castle stairwell's highest level, Nessa gave a smile to the harried Will. He took his duties so seriously that any block in their doing distressed him. In need of a few quiet moments, she'd returned from delivering Lord William's midday meal by way of the parapet path, dawdling in the sunlight and fresh breeze. Then she had paused here in the privacy of tower landing, but as this window faced away from the courtyard and castle approach, she'd not seen the arrival of guests.

''Who are these visitors?''

''Sir Rufus doesn't know them, nor do I, but the lady asked for you.''

''Lady?'' Nessa's knew many nuns but few secular women and fewer still of those who could be termed thus.

''A golden-haired lady with knight at her side. He didn't speak, but she said as she didn't want to see the earl, only you.''

Lady with golden hair—surely not, not here. Nessa set

248

off, descending winding stairs at a brisk pace leaving Will hustling to keep up as she continued questioning him.

"These guests, did they come alone or with guardsmen?"

Having already run from near one end of the castle to the other in his search, Will's answer was breathless. "Alone."

Nessa came to a halt at the foot of the steps, dreading what likely waited around the corner. Matters between her and Garrick had been strained since the past night's scene. He had returned to their bedchamber, but not until he could expect to find her asleep. She'd held her breathing steady, pretending it was true while he turned a cold shoulder to her for the first time since they'd begun sharing the chamber. Her heart felt bruised and if her fears were true, the strain on their bond would worsen. Head bent over the joined hands pressed to cold lips, she urgently called on her abbey training to endure all trials without complaint. Squaring her shoulders, she took one step forward and learned the difference between gloomy suspicion and depressing reality as her already battered heart fell to abysmal depths.

"Nessa!" The squeal was all to familiar, and Nessa's arms automatically opened to the beauty who was sister, just as the earl stepped into the hall behind Reynard. In a black scowl she read Garrick's irritation with not being summoned to greet visitors come to his castle. She gave him a tentative smile. It appeared to deepen his annoyance. After their disagreement, having two of the queen's supporters suddenly arrive had doubtless upset him the more.

Worried about the dark man's response to unwelcome guests, Nessa leaned back to meet azure eyes and ask, "What brings you to Tarrant Castle?" She'd spoken more sharply than intended, and Aleria burst into tears. For once Nessa's own irritation threatened to overwhelm her overstrong sense of responsibility.

"Come, let's retire to the solar above where you can tell me all that's happened." Nessa had little choice but to take the weeping beauty to privacy yet hesitated to leave the prickly Reynard alone with an ice-cold host. As she turned to lead Aleria above, she cast her husband a glance soft brown and pleading.

Garrick found himself not so immune to his sweet lady's wordless entreaties as he'd meant to be. With a deep sigh he gave his guest a smile which, though chilly, at least lacked the freezing bite he'd have bent upon the other without Nessa's gentle intercession. Holding himself under tight control, he commanded a belated meal for the young knight.

Reynard, stiff with easily offended pride, knew his welcome insincere and accepted the hospitality with rigid courtesy.

Above stairs Nessa settled Aleria into a chair beside the fire before returning to firmly close the door. Then, taking the chair opposite, she exercised her carefully learned patience to await her sister's words. Aleria, she knew from experience, would first deliver a long tale of woe, justifying her complaints and emphasizing the urgency of the pitiful plea sure to follow.

"We went north to where the queen told us we'd be welcomed." The beauty leaned forward as if imparting some important state secret. "It took days, and it was so cold, so miserably uncomfortable that I vow I'll never sleep aside the road again!" Chin tilted with disgust, she sat back.

Despite her intent to console, Nessa's brows rose. Was this not the same woman who'd sworn she'd bear anything if only she could have her love? The spoiled beauty clearly hadn't considered what true hardships she might be called to face and, now that they'd come to be, even less was she prepared to accept them.

Her sister's mock amazement brought a delicate flush to Aleria's soft cheeks. "Well, it would have been all right if once we arrived our journey's goal had met with success, but the man to whom the queen sent us had fallen victim to an old injury and his nephew was lord in his stead. The nephew is Henry's man and Eleanor's letter carried no weight with him. Indeed, he seemed to believe it branded us his foes. He refused to let us spend so much as a single night in his castle! Not one night." Aleria's tone ranged from self-pity to amazed disgust for the man who'd failed to see the necessity of comfort for a fragile beauty such as she. "We'd no option but to return—to repeat the whole miserable journey." As if recounting a final blow of injustice she nearly wailed as she added, "And it rained every, every day!"

Though love further softened an already compassionate heart, Nessa was saddened to find her sister more concerned for herself than her husband's pain in finding his services unwanted, a rejection Aleria's demands and condemnation surely made worse. "You came directly here?" It didn't seen possible. Too much time had passed.

"Nay." Firelight glowed on coils of golden hair as Aleria shook her head. "First we traveled to Swinton Keep. I felt certain Sir Gilfrey would welcome us. As castellan of your lands and mine how else but that he should share the keep with me?"

Clearly the fact she'd given up her claim to the keep in exchange for her marriage to Reynard meant nothing to Aleria. Nessa was not surprised. She'd always assume whatever belonged to Nessa was hers to take.

"But to our horror we found Sir Gilfrey banished and the earl's insensitive companion in residence." Sitting straight, mouth pressed into an unattractive line, Aleria glared at Nessa as if she were the offender.

Aleria's description of the open and amiable baron made her vexation with the foiler of plans plain. Although 'twas the last thing Nessa needed when already she had her love's safety to worry about, she could see a huge problem looming in this sister who assuredly expected a miracle from her.

"Lord Conal is a fair man, and an honest one—which is certainly more than can be said of Sir Gilfrey." Nessa quietly defended the man who had proven himself a friend.

"Humph." Aleria gave a dainty snort, but she knew better than to argue with the person whose aid she'd come seeking. "He invited us to tarry the night but made it clear the keep was now the earl's and not mine."

"And he spoke true," Nessa affirmed.

Azure eyes narrowed on the one daring to agree with so unfair a statement. "Reynard is too proud and refused to ask a longer visit. Yet, knowing a well-bred woman cannot be expected to travel too quickly nor for too long a time, he asked that I be allowed to remain while he returned to Queen Eleanor."

Nessa feared she knew just how Reynard had come to possess such important information as what a well-born woman could or could not be expected to do, and restrained a crooked smile.

"And thus I stayed." Deeply involved in the grievous trials of he story, Aleria failed to see Nessa's wry amusement. "He was gone for several days. We truly thought she'd have some answer for our dilemma, but though she promised to seek a new position for Reynard, she said it would take weeks at the least. Moreover, she said we couldn't come back to Salisbury for Henry had heard of our 'treachery' and forbidden our return to his board." Aleria's perfectly formed lips pouted in a curve appealing and well practiced—yet a very real shadow darkened blue eyes. "Reynard's been as grouchy as a baited bear since his return to me. I told him he must demand of Lord Conal that Swinton Keep be put at our disposal, but he refused. Now he hardly speaks to me." Aleria had worked herself into a gloom over the injustice of it all. "What use has your husband for it when he has this great castle—" Tiny hands spread wide. "—and we have no home at all?" Aleria's voice had faded into a poignant lament.

Nessa understood why the girl they'd both been raised to believe born for pampering was upset at the prospect of being homeless. How else but that one as spoiled as she would find unpardonable Reynard's refusal to see to her long-term comfort. After all, never before had anyone failed to put her needs first. By her distorted logic such inaction could only be proof that her husband lacked appropriate emotion. Nessa's dread of where Aleria was leading intensified. With all her heart she wished she'd long ago learned how to firmly deny her sister's demands.

"So I insisted that Reynard bring me to you." Aleria brightened. "I told him you always have the right perspective. You know the importance of seeing me comfortable. You always solve my problems, and this one will be no different. I know you'll tell Lord Conal that the keep is mine to use as I will."

Looking into the other's confident face, Nessa soothed her impatience with the impossible request by reminding herself that this beauty—who could be sweet and loving—was simply a child never forced by life's realities to grow up. A lack for which she was largely responsible and must now pay.

"Nay," Nessa quietly responded, slowly shaking her head. "I cannot for the keep is not mine to give. Recall the bargain you made with the queen that saw you wed to Reynard? You claimed to be willing to give the keep over to the earl as the price for your happiness. Give it over you did and not to me but to him."

* * *

Nessa sought always to dress appropriately and never be a shame to her lord, yet previously she'd been unconcerned by the severe limitations of her wardrobe. This evening was different. After the younger girl—pouting and clearly determined to pay a disobliging sister back for desertion—had been settled in her room across the corridor, in the privacy of the lord's chamber, dismayed hazel eyes studied her few gowns each of which had often been worn. She'd have preferred the cranberry gown which offered hope of reflected color in her cheeks, but instead changed into the forest green wool. Busy preparing the chamber for their guests and helping in the kitchens, Merta couldn't come to her aid, and this gown at least laced down the side where she could reach.

She loosened toil-disordered hair as she moved to pick up a horsehair brush from the chest beside the bed and stroke repeatedly through thick curls. At length she tossed the bone-backed instrument aside in disgust. No amount of brushing would change brown to gold, no wonderment of a gown would make her a beauty to match Aleria. What use in such care when she would, as Erdel had so aptly put it, "fade into nothing" beside her sister. Yet, useless or no, Nessa found she must do all she could and plaited heavy tresses with golden ribbons before wrapping the braids in a shiny coil at her nape, allowing short curls to spring forward and lie against smooth brow and pale ivory cheeks.

As she adjusted her creamy camise's gold embroidered cuffs, she drew a deep breath for courage. Below she would stand beside Aleria and all in Castle Tarrant would see how inferior a substitute had been foisted upon their earl. Worst of all, Garrick would have living demonstration of the poor bargain he'd been trapped into accepting, of the severity of his loss. Her long-ignored conscience revived and made a noble stab at pricking her to bravery with a virtuous reminder that there was no point in self-pity nor value in pain over the lack of a beauty which justified sinful vanity.

Unwilling to linger until visions of inadequacy swelled to daunting proportions, she opened the door and moved to descend the broad staircase. With each downward step the dull roar of those gathering for the evening meal grew stronger, and with each step her apprehension grew. Would their laughter turn to disgust for her foul deed or to pity for her lacks compared to Aleria? A second time in one day she paused at the corner's edge, fearful of what waited beyond. Feeling as if she were walking to her own execution, she proudly tilted her chin and stepped into the hall.

"I've been waiting, praying you'd come afore they all take their seats." Reynard's nervous fingers engulfed her folded hands.

Nessa was surprised, but gave the high-strung man, already anxious to be done with whatever chore had sent him to her, a reassuring smile. Glancing around the vast room, she found people milling about, moving from one small group to another—but no sign of Aleria. Nothing strange in that, Nessa acknowledged. Aleria preferred to make a grand entrance after others were seated and quiet enough to take note. Her smile turned wry. Seemed the earl's cynical view of human nature's petty vagaries had spread to her, or else this castle truly instilled such jaded responses. Stricken with guilt for such uncharitable thoughts, she rebuked herself but had no time to dwell on her wrongful ways.

"The queen sent this to you." Reynard freed one hand to pull a folded parchment from its resting place behind his leather belt and hastily thrust it into the small fingers he yet held.

Pleasure drove bleak expectations and shame for unworthy thoughts from her mind. Hazel eyes glowed as she happily accepted the letter before backing into stairwell shadows to read its words.

Poor Reynard has but his one horse and it too well loaded already, but you have my oath that you will see the Saracen carpet soon for I am well pleased that your marriage is so much a success you wish to give your lord a thing of such value.

The message went on to speak of the queen's regret in being unable to aid Aleria. After the discovery of their trickery, Henry had tightened her constraints. Even had she been "blessed" with a visit from her youngest son, John. The rarity of that event had increased her suspicions. Likely the prince had been sent by the father to spy into the truth of her affairs. She was certain that any supporters she

254

contacted to seek employment for Reynard would fall under Henry's displeasure. She couldn't take on the burden of their ill treatment, not even for Aleria's sake. This time the girl must accept the consequences of her own choice.

This decree lent a twist of despair to Nessa's smile.

Aleria clearly hadn't taken such responsibility but rather had come here expecting her to give over Swinton Keep. Nessa felt doomed by the certainty her little sister would never understand that the Keep was not hers to give.

"The meal waits on your coming." A piercing silver gaze had observed Reynard delivering a folded parchment to Nessa, and her quick withdrawal into shadows. Garrick was not pleased.

Startled, thinking only of the gift meant to be a surprise, Nessa hastily stuffed the letter beneath a wide forest-hued sleeve but not before the waiting man had seen its royal seal.

"I'm sorry to have delayed you," she apologized, quickly stepping beyond his piercing gaze.

To Garrick the guilty action seemed confirmation of intrigue between his wife and the queen. Even had he not seen the seal he'd have guessed. Who else did Reynard know likely to write Nessa? Weighted by the pain of his suspicions, he followed her to the dais, his cold glower leaving silence in their wake.

As they approached the dais, Nessa saw Aleria waiting already behind the chair to the left of Garrick's. The stunning gown dyed to match her eyes lent a shocking vividness to a gaze full of childish spite, and the candles massed on metal rings suspended from heavy ceiling beams seemed to pale before the brilliance of golden hair. Nessa stumbled and cheeks once too pale burned bright with humiliation. Her awkwardness was a glaring contrast to Aleria's grace. The soft melody of her sister's giggles did nothing to alleviate her embarrassment. Unable to look up, she failed to see the flare of silver anger in the eyes of the man who'd deftly caught her near, preventing an ignoble fall.

Aleria did see the earl's irritation and recognized her mistake but had assurance enough in her own charms to count it as naught. Nonetheless, a strained silence stretched over the high table as its occupants took their seats. Aleria had claimed the chair on Garrick's left, but Nessa sat on his right, her due as countess. This left Reynard no choice but to sit at his wife's left, the farthest point from Nessa, and Garrick was pleased.

Nessa felt suffocated by the two men's tension and lifted her gaze no higher than the platter she shared with Garrick. She was all too aware that it would have been as proper, or more so, for Reynard to sit at her side and Aleria beyond him, as far from Garrick as possible. 'Twas clearly by Aleria's choice they sat thusly and just as clearly Reynard found it distasteful. Nessa's hands came together palm-joined in her lap. She knew as well as if it had been written across the table's white cover that Garrick viewed Reynard as a traitor to his king while Reynard saw Garrick as a threat to his marriage. What a hopeless situation! One that did not bode well for enjoyable meals or comfortable days.

"Garrick?" Aleria purred. "As brother I may name you thus?"

Light gleamed on black hair as Garrick politely nodded.

"Then I shall, for to say always 'my lord' would be too remote, too unfriendly." She peeked coyly at him from beneath flirtatiously lowered lashes.

"It would be unnatural for sister to call brother 'my lord.'" Garrick lightly stressed her position as close relative but plainly no one caught the significance. Aleria was too involved in her own conceit, Reynard in his irritation with her, and Nessa—well, she seemed too withdrawn to note anything at all.

Reynard's unhappiness increased as Aleria persisted in turning her considerable charms not to him but to their host—the man she'd nearly wed. The pain of losing his beauty's attention was harsh enough without a blatant display of her regret for the choice. His sulky frown deepened as he slid into a wordless pout.

For Nessa's sake alone and despite his barely hidden annoyance with the self-centered young woman, Garrick gave Aleria's too obvious ploys a polite reception, but no more. As he had on first meeting them in Salisbury, Garrick watched the two women and found the older sister far more alluring.

"Garrick—" Aleria's voice fairly dripped with honey and Garrick felt an urge to brush its sticky touch aside but forced himself to smile as he turned with a look of inquiry.

Aleria was pleased with the earl's response and even more

256

pleased by Reynard's. She planned to punish her husband for his recent inattention by proving she could beguile a handsome, powerful lord. Such a display ought to make him sorry for his treatment of her, make him think twice before subjecting her to such actions again. Besides, the earl's admiration would provide a soothing balm for her battered ego. She'd not enjoyed herself so well since she had accompanied the queen to the continent where so many noblemen had given their flattering approval.

"I'd be pleased to help you plan improvements for Castle Tarrant. It's so—so—austere." Sweet smile soured with disdain as Aleria slowly surveyed stark white walls. "Of course, Nessa's abbey background provided her nothing to compare against, no talent for creating the beautiful surroundings appropriate in a fortress so important. But I, raised by a queen and having visited the loveliest castles in France, could make suggestions." She peered at the handsome earl through flirtatiously lowered lashes. "I could even arrange for the purchase of a few choice tapestries, a finer service for the table." Without looking away from silver eyes, she waved dismissively at plain goblets and practical wooden serving platters.

Beyond wanting her sister to pay for her refusal of immediate aid, it never occurred to Aleria to consider Nessa's feelings. Her feelings for Garrick least of all. She'd married the man for her sake alone and, once nearly a nun, could surely harbor no romantic interest in him. Moreover, if Nessa would not give her the keep, 'twas only just that she charm it from the earl.

To hide annoyance, more like disgust, with the beauty's insult of both her sister and the outcome of all her sister's hard work, Garrick forced a brilliant smile as he responded with tightly controlled softness. "I thank you for the generous offer, but I am far too busy at present to embark upon such endeavors. Mayhap during one of your later visits."

Beyond the hurtful truth of Aleria's initial comment on her lack of talents to beauty, Nessa barely heard their words. Pain of another sort had struck her too deeply. After days of sitting at Garrick's side, basking in his attention, the feel of it shifting away seemed to wrap a sharp metal band about Nessa's heart, tightened by each smile, each quiet word given to another. Jealousy? She feared it true, and it was a sin although she knew no penance would ease the grip on her heart. Fingers twisted tight together, she tried to calm the sting with an application of cool logic. Aleria meant to punish her for not giving all that she'd asked, and for the same reason to punish Reynard as well. Furthermore, 'twas simply a part of Aleria's nature to prove her ability to add every attractive male to her collection of admirers. Unfortunately, another specter hovered behind soothing excuses. Had Aleria (as she'd been told many beauties had) found it impossible to resist the tempter's lures? No beauty and nearly a nun, she had.

Nessa surreptitiously peeked and found Garrick gazing steadily into azure eyes. Tears threatened to brim over in her own, and she held them open wide to prevent a silent flood. For a time she'd been happier than ever before, able to fool herself that Garrick might come to love her as she loved him. Leastways to bear some small fondness. But with Aleria so close how could he see her, a mere shadow of so bright and vital a being?

From her own well of distress she recognized Reynard's. His wife occupied with charming another man, it was plain that his control was sorely strained and his ability to be civil slipping dangerously low. He sat in pained jealousy, ignoring them all.

Garrick saw the other man's anger. Man—a generous use of the term, for Reynard was little more than a boy. Aye, a young and foolish boy doubtless easily manipulated by the the queen. He assumed Nessa preoccupied by her letter from Eleanor. Thus, to escape the blatant ploys of a beauty who hid a mind of no depth behind coy words, he spoke above golden hair to her husband.

"You've recently visited Salisbury?" In truth, there was no question on the matter for Aleria had already prettily complained about his 'desertion' of her for long boring days, but it was excuse enough to draw him into conversation.

Reynard turned a petulant face to his host but knew his manners well enough to respond promptly. "I made a hasty trip in hopes of aid in securing a new position."

Garrick nodded and silently continued to meet dark blue eyes. Such tactics most oft drove the recipient to speak further.

Reynard cleard his throat, nerves at fever pitch beneath

258

the compelling gaze that had forced many a man into retreat. "I wasn't there long but, as it happened, Sir Gilfrey was present when I arrived." This trivial news was the only thing he could think to say and say something he must. "But I believe his quest came to no happier ending than mine. I heard it said that he'd come seeking the queen's support in seeing Swinton returned to his hold, but she refused." Reynard nearly quailed beneath the ice in eyes gleaming silver. "Leastwise that's as I was told."

"He's got no right to our home!" Aleria gasped, clutching not Reynard but Garrick's strong arm between her small hands. This was the first she'd heard of the former castellan's claim.

" 'Struth." Garrick's voice was as cold as his eyes. "He has no claim, for Swinton is mine and what is mine I keep."

Even Aleria knew better than to argue. No matter. She had confidence that in time she would win the gift from a willing admirer. Her hold gentled to caress while she smiled with seductive warmth. "What's yours then is clearly fortunate to be held so dear." Her words were soft and full of unspoken meaning.

Aleria's words and action together with the fear raised by Reynard's talk of Sir Gilfrey hit Nessa with the power of a double fisted blow. At the dainty fingers clasped about an iron-thewed arm she stared so fiercely they must surely sting.

Garrick sensed Nessa's unhappy gaze on the hands touching him and was hard put to restrain the urge to shake them off as sharply as if they were leprous. Instead he let them fall away as he pushed his chair back and rose to his feet.

"The meal is past; and, as even late spring nights are cold, let's move nearer the fire to share mulled wine and cheese."

The others at the high table were forced to rise and move as a group to chairs arranged near the huge hearth. Nessa wondered why he had suggested they retire here rather than in the solar above. Yet, she was glad. The solar meant something private and warm, and she preferred not to see its remembered harmony sullied by the sight of another as recipient of her love's attention.

Stepping into the blazing fire's ring of warmth, Aleria claimed the padded bench closest to the flames. 'Twas wide enough for two and she smiled enticingly at the earl. Garrick ignored the invitation and took up a position with his back to the fire, feet planted wide and arms crossed over his powerful chest—a battle stance. Aleria was miffed but hid her vexation well.

Nessa hesitated, wondering where best to sit. Beside Aleria? Nay, she could not bear to be so near while the beauty, meant to be his, sought to kindle the temper's fires. A light touch on her arm was a welcome diversion, and she turned to find Reynard near. For a second time he'd sought her company, and she could see that he needed her support against this wound as badly as she needed his. By wordless consent, they moved to the fire's far side and settled into chairs placed close together. Anxious to take advantage of an unexpected opportunity, Nessa searched for some method of drawing him into the subject she wanted to discuss, without raising undue curiosity for her reason.

"In the letter she sent," Nessa began, hoping to sound as if the subject were of only passing import, "the queen mentioned a visit by Prince John. Was he with her while you were there?"

Reynard nodded and an unruly lock fell rakishly across his forehead. "Aye, he and his guardsman and, as I said, Sir Gilfrey. The queen said as she'd had more guests in the last month than in all her years within those walls."

Remembering how the queen had claimed to have no experience in hosting guests at Salisbury Tower when the earl first arrived, Nessa smiled. The warmth was short-lived. Reynard's words confirmed her worst fears. Garrick's two most dangerous enemies had surely met, and she'd no doubt but that in Sir Gilfrey, Prince John had found the perfect accomplice for his black deeds. Once again her hands came together in the old palm-joined gesture. She lifted them against her lips, worried about the plot she was certain Garrick would not believe. Trying to talk with him about it would only make matters worse. She'd no choice but to find a way to forestall it alone. Involved in dark fears, she didn't notice the silver glare directed at her and her companion.

While Aleria chattered of matters uninteresting to him, Garrick watched the other two. His doubts about his wife's loyalties were increased by the sight of her in close conversation with the young knight so recently come from the queen. Had the royal schemer sent this boy with new tactics to sow further seeds of distrust between him and his king, between his people and their lord?

None among the four recently descended from the dais were aware of the steady interest of another. Erdel turned his penetrating scrutiny upon the earl. Since their return with an unworthy countess, Erdel's arrogant disdain for the lord who'd repeatedly insulted him had simmered until it heated to a burning hate. He meant to see the earl rue the day he'd underestimated a worthy knight's superior talents. Though subjected to the beauty's enticements, still the man of ice glared at the woman's husband—in conversation with his countess. Next Erdel studied Reynard, who brooded beneath the earl's freezing dislike. A cruel smile curled Erdel's lips into a satisfied sneer.

❧ Chapter 20 ❧

I s it too heavy?" Nessa questioned a sensitive boy so quietly no one else in the busy kitchen would hear.

"I'm strong enough to heft a broadsword, and this is nowise so great a weight." Will's tender pride rebelled against the slight on his abilities. Chest puffed out, he held the metal pitcher before him with carefully steady hands to prove his claim.

Nessa smiled, nodding recognition of the feat. "I didn't intend to demean your strength, only for me 'tis so heavy I often fear 'twill tumble from the tray or tilt the whole from my grasp."

"With me to help, you've no reason to worry." Pleased by the lady's choice of him for the task, Will meant to see her faith justified.

Lifting the waiting tray of food, Nessa led the way from the kitchen and into the passage toward the West Tower, Will with his liquid burden proudly in tow. Happily the boy hadn't thought to question why, after weeks of carrying the whole by herself, she suddenly felt in need of aid. The old earl refused to leave his solitary life though with energy restored, he prowled the confines of his chamber like a wild animal locked in a cage—a cage of his own making. If he wouldn't come to others, then she would take others to him. And who better as guest than the grandson, acknowledged or no, whom Lord William likely did not realize now resided in Castle Tarrant. While convinced that a sensitive and loving heart dwelled beneath the old earl's bitter facade, she recognized that by leading the lad to the West Tower she risked raising wrath, even his banishment and every step of the way sent prayers for success winging heavenward.

They journeyed in silence; their footfalls echoing against the corridor's stone walls and padding over the stairs they climbed the only sounds. At the chamber door she glanced down and nearly turned back. Will looked at her with such trust that she was assailed with doubts for the wisdom in leading him to a possibly stormy scene. He'd followed unquestioningly and without pausing to consider to whom they'd come. Before she'd made up her mind to one action or the other, the door was flung wide.

"I thought I'd heard you arrive. Why do you linger so long outside that my meal grows cold?" William's booming voice was more bantering than condemning, and his smile was welcoming.

Nessa's breath caught as dark eyes slid from her startled face to the youngster. His smile disappeared and eyes went hard as black stone. Yet, he stepped back and waved them inside.

She set the tray on the table beside his favorite chair, as always, and turned, dismayed to find not only her father-in-law but Derward watching. The cruel pleasure in the latter's beady eyes informed her that she'd been mistaken in believing the old earl unaware of the boy's presence. Derward's satisfied smirk told her as plainly as words that she'd done the unforgivable. Her worried gaze fell to the boy equally apprehensive but standing brave against the black scowl of the man who denied him as kin.

"Pour Earl William a goblet of wine." To lessen her helper's distress, Nessa forced her voice to remain even and reassuring.

Despite slightly shaking hands, Will spilled not a drop as with slow care wine filled the goblet she held. While she sat the goblet on the tray and he put the pitcher on the table behind, Nessa struggled to find some soothing talk to fill strained silence. If only Derward had not been present.

Chin tilted, she faced disapproving eyes with a steady smile. "I've appreciated the help in my task. The pitcher is heavy, and I've already proven what harm can follow an off-balance load."

"Lord William, you see my warnings are true. This wicked creature has brought insult to you and—"

Derward's words were cut short as the old earl spun to deliver a cold glare. "Nay, I've said I'll listen no more to your spite and no more will I. Be gone with you and keep your malicious lies to yourself or I will banish you for good and all."

Derward cast a venomous glance at Nessa but quickly scurried from the chamber. Lord William then turned a still cold gaze to the boy standing fearlessly before him.

"Your name?" The question was short and its tone harsh.

Prompt and unwavering came the answer. "I am William, but most call me Will."

Lord William gave a grunt and nod in return. Though he spoke next to Nessa, his deep brown eyes remained locked with a pair of precisely the same hue.

"You expect to need his help again?"

"Mayhap." She'd not commit the boy to a deed he might prefer to deny.

"You would come back to this place?" This time the old lord spoke directly to the diffident youngster.

"Be it the lady asked me to." Will agreed without hesitation, never flinching beneath the man's penetrating stare.

"Worked her mystical charms on you, too, eh?" A slight smile came to William's hard mouth as his gaze moved to the woman whose subtle beauty seemed clearer each time he saw her.

"Aye," Will spoke with never a thought to hide his youthful admiration.

Only as warmth spread through her did Nessa realize how cold she'd become under her love's chilly disapproval. Both the old man and the boy found her acceptable, even if the one most important did not. Her dimple appeared but to conceal her pleased embarrassment she quickly moved toward the door.

"Come, Will. The meal waits for us, so best we be there before others grow impatient."

Will's face split with a bright smile more telling of his

relief in their departure than he knew. Happily he followed as she made her way from the chamber, down West Tower stairs and into the narrow corridor leading to the next tower.

As they neared their destination, Nessa froze. Two familiar voices carried through the tunnel's hollow silence. Clearly the speakers had moved into the shadows only moments before else they'd have heard approaching steps and held their tongues.

"You have it?" Erdel's impatient voice was unmistakable.

"I've the seeds you requested, but beware the effects of a poorly made potion." Derward's sibilant caution was all the more ominous for its being plainly meant as jest for the preparation's true use. Nessa's breath caught painfully while she strained to hear what followed. "This amount brews sleep but the whole renders slumber eternal."

"Give it to me and have done." The sound of a package snatched was so clear to the motionless pair beyond the corner to stairwell landing that they'd as well seen the action.

"Humph." Derward's initial irritation slid into a whine. " 'Tis yours then but remember your oath to me."

"Aye, 'tis all on the lady's head and neither yours nor mine." Erdel's tone was a sneer. "It fulfills my needs as well as yours."

Receding steps echoed and faded into a silence as cold as death. Caught by the horrible meaning of overheard words, Nessa felt frozen in place. That the seeds had been given in secret and that the two men had whispered of the deed confirmed her worst fears. She was positive that the potion was meant for Garrick and intended to see him consigned to the grave's eternal darkness. That she was to be blamed for the action meant nothing. Were the black deed successful, she had no care for what followed after. Her alarm was intensified by the absolute certainty that Garrick would not believe the danger. Even were he driven to investigate he would find no more than an innocent powder for a sleepless Erdel's relief. The request for such medicants from the castle's physician was reasonable and there was no wrong in his providing it.

Will's warm tug on her hand called her back. She gave him a weak smile, praying he hadn't understood the men's talk as the threat it was nor would speak of it to others. Such an action would all too likely call upon him a dreadful retribution.

With a select few of his guardsmen, Garrick had taken Reynard out on a hunt. Thus, only Nessa and Aleria took their seats at the high table for the midday meal. And Nessa had as well been alone, as Aleria chose to continue punishing her sister by determinedly ignoring her presence. Nessa had watched her sister and brother-in-law closely the previous night and then again this morn, and her earliest assessment had been confirmed. They both were still children; neither of them mature enough to consider the other's feelings, anxieties, or hurts.

She wished she had the heart to find amusement in Aleria's childish pout, but she'd no time to waste over paltry insults. Indeed, even the growing wall of ice between her and Garrick—the wall that separated them as effectively as stone even while they slept in the same private chamber, same once fiery bed gone cold—seemed trivial compared to the immediate threat recently revealed.

From the corner of vivid eyes, Aleria peered at her sister and found her totally preoccupied, showing no sign of the remorse their wordless meal was intended to earn. Even the watching eyes of those at tables below and those that served seemed more to condemn her! Until she'd left the queen's company, in all her life she'd never experienced such unpleasant responses from others; and, beneath her injured pride and virtuous outrage, she was deeply confused. It was a relief when the meal was done, and they could rise to move away from disapproving observers.

The sound of many feet tromping through the entrance tunnel was a welcome diversion for the two ladies who'd just descended from the dais. The earl was first into the room. Towering above his companions, he doffed his helm, ruffling night-black hair. His attention went immediately to the two caught halfway between dais and stairwell arch. Silver eyes passed the beauty as if she were not there to settle on the one beside.

Unable to sustain the added burden of a frost-filled gaze, Nessa looked down and missed Garrick's soon hidden regret. He wanted desperately to believe his wife innocent—but damning facts seemed to be piling against her with alarming speed.

266

At the earl's side and full of an excitement that left him looking even more the immature boy, Reynard fairly burst with the news of their morning's adventure. "We went a'hunting, only to become the hunted!" As his words tumbled out Reynard strode toward the startled women. "Leastways Lord Garrick was near struck down."

Nessa's hands flew up, their joined edge pressed to tight lips as her eyes clenched shut in a face blanched white. The expectation of some further wicked ploy had not prepared her for the actual event. Dangerous threat again fulfilled, she could only send upwards a paean of thanks for her beloved's escape—and simultaneous plea for continued protection.

Cheeks prettily flushed, whether with excitement or concern none could say, Aleria hurried to Garrick's side. "Oh you poor, poor man. How awful! But come, sit down. The wretched deed must have left you in need of a bracing drink." She tugged at the strong arm between her hands, but her prey would not budge. Refusing to admit his lack of action a rejection of her surely flattering solicitude, she stepped back. "Let me fetch one for you." She rushed to the high table on her self-appointed errand of mercy.

"There's no need for your—overwhelming—concern." Garrick's irritation was as plain in his denial of Aleria's overdone distress as in the look of disgust he cast Reynard. Shrugging the younger man's dramatic assertion aside, he gave his account of the matter. " 'Twas no more than an unfortunate accident. An arrow gone astray from its target. No more than that and a common enough happening." He did not add that the arrow had ominously lacked the distinguishing marks of any member of his party, any distinguishing marks at all.

Nessa's lashes lifted and worried hazel steadily met eyes deepened to cloud-gray. She'd heard this excuse before and no more believed it than surely he could this second time. Knowing he'd seen her rejection but just as aware that arguing with his logic was futile, she turned to wearily climb the stairs alone.

"You are so oft on your knees you accomplish little else." The verbal assault jerked Nessa from her prayers, and she twisted toward their speaker. Garrick stood only a pace or two behind. Despite knees stiff from an afternoon spent in earnest supplication at the prie-dieu she'd moved to an unused chamber, she rose gracefully to meet his glare with proudly uptilted chin.

Knowing the attack unfair, considering the long hours she'd spent reordering his home for his comfort, her steady hazel gaze and calm pride nearly forced an apology from the strong lord who'd seldom admitted error to another. His lips parted but before he could begin she spoke.

"My prayers are on your behalf and seek only your safety against Prince John, Sir Gilfrey, and all others who wish you ill."

"Prince John!" Impatience already needled by the length of time it was taking to eradicate the seeds of rebellion scattered across his lands increased Garrick's frustration over his inability to name this woman either evil or good, even to settle his own emotions. It erupted from him in words of angry disgust. "You pray for my safety against *John's* plot!" Seemed to him that, now when another confrontation was so clearly coming, Nessa was using even her apparent religious fervor to drive a wedge between him and Henry. 'Twould be a strategic blow to sunder the bonds of loyalty tying a powerful earl and his sovereign. "More likely yours and that queen you so admire."

Nessa stood firm before eyes that flared like ice on fire. A silly thought but a true observation that lent no humor. When Garrick whirled and strode from the room, his each step away felt like a further condemnation. Only when the door had closed upon his broad back did she sag against the wall. Clearly he believed she'd joined Eleanor in a plot against him. That she was behind dreadful deeds. The depressing certainty drove a shaft of pain to her soul. Garrick was a man of honor, a man of justice who loved the truth. That he found her so unworthy of trust was understandable given the method of their coming together, yet unbearable still.

Nessa stumbled to the stripped bed and let herself find rough comfort for slow falling tears in the depths of its homespun-covered mattress. Once the worst of her pain had been driven deep inside, she seriously examined Garrick's suspicion of the queen's part in a plot against him. Disallowing affection for Eleanor to sway her logic, Nessa found it easily possible to believe the royal woman was the source of

268

rumors which bred discontent. She was certain, however, Eleanor was not responsible for the inept attempts on Garrick's life. While verbal sieges, even assaults, were indisputably the queen's forte, stealthy attack with stones and arrows was not her style—and even less her style to employ those inept enough to miss.

A loud crash from below at last roused Nessa from morose contemplations, and in the subtle noises that followed she recognized the sounds of the evening meal's preparations drawing to a close. Sitting up, she was surprised to find dusk settling its color-stealing shroud across the room. She quickly stood and slipped up the stairs. The lord's chamber was also gloomy and, with no one to tend its fire, had grown cold. Although spring was nearly past, thick stone walls left the rooms within always chilly. She briskly stirred coals burned low to renewed life and carefully added a few chunks of wood taken from the pile at one side of the hearth a safe distance from open flame. As she rose, the brighter light of snapping flames revealed the crumpled condition of her soft gray gown. She heaved an exasperated sigh. Wasting time on self-pity had kept her from remembering a planned task she'd thought needful then but more so now.

Anxious to see it done, Nessa stripped off the ill-used gown and hastily donned the one of misty green whose side lacing could be managed alone—and which had not been attractive on Aleria. Her conscience, growing in strength again, rebuked her for the uncharitable thought. Mentally confessing her offense, she rushed from the chamber and began the downward path, all the while running hands over coiled braids to tuck in sadly errant curls.

From the shadows of the stairwell passage Nessa peered through the growing crowd, searching for a tall dark man. Nay, she smiled at her own easily mistaken description. Not Garrick but Reynard. At length she spied her goal and again scolded herself for failing to move with more speed. The lanky man she sought was already deep in conversation with Sir Rufus. Having little choice, for 'twas important to her that she talk with him as soon as could be managed, Nessa wound her way through the milling crowd to Reynard's side. She'd not have chosen to approach him publicly, but mayhap that was the best course. So open a meeting would be less likely to annoy their spouses.

"Prithee, Reynard, a private word." Nessa lightly touched his arm and spoke quickly to block her embarrassment in coming to a man, though brother-in-law, and with a request so unseemly.

Surprised at being so boldly summoned by a woman trained as a nun, Reynard's brows rose to disappear beneath the dark, unruly locks fallen forward. He nodded and turned his back on the older knight. The one thus dismissed melted into the group behind.

"When you wed my sister you gave an oath to willingly come to my aid whatever the need." She began with a brave claim and steadily met startled deep blue eyes.

"Aye, and 'tis an oath I will keep." Reynard's confirmation was immediate, if curious.

"You saw the arrow barely miss my husband and likely won't be surprised to learn it preceded by a rock which missed as narrowly." Nessa's voice dropped near to a whisper. She'd rather not have spoken of such matters in the midst of so many. "He claims both were 'accidents' and refuses to admit he's in danger."

Nodding, the tall Reynard bent closer to hear the small woman's each soft word.

Thick lashes swept down to shield eyes gone doe-brown with pain. "You had as well know he suspects me in league with the queen and likely their source."

Reynard jerked back as if her statement was an unexpected physical blow. "Surely not!" His reaction was vehement enough to draw the attention of most standing near.

Hiding dismay over her companion's too loud response, with a bland smile for those now watching, she motioned Reynard to accompany her to a small, almost deserted area near to the outgoing passage. He bent close again to listen intently as she continued in a tone so low no others would hear.

"I believe the danger comes from a terrible alliance between Prince John and Sir Gilfrey."

Reynard's dark brows puckered questioningly.

Nessa tried to explain. "John hounded his father into promising him the lands and title of the first earl to die without heir, thus gaining what he seeks without need to wed a woman he plainly finds distasteful. Garrick has no heirs." Nessa paused to let her meaning come clear, then

270

continued. "Sir Gilfrey's spite leaves him willing to wreak any violence upon the earl who claimed what he'd come to view his own. Particularly if the reward is the holding he believes unfairly taken from him."

Glancing nervously around, Nessa realized that the crowd was quickly dispersing to take their seats for the meal. Her gaze flew to the high table and clashed with a silver scowl. She hurried to conclude her tale and request that he honor his oath.

"Moreover, I've reason to fear that Sir Erdel, too, plans the earl harm. When we've a moment in privacy I'll tell you why. For now I'll say only that Garrick will not believe my warnings, forcing me to find my own methods of protecting him." Moving slowly toward the dais, she looked directly into Reynard's eyes and said, "I call on you to discharge your oath by lending me aid in the task."

Although privately doubtful of any woman's ability to plan a defense able to change the courses set out by men, Reynard was pleased by her trust and gave her a bright grin. "I swore to do whatever you asked and uphold my oath I will. Tell me what service to perform, and I will see it done." 'Twas an easy promise to give as he'd no expectation of being asked to fulfill it.

Nessa had no specific plan in mind but was relieved to have the promise of help in attaining her goal and rewarded the provider with a sweet dimple-bearing smile. As she stepped up to the dais, Nessa was surprised to meet a fierce azure glare. Surely, the beauty could not consider her a threat to Reynard's fidelity? Nessa nearly laughed at the foolish notion of herself enticing him or any other man into a passionate tryst. But then, mayhap a little jealousy would be a salutary lesson. For her conscience's sake she dare not openly admit that, after Garrick's cold treatment, the idea of Aleria being jealous of her was a precious, confidence-restoring thing.

Aleria was furious. Reynard had given Nessa his undivided attention when for days he'd been so very distant with her. For the first time she truly looked at her sister as a woman and in mysteriously changeable eyes and soft gilded curls found enough to fear. Shaken as much by Nessa's sudden transformation to attractive rival as by her husband's

271

apparent defection, Aleria turned well-practiced wiles upon the devastating earl with fervor.

Garrick had a very different interpretation of the scene between Nessa and Reynard. He thought it more than likely they'd been plotting. Surely, for no other reason would they speak so intimately. At the mere notion of his wife being drawn to the boy his lips clamped into a merciless line. He had seen the dimpled smile she'd given him. Then, too, there'd been green sparkles in her eyes. One way or the other her intentions were damnable. His hand tightened into a fist around the small, sharp knife he held.

When it finally sank through Garrick's disgust with the ill-matched pair that Aleria was pursuing him with retribution in mind, for like reason he no longer endured but rather returned her attentions full well. To her he gave a rare smile so potent that she very quickly forgot the reason she'd begun.

In the boisterous noise ever an accompaniment to evening meals where ale and wine were plentiful, Nessa sat at her love's side, ignored, while he opened his ice armor and bent the power of his tempter's charm on another woman—her sister. Knowing his admiration was justified did nothing to lessen the pain. Now, for the first time, she truly understood how Eleanor must have felt when Henry put the beautiful Rosamund in her place. 'Twas an anguish beyond measure.

⤚§ *Chapter 21* §⤙

During the next several days the skies were filled with ominous clouds that, of a morning, hung low and trailed patches of mist across the land. Even at midday they blocked the sun's warmth from the chilled earth and offered no sign of reprieve. Shivering as she moved down winding stairs, Nessa acknowledged that the dreary days were a fine reflection of her mood or, more truthfully, of the man whose ice armor seemed thrice thicker than ever before—black ice, dangerous and unrelenting. Though having felt the weight of a silver gaze all too oft upon her since she'd been charged with disloyalty, she was certain 'twas filled with a condemnation which added to her already near overwhelming weight of guilt for the action which had forced her upon him.

The plan had not been of her own devising but had come to be only after she, taught to be giver and never taker, had sought another's aid. Thus, her conscience relentlessly repeated, she'd been the source of the scheme whereby Garrick was bound to her and Aleria to another. Had she been the strong woman she'd long tried to be, she'd have insisted they two sisters remain true to their mother's plan—she remaining behind abbey walls while Aleria wed an earl. By her strength both Garrick and Aleria would now have been happy and, though lonely, she'd never have known this misery of guilt. A small voice of honesty reminded her that she'd also never have known the fiery pleasures of Garrick's embrace, the golden days spent in his company—things she could never regret no matter the price. Her forlorn smile faded into a dejected droop. Nay, for her beloved's happiness, she would sacrifice even her precious memories of joy.

That Garrick rued their marriage she could not doubt. Nor could she doubt his justified admiration for her beautiful sister. Whenever Garrick was in the castle, Aleria was near and the recipient of the tempter's luring smiles and soft words. All the while, he seldom spoke to Nessa and came to their bed only after he could suppose she slept. With an example of ravishing womanhood so near, Nessa was determined never to force upon him an unwanted closeness with one as plain as she. Thus, though unable to sleep until he laid at her side, she'd never revealed herself wakeful.

Caught in depressing thoughts, Nessa walked through the hall nearly blind to the serfs laboring to assemble trestle tables for the midday meal. The strained smile she gave as return to their greetings heightened the concern of those following her progress with worried eyes. In recent days they'd watched the lady who'd become the vital center of the entire demesne begin to lose her vibrant spirit. She'd toiled as hard as they to restore the castle and since then had shared joy in their marriages and births; sorrow in their ills. To them she'd proven herself a true beauty, and they considered themselves fortunate indeed to have her for their countess rather than her self-centered sister. Moreover, although previously they'd taken pride in their earl's reputation as the Ice Warrior, now they watched with disapproval as he turned his cold gaze to his lady yet smiles to her sister.

"Thank you, Oram." Answering the stocky man's good wishes, Nessa failed to see his bride standing in the kitchen doorway, hands on hips and worriment darkening her normally cheery face.

"Young Will's been put to spit-turning duties this morn, though he says as you needs his strong aid," Merta told Nessa when she came near enough to hear. "As an end to his argument, I promised as I'd take up the old earl's meal." Merta welcomed the excuse to ease the clearly unhappy lady's path in some small way.

"And leave me with nothing to do when already you have duties aplenty?" Nessa's smile warmed with affection. She knew the other woman fretted about her but refused to be coddled until she became self-pitying indeed. Nay, far better to stay busy.

"Be it you are determined to go, then leastways I'll carry the pitcher like as Will does." Merta turned toward the meal already laid upon a tray and lifted the heavy crockery vessel.

Nessa reached out gently to pluck the dull brown pitcher from Merta's hands. "Young Will I take not for a task I can easily perform myself, but for other purposes. If today he cannot be my aid, then I go alone."

Merta started to argue but saw the determined narrowing of hazel eyes and knew the cause lost. Affronted by the rebuff of her concern, she shrugged and turned aside.

"My thanks for preparing the tray, Merta." Nessa's words were soft and intended as atonement for the apparent insult.

Ashamed of her too quick temper, Merta looked over her shoulder and grinned. She'd meant to relieve, not add to the lady's trials with sulky behavior. "No burden to me as I already divides the portions." She waved toward the long table bearing platter after platter of foodstuffs waiting for pages to serve at table.

Thankful for her friend's cheerful spirit, which never let a grudge fester long, Nessa lifted the tray. "One thing you can do."

Merta spun to face the countess, anxious to be of help.

"The earl has gone to Sutton Mill, where he oversees the rebuilding of a wall fallen 'neath a winter snowfall, and will not return until hours hence. Thus, I'd be grateful if you'd see that my sister and her husband partake of the midday meal without me. Tell them I'm with Lord William or visiting an ailing villager or—." Shrugging, Nessa let the words trail away. She'd no appetite and without Garrick at table there was no need to prove herself unaffected by their disharmony. This chance to escape the uncomfortable ritual of pushing food from one side of the trencher to the other in imitation of eating was welcome.

Merta nodded her willingness to fulfill the request; but, although she understood Nessa's lack of hunger in the face of her husband's inexcusable actions, worried for her health.

Load somewhat lightened by the removal of her most

immediate difficult duty, Nessa made her way to the old earl's chamber. Still she labored beneath bleak clouds of depression so heavy she hardly noticed the once fearsome dark passage she walked through.

William was waiting in his chamber's doorway. "I heard you coming up the steps," he explained with a welcoming smile even as he leaned to peer behind her. Discovering her alone he looked back, brow quirked with an unspoken question.

"Will had other duties." Nessa was happy to see a momentary flash of disappointment pass over rugged features.

"Other duties—by his request?" His dark gaze demanded the honest answer which Nessa was happy to give.

"Nay. Indeed, he protested that he was needed here." She offered the reassurance while fighting to restrain a pleased grin. Here, at least, something was going as she'd hoped. "And likely he'll be free to help me with the evening meal."

Iron-gray hair brushed broad shoulders as Lord William nodded, face carefully devoid of emotion. He took the tray from her hands and tilted his head to the side, motioning her to precede him into the chamber.

Glad that she needn't rush and return to the hall for the meal, Nessa entered. Despite shuttered windows the room was well lit by a multitude of candles and a blazing fire.

With his back to Nessa, William set the tray in its usual place on the table next to his padded chair. When he turned, he leveled a penetrating gaze on her.

"Lest you should believe me too age-fuddled to recognize my own blood, rest assured I know the lad is my grandson."

Nessa blinked, startled by his sudden claim of the boy whose mother he'd denied.

"How—" She'd known from the first day that he'd known Will's identity, but still she questioned.

"The day he trailed you here and stepped from behind your skirts 'twas like looking at myself a goodly number of years past." William shrugged and settled into his chair waving her to the one opposite. "You could never understand what pleasure it gave to learn he'd been named for me."

His melancholy smile lent an already overly emotional Nessa a sudden urge to tears. By concentrated effort she

276

gulped them back, and her voice held only a slight waver when she asked, "Why then did you not give the name to your own son?"

William's lips thinned into a harsh line of self-disgust. "I lacked the courage even to look upon that tiny replica of what I'd lost. He seemed not mine but hers. I couldn't allow myself to love the boy after loving the mother too well; couldn't bear to lose another precious to me. Instead, I lost the opportunity to be father to my son, to help my heir grow and learn."

"You blame all this on the love you bore your wife?" Here in the fire-warmed intimacy of a powerful lord's chamber she asked a personal question she'd never else have considered.

The man's rugged face was filled with mingled anguish and despair. "I loved her too well and blamed not her but the one who stole her from me."

Nessa was dumbfounded. The woman had not been stolen away but had died in childbirth. She'd not been foully murdered, but had died of natural effects.

William's lips twisted into a parody of a smile more pained than amused. "He took her from me, took her life in exchange for his own."

On Garrick's behalf Nessa's long dormant temper rose. "A baby stole her from you? A tiny being with no choice but to enter an unwelcoming world?"

Wry laughter gleamed in dark eyes as the subject of her ire raised both hands as if to protect himself from her attack. "I know the irrationality of it. I knew it then but pain befuddled my logic. I sought a scapegoat for my loss and to my shame I placed that burden on the helpless child in my charge. A sad fact that I regretted sooner than any would believe. But, after I recognized my error and longed to repair the damage, I knew myself unworthy to instruct another on how to meet life with the bravery I lacked. I'd failed to manfully face my hurtful loss and retreated from the struggle a coward. In the years since I've discovered that once you've closed the door upon another, mere opening will not call the rejected one back."

Nessa's compassionate heart bled for both the rejected boy and the father who had lost the path to a son's love. Crystal tears silently broke their earlier barriers and laid

277

shining tracks down pale cheeks. Unashamed, she wept not only for the two men who had lost each other but also for the cold distrust with which that loss had filled their lives.

William was amazed to see the sweet girl crying for his unhappiness. Although many there were who'd sought the favor of a man in his position and with his wealth, since his wife's death no one had cared for him, save loyal Sir Rufus. Feeling as if he'd been called from a frigid winter storm into the welcome warmth of a cozy home, he was deeply affected by this young woman's action and wished he knew how to thank her.

Through tear-blurred eyes Nessa saw his mingled wonder and puzzlement. Misunderstanding his expression of helpless query, she softly spoke. "I weep for your unhappy decision to allow the pain of your wife's death to bottle God's sweet gift of love so tightly inside that it's turned to sour bitterness."

William's voice was suspiciously husky as he responded. "Your abbey training stands you in good stead, for you've more compassion and understanding than I've encountered in many a year."

Nessa's gentle smile peeked through the retreating rain of tears. "Aye, there I was raised to belief in forgiveness and hope eternal, of repentance and rebirth. And sincerely I believe you must unlock your heart and body. Scripture says God forgives all who humbly confess. Forgive yourself what God has already and enjoy what life is left—don't waste it by choice in seclusion."

A silence full of weighty matters fell between them. Bushy brows furrowed, William stared into the hearth so fiercely it seemed he commanded the battle between flames yellow and flames orange. Coming to a sudden decision, he rose and held out his hand.

Without hesitation Nessa laid her fingers in his palm and rose. He placed her hand upon his arm and led her to the chamber door. In Nessa hope soared that he intended to immediately accept her invitation to leave the tower's solitude. When he walked straight across the corridor and stopped before the chained portal opposite, she was startled. Massive metal links, although no longer caked in dust, were ominous and forbidding, guarding a chamber she'd no doubt had gone years unopened.

Lord William pulled a fine golden chain from beneath his tunic. Ducking his head, he lifted it free. Nessa watched perplexed. The chain was so delicate it must have been intended for a woman's adornment. His wife's?

Holding the object suspended on the chain up before her eyes, he said, "This has been with me day and night since my Odlyn died, a guard against exposing what I hold dear, exposing my pain."

Nessa saw that it was a key, ornate and well polished. Once it was placed in the lock melded to heavy chains and turned with a difficulty lent by disuse, the metal links fell away, scraping against thick planks. Hanging in useless strands, the abandoned chain dragged on the floor as Lord William steadily pushed the stubborn door. In the moments between closed and open wide, Nessa's heart beat hard in apprehension of what was hidden within.

"Ah-h-h-" Her held breath sighed out. Decades of dust could not dull a richness surely rivaling even Solomon's treasure.

"Odlyn's prized possessions. But even their beauty faded to tarnished dross next to her loveliness." As if sundering an invisible barrier, he stepped into the chamber and lifted a tapestry of muted tones and delicate stitches, next a silver goblet intricately embossed. For long moments he visually examined the chamber's contents, lost in long barred and bittersweet memories. At length he roused himself to search for a particular item. When he spied what he sought, he strode straight to a richly carved chest and from atop it lifted a small golden box inlaid with precious jewels. As he returned to face Nessa, he was amused to see hazel eyes still rounded with awe for the vast wealth accumulated in this one room, sizeable as it was.

"In thanks for releasing my soul from a self-imposed purgatory." He held the gleaming box toward her. "This is for you alone, but all the rest you may use wherever you please."

Had the object offered her been a poisonous adder, Nessa could not have recoiled quicker. He'd described his wife as so great a beauty that even these exquisite ornaments paled beside her. Nessa could not bear to stand amidst them so plain, so unworthy and such a great contrast. Already revealed for what she lacked by Aleria, this much more she did not need.

Lord William was amazed. From her initial awe he knew she found beauty here. How then could she recoil from this token?

Fool, she berated herself, witless fool. *You strive to restore a man's link to reality and then scorn his gift.* But even her desire to offer compassion to the one wounded by life could not force her hand to receive the symbol of her inferiority. With a weak smile she tried to explain. "If I can help you find peace, then your peace is all the reward I will accept, for I cannot take your beloved wife's lovely possessions—I am not worthy of them."

The old earl noted the pained regret in the soft brown eyes still staring at his outstretched gift. So, what his informants strongly hinted was true—there was trouble again between her and his son. Trouble likely born of a beautiful sister first meant to be countess and recently come to cast Nessa into the shade of her loveliness. Even the men Garrick had termed his "spies" had clearly been irritated with their earl for his treatment of his wife. Although they didn't like to report on the young earl's doings, they'd been driven to do so by their disapproval.

William's eyes narrowed as he withdrew his hand. Aching with sympathy, he went back into the chamber and replaced the box where he'd found it. She had done much for his sake, so now he meant to venture forth and do his best for her. When he returned, his frown was gone, and he smiled at her with gentle understanding.

"I will again lock all of this away if you would have it so. But this time for your sake, and not in pain of my own." His thick brows rose inquiringly.

"Please," Nessa softly implored. "For now leastways. Mayhap later you will wish to bring them out." An idea was taking form, a plan whereby both Garrick and Aleria could have their heart's desire. And if ever her sister were countess here, then these magnificent items should rightfully fill her home.

"For you." William bent, lifted the chains, and turned the key in the lock between to again form a barrier against pain—not to hold his inside but to hold hers out.

When he straightened, he swept Nessa into a quick hug of

280

such strength it forced the air from her lungs, yet she returned it full well.

One step from the archway between stairwell and great hall Nessa caught the sound of a familiar voice and froze. What possible excuse could Sir Gilfrey have for coming to this castle? Useless to stand and wonder. More useless to wait until anxiety left her knees shaking and even the weakest of bravado absent. Squaring slender shoulders and taking a deep breath, she lifted her small pointed chin and slid into the hall with a smile pinned on lips nibbled to rosy color.

"Sir Gilfrey." Before she could lose her nerve, she went right to the core of her alarm. "What brings you to Tarrant?"

"Ah, countess." The knight reached for a hand not offered and bent to lay a cold, lingering kiss on her fingertips.

Nessa suppressed a tremor of revulsion and concentrated on not giving him the satisfaction of jerking her hand from his hold as every instinct demanded. He was as repellant as she remembered and as insistent upon familiarities unwarranted. He straightened but retained her hand and his smile, more a sneer, was all too knowing of the distaste he yet wielded over her.

"I came at Queen Eleanor's request to bring you this package."

At last he dropped her hand. Nessa couldn't keep herself from rubbing the back of it down her skirts, ridding her flesh of his contaminating touch while he turned to lift the parcel wrapped in homespun that laid earlier unnoticed at his feet. As Nessa accepted it she quickly glanced around, worried about who had seen her receive this package once intended as a surprise gift.

"My thanks for making the journey for so trivial a reason." Nessa stiffly gave the formal appreciation courtesy demanded, praying the few guardsmen lingering at the hearth all too near had either taken little note or would be convinced by her words that it was of small import. "The kitchen is behind the dais and though you've arrived between midday and evening meals, those who labor there will provide you with a light repast to ease the hunger of travel while I see this tidied away." She shifted the bundle in her arms. Then, waiting for no further words, she escaped to the stairwell opposite where she'd directed he go.

281

Nessa rushed to the unoccupied chamber where her prie-dieu waited. Laying her burden on the floor, she tugged the large structure out from the corner it angled across. Lifting the long, narrow parcel, she upended it to lean into the niche behind. It had been meant as a betrothal token, a commemoration of the deed she was certain Garrick deeply regretted. Shaking her head in sorrow for lost dreams, she acknowledged the impossibility of giving him a daily reminder of what he'd rather forget. She refused to let threatening tears fall and mentally shook herself from melancholy thoughts. Only as she started to back away did a glimpse of something creamy tucked amidst dull brown homespun catch her eye. Sliding her fingers into rough folds she withdrew a folded parchment closed by the queen's seal. Breaking it open, she quickly read Eleanor's words:

I have not sent to you this man I know you have no liking for, merely do I send this requested item with one who says he is coming. This package and a warning I send—watch Sir Gilfrey closely for I fear he means your husband harm. Garrick would not believe a warning from me, so I send it to you. Watch and beware.

Nessa refolded the parchment and tucked it again into layers of homespun before pushing the prie-dieu back until each side touched a wall and hid her now useless gift. Her earlier wrongful self-pity was forgotten in the face of the living danger newly arrived in their home. 'Twas enough to overshadow all else. She sank to her knees on the padded bench created for that purpose and earnestly sought divine protection for her love and inspiration for steps to take in aid of its doing.

An unmeasured time later she roused herself. Likely Garrick would soon be here, and she meant to meet him outside, give him advance warning of Sir Gilfrey's presence. Rising, a grimace crossed her face. Her knees were sore despite their padded perch, and her neck ached, as much with tension as with the sore muscles of a head held too long bowed in humble supplication.

Anxious to be in the stable before Garrick returned, she hurried down the stairs, unnerved by the very real threat lurking near. Too near and, she discovered when she stood in the great hall's shadowed entrance, too late to deliver a forewarning.

"For all the years I spent caring for Swinton I deserve payment!"

Nessa's eyes widened at Sir Gilfrey's audacious demand.

"In the years you spent 'caring' for Swinton you stole tenfold more than your care was worth." Garrick's words were softly spoken but so cold they'd surely been blown off the ice floes of the great North Sea. He could hardly believe this knight's effrontery in coming to him with so feeble an argument after he'd made his position abundantly clear when ordering the treacherous man off Swinton lands in the first instance. Only could Garrick wish that Sir Gilfrey had gone straight to the fiery end he deserved rather than lingering near to tend the fields he'd sown with rebellion.

Garrick's broad back, still cloaked, was turned to Nessa but she was certain his eyes were as frost-filled as his words. Sir Gilfrey stood slightly to one side, which allowed her to see the poorly hidden alarm which drained color from his face. She was pleased to find him flinching before the latent force of her Ice Warrior. An uncharitable emotion perhaps, but how else should she feel about the one who offered a threat to the man she loved?

"So again you will send me away into the night?" He sneered.

"Nay, you may eat at my tables, spend the night in my castle, but this one night only. On the morrow be off and never return." Garrick recognized the man for precisely the peril he was. Yet, surely knowing his whereabouts was a stronger defense than sending him out to continue slinking unseen through forest gloom. Besides, what danger could a single knight with but two guardsmen be to him here in the midst of his castle and its mighty garrison.

Garrick abruptly turned and strode toward the stairwell. Seeing Nessa hovering there, he let his gaze drift over her. The apparent concern deepening hazel eyes to soft brown brought a cynical curl to his lips and an agonizing ache to his soul.

Will, the earnest young orphan he'd taught to ride, had been in the stable when he arrived, waiting to warn him of Sir Gilfrey's arrival on the pretext of delivering a parcel for his countess from the queen. The boy, Nessa's ardent admirer, had found no wrong in his lady's deed, but after learning of Nessa's hasty retreat with the package, Garrick believed it proof of her involvement in some plot of Eleanor's. Likely a plot involving Sir Gilfrey, once her castellan and the queen's supporter. His worst fears seemingly confirmed, Garrick could only name her a master of intrigue. Her ability to appear guileless while her loyalties were given to another smote him with a near unbearable pain, like a well-aimed dagger's deadly strike straight to the heart. He brushed past her with no more than the briefest of nods.

Beneath Garrick's disdain, Nessa fell back and she watched as he steadily climbed the stairs. Then, escaping into shadows, she sought the once fearful dimness of the corridor betwixt one tower and the next as if it were her only comfort. Garrick's coldness toward her had crystallized from detachment to disgust, like frost to solid ice. Leaning against the chill stone wall that felt warm in comparison to the man who'd passed her by and welcoming the frigid embrace of darkness, she loosed the long threatening flood of tears into anonymous, unseeing gloom.

Settling into her seat on the dais for the evening meal, Nessa clasped her hands tightly together beneath the table's white cover. She fiercely repeated the already oft delivered command to hold her emotions in check, to present a calm face to the hall's company—even when her husband turned stunning smiles upon her sister, complimented her beauty and grace. Nessa didn't wish others to share her distress. Still, although she knew herself to be no competition for Aleria, she hadn't demurred when Merta came to lace her into the cranberry gown. Nor had she argued when her friend insisted its deep cheery hue lent color to her cheeks and emphasized the golden highlights in ringlets escaping plaits intricately wound at the back of her head. There was little purpose in pointing out that whatever limited appeal she might possess was as nothing compared to Aleria's beauty.

Garrick was all too aware of the anguish in the gentle woman at his side—a pain laid at his door? How could it be that he ached for her hurt? Staring blindly at the heavily burdened platters being distributed to each table, he mutely fought against the guilt he felt. Why shouldn't he have responded as he had to the certainty that his wife gave her loyalty to another? His father had spoken true when he warned she'd steal his heart and trample upon his soul. The unbidden thought shocked a silent groan from his depths. Had she stolen his heart from him? Impossible. Were it gone, it would not ache so. Determined to deny the fall to a scheming woman's wiles, he reached for the platter and, using his sharp knife, attacked the roast pheasant atop it with a fierceness that would terrify any foe.

'Twas not a sudden noise that broke his concentration on the hapless bird, but rather a silence more telling than words. Silver eyes followed the path of many others to the man walking firmly down the hall's length toward them—Lord William. Garrick carefully laid his knife across the trencher he shared with Nessa and nodded to his sire before commanding another trencher be brought and a chair be set at Nessa's side.

For the first time since leaving the approaching man's chamber that morn, a warm smile came to Nessa's lips. Again he'd accepted a challenge from her. This time he'd forgiven himself and descended from his only tower to rejoin the world.

"You've made a wise decision," she quietly congratulated him as he lowered himself into a hastily supplied chair.

"Your wisdom pointed the way." His answer came with an affectionate smile that surprised those watching—and nearly the whole company were.

Knocked out of stride by both his father's appearance and the curious conversation between the man and his wife, Garrick began distributing the now carved pheasant and the meal began in earnest. Nessa was relieved to have Lord William's pleasant company when Aleria resumed her campaign for Garrick's attention.

"I congratulate you on refusing Sir Gilfrey's witless request." Aleria's voice was filled with overdone admiration as she stroked Garrick's arm, determined to win his thoughts from the odd pair at his other side.

"Witless, indeed," Garrick responded with a potent smile meant more to pain his enigmatic wife than to dazzle Aleria, although it succeeded at both. While Aleria prattled on with ridiculous praise, he looked above her head and noted the sulky droop to Reynard's lips, the way the boy-man withdrew into moody solitude. To his own surprise, Garrick felt some empathy with him. They were both possessed of wives they didn't understand and could not honestly communicate with.

The talk of Sir Gilfrey drove Nessa's hurt over Garrick's absorption with Aleria into the aching corners of her heart, leaving her mind occupied by more ominous concerns. Hazel eyes found the visiting knight where he sat with the knights of Tarrant's garrison near the top of a lower table, beside Sir Erdel. She was horrified to find Sir Gilfrey's strange eyes trained unwaveringly on her husband, menacing and so clear a threat it almost stilled her heart. Certain he was in Prince John's employ, her alarm for the true purpose of his visit grew to oppressive dimensions.

Lord William watched the table byplay through narrowed eyes. As earlier suspected, all the rumors reported to him were true. Garrick did seem a willing victim of the beauty's wiles and truly treated his tender wife with bruising inattention. A terrible deed which William feared, in part, his fault. Earlier he'd told Nessa it was too late for him to offer instruction to his son, yet he meant to try—the goal was too important to fail.

When the meal was done, as had become their habit since the arrival of Reynard and Aleria, the high table's occupants moved to the chairs grouped near the hall's vast stone fireplace. Again happy to have distraction of her own, Nessa asked Lord William if he approved of the whitewashed walls. The old earl, willing and more to lend support to the woman who'd done much for him, heartily praised her efforts and continued the conversation with amusing tales of past visitors and feasts. His unexpected wry humor soon had Nessa softly laughing and so engrossed that she almost failed to notice as Sir Erdel handed a goblet of mulled wine to the frowning Reynard who leaned against a stone wall just beyond fire warmth and light. Her attention was firmly caught, however, when the moody man shrugged and forced his shoulders away from the supporting wall to approach Garrick with the brew.

"The mulled wine you always have." Reynard's affronted tone made plain his irritation at being reduced to so menial a task.

Nessa's gaze flew back to Sir Erdel and recognized cruel satisfaction in his eyes.

Garrick lifted the goblet high in mock toast to the disgruntled boy-man before lowering it to his lips.

"No!" The anguished cry burst from Nessa's lips but others did not understand until after they'd seen the blur of her deep red skirts flying across the space between her and the earl. She knocked the vessel from his surprised hold, spraying the rush-strewn floor with crimson liquid.

Stunned, Garrick instinctively caught the body hurtling toward him. While the ringing sound of the metal chalice bouncing against the hard floor beneath rushes died away, over soft curls he watched bemused as one of the many dogs ever creeping near the fire's warmth lapped at the spreading red stain.

He sharply shook his head to clear the cloud of confusion and growled, "What madness is this?"

The question rumbled from the chest beneath Nessa's ear, but she could not distinguish the words above the wild pounding of her own heart. Her eyes, too, were fixed on the dog. She, nearly alone, was not surprised when it began to wobble, then fell—a discarded hide upon fouled rushes.

"Poison. Poi-s-s-ion." Like the hissing of a venomous snake the word was repeated in hushed whispers from one edge of the curiosity gathered crowd to the other.

"Reynard—" Garrick's one word stripped color from the man it accused.

Nessa's gaze went straight to Erdel and found a nasty smile. But another screeched from the back of the people gathered to form a half circle about the deathly play.

" 'Tis the witch's work!" The crowd parted as magically as the Red Sea at Moses' command to reveal Derward, flushed with animosity and determination to rid himself, indeed the world, of his opponent. "She be the one who charmed Lord William's mind." He sidled into the center, pointing at Nessa. "She be the one who takes revenge on her erring spouse."

Garrick held Nessa a breath away and looked down into her horrified face. In a flash he dismissed the wild accusation that named her witch. Might be she plotted with the queen, but she thought not to kill him, certainly never by so obvious a ploy.

"You blackhearted fool! Be gone from this hall and never set foot on Tarrant soil again!" William roared his banishment of the despicable worm without thought for the fact that his son was now earl and had right to such deeds. "You are the one who possesses the seeds of life and death. Because her good sense proved the folly of your cure, you've repeatedly sought to brand her thus. I've no doubt you were willing to commit any villainy to see it so, but I warned you that making the accusation once more would see you banished, and now you will go."

The people were grinning. Their old earl had truly returned to them, hale and hearty, and they were not surprised to learn their sweet countess was the miracle's source.

"True, he gave me the seeds to put in the wine." Erdel shouldered his way to the front of the crowd. "Claimed it was a potion to 'sweeten' your foul mood." He met Garrick's steady gaze with a shrug. "We all had reason to covet that end."

Nessa looked up. Ice glinted from narrowed eyes but firm lips were curled into a cynical smile. Obviously her husband's sense of justice demanded he accept the knight's explanation as an understandable quest and forgivable deed. Likely he'd find unbelievable any word she spoke of Erdel as a threat, and as unreliable as her talk of Prince John. Weighted by defeat, in the hubbub that followed she slipped away and slowly climbed to the chamber shared with a man who neither trusted nor even liked her.

Lord William watched the young woman he'd defended when her husband seemed slow to do the same. He ached for her but hoped to do more good by speaking with his son than by following to offer compassion.

"Garrick," William called to the man being fussed over by a beautiful woman. "I ask a private moment with you."

Black hair gleamed as Garrick nodded his assent. "Join me in the solar above." He led the way, conscious of how rare were the times he had walked this far with his father. Once in the chamber, he moved to the bench at one side of the blazing fire, leaving the large padded lord's chair for his father.

"You keep a fire burning here always?" Now they were here, William was uncertain how to broach a subject so private. This cold man was his son, but they'd never shared close moments. Of truth, their only talk of such matters had involved either warnings or arguments. His hands gripped the chair's armrests so tightly 'twas fortunate they were made of stout oak.

"Nessa often spends evenings here with the orphans who arrived with our castle cook, Maud." Garrick watched to see his father's reaction to the return of the woman he'd once banished.

"Maud?" Thankful for the opening, William gave a mirthless smile. "Aye, that's when it began, my denial of womankind. My rejection of them all a famous—infamous—fact you know well. What I fear you do not understand is that 'twas not for hatred or distrust that I barred all of their number from me. Simply did I love too well and dread the pain of again losing what was precious." Through flickering firelight William studied his son, hoping he would understand the confession's intended purpose.

Dark brows were drawn over cloudy gray eyes. Garrick had earlier learned that they didn't share the same reason for their rejection of women, yet he was surprised to discover their mirror attitudes sprung from nearly opposite sources.

William saw that Garrick failed to recognize the confession as the urge to marital bliss he'd intended and tried again to make his message clear. "By my own choice I wasted many years in lonely solitude—until Nessa took the time to find the path through my pain and lead me out again. She's a wonderful woman and well worth any hurt that might follow loving her. I beg you not to make the same error as I, even if born of a different rationale. There is no reason important enough to risk losing the joy of love returned."

Looking into a steady dark gaze, Garrick found he had not the heart to disillusion one only now coming out from years of bitterness by giving his excellent reasons for believing Nessa unworthy of trust.

In the growing silence, William was uncomfortably aware that he'd failed in his first goal—but he'd another. Summoning the courage he'd recently believed gone forever, he leaned forward to earnestly state, "I've been no real father to you, yet I hope you will accept our talk as proof of a love which, though never spoken and less often demonstrated, has always existed."

This attempt to form a relationship between them Garrick could answer and freely did. He rose and extended an arm to his sire. William's smile gleamed as he stood to clasp his fingers about the other's forearm below the elbow in bond of kinship.

"Nessa—" A tiny voice broke the two men apart and both turned to find a small girl timidly hovering in the doorway.

"Beata," Garrick's voice was a purr as he motioned the girl forward. "You've come for a story?"

Although she did not speak, her emphatic nod set fine brown hair to dancing on delicate shoulders.

Kneeling beside the girl, Garrick looked up into William's questioning eyes. "Before our visitors arrived, the children—two girls and two boys—came here every night. Nessa would tell them stories from scripture or from the book I gave to her. In recent days they've gone without."

"Fetch the others," William gently directed. "When you're all here, I'll tell you one of the legends I learned from the minstrels in my early years." He was certain his grandson would be among their number and, as he'd come down for the meal, he'd not seen the lad this whole long day and missed him.

Knowing his father had long forbidden the presence of children in his castle, Garrick was amazed by this easy acceptance of the orphans, even more by the man's willingness to join in their entertainment.

While Garrick watched the tiny girl hurry off, William felt compelled to speak on another matter. "One more secret I have that you should know. Young Will has helped Nessa bring my meals to the tower." William believed Garrick deserved to be told of the boy's heritage and did not even try to hide his pride as he added, "Will. You see, he was named for me—his grandfather."

Garrick was no more than momentarily startled. From his first sight of the boy, Will had looked familiar. Now he knew why and wondered how he could have failed to earlier interpret the child's claim of a shared heritage. Surely only knowing his father's woman-despising ways and his own preoccupation with threatened rebellion had kept him from recognizing the link sooner.

"I've lost years of joy and nearly destroyed the hope for a relationship with my son, this I won't do with my grandson,

290

even though he be of illegitimate line. And that my fault as well. The day your mother died I drank until I was so sotted I knew not what I did when I took a serf-girl, likely against her will. To add to my shame, the next morn I did not remember the deed and rejected her claim when she came to say I'd sired a child upon her. The daughter she bore I never acknowledged. Both mother and daughter are dead, leaving the boy alone. I cannot atone for my mistakes, but mean to see the boy neither abandoned nor denied."

Garrick nodded. Although he was not sure what his father intended for the boy, he would agree and do his best to see it carried out. Before he could question further the children came hesitantly to the chamber's door. Will was plainly shocked to find his grandfather in this part of the castle, but grinned in response to the old earl's welcoming smile.

"Come, Will, sit beside me," Lord William invited, making room for the child in his chair. "I'll tell you all a tale of a famous warrior. One about whose valor the minstrels wrote many songs and performed often when I was a lad your size—the Bastard of Warmaine."

❧ Chapter 22 ❧

Nessa stepped through the castle's massive entrance door and paused atop the steep stairway just beyond to gaze across a muddy courtyard. During the hours of early morn the long brewing tempest had broken to spew its fury upon the earth below. Adding to the aura of foreboding that Nessa felt closing in around her, Sir Gilfrey hadn't departed at first light as the earl had originally commanded. Garrick had chosen not to send the knight into nature's wild assault, like he had that night in Swinton Keep, and the day was more than half gone before the storm had finished venting its anger, washing even color from the sky.

As Garrick was truly temptation's lodestone and she the iron filings unable to refuse his call, her gaze unerringly settled on the man standing amidst shadows below the curtain wall. Although apparently extending a courteous farewell to the unwelcome knight, Nessa knew that he, as she, actually meant to be certain the man departed. Surely she'd feel easier once this particular visitor had disappeared through the bailey gate, taking with him his immediate danger to her love.

A movement on the wall above caught her attention. She saw a dark figure silhouetted against pale blue. It bent, straining to move a weighty object, and sheer terror blocked her throat. But when, with a final heave, the object was dislodged, she screamed.

Garrick whirled at the sound of desperate panic in the voice most special to him and took one step forward.

Stunned horror held Nessa in its grip as a monstrous rock fell with the unbelievable slowness of thistledown. Only as a wide ring of mud splayed out from the point where her husband had been meant to die, did a wave of overpowering relief sweep strength, even thought from benumbed mind and form. She slid into blessed nothingness.

At a mighty crash Garrick spun once more. On the very spot where he'd stood but a moment before a massive stone lay buried deep by the force of a landing loud despite mud cushion. He instinctively glanced up into the face of the mounted knight and found a shocked surprise too real to be feigned. But Garrick wasted time on neither his worthless foe nor consideration of his near end. He'd no room in his thoughts for aught but the fragile woman now a crumpled heap atop entrance stairs.

"I'll sit with Nessa while you change out of those mud-befouled clothes," Aleria offered, more distaste for his state than worry for her sister in the words.

Garrick had no patience for such foolish distractions. He curtly shook his head, and the fingertips pressed against one of the bed's canopy posts were white. Turning his back on the woman, he eased down beside Nessa who was still deathly pale and unmoving.

"But you've had a dreadful experience and must need time to recover." Aleria was not quick to accept a man's dismissal.

"Go and leave us be." Garrick bit out between clenched teeth. If Aleria failed to depart soon he'd likely wring her neck. In respect of their honest concern for his lady's well-being, he'd been gentle in fending off both Merta and Maud, accepting a bowl of cool water to bathe pale cheeks and a goblet of restoring wine for when she awoke. But put up with Aleria's false act he would not. Aye, at the first when he'd strode through the hall she'd been frightened for the limp woman in his arms. Yet, as soon as she'd learned the danger was to him and her sister's condition a mere reaction, she'd turned upon him her overdone and irritating words of distress.

Finally, Aleria rightly read the earl's growing ire and crossed to the door of the lord's chamber—once nearly hers. "If you've need of my aid, I'll be just across the corridor."

Having already turned his mind from her, Garrick barely heard the words. Holding delicate fingers within the gentle strength of his hand, Garrick studied the subtle loveliness of the women he'd wed. Nessa looked so small, so helpless yet she'd revived the castle's spirit, brought his father back from the brink of a solitary death, and saved his life—not only today but last night as well. He desperately wanted to believe she'd taken the actions for love of him. A heart-wrenching admission which demonstrated the depth of the undeniable love he bore for her.

Garrick dipped a cloth in cool water and wrung out excess moisture before stroking the satin cheek and smooth brow buried beneath escaped curls. Her actions surely proved she was not the source of deadly deeds. Couldn't have been and yet be this terrified by their near success. Gray worry went to silver ice as long training to doubt refused easy faith in a woman. In his soul raged a battle between loving trust and dark suspicion.

The fact that another was the source of mortal peril did not acquit her of intent to breed in him a suspicion of his king. His hands went still as a new possibility arose. Did others manipulate her, unknowing of the ploy, so that by her obvious concern for his safety he'd be led to believe Henry willing to see him dead for the sake of rewarding a beloved son?

He couldn't believe Nessa involved in the attempts on his life, but Reynard, her "friend" and perhaps cohort, was another matter. Reynard had been hunting with him, although not in sight, when an arrow narrowly missed his heart. The past night, no matter the source of the seeds, 'twas Reynard who'd handed him the poison brew; and Reynard, who'd he'd not seen today, could easily have been atop the parapet. Reynard, the queen's supporter.

Cool strokes brought Nessa to awareness, but only when they stopped did she risk opening her eyes. She found silver ice staring blindly through her and a damp cloth twisted so

294

tight between knotted hands that a steady stream of water pooled on the coverlet beneath. Although he bent over her in dutiful care, his mind was elsewhere. With another? With Aleria? An ever present guilt faced no difficulty in convincing her that his distress was the result of frustrated longing for the beauty he'd of recent days lavished with potent charms. The beauty he'd been meant to have, would have had but for her meddling.

"I'm sorry, so very, very sorry," Nessa blurted out, disoriented and speaking thoughts aloud. She loved him, loved him enough to give him all that he desired—even another woman.

Preoccupation broken, Garrick's gaze dropped and fell into doe-soft eyes. Black brows lowered. For what was she sorry? For the attempt on his life of which he'd just absolved her?

His dark frown brought Nessa to her senses with unpleasant suddenness. Yet, by her training to endure the carrying out of unpleasant chores for the good of others, she continued on the path toward offering Garrick the gift of happiness.

"I know what a disappointment I am, how difficult it must be to find yourself foisted off with me rather than the beauty meant to be mate for you. One who matches your incredible—" At a loss to describe his masculine perfection, she ineffectually waved toward him and continued with grim determination. "From near the start of my life I've known I was made to perform practical duties, not to arouse men's passions. I lack the golden hair, the vivid eyes, and the—" Again the words to explain what she meant failed her. Her voice trailed into a mournful quiver, and she motioned at her insufficient curves even as she berated herself for sinking into selfish pity as well as losing the power to speak with a modicum of wits.

Her self-denunciation was so different from the confession Garrick had expected that it took a moment to sink in. When it did, dark brows arched in surprise. Not arouse men's passions? What in Sweet Mary's name did she think had set him ablaze in their bed again and again? Before he could respond she went on.

"By my blameful action were you landed with me and, to see the wrong put right, I will submit if you choose to set me aside, send me back to the abbey." Her heart would wither and die but she must pay the price. To contain tears of misery, she let thick lashes drop and hurried to finish before her voice dissolved into sobs. "As 'tis commonly known that such a path was planned for me long ago, no one will question your decision. Then, on grounds of prior commitment—I to the church and Aleria to you—with your king's aid you can petition a release from marital bonds for both you and her."

Garrick was horrified. He first wondered if this were a scheme devised to see her returned to the cloistered life she preferred. The steady stream of tears spiking gold-tipped lashes and glistening on flushed cheeks disputed that possibility.

"For your sake, only yours, I will try to be a good brother to Aleria, but bear a lifetime of her company could I never! If the religious life you pine for, you've my oath to see it yours once more—though if you go, my heart goes too."

The fervent declaration shocked Nessa into looking up into serious eyes gone dark with pain at the prospect. Could it be that he loved her? Oblivious to the warm wetness of her tear-washed face, she slowly shook her head in disbelief.

"My father I understand at last," Garrick's words were husky, "for if I must give you up, I'll live out my days alone."

"No." The word hurt. "Never alone. Not you." The idea of him closed within his icy shell, lonely and longing for what he could not have was more distress than she could bear. She reached out to smooth the lines of anguish from beside his mouth.

Garrick caught gentle fingers and buried his lips in her palm. Was her response merely compassion, pity? Almost could he accept the crumbs from her heart, yet he hungered to feast on the whole, knew himself unable to survive on less.

"Is it St. Margaret's cold cot you want or the fire of my bed?" He couldn't help but argue his case as persuasively as possible and tugged on her hand to pull her up into his arms. "I love you and want you in my life." His rough velvet voice stroked like passion against her ear. "Stay with me."

Nessa marveled at the tremor in arms cherishing her against a broad chest. She must be dreaming. Only in her dreams could he love one such as she. Only in her dreams. But if 'twas the only way it could be true, then she'd pray never to awaken. Eyes shut, she wrapped her arms about him and sought his mouth with hers. For the length of this dream she'd blind herself to the inhibitions which kept a plain woman from seeking a man's desire.

"You are everything I secretly longed for." She confessed, no longer able to hide intimate transgression. "The tempter to delights forbidden me." The words dissolved into throbbing silence as his mouth took the ardent offering of hers with restrained ferocity.

Her longed-for admission broke wide the dammed well-spring of tenderness within Garrick, and it flooded into the raging sea of his need. He welcomed her advances, the feel of her melting against him and reveled in this undeniable proof that she was his the moment he touched her. "If I am the tempter, then you are truly my mate for beneath your cool control hides the fiery angel who tames him, a being of such enticements as I've never known—and mine alone! Release her to me," he growled, again lowering a mouth hard and warm, his breath mingling with hers.

She yielded eagerly to his demanding kiss. Drowning in his desire, she felt only his slow, burning caresses and gave no notice to the deft motions that loosened the gown's laces and the ribbon gathering camise about her neck. His hands pushed hers away; and, while her passion-hazed eyes blinked in confusion, his fingers moved to her throat. Slowly he widened the flimsy camise and stroked downward, brushing garments aside and revealing the pale cream and tender coral of her sweet body to his visual possession. He leaned forward, forcing her back against the bed as he dragged cloth free to be discarded, unnecessary, unwanted.

Interlocking his fingers with hers, he held her hands immobile against the pillow above her head and hovered a tormenting whisper away. Touching only at joined hands and lips, he ravished her mouth—deepening the kiss with devastating slowness until she writhed against rumpled sheets and gasped in an agony of need. Freeing her hands, as if afraid that to touch her at any point was to lose control, he pulled back but silver flames scorched over her elegant curves. This exquisite creature was his to caress as no other hands or lips ever had. His alone were those sweet little cries. He was drunk on the private pleasure of her.

Looking beyond glittering silver and straight into eyes gone to smoldering charcoal, she tumbled headlong into his molten core. Driven to incite a response in him as unmanageable as her own, she arched in wordless invitation. Drawn by a craving stronger than his will, with a groan Garrick bent to her body, and she helplessly watched, fascinated, as he put his open mouth completely over her breast. She trembled and a moan welled up from her depths. Twining fingers into midnight dark strands, she drew him nearer, certain that never again in her life would she recover from this sensation, shaking her, making her wild as again he played the tempter's song on her willing flesh.

Lost to rational thought, she tugged at his tunic. She wanted his clothing out of the way, wanted to smooth her fingers down the strength of his body and perfect her accompaniment to his wicked tune, return hot pleasures.

Seduced by her glorious abandon, a shuddering Garrick rid himself of clothes and came back down before Nessa had time to catch more than a glimpse of his magnificent form. In silent praise her hands explored the erotic combination of hard muscle and abrasive hair, moving up to measure the width of his shoulders with awe. Reveling in the feel of his powerful body, the clean male scent of him, she leaned forward and her small, pointed tongue ventured forward to taste him as he had tasted her.

Garrick's labored breathing caught on a harsh cry of starving need. He pulled her full into his embrace, crushing her against his whole long length and swept his hands down the satin curve of her back, urging her deeper into his embrace, mindlessly bringing her hips into contact with his. Lost in blazing sensations, Nessa shifted recklessly. Her nails dug into the firm flesh of his neck in a silent plea for relief as she offered herself up, a willing sacrifice to the tempter's consuming fire.

He moved to settle his whole long length atop her—hard chest against soft breasts, hip to hip, thigh to thigh and the intimacy dragged a shattering moan from her throat. Inhibitions long past burned to cinders, she clasped his hips nearer and provoked him to the final verse of the tempter's song. Their bodies merged, twined, and surged in the hot, wild rhythm of passion. She clung to the source of sweet, fiery music, striving to match its power while her nerves stretched so taut they must snap under the increasing tempo until at last it flared and crashed into a searing crescendo.

After long moments at the pinnacle of delicious fulfillment, they fell into the soft, welcoming mists of love admitted and shared. Garrick held Nessa close, dropping gentle kisses on her forehead, eyes, and cheek until, at last, she drifted into dreams.

An unmeasured time later, the gentle tug of a curl at her temple roused Nessa from a euphoric lethargy she'd never known—their previous passionate play had provided satisfaction but only acknowledged love could give such complete contentment. Incredibly happy, Nessa smiled, dimple peeking, at the man holding bed draperies open on one side. Seeing chausses tied about his waist, her smile slid into a puzzled frown.

"I've just returned, slugabed." Garrick grinned.

Nessa apprehensively glanced toward the shuttered window. Had she slept the whole night through? Was their precious night already at an end?

Soft laughter told her it was not so. Having missed the evening meal, however willingly, Garrick had been awakened by hunger of a more mundane sort. Not wanting to give over even a moment of their time, he'd risen and called for food to be delivered outside their chamber door.

"If my lady is ready to sup, her repast awaits." He stepped back and waved gallantly toward the small table in front of a blazing hearth. Upon it rested a tempting array.

Eyes wide at the luxury of a private feast, Nessa rose on an elbow to study the elegant offering—silver goblets with a flagon of mulled wine and a fine assortment of dishes she hadn't known Maud could prepare. Garrick formally offered his hand, and she accepted. Wrapping coverlet about herself in haphazard fashion, she walked with her lover to the intimate supper.

Passion-tangled curls falling past her waist and coverlet dipping provocatively, she nibbled on tasty morsels while studying the man she'd wed with open admiration—superbly masculine, handsome, and hers!

Garrick felt the sweet stroke of hazel eyes and leaned down to whisper against her ear. "You hold me in your gentle hands, lure me with innocent wiles I know never given to another.''

His dark tempter's murmur strummed across sensitive responses and she quickly lowered her face while a lack of confidence as ingrained as her sense of honesty insisted she speak the plain truth. ''I am not worthy of you.''

''I've traveled to the ends of Christendom and back, and you are the loveliest woman I have seen.'' The power of a silver gaze once again commanded Nessa to look up and see his sincerity. '' 'Tis I who am unworthy, but I'll cherish you until the earth falls away.''

Nessa smiled, ruefully shaking her head. ''Either you suffer failing vision or have learned in your journeys to tell pretty lies.''

''I don't lie—ever.'' He quietly stated.

''I know,'' she answered without pause, serious expression spoiled by green sparks of teasing laughter. ''Proof your eyesight is fading.''

Garrick grinned, pleased to find her spirit still healthy and willing to risk his ire. ''My vision is acute, 'tis simply that you cannot see what only a privileged few do. Like mists of enchantment suddenly lifted to reveal paradise, your pure loveliness is a magical vision all the more beguiling for its rarity. Unpredictable, breathtaking and a secret treasure which is mine and no other's.''

His pride was as clear as his sincerity. Knowing he really never lied, Nessa believed it was true, at least for him. And this magnificent man was the only one who mattered. Amazed that he could love her and thrilled by the freedom to do so, despite bright cheeks, she studied his lips with eyes melted to misty green. The unfinished meal was forgotten. Garrick swept her up into his arms and carried her back to the tempter's cavern, demonstrating his admiration with slow unmistakable fire until the welcome blaze consumed them once more.

After the castle had settled into the quiet of night hours, missing the curled warmth that had so quickly become vital to his happiness, Garrick came back through clouds of contentment to see a cloaked figure slip through chamber door. Warrior training held him immobile, tense and ready for whatever the stealthy visitor sought. He refused to allow the doubts engendered by a lifetime of suspicion to chill newfound trust or even momentarily to entertain the possibility that Nessa had gone from him to arrange for another to come upon him while satiated and unprepared.

The hood of Nessa's dark cape fell back as she bent to lay her burden quietly on the floor beside the bed where Garrick would step when first arising. Loosing the cloth wrapping, she rolled the rich Saracen carpet out and lips curled in gentle pleasure as she stroked its soft nap.

By the hearth-fire burned low Garrick saw the shy smile on passion-swollen lips and rolled toward the kneeling girl.

Beyond being surprised by her husband's unerring knowledge of her whereabouts, she looked up into questioning gray eyes. "When I came to you the night of our first coming together, I told myself that I sought only to give you the one betrothal gift you would appreciate from me—an heir."

The thought that it had been no more than that which had laid her in his bed was unpleasant.

Concentrating on her confession, Nessa failed to see his discomfort, and by continuing unknowingly soothed his pain. "During the hours of that night I was forced to admit that 'twas no boon to you, merely an excuse for selfishly giving to myself the gift of pleasure. I've spent days seeking some token that you might enjoy and when one morn you rose and spoke of cold floors, I remembered the luxury of this foot-welcoming carpet beside my bed in Salisbury Tower. I wrote to Eleanor and asked that it be sent to me. I realize now that my keeping it a secret left you to misunderstand my purpose, but 'tis here. Only do I regret that it was tainted by Sir Gilfrey's hand."

Such a simple, harmless reason for her correspondence with the queen, for the package exchanged. Garrick was all the more ashamed of his mistrust of her when she had tried so hard to please him, accepting even his censure to see the deed done. His father had spoken true—the risk of future pain was worth the golden joy brought by love of this special woman.

"You hold the power to take my wary heart and sooth its fears." Garrick spoke his thoughts aloud as he lifted Nessa into their intimate haven, gathering her into a tempter's embrace, past icy armor open only to her and into his molten core.

* * *

While fires burned and love flowed in the lord's chamber, in the cold and musty damp of the deep forest beyond Castle Tarrant two men argued.

"What foolishness led to two witless actions within the length of a single day?" Gilfrey's sneering contempt scraped across his listener's pride.

"Had either succeeded, 'twould not have been foolish!" Erdel defiantly snapped at the shadow so shielded by impenetrable night gloom that he recognized the speaker only by voice. Surely his attempts to secure the goal were heroic, if naught else. He was tired of being spurned by those in command, even by serfs, and had meant to prove his superior cunning to them all—and punish the perpetrators as well.

A low growl of disgust was his answer.

"If a new order is what you seek by removing the earl from his position," Erdel impatiently explained the rationale behind his acts, "then 'twould be better if blamed on one of his own."

"And so it will be," Gilfrey agreed, pausing for emphasis, "but 'tis important that the people be a part of the deed."

"Important to who?" Unseen in the dark, Erdel's brows creased as he questioned the other's statement. "By their uprising will they earn only harsh suppression, not the freedom you've promised."

"Aye." Satisfaction purred the word. "But 'twill leave a fief in need of immediate leadership with no time to waste and no reason to reinstate an aging man known to be failing in health."

"Lord William is restored," Erdel instantly answered.

"'Tis a fact that King Henry doesn't know nor will he before the fulfillment of a promise is demanded and given."

This talk of kings and promises was unfamiliar and had no bearing on what Erdel knew of Sir Gilfrey's plot. But one thing seemed clear as water from a mountain spring—his talents had again been spurned. "Then you've no need of my aid?"

"Indeed, we do." Gilfrey's mocking smile spread thin lips wide. He and his cohort could manipulate this young fool to, at the end, bare the brunt of the blame as leader of rebellious serfs. He went on to awe the ambitious knight

302

with talk of a prince and a masterful plan, ending with a flattering show of trust and an important charge. "You are to keep us apprised aforehand of what actions the earl takes, prevent us from walking into danger unaware. Aye, and more importantly, you we need to take command when the unexpected army appears."

The pleasure of being given a position of leadership did not blind the crafty Erdel to the possible dangers of such a role, but he deemed himself capable of avoiding them. After all, twice already he had walked free of blame from failed plans. No need to remind this man that to see the proud earl dead was a shared goal. No need when to hold his tongue might see him paid for an action he meant to see complete one way or another. "What is my reward for services rendered?"

"A fief, albeit small, of your own." Knowing that the intended result of the younger man's task would leave any future payment impossible left Gilfrey free to offer what was not in his power to give. "Only be at Hydatha's Tor two nights hence for a final meeting of your warriors." Cynical amusement pulled Gilfrey's lips into a sneer but his voice he held free of emotion while talking of the untrained and unprepared serfs whom he'd stirred up to do battle with warriors well able to dispatch them hastily and without strain.

Trees grown so dense that their branches twined overhead, disallowing so much as a stray shaft of moonlight from penetrating the gloom below, prevented Erdel from seeing his companion's expression. Without further hesitation, he accepted the dimly seen outstretched arm and firmly shook it as he solemnly responded to the offer.

"Done."

᭗ Chapter 23 ᭗

B ut Reynard was there and he says both Sir Gilfrey and
Prince John were in Salisbury Castle.'' Gentle hazel eyes
pleaded for belief from the man dressed and standing with
one hand on the chamber door's latch while she was still
abed.

"Even did I believe Reynard speaking true," Garrick
answered with a consoling smile, "I would find it difficult to
accept an alliance between a supporter of the king and a
supporter of the queen." He wished she'd not waited until
now to speak of serious matters. After seeing her faint and
his own panic while he'd carried her here and as they'd
missed both evening and morning meals, the people of the
castle likely feared them all too shaken by the previous day's
events. It was important that he rejoin them soon and see
the whole demesne returned to its natural order. Yet, he
couldn't bear to abruptly leave his love full of anxiety.

"Mayhap they do not share the same loyalties, but they
do possess a single goal." Nessa earnestly sought to make
the looming threats clear. "Sir Gilfrey has said he'll see you
dead while the prince has Henry's promise to see his greed
rewarded by the end of your line."

Dark brows arched, Garrick asked, "And you believe one of them was responsible for yesterday's incident?"

Nessa nodded, silky curls tumbling over her shoulders as she leaned closer to the opening between parted drapes.

"Then, my sweet, you haven't applied your praiseworthy logic," he lightly answered, with a faint hope of jollying her free of preoccupation with his danger. "Prince John has never been to Tarrant, and I was talking with Sir Gilfrey when the deadly stone slammed to earth." Even more, in an honestly shocked face he'd seen the proof of the admittedly unsavory knight's innocence.

Her lover was laughing at her, although without malice, and Nessa could only shake her head in despair. "I'm not blind to those facts but, even if their hands were not upon the stone block, it may have been they who directed the deed."

"Beyond Sir Gilfrey there were no strangers visiting Castle Tarrant." The words were a cold statement of fact.

Squaring her shoulders to bear an unpleasant reality, Nessa nodded her agreement. "No strangers, but many others."

Silver eyes narrowed, against not her but the hurtful thought. "You are suggesting one of Tarrant's own is a traitor in league with my enemies?" Though buried first beneath concern for Nessa and next beneath the joys of love returned, he'd earlier known it true. Whoever the foe behind, the perpetrator had to be one familiar enough with castle routine to take advantage of the short time during which tower guards changed and the parapet path went unwatched. Then, too, the perpetrator had to be a familiar face able to easily blend into the momentary chaos breaking out in the wake of the unsuccessful attempt.

Nessa bit back a spontaneous accusation of Erdel. Having no proof beyond an overheard conversation that could be interpreted to mean either something or nothing, she dare not speak and had to content herself with another slow nod.

Cloaked in a luxurious mass of cloud-soft hair, the fragile woman in the midst of his huge bed troubled Garrick. He saw the unhappy droop to her lips and the apprehension darkening eyes to gentle brown. Did she fear he'd blame her again for speaking of it? And did she see his sidestepping of the issue as a rejection of her concern, a concern he now

305

believed born of love? He rushed to reassure her with words he would otherwise have left unsaid.

"Clearly, someone is intent on seeing me fall to mortal danger. However, and I tell you true although you will not like what I say, I do not believe Prince John is at its root. Nor do I believe the prince was with his mother as you were told. Since the disaster he made of his campaign in Ireland, Henry seldom lets him wander far—to his mother least of all. Nay, I fear it more likely that your informant, long a supporter of the queen, has merely repeated the story as Eleanor instructed him to do."

Garrick smiled his encouragement but chose not to add that he believed Reynard was the most likely culprit. The boy's convenient lack of employment and need to seek shelter in Castle Tarrant was too opportune. Each accident had occurred while he was near, but not in sight. Even that first "flying rock" had happened when, by Reynard's own admission, Aleria had been at Swinton Keep and he riding alone in the area.

Nessa could see in a steady gray gaze that Garrick believed Reynard guilty not only of spreading false tales but of the attempts on his life. Therefore, he must believe the pair had come to his castle under the cloak of a deceitful excuse. They were now so close in personal matters, yet this subject of his peril they saw from opposing viewpoints for she was certain there was no untruth in the reasoning behind her brother-in-law and sister's arrival, couldn't be. Reynard's wounded ego and jealousy were too real to be pretense. Still, knowing what Garrick believed, Nessa was aware that 'twould be impossible to convince him of the dangers she saw. Her gaze dropped to hands once again palm-joined, fingertips white under the pressure imposed.

Although on the point of departure and convinced of the necessity of rejoining to his men with all haste, Garrick returned to his anxious bride. He stepped across the lush carpet without allowing dusty shoes to touch the precious gift.

Nessa gave her tempter a tremulous smile. He bent, tangled fingers into the rich silk of sleep-mussed tresses and touched her lips with a brief kiss of fire.

"Don't stew on the matter," he softly commanded, holding her with gleaming silver eyes. "I swear I'll be on my guard and prepared, whatever the threat or its source."

Nessa nodded but her smile had a forced brightness. Garrick backed to the door and departed, after pressing fist to heart as he bowed in a farewell salute. Her smile faded to worriment. He would 'be on guard' but doubless he had been the same before and see how often he'd narrowly missed death. Nay, she'd have to find some way to save her love. The ultimate weapon, the babe she prayed nestled even now within, would be neither believed nor yet considered adequate defense. Without warriors of her own, 'twould be difficult to fight a prince, but for Garrick she would.

She must take advantage of the few who would accept her tale of imminent danger. They constituted her meager resources. Quickly she rose, dressed in the gown of deep brown and a cream-toned camise, and, with plaited hair coiled at nape, was stepping out of her chamber when Merta arrived.

"I must hasten to the West Tower," Nessa began before the other could speak.

"Lord William has had his breakfast, milady. He comes down to table with everyone else—almost everyone else," Merta teased.

For once her friend's cheerful spirit was lost on Nessa. Her feeling of impending doom and pressing need for action led her to speak more briskly to the woman than ever she had before. "Between first and midday meals I ask that you and Oram meet me in the kitchens." She had no specific plan beyond a vague idea of asking their help in keeping watch over the earl while he was within the castle proper and hoped Lord William would have suggestions for more useful tasks.

Merta was startled by her lady's odd behavior, and odd request—considering it was already the time of which she spoke. Even in the days of her estrangement from the earl the countess had never spoken thusly, but Merta nodded and with brows raised over mud-brown eyes watched the smaller woman hurry away.

No thought to spare for its once fearful shadows, Nessa moved through the corridor leading to the West Tower with steady purpose. She knocked on Lord William's door—no answer. She was on the point of turning away when a voice spoke from behind.

"You've come to visit me in this chamber after struggling so long and valiantly to win me free of its confinement?" William's dark eyes sparkled with amusement.

Nessa spun to meet the one she'd come seeking. Knocked off balance by the unexpected hallway reception, she lost the words to begin. She'd suddenly realized that he, who was also the king's man, might share Garrick's view. Her hands twisted.

Laughter wiped away by his visitor's distress, William reached out to throw open his chamber door and motion her inside.

"What is it that troubles you?" The question came the moment the door thudded shut behind.

Nessa drew a deep breath and dove into the possibly icy water of the telling. "Garrick is in serious danger."

Dark brows furrowed beneath iron-gray hair. By now surely this much was known to all on Tarrant land—and likely far beyond the fiefdom's boundaries. Truly a matter for concern but surely a deeper purpose had sent her to him.

Seeing her host's questioning expression, Nessa hastily added, "I've known Sir Gilfrey since I was a child. He is a spiteful, devious man who wishes ill upon your son and me as well."

This, too, William already knew. He merely nodded.

Nessa recognized that, so far, he'd found no reason to dispute her words and braced herself for his possible reaction to what next she said. "Prince John also has reason to wish Garrick dead." She peered into Lord William's unsmiling face.

"A nasty piece, the prince. But what possible motive would he have for seeking my son's demise?"

"He hounded his father for more lands until, to still the nagging tongue, Henry rashly swore to give him the lands and title of the next earl to die without heir."

"Sweet Mary's Tears!"

The old earl's exclamation gave hope that he accepted the disgusting deed as fact. Nessa nearly sagged with relief. "Garrick will not believe his foster father could be even inadvertently responsible for so dastardly a trap and though he says he will be on his guard, I fear it impossible when he protects himself from the wrong threat. I've come to beg your aid in seeing him safe."

William could easily believe his king had made the impatient promise yet, although certain Nessa believed every word she spoke, he needed more proof to see John as a threat. Still, he chose not to wound her by openly disputing her claims. He motioned her to a seat in front of the fire which he bent and stirred to life.

"Tell me how all this came to your ears and mayhap I'll see the path from which the danger came and from the knowing be able to end it before it grows out of hand."

Nessa shifted uneasily. She'd just told him its origin. Still, she obediently detailed her sources of information from the traveling minstrel at Swinton to the peddlar who'd seen men in Prince John's colors and the many revelations upon Reynard's arrival. She told him of Reynard's oath to do her bidding and in the end Lord William's open attitude allowed even her unprovable suspicions to find voice.

"I believe, but cannot prove, that 'twas Sir Erdel who sought poison of Derward for I overheard them speaking of seeds able to render eternal slumbers as I walked through the dark corridor below. Will was with me and heard the words though I doubt he understood their threat. By them I knew 'twas poison in the goblet of mulled wine that Erdel gave to Reynard and he to Garrick."

William was convinced of the truth in the threat offered by Erdel and Gilfrey but found the prince's involvement unlikely. Nonetheless, as the whole was equally ominous whether or not John was part of it, he didn't argue. He was willing to investigate and guard against all possible sources of the danger that must be stopped, and he shared Nessa's ultimate goal—Garrick's safety.

"I go from you to meet with two more whose aid I can trust, Merta and Oram. Them I will ask to watch over your son while he is within the castle. But 'tis not enough. Not nearly enough. Fighting a prince without an army is a difficult chore."

"Perhaps, perhaps not," William immediately answered, continuing with a touch of amusement, "I very much doubt that the prince would dare bring an army to bear against one of his father's strongest supporters."

It was a cheering thought and Nessa brightened.

Even though he had little faith that what she believed was true, he would see his son guarded against it. "What it will take," he stated, "is a deeper knowledge of the inner workings of Henry's court than either of us possesses. I've been a recluse for years and, as Eleanor's foster daughter, you've none."

"Reynard?" Nessa tentatively suggested, but the shallowest logic quickly wiped that hope away. "Nay, he's been at Eleanor's castle-prison since coming into the king's employ and has never been privy to the court's inner circle."

" 'Struth, but as I said, by telling me how you've learned all that you know, 'tis possible to trace back the line. Beyond your early years with the treacherous Gilfrey, from whom did you first hear reports of danger?"

"The minstrel of Swinton Keep." Nessa's answer was immediate but as quickly amended. "Nay, in truth from Conal, Baron of Wryborne." Hazel eyes widened. 'Twas he whose help they needed. She was irritated with herself for not seeing it earlier when they'd already made a pact to watch over Garrick. "Conal has been with Henry near as long as Garrick and is as knowing of the court. Conal is Garrick's friend and was first to warn of the threat. Aye, Conal will help us any way we ask."

William beamed and nodded. "Now I'll tell you of dangers more than you may know." All warmth had drained from his voice and expression. "There is rebellion simmering amongst Tarrant and Swinton serfs, even free-born farmers, and Gilfrey is the brewer stirring the whole. I've been out since dawn seeking old supporters and striving to discover the identities of the misguided few—to no avail. The knights Gilfrey and Erdel are the only two names I repeatedly hear."

Nessa hadn't paused to think on it, but she'd heard Garrick complain so oft about rebellion that the old earl's words were not a surprise. She solemnly asked, "What can we do to halt wicked deeds?"

"I suggest directing friend Oram to follow Erdel whenever and wherever he goes during the next few days—I do not believe the confrontation will be restrained much longer."

Nessa's vigorous nod freed several ringlets to curl against flushed cheeks. Here at last was a path, a beginning, some action to take. "I will see that Oram begins the task without delay. Moreover, I'll send Will to Swinton with a message

310

for Baron Conal and on the morrow meet him at Hydatha's Tor.''

William admired the girl's unhesitating support of his plan and how she carried it a step further. He grinned his approval. "A fine notion, and I'll join you on the journey if you allow?''

Nessa was pleased to accept his offered company and told him so as she rose. Mindful of the two waiting for her below and anxious to get the strategy for defense underway, she excused herself and made her way to the noisy kitchen filling with the preparers of the noontide meal. Under the unexpected shield of a boisterous group still lacking the firm guidance and restraint of their leader, she led her two friends into the shadows at the far end. With them she sat at a crude work table and, too quietly for others to hear, explained the need and the assignment for each—Oram to shadow Erdel and Merta to watch closely for unexpected dangers while the earl was within castle walls.

By the time Nessa was finished, Maud had arrived to firmly direct the kitchen crew's chores. Waiting until all were busy with assigned tasks, the countess took the heavyset woman aside and again quietly explained the dangers before asking permission to send Will with a message to Swinton. Although it was the right of a lady to command any serf on her land, Nessa wouldn't offend this woman by ignoring her right to motherly concern. Maud beamed with approval of a consideration few well-born would give and agreed, sending for the boy immediately. She, too, would do much to see to the safety of a man once boy in her charge.

After Will was on his way, Nessa hastened to the great hall for the midday meal. Disappointment left a downward droop to her lips as she saw Garrick's empty chair. Clearly his business today was too far afield to allow for returning home. She'd not questioned him for his path this morning— her thoughts had been too taken with trying to convince him of his danger's source. Tension brought her hands together palm-joined. She'd pray for his safety for already had it been proven that even the company of his well-trained and battle-honed guardsmen was no protection.

So involved was Nessa in her worries that she'd failed to realize Aleria absent until she, Reynard, and all those at lower tables heard the approach of a familiar flirtatious giggle. Startled hazel eyes flew to the golden-haired female hanging on a powerful man's arm while walking with him to the dais.

Garrick saw Nessa recoil as he arrived with another. It had not been his idea. He'd hurried his return to be with her even publicly—a few bright moments in the midst of a day gloomy despite strong sunlight—only to be met at stable door by this conceited creature.

Once past the immediate shock and instinctive pain in seeing her beloved caressed by another, Nessa saw beyond a cold mask to the barely restrained irritation forming silver icicles in gray eyes. She couldn't help but smile.

The dimple-revealing curve of sweet peach lips washed Garrick with relief. He had her trust, and he gave it back with a smile so warm she blushed with pleasure.

Garrick politely aided Aleria to her chair but turned to Nessa as soon as he slid into his own. "How has the morn treated you?" The question, low and intimate, was a verbal caress.

"I fear I was late in arising." Bashful eyes twinkled beneath half-lowered lashes. "By its shortness, therefore, 'twas busy." She couldn't explain to him exactly what had kept her so occupied and hoped he would not ask. He'd no chance.

"Garrick." Aleria again demanded the earl's attention, azure stare hard upon Nessa. "Won't you take me for a ride? The sun is cheering, and I am so bored." She was unused to a man, any man, turning from her to another and to her plain sister least of all.

A silver gaze narrowed so pointedly on the dainty fingers stroking his arm from elbow to hand that 'twas a miracle it did not cut. Garrick looked from the hand to the owner's husband. Why couldn't the foolish boy entertain his wife, keep her from being such a pest.

Reynard felt the other man's disapproval and straightened his back to glare in return.

Nessa saw the visual battle and, ever the peacemaker, jumped into its midst. "Aleria, I have plans for us."

Aleria was torn between pleasure with her sister's clearly jealous wish to halt the proposed ride and the curiosity her attempt at disinterest could not hide. The younger girl's raised brows silently questioned the details.

Nessa improvised. "I'd hoped you might be interested in seeing the view from the battlements." She could have bitten her tongue the moment the words were out. The last place she wanted to be was the site of yesterday's distressing action.

Aleria looked skeptical.

"What a fine idea," Garrick reinforced Nessa's timely offer. "I've a private meeting some distance from here and have no time to ride with you, but your sister will see you entertained."

Aleria recognized the trap she'd set for herself. Though she'd far rather stay indoors, now that she'd sought an outing she was forced go through with it. Her smile was brittle as she curtly nodded assent.

After the meal was done and hazel eyes had followed a figure of power and grace until he disappeared, Nessa reluctantly rose.

"Shall we begin the tour?"

Aleria stood but made the lame excuse of wanting to wait until the sun's power to darken fair skin had lessened.

Nessa feared the sun would only grow stronger as the day progressed but welcomed the postponement and offered an alternative. "At nones, then?"

"Bells do not mark the hours in a castle, and I've not learned the timelines by repetition as have you," Aleria sniffed. Such religious schedules were not hers to know.

" 'Tis when the sun is half done with its downward journey, and I will send someone to fetch you."

"Nones," Aleria mutinously agreed. She sensed a reason behind Nessa's insistence on this time together and was certain she'd not enjoy it.

"With your guide's aid, we'll meet in the stairwell landing aside our chambers." Nessa was relieved to have the time to ponder the best method for speaking as plainly with her sister as she must, and settled once more into her high-backed chair before the table being cleared while Aleria climbed the stairs alone. From hive of activity while trestle tables were disassembled to near deserted quiet, the atmosphere in the great hall changed unnoticed by the gently frowning countess seated alone on the dais. All too soon the sun was in the appointed position, and she made her way to the meeting place, dreading the conversation she still felt

313

supremely unequal to conducting. It had been put off too long, this task of helping Aleria understand that the time had come for growing up, for thinking of the needs and feelings of others.

An irritable Aleria stood waiting, wrapped in a cloak doubtless intended to block damaging rays as effectively as it warded off winter chill. Her small foot tapped impatiently. "I've been waiting for hours."

Having sent a servant to lead Aleria here only moments past, Nessa's brows rose but she let pass the obvious exaggeration which would have put her sister here before noon meal. "I'm sorry. However, I've duties which I cannot always set aside for my own pleasures." The gentle rebuke fell on deaf ears.

In silence Nessa led the way up another flight of steps and struggled alone to shove open the massive door on the highest landing. Thankfully, the guard just beyond heard the sounds and pulled it wide. That Aleria had offered no aid merely reinforced Nessa's guilt for her lack of right guidance in the past.

As Nessa stepped out onto the parapet walk, hazel eyes flew to the pile of rubble from whence a stone block had been dislodged with deadly intent, but she forced her attention back to the matter at hand. Halfway along the battlement walkway, Nessa stopped, much as Garrick had the first time she'd crossed here. She turned to find Aleria clearly fearful of the sharp drop from their path to courtyard floor and near clinging to the outer wall. Nessa gestured toward the view.

Sunlight glided the moving moat waters below, brightening the fields to an emerald hue, and bringing a peaceful smile to Nessa's lips. Not a cloud marred the sky's blue dome allowing a welcome warmth that penetrated the skin and soothed the soul—or was it love returned which made the world below appear clean and crisp, lending courage enough to begin the task too long undone?

"There is a wall growing between you and Reynard near as high as this one, and I fear 'tis of your making."

"*My making!*" Aleria bristled, turning to advance on the sister standing behind. " 'Twas not I who refused to do all to provide a home."

"But it was you who swore to be willing to abide any-

314

where as long as it was at your love's side." Nessa stood steady to respond calmly. "I am certain the choice is no more his than yours."

"He most assuredly could have done more!" Aleria straightened, righteous indignation flaring in blue eyes. "He could have demanded the queen give him employment."

"Nay, that he could not. No man may make demands of his sovereign." Nessa's denial was firm.

Self-centered reasoning flailing against a logic far stronger, Aleria retreated a step as she retorted, "He certainly could have demanded it of the stranger in my keep."

" 'Tis *not* your keep, nor even mine." Nessa was forced to speak bluntly to the one who chose to conveniently ignore an undeniable fact. "It and half of Swinton belong to Tarrant, not to either of us. Reynard could no more demand it be given him than he can command that this castle be his."

Aleria backed away until she stood flat against the stone wall, looking like a cornered animal.

"Don't you see how your reversals have hurt Reynard's too tender pride, how your continual nagging and belittling make it only worse. I strongly fear your attitude may render a death blow to his love."

Attacked by a supportive sister for the first time, Aleria lashed out. "You're simply jealous yourself—and who'd have thought it of a nun?" Her laugh held not mirth but bitterness.

Though clearly not intimidated by her sister's attack, Nessa was wounded by the girl's pain and ruefully shook her head. "I am no nun, nor could ever again consider that path as I am much too happy in my husband's arms—as you would be in Reynard's if you would only give of yourself to try."

Like any trapped prey when the chance avails, Aleria fled. Nessa had repeatedly stolen Reynard's attention and now sought to humiliate her with an unspoken claim to be the one preferred by the earl. Well, she'd find the powerful lord, make him admit he found her the most attractive, and prove Nessa's hopes unfounded.

Nessa watched the startled tower guard swing stairwell door wide for the rapidly approaching beauty. Feeling her sister's confused hurt and wanting to offer both sympathy and support, she followed, steps slowed by a futile quest for a new avenue to Aleria's understanding.

Aleria was out of breath, cheeks flushed and shiny curls tangled by the time she'd reached the bottom of winding stairs, but she ran through the near empty great hall, drawing the puzzled glances of only a few and never hesitating. Once this day she'd successfully caught the earl in the stable and meant to do so again. She hurried down the castle entrance steps and across a courtyard already sun-dried and packed by the day's traffic.

Garrick was rubbing his huge steed's silky nose when, over the meaningless words he murmured into the beast's ear, he heard another's rapid approach. Dark brows were low over flashing eyes as he turned, prepared to harshly warn an unthinking stable boy of the folly in startling these massive beasts, not all trained to war and impassivity. The body that hurtled itself against his chest was most decidedly not a boy's.

"Nessa is cruel, cruel." Crystal tears were prettily clinging to dark gold lashes when rough hands grasped Aleria's shoulders and held her away. Looking up with her most enticing pout, Aleria mournfully added, "She won't understand that I must have a home, and she preaches at me to pity Reynard who refused to see me provided for."

Garrick felt only disgust for this woman who epitomized all he'd learned to detest and against whose image Nessa was more clearly revealed for the rare and lovely creature she was. "If you seek sympathy, you've come to the wrong source." The words were shards of ice. "Best you seek it of the one you wed. I've none for a woman unable to appreciate how very fortunate she is to have a sister as loving as Nessa. A sister who has sacrificed for you again and again. You should strive to emulate her selfless, honest spirit."

The mouth fallen open under his attack snapped shut into a most unattractive line, and she straightened to sneer in return. "Those are the traits of a nun. A beauty doesn't need them." A dainty hand smoothed over the golden hair intricately coiled at the back of an elegant white nape.

Freezing eyes slowly examined the woman, and the smile brought by the sight held no admiration. "Outer beauty fades and I fear you'll become more a trial than a joy, indeed even your husband now finds you so, while Nessa's sweet

316

loveliness endures and her company is ever a pleasure to all around her."

Nessa had arrived at the open door in time to hear Aleria's contempt for a nun and Garrick's defense. Though already near convinced, 'twas further proof that her husband meant what he'd said in dark hours and that his words had been more than mere comfort for a plain woman. They put to rest the faint doubts lingering around the tender edges of her newborn self-confidence, and she quietly slipped away, certain that 'twould only add to Aleria's shame were she to know her sister privy to the scene.

⋧ *Chapter 24* ⋦

In the night gloom above Oram's head a bird loudly protested the intrusion of man. His heart stood still. As silently as possible he'd crept along behind Sir Erdel to this well-known landmark. Before the wild creature's unexpected reaction, he'd been congratulating himself on his skill at playing the unseen observer. Now Oram could only pray he'd not be discovered—surely a dangerous possibility. Peering apprehensively through the thick leaves of an overgrown bush, he realized that the handful of men hanging back in shadows beyond a small fire's ring of light seemed as reluctant to be seen as he and, occupied with their own fears, hadn't noticed the bird's disgruntled cawing.

Impatiently waving his audience nearer, Sir Gilfrey spoke. "We'll wait no longer for the others. To you I will tell my design and expect that you carry it to your neighbors."

Afraid to move and draw unwelcome attention, Oram struggled to see the faces of those who mumbled their assent. His eye was caught by one who took several steps back to lean negligently against the upright stone which was Hydatha's Tor. The action earned Oram's contempt. How natural for a man as condescending as Sir Erdel, one who ever sought to prove his superiority by relaxing while others toiled. The knight never stood when he could lean, nor walked when he could ride, nor did even the simplest task for himself when he could command another to do it in his stead.

A haze of smoke from the blaze beginning to smolder and die away drifted across and partially obscured Gilfrey's face, but as he continued his words were clear.

"The moment we've been waiting for is near at hand. Within the week the signal will be given. I'll not know the day until our friend in the castle," he waved toward Erdel who straightened and stepped to Gilfrey's side, "brings to me the news. But when it arrives, and you hear my call, gather up your weapons and fellow freedom lovers. Join here and follow Sir Erdel's command. I will come and together we will defeat our common foe."

The dull gray of a cloudy dawn stretched overhead, echoing the morning mist rising from fertile fields to obscure the feet of Nessa's dainty mare and Lord William's great destrier. Nessa tucked her cloak near to hold off the damp chill of early hours and settled more comfortably for the long ride ahead. Garrick had been called from their bed in the middle of the night and with a large contingent of guardsman had ridden out in response to a vassal's plea for aid in the face of a dam broken and flooding valuable farm lands. 'Twas not the first time an emergency had summoned him at odd hours; nor, pray God, was it likely to be the last. She pushed aside her fears, however, by acknowledging that this time it had eased her own plans. She'd thank God for the aid, as she'd been unable to think of a believable excuse for her own early morning departure. Now there was no need.

As they entered the woodlands, Lord William again reviewed the news Oram had brought to him before even the faintest light had appeared on the horizon. The names he recognized and the men he would visit, such were the positive results of Oram's task. It was unfortunate that they'd no certainty of the date nor the place of the confrontation looming ever closer. More unfortunate still was the proof that a traitor lurked in their midst.

Trees lush with new green leaves lined their path on either side, and the scent of damp earth and fresh sprouted vegetation laid heavy on the air. The going was slow for the haze-hidden path was made dangerous by unseen stumble-holes able to maim both horse and rider. Nessa was impatient, anxious to meet with the baron and set firm plans for defense, to accomplish something although the threat had only begun to take shape. Oh, indeed, the participants were known, but the method was still as befogged as the path at their feet.

"If this cursed mist lifts afore we return," William rumbled, "I'll show you a much shorter route to the Tor than this commonly traveled path." He hardly noticed that his trivial comment faded away without apparent response from his worried companion.

Each caught in their own concerns, they traveled in silence. Before reaching the outer bailey wall they'd exhausted the topic of what little was certain and by unspoken agreement had realized that to speak further would merely increase nervous strain.

At last, in a small clearing amidst dense green forest, they sighted the stone monolith of their goal rising out of low rolling mists. No sunlight broke through the clouds overhead, but Conal's tawny hair gleamed near as bright as his broad, white smile.

"Welcome, friends," he called out, moving forward to hold their horses' reins.

Before the baron's lips had closed, Nessa began. "You had the message I sent with Sir Jasper? The one telling of attempts on Garrick's life and his refusal to take them seriously?"

Lord William climbed down and tied his steed to a low-hanging branch at the edge of the wood, freeing Conal to aid Nessa in dismounting as he nodded his answer.

"Since then a poison brew was given him and a block dislodged from the parapet walk missed him by no more than a step. Now he believes his life in danger but not our warnings of the prince's involvement." She studied a cheerful face gone serious.

Conal glanced toward the older man who listened with arms folded across a wide chest and saw the skepticism in dark brown eyes. 'Twas a miracle he was here at all. They'd met but once, and he'd had the impression that the father cared little for the son, yet here the older man was and come seeking aid for his son's protection. In truth, a miracle, and he'd no doubt that its creator was the lovely woman standing near.

"I know 'tis difficult to believe, Lord William." Conal met a brown gaze directly and spoke with conviction. "But true it is."

Iron gray hair fell forward as William bent his head, but whether in agreement or mere acknowledgment of their belief neither Conal nor Nessa could be certain.

"Whatever the danger's source," William quietly said, "the threat is real, and the outbreak of rebellion is very near. Nessa assures me you are a true friend to my son and will do all to help our cause. An obvious truth as, in a difficult period, you've given of your own time to care for his fief."

Impatient with the waste of precious moments on matters other than solutions, Nessa explained. "Garrick believes Eleanor is the one who foments rebellion, the one who threatens him, but I know it cannot be so." Nessa looked between the two men and realized that neither would believe so simple a statement. "I've talked with her, and she has wished me well with my marriage, has sought to ease my path." If anything, her argument had deepened the others' suspicions. "She even sent warning of Sir Gilfrey's danger to my husband." At last the others' narrowed eyes showed them questioning their distrust, and Nessa went on to speak of what was surely the most dangerous threat. "When my sister and her husband arrived at Tarrant, Reynard told me that John was visiting his mother while Swinton's former castellan was there. What more natural allies than the two who both wish Garrick ill?"

Conal's brows rose at the news his one-time visitor had not shared with him. Yet, it was not surprising that the diffident Reynard had kept his knowledge to himself for they'd hardly been on cordial terms. Moreover, Conal didn't believe Eleanor was at the bottom of this particular danger, but neither did he trust her. Only was it that, at the moment, her actions were not those in question. Aloud he mused, "I can believe that Sir Gilfrey has become John's accomplice and am certain that John is responsible for the ills befalling Garrick. And, too, I know that Garrick has long believed Sir Gilfrey, as the queen's man, is the inciter of rebellion. What is more logical than that the knight use his own ill will to his advantage, supporting John for personal gain. I've no doubt his loyalties are shallow and easily bought.''

''Then,'' William startled the other two who'd nearly forgot him present, ''if John is responsible, 'tis necessary that we prove his guilt to Garrick so plainly that there can be no question.'' Under the others' absolute conviction of the prince's involvement, William had begun to believe.

Knowing the strategy of warfare if not the subtleties of politics, Conal suggested. ''As simple accidents have failed, no doubt John will use Gilfrey's rebellion to draw Garrick from his castle's safety, see the deed done, and blamed to others.''

''Aye, they cannot attack a well-defended fortress, dare not fight on trained soldiers' familiar ground,'' William calmly agreed. ''They must draw Garrick out without the suspicion that would see him accompanied by an armed force of size.''

The wicked plan was devastatingly simple and hearing it so unemotionally discussed sent a cold tremor through Nessa, as if a chill wind blew. Standing close, Conal felt the involuntary action, glanced to the side, and saw the outward sign of her apprehension in palm-joined hands against tender lips.

The mists had disappeared as they spoke and, deep in thought, William stared sightless at the ground now visible. ''As Garrick knows the danger, only a message from one he trusts could summon him without adequate protection.'' He paused and the silence was heavy with possibilities. ''A message from the king?''

''That in itself would raise suspicion as such communication must be delivered by one in the king's colors, a formal garb that they cannot risk falsifying.''

'' 'Struth,'' William conceded, lapsing into silence again.

Nessa stirred and broke the glade's quiet to venture a suggestion, ''Would the king's chancellor and son, Geoffrey, send letters through the king's couriers as well?''

Both men looked at her in surprise.

''Nay,'' Conal immediately answered, ''only official writs. He would send personal greetings with a traveler journeying this way.''

''You've provided the riddle's solution—again.'' William gave Nessa a broad smile. ''At least in part. And I can provide the rest.'' Relieved to have the near certain answer to who, he explained the how. ''There are ways and ways to 'borrow' a man's seal. Be the reward high enough, any number of people in the court could be bribed to find a method for using the chancellor's personal seal to close a parchment.''

Pulling her cloak closer against a day that had for her gone winter-cold despite full daylight, Nessa summed up their course of action. ''Lord William and I will watch closely for a message from Geoffrey or another in Henry's court. When it comes I'll find some way to learn its contents and send word to Conal.''

The baron continued the verbal outline from there. ''And I, with Swinton's men, will meet Lord William and the balance of Tarrant's garrison, at whatever site the conflict is meant to occur—where I hope to bring a surprise of my own.''

Hazel eyes questioned but Conal laughed and shook tawny hair. ''I may not be able to see it done, and I'll not speak of it now.''

''But what will be my part in the final act?'' Nessa questioned, determined not to be left behind to worry while others took the responsibility for a triumphant end to their plan.

''You we ask to pray,'' William answered without pause, ''exercise your special link to heavenly powers and beg the Almighty for success in our endeavors.''

Nessa nodded. Of course she would pray. She'd been praying for Garrick's safety since first she'd learned of his danger, and would likely not stop once this immediate threat was past. But it was not enough. She couldn't sit quietly home while others protected her love. Twice had she saved Garrick by her own action while strong but unprepared men stood near. She could not, would not sit idly while he rode into much greater danger. Their arrangement was no guaranty of Garrick's safety. Moreover, it left undone a task whose importance they'd all agreed upon.

''I doubt that halting the rebels in their deadly intent, though a rightly desired end, will prove more than the involvement of Sir Gilfrey. Surely cowardly John will be far removed from the scene and able to deny his part.''

" 'Tis shame for that cowardice which, if I am successful," Conal grinned, "will send the prince into our hands."

Reynard tightened the cinch on his horse—too tight. The huge beast sidled away and he felt guilty. Useless to take out his frustration with his wife on an innocent animal. Aleria had grown ever colder since they'd come to this great castle. In truth it had begun with their first disappointment, nay, with the first night she'd slept on hard ground beside the road north. It was too late for them. The dream was dead. He'd disappointed her, his mouth tightened defensively, but she'd disappointed him as well. Clearly her great beauty hid the shameful fact that no heart beat beneath it, else she'd have understood 'twas not his fault. Not his. He'd done all he could to see her well cared for, although beg from others he would not! His bundled personal possessions landed roughly atop the already abused steed.

Aleria flung wide the stable door, irritation marring her lovely face. She didn't like having to go in search of her husband. He ought to stay near, be more considerate of her comfort. A hopeless demand as already had he proven he'd no care for that. As she rounded the corner of a stall near the front of the central aisle surprise brought her to a halt. Delicate brows arched over azure eyes. What was Reynard doing? Going for a ride? Nay, couldn't be. A pack was loaded atop his horse. Breath caught deep in her throat. Was he leaving? Going without her?

She gripped the post of a neighboring stall, the only unmoving thing in a suddenly spinning world. Reynard meant to leave her? Nessa's warning that her selfishness would drive him away, would render a death blow to his love, sounded as clear in her ears as the moment it had been spoken and brought a pain sharper than any she'd known. Tear flooded eyes closed against the hurtful sight.

A gasp nearby shook Reynard from his preoccupation. Turning, he found a pasty-white Aleria, cheeks drenched, and didn't move. He'd not let her tears affect him this time. Too well he knew she wielded them as effectively as did a fierce warrior his sword.

"Don't go." Desperate words blurted out lacked Aleria's customary coyness.

Reynard stiffened, chin up, and refused her call. But when

324

Aleria stumbled toward him, he had no choice but to catch her before she fell. An unfair advantage for she clung to him with more strength than he'd believed her curvaceous body possessed.

"Please don't go, don't leave me." Her words were nearly incoherent, further proof of her panic.

Reynard gripped her shoulders, forcing her away, but couldn't prevent himself from responding, although the answer was not the one she sought. "I will no longer live on another man's bounty."

"But, Reynard," Aleria instinctively argued, "what choice have we? We cannot starve."

"I had rather starve than eat through no toil of my own." Dark blue eyes hardened as they swept over the confused speaker. "It steals a man's pride, kills his honor."

Aleria was at a loss to understand his reasoning. Having been cared for, indeed, pampered by others all her life, she'd never thought of it as a burden upon them. Rather 'twas their responsibility—her sister's most of all. Taking a hesitant step forward, she confidently assured him, "Nessa doesn't mind, truly."

"Nessa may not, but I do." Reynard gritted out his words between clenched teeth. "Moreover, her husband is not so welcoming."

Remembering her humiliating scene with the earl the previous day, Aleria nibbled at her lower lip while fresh tears spurted.

Believing his mention of the man had reminded her of her loss of the earl for mate and certain her sorrow born of regret, he took step back. "You are right. I am unworthy of you. You should have wed the earl when you had the opportunity. He would have given you the life you seek. I know you'll ever rue the mistake you made, and resent me for being its cause."

Terrified by the prospect of losing the man she loved deep down, she flung herself against his chest, nearly oversetting them both. "Forgive me! You must! I cannot bear to lose you. I'll willingly follow wherever you go. I'll sleep on the cold ground for a lifetime if 'tis the only way I can be with you." She leaned a breath away and, seeing disbelief in wary eyes, wrapped her arms tight around his neck. "Truly I will."

325

"Milady." A young voice piped from beyond the still open stable door, interrupting the emotional scene. "Need you aid with your steed?"

"Nay, Will," Nessa immediately answered, embarrassed at having been revealed as an eavesdropper. "But Lord William soon returns. Why don't you go and meet him at the bailey gate." Praise the saints the man had left her to cross the drawbridge alone while he called upon an old supporter in the village.

Nessa stepped inside, sheepishly meeting the eyes of the two within. Not wanting to intrude but unable to lead her horse away without drawing attention, she'd overheard their quarrel. "I'm sorry for the poor timing of my arrival." She waved aimlessly. "But, Reynard, though unintended, I heard what you plan and must ask if you've forgotten your oath to me?"

Reynard flushed but did not answer. In the heat of his own problems, he had forgotten and was ashamed of his error.

"As a knight of honor, will you not keep it?" Hazel eyes steadily held dark blue.

Reynard nodded, a lock of hair falling forward to lie in a dark, boyish curl against broad brow.

"We've spoken already of my need for your aid in giving the protection that, although he denies it, the earl is in need of."

"Whatever I can do, for your sake, I will," Reynard claimed, determined to make amends for having nearly forsworn his oath.

"Then stay, help me protect the man I love." Nessa glanced from the embarrassment-reddened face of the young knight to the pale one below. "Then, too—for her sake, not mine—give Aleria another chance to prove her love for you."

Reynard looked down at the woman nestling against him. No matter her failings, he adored her, had since she was a tiny child leading the young page he'd been from one mischievous scrape to another.

"Please," the teary-eyed beauty earnestly pleaded, thankful for her sister's intervention and sincerely determined to honor the chance. For the first time in her life someone was more important to her than she herself. It was a frightening fact, but not nearly so frightening as the possibility of losing him.

"But I am unworthy of you," Reynard repeated, his final cry in a clearly lost battle.

"Nay, 'tis I who am unworthy of you," Aleria gently argued. "But, though I'm certain to fall again and again, I promise I will try to change. Really, I will try."

Reynard smiled at this solemn love. "Then I'll try to learn patience, and mayhap together we can find the path to happiness."

Filled with gentle amusement at lovers' talk of worthiness, nearly a mirror of one she'd shared with her beloved, Nessa led her mare into a stall and tied him there. After a discreet time had passed, she'd send a stable lad to see her horse unsaddled and rubbed down. The two in the neighboring stall were so wrapped in each other that they little noticed as she departed.

❧ Chapter 25 ❧

For the next two days bright sunlight and the sweet scents of spring blooms mocked the gloom hanging over Castle Tarrant but could not break nor even lessen its hold. By the end of the second day, the sense of foreboding was so strong that even the lowliest inhabitant walked carefully, glancing over a shoulder as if some unseen foe stalked silently behind. Clouds began to gather on the western horizon in time for the setting sun to stain their edges a blood red that clashed with the violet washed sky.

At the high table Garrick presided over an evening meal so subdued 'twas if someone of import had died. All spoke in hushed whispers. No jests were heard nor laughter sounded. Not even a smile was seen. Clearly the whole demesne was aware that a confrontation was near. He only wished he knew how many of Tarrant's own would stand against him, for his father had warned that Sir Gilfrey had once more met with men from amongst their number—Sir Erdel one of them. Although confident of his own ability to triumph in open battle, Garrick's nerves strained under the cautious waiting for a stealthy assault which he, as a man of action, found more disquieting than an actual fight.

"Aye," Nessa's voice broke through her husband's preoccupation. "Merta will help us gather the blooms we then dry for scenting fresh floor rushes."

Garrick watched as his love leaned forward to quietly answer the question he'd not heard her sister ask. Amazingly, the beauty had settled into the role of loving wife. He'd no idea what had effected the change—his rejection or some further personal disaster—but hoped 'twould be more than a temporary improvement.

"Will we go early on the morrow?" Aleria questioned.

"Either then or in late afternoon, so long as we avoid the quick-wilting heat of day." Nessa gave a gently encouraging smile to the younger woman who seemed truly determined to be worthy as wife and mayhap one day lady of her own home.

"Whatever you choose," Aleria agreed quickly enough, but Nessa saw her crestfallen expression and her heart skipped a beat hoping the girl wasn't falling back to old ways so soon.

"I promised we'd go hawking if the afternoon is fine." Reynard saw Nessa's fear and hurried to explain Aleria's disappointment.

Glad that the couple meant to spend time together, Nessa smoothed their path. "Then early on the morrow it will be."

A blush warmed Aleria's cheeks, and she had to bite her lip to restrain an embarrassingly broad grin of pleasure.

Garrick was happy that Nessa had activities planned beyond castle-care. He appreciated any distraction for her all too obvious apprehensions. The waiting was hard for him, but he at least would be able to respond while she could only wait—and pray. Strangely, he had almost more faith in her prayers than his own considerable physical resources. After all, more than once he'd escaped mortal injury not by his prowess but by chance—or the hand of powers unseen.

It was a measure of their tension that although the hall was filled with members of the garrison, castle-serfs, and the well-born, no ear failed to hear the opening of the outer door. The silence was complete as a guardsman in Tarrant's gray and crimson appeared through the shadows of tunnel entrance, formally escorting a slender, elegantly garbed man. Between two lines of trestle tables filled with motionless onlookers which stretched from either end of the high table in a massive U-shape the guard led their visitor to a position directly below the earl.

Expression closed into a cold mask, Garrick nodded in response to the stranger's polite bow and lifted dark brows.

Standing relaxed and meeting the earl's chilly examination without flinching, the visitor gave the explanation so clearly demanded. "The chancellor sends you greetings and asks that I deliver this to you." A folded document of creamy yellow was produced from the folds of fine blue wool across a narrow chest.

Nessa swiftly glanced to the older man on her right. Mouth flattened into grim lines, William nodded. They each intently studied the seemingly innocent sheet of parchment closed not by the chancellor's official seal but by Geoffrey's own signet.

Forgotten was an instinctive distrust of any man so at ease in unfamiliar places, and a slight curl of pleasure warmed Garrick's mouth as he reached out to take the missive. He hadn't heard from Geoffrey since leaving Henry's court and amidst the tension rolling through his world, this reminder of an enduring friendship was welcome. On the point of breaking the folded document's wax closure, its possible purpose struck him. Did Geoffrey send news of Eleanor's plot? Did he warn of a specific threat? Nay, surely not. If he knew such a thing he'd come himself to a friend's defense. Of a sudden, strong hands held the parchment as gingerly as if 'twere a danger in itself. It was possible that Geoffrey knew his coming would incite immediate attack and dared not tempt such fate.

Nessa nearly moaned her frustration when Garrick tucked the unopened parchment beneath the wide leather belt about his waist. William unobtrusively covered palm-joined hands lying atop the table in too plain a sign of fear for the seemingly innocent message. If Garrick suspected they'd particular interest in it—in defense of a friend, however misguided—he'd be certain they never learned its contents. A task now this young woman's.

"I'll direct young Will to linger near the stairwell landing to your chamber." William's whisper was almost inaudible. "Then to me first and Reynard second he'll come before doing the deed." He squeezed the fingers in his hold before casually leaning back to nibble on a golden crust of bread.

330

Nessa relaxed her fingers but kept her eyes closed. Fervently she prayed that once in their chamber Garrick would reveal or divine guidance would show her the path to the facts she must know in order to set the plan for his protection in motion.

Her prayers were answered. No sooner had the meal ended than Garrick suggested they retire. When the chamber door had shut them into privacy, he wasted little time opening his friend's letter. Nessa sat unobtrusively in one of the chairs flanking the small table before the hearth, tension increasing. She realized that if Garrick had been less caught in his own concerns, he'd have sensed her anxieties. As it was, she watched black brows furrow over eyes flashing with silver warnings of danger.

Lost in his own thoughts, Garrick mused aloud, "I feared as much." He paced to the bed and leaned against one of the posts holding drapes aloft while Nessa gripped her hands tight together, afraid to breathe as she waited, listening intently. "He dare not come directly here. On the morrow. Hydatha's Tor."

"Hydatha's Tor?" Nessa whispered without thinking. The very place she and Lord William had met with Conal. Perhaps not so unusual as it was the only landmark of note in the area.

Having forgotten her present, Garrick was surprised by the sound and glanced toward the dainty woman so stiff with tension that she'd surely shatter if touched. He felt guilty for speaking of what had likely increased her irrational fears. "Nothing to worry you, sweeting. Only do I go to meet with a true friend who would never be a threat to me."

Nessa struggled to ease his concern for her with a sweet smile that failed abysmally. Aware of its lack of success, she turned her gaze to the soot-darkened hearth. To her stress-heightened imagination the fierce clash of orange and yellow flames which burst into showers of sparks seemed a demonstration of the confrontation only hours away.

After Garrick turned his attention back to the letter, Nessa quietly spoke, hoping her words would seem of little note. "In the excitement of our unexpected guest's arrival, I forgot to tell Merta that we begin gathering herbs early on the morn." Hazel eyes studied the man so absorbed in rereading his letter that he merely nodded absently, firelight gleaming over black hair. "I asked Will to bring more wood to Aleria and Reynard's chamber and should go to be certain he's remembered. Then he can take a message to Merta as well." Garrick glanced up as she passed him on the way to the chamber door, and she affected a somewhat more natural smile.

"Will," she called from the open doorway. Within a few moments, the sound of running steps was heard.

"Aye, milady." Will's cheerful voice carried to the man still leaning against the lord's bed.

"I've a message for you to deliver after you've replenished the wood pile across the corridor." Facing Will, Nessa winked and hoped the intelligent boy would go along with her ploy.

"I already fetched the wood, and so can take your message now." Will grinned at his lady's relieved expression as she stepped into the corridor and pulled the door shut behind her.

Voice no louder than a murmur, Nessa immediately said, "Swift as you can go first to Lord William and then to Sir Reynard. Tell them that 'tis Hydatha's Tor and on the morrow."

Will nodded as Nessa continued. "Most importantly, hasten to Swinton Keep, give the same message to the Baron of Wryborne."

Straightening with pride for the importance of his charge and the trust its giving demonstrated, Will again nodded. While the countess slipped back into her chamber, he hurried away on the secret task to be done in dark hours.

Dawn laid a dull gray glow across the heavily overcast sky, and as Nessa crossed the near deserted courtyard to the stable built against bailey wall she prayed the weather did not portend the day's outcome. It was dark inside the low-roofed structure. She paused a step within, and in the moments before her eyes adjusted to the gloom she listened to men quietly soothing their destriers and murmuring amongst themselves. Once clear vision returned she had no difficulty locating the one she'd come to wish Godspeed and safe journey. Dark head and black-clad shoulders turned to her, he was an impressive silhouette amidst lesser shadows—the focus of her world and threatened by what lay ahead though he'd never believe that certain truth. Palm-joined hands were pressed against soft lips, but her eyes never wavered from the man whose protection she implored the powers above to provide.

Garrick had checked the bridle and, as he patted his steed's nose, glanced over his shoulder to see a gentle lady standing quietly beside the stable door. With a wealth of silk-soft curls tumbling over shoulders and down the elegant curve of her back, in her dark green gown she looked like a woodland sprite borne on morning mists. He should be upset by the publicly unbound state of her hair, yet his will was stolen by the knowledge that the anxious woman had failed to do the deed in order to be with him once more before he departed. After a night of fiery delights during which he'd felt her desperate need for his strength and love, as if it were her last opportunity, he'd suggested she stay abed. No need for her to rise as early as he. But clearly she was too concerned for his safety to be calmed by his reassurances and was here to bid him farewell once again.

Bridles jingled as steeds were led past the waiting countess into the light of morn. Then came the sound of creaking leather as chain mail weighted guardsmen mounted. With most of the earl's men already ahorse, they were near prepared to depart, waiting only for Sir Erdel. Garrick had chosen not to leave the treacherous knight behind—indeed, meant not to let him out of sight—and was irritated by his habit of tardiness.

Aching with fear that this might be the last time she would see him all of a piece, Nessa watched her dark tempter approach with loving eyes, visually stroking each line and contour.

Towering above his wife, Garrick bent to brush a light kiss across her lips. Only as he straightened did he notice the crystal tears in soft brown eyes widened to prevent their fall. His dove, truly his symbol of love and peace. "Sweeting, I swear I will return by the time the sun is done with its day's journey. Geoffrey is no threat to me, and to protect me on the path I take a full complement of my men, all battle trained and tested."

Nessa dare not speak else tears would of truth overflow her restraints, but let him ride away with no more than a chaste kiss she would not. Standing on tiptoe, she threw her arms around broad shoulders and pressed her lips against his strong jaw, the highest she could reach.

Knocked off-stride yet again by the woman he'd hesitated to subject to such public embraces, Garrick's arms closed about her. Enfolding her within a strong embrace, he drew her near and nearer still as his mouth took hers in a searing kiss. The deserted stable's silence blazed with the aching passion of two who for tense days had lived on the edge of an overshadowing danger.

"My lord, I bring distressing news."

Though nearly lost in her desperate hunger for the man too soon going into mortal peril, Nessa felt Garrick freeze at the sound of Sir Erdel's mocking voice.

Garrick held his trembling love protected even as he realized that his tardy knight sounded more pleased than upset by the message he brought. He looked up to see Sir Erdel sneering at him from the open doorway no more than two steps away. Dark brows rose in question above eyes glittering with silver ice.

"Your guest, the prickly knight, is mysteriously gone." Erdel felt Reynard's action was the gift of an approving fate. Even should something go awry with the day's plan, he had a scapegoat to carry the blame.

Feeling the woman in his arms tremble at the news, Garrick glanced down. Nessa appeared to be the one distressed. But how else than that she be upset at hearing this proof of her brother-in-law's betrayal? Without comment and looking grim, he motioned Erdel be about his duties. Once the other man had moved away, Garrick stepped back to fetch his destrier.

Hands pressed tight together, Nessa stood to the side while the two men led their horses from the stable. She was certain that Erdel had imparted this last bit of information to sidetrack the earl from questioning his own late arrival. Without doubt, the moment Erdel had learned their destination, he'd hastened to the waiting Gilfrey's side. The plan for dark deeds was underway and could not be stopped although hopefully the conclusion would be far different than its plotters intended.

Mounted and at the head of a sizeable force, with closed hand against heart, Garrick nodded a departing salute to his fiery dove before motioning the waiting guardsmen forward.

334

Nessa watched them disappear into the tunnel through inner bailey wall, then spun to dash across the courtyard, up castle steps, and into the great hall with no care for her lack of ladylike grace.

"Where is Lord William?" Castle-serfs bustled around setting up trestle tables for the morning meal of those left behind and tried to hide the curiosity roused by their lady who gasped for breath while questioning Sir Rufus. As on her first morning in Castle Tarrant, he stood honing a blade by the light of the massive hearth though this time 'twas a bone-handled dagger, one from the pair he'd told her he shared with Erdel.

The white spikes of the aging knight's hair seemed an extension of his shock at seeing the countess so agitated. A shock that appeared to have robbed him of the words to respond.

Horrified by a desperate and wrongful impulse to shake an answer from him, Nessa crushed her hands together and forced a smile. "I've an urgent need to speak with him so, please, can you tell me where he is?"

Sir Rufus regained his usual composure and spoke. "If you needs him now, then I fears you'll have a time of it. He rode out hours ago, in the dark of night, and 'taint yet returned."

Thick lashes hid anxious eyes while Nessa fervently prayed for inspiration. In the plan laid out on the return from their meeting with Conal, she and Lord William had decided that as soon as Reynard had been told the destination, he'd go out to search Garrick's path for hidden traps and warn the earl before he could ride into one unaware. Already suspicious of the young knight's intentions, now that Garrick knew Reynard's whereabouts were unaccounted for, he'd never believe any word he spoke. Far more likely was it that Reynard would be found and harshly treated as foe. It was left to her to arrange an alternate method of ensuring her tempter's safety while worrying about the fate of the man endangered by fulfilling an oath to her.

"Merta? Oram?" After navigating past the lump of anxiety in her throat, Nessa's one word questions came out as whispers.

Sir Rufus cleared his throat. "They's both gone with him."

Nessa felt as if the breath had been knocked from her body. Why had her father-in-law departed in the night without telling her? Most importantly, why had he taken her friends with him but not her herself? She shook her head and heavy tresses danced about her shoulders, catching flamelight in each curl. No time now for questions without hope of answer. She'd only herself to rely upon and could afford to waste not a moment more.

Rushing out of the castle and back to the stable just as quickly as she'd come, she left a startled Sir Rufus and a great many others staring after her. Not bothering to saddle her mare, she climbed atop the bare back and madly urged the dainty creature into a wild gallop. Hooves clattered across the wooden drawbridge, then thudded down the packed track between green fields toward the gate in the outer bailey wall. Once beyond that last barrier, she turned her steed from the commonly used path, choosing instead the more hazardous but shorter route to Hydatha's Tor that Lord William had taught her a few short days past.

The gray sky offered little enough light and when Nessa entered the dense forest where towering trees blocked even its weak attempt, she was forced to slow the pace for fear of stumble-holes hidden beneath thick undergrowth. Though it had not rained for days, here where sunshine found difficulty in penetrating, the odor of damp earth mingled with the scent of spring flowers, details for which the woman, impatient with possibly deadly delays, had no thought to spare.

After an agonizing time, the nearly impenetrable woodland curtain abruptly parted to reveal a stone monolith springing from the center of a small but fertile meadow. She had arrived and apparently arrived firstly. The problem was what now to do?

On reaching the goal of an uneventful journey, Garrick was not surprised to discover that he and his men were the first to arrive. They'd set out early and doubtless from a closer point than his friend. So much for Reynard's desperate talk of hidden dangers along the way. Cold eyes full of silver scorn narrowed on the young knight trussed hand and foot and slung over his horse's back like a sack of grain for the mill. He'd no doubt but that the danger had been that selfsame knight and his ravings of imminent attack simply a last attempt to protect his own hide. Certain that the threat to his life was past, he had only to wait for Geoffrey's aid in defeating a poorly armed and poorly led rebellion. Having the key in hand to return peace to his land, Garrick dismounted and lowered himself to sit on the trunk of a fallen oak. More at ease then he'd been in a very long time, he allowed his thoughts to dwell on the gentle woman of soft, clinging curls and peach-sweet lips who turned to fire in his arms, melting the ice block that had been his heart.

Nessa was grateful that in her early years she'd learned to clamber into any conveniently placed tree to hide from Sir Gilfrey's torments or her father's anger. She peered now through dense foliage halfway up an elm, feeling helpless as she watched her love relax as a fighting man should never. What could she, alone and unarmed, do to protect him where even his fierce warriors were likely to fail? In the face of her fears for him, logic had completely deserted her, and she'd ridden into the wilds without a weapon of any sort. Of course, even if she'd had one to bring, she possessed no training in their use for 'twas a subject seldom taught to gentle-born girls and never to postulants in an abbey.

Prayer was her only hope. As she watched men at their leisure, bantering amongst themselves, ignorant of and, therefore, unalarmed by what surely hovered near, she fervently begged God and every saint she could think of to see that Conal and the men of Swinton Keep arrived in good time or, failing that, that she'd chosen a perch from where she could disrupt the plot. *I must have perfected the method for praying with open eyes,* Nessa chided herself. All too often her anxiety for Garrick had prevented her eyelids from closing while she sought heavenly intervention on his behalf. No sooner had the thought passed through her mind than once again she was thankful for the action.

A silent movement in the tall grasses and ferns on the glade's outer edge caught her attention. Breath caught painfully in her throat until she could hear her heart pounding in her ears, then whooshed out as straining eyes saw the source. Young Will lay shielded by tall green spears. Nessa silently gasped, and on rough dark branches her fingertips showed white. Had he never made it to the keep? The horrifying possibility nearly blinded her to newcomers hidden in the bushes clustered about the base of her tree—Sir

Gilfrey and a small, slender man with lank dark hair. A far more fearful sight.

The company from Tarrant had settled on the ground or were leaning against the massive upright stone at the glade's center, relaxing as they awaited the arrival of friends.

"You're fools!" From where he'd been deposited on the far side of the clearing Reynard's voice rang out above other's quiet talk. "Beware and stand prepared to meet the approaching threat."

"You are the fool," laughed a young guardsman, laying back propped on his elbows amidst lush meadow grass. "Think you there is still hope we will believe the witless claims you've been spouting for hours with no sign of truth?"

Desperation lifted Reynard's voice to an uncomfortable level as he implored, "If your leader will not take his mortal danger seriously, then 'tis your duty to protect him—beware—"

Wincing, the guardsman languidly rolled to his feet and turned to the earl. "I beg leave to muffle the howls of this irritating hound, my lord." Eyes twinkling with mockery, he approached his lord with hands clasped together below his bowed chin in the manner of a beggar come seeking alms.

Nessa's blood froze as, one last time before the gag was secured in his mouth, Reynard persistently repeated his dire warnings—impassioned words of the young prince and a vengeful knight, of rebellion to mask murder. The guardsman's foolery drew laughter from his companions, even a smile from the Ice Warrior. Indeed, he'd amused them all, all except the unusually nervous Erdel who tensely awaited the culmination of his long anticipated retribution.

Like an immobile tableaux in a Christmas pageant the four unseen observers watched while time stretched ominous and unending. Only when the stranger directly below lifted his bow and drew back an arrow pointed through thick greenery straight at a laughing earl did Nessa instinctively respond.

The glade's peace shattered beneath a sudden scream, almost simultaneously accompanied by the zing of a wildly shot arrow. Ignoring the missile harmlessly embedded in the trunk of a nearby tree, Garrick leaped up. The grunts and curses of an unexpected struggle came from a thicket of berry bushes on the forest edge. He scrambled toward the

338

sounds, followed by every member of his guard. Eyes shooting dangerous shards of ice widened when met with curious sights. Trying to shake from his back a young boy who clung like a limpet Sir Gilfrey staggered about but Garrick gave the two only a quick glance. His stunned attention fastened upon an all too familiar male figure lying prone and desperately attempting to disentangle himself from a small woman. Nessa would not release her death grip on the man's hair until, with a growl, Garrick jerked her opponent up by the scruff of his neck to hold him dangling above a badly crushed patch of brambles.

"Tarrant Beware!" At the sound of his family battle cry, Garrick swung around, never loosing his grip on the man futilely struggling against his hold. Conal was bearing down, unsheathed sword glittering above the tawny head he'd always refused to see helmeted without a full-scale battle in the offing.

Bewilderment brought Conal and, obedient to his example, the men of his company to a halt.

Concerned for the woman doubtless battered and bruised by her struggle on his behalf, Garrick hardly noticed the big man at the baron's side. Sir Jasper was the first of the newly arrived to dismount, and the earl thrust his squirming burden into the surprised knight's hands.

In her desperate struggle, Nessa hadn't noticed the discomfort of her landing. Only now that the baron had arrived to take from her the burden of her love's protection did she begin to feel the many thorn stabs and scratches torn across her flesh. She couldn't move without making it worse and with no thought to the paradox in her view, looked to the man she'd named tempter for savior. Garrick lifted her completely into his gentle arms, cradling her close while gray eyes darkened to smoldering charcoal said everything words could not in so public a place. Neither of them heard the men congratulating Will on a splendid defense as they tied a sullen Gilfrey's hands behind his back.

"Saints be blessed, we've been honored by a visit from our beloved prince," the baron drawled in feigned surprise from atop his steed. Golden brows ached above sparkling brown eyes slowly examining the subject of his words from rumpled hair down a narrow but expensively garbed form to the elegantly shod feet at last touching ground. "Garrick, I know you've better things to do, but take a moment to greet our royal guest.''

In answer, Garrick turned a gaze gone to ice upon the one whose threat Nessa had repeatedly warned him of. Under the freezing assault, John began to whine his excuses.

"Be quiet." Sir Gilfrey's disgust was a snarl. " 'Twas witless to attack while we stood alone. Still, they've not yet won, though they believe elsewise." Contempt and defiance met and joined in his tone. "We've a force of our own and will see them brought low, humbled by our might."

"This force?" Unnoticed in the excitement, more than two score men had arrived, an odd assortment of serfs and garrison guards led by Lord William and accompanied by Nessa's missing friends. With a mocking smile the old earl informed the slack-jawed knight of his error in judgment. "Thanks to Oram's brave completion of a dangerous assignment, I learned who you'd lured with false promises and spent the night calling on each—only to discover none of them meant to do your bidding." Pride deepened his voice as he added, "They know my son as a man far more trustworthy than you who meant only to use them to accomplish your deadly goal and then let them pay the price for the deed."

Gilfrey's shoulders went rigid and he glared through rage-slitted eyes at the man who continued speaking.

"Nay, even without my intervention they'd have allowed you to come, full of your own importance, and fall beneath the Ice Warrior's freezing power, answerable to his just retribution."

"I fear not, father." Garrick's voice rumbled from the chest below Nessa's ear. "Retribution would have been left to you had our royal guest been successful in his attempt but moments past. Only by my protective spirit, amazingly fierce for a peaceful dove, was he forestalled."

Gray eyes gone soft felt like a velvet caress to Nessa who hid peach-tinted cheeks in the curve between a strong neck and broad shoulder.

"My life was spared by her determined defense of a man who'd not believe and the valor of a young sir whose aid I will see rewarded." Garrick looked over Nessa's curls to the boy kneeling to free a wrongly trussed knight. The limp cloth of the gag he'd removed from Reynard's mouth dangling

340

from his hand, Will's pleased grin went undimmed by his attempt at manly nonchalance.

The attention of all was upon this satisfactory end to a long dreaded drama, all but the one whose frustrated spite welled into irrational fury with a man impossible to see die—until now! A low growl, like an animal in a killing frenzy, broke the warm peace.

"Your back, Garrick!"

Instinctively heeding Reynard's shouted warning, Garrick stepped to the side and whirled, dropping Nessa to her feet and shoving her safely away. She watched in horror as Sir Erdel fell on the spot where they'd been only moments past, the bone-handled dagger in his outstretched hand a duplicate of the one protruding from a spot between his shoulder blades.

A movement pulled Nessa's attention away, and she looked up to see Sir Rufus step apart from Lord William's odd force. Slowly he made his way forward to kneel in sorrow at his grandson's side. "I had to do it, my boy," he murmured to one who could no longer hear. "Your actions have now and always been a disgrace to family honor, to Tarrant." Age spotted hands tenderly tucked ruffled hair behind the dead man's ear. "But the blame is mine," he whispered in a broken voice. "I failed to teach humbleness for your arrogance, restraint for your greed and as the price for my failure had to see you die by mine own hand."

Though Nessa could not rue the action that had saved her beloved's life, still her heart bled for the grieving man. She moved forward and sank to the crushed meadow grass at his side.

While Nessa gave gentle comfort to the grandfather and prayed for the soul of the one beyond human help, Garrick strode to Reynard's side. The lanky man hesitated uncertainly at the woodland's edge, rubbing recently freed wrists to restore feeling in tingling hands, and warily eyed the powerful man approaching.

"I've wronged you in both thought and deed, and I seek your pardon—brother." Garrick extended an arm to his relative by bonds of marriage. After a long pause during which gazes met and held unwavering, Reynard grasped the offered arm below the elbow, joining forearms in kinship accepted and forgiveness granted.

341

"And if you are my foster brother's brother, then you are mine." The two men still clasped looked to the side and found the one who had arrived with the baron. Garrick laughed and with his free hand clapped the speaker on the back.

Tarrant guardsmen rolled Erdel's lifeless body into his outspread cape, laid it across his steed, and quietly helped their sorrow-laden captain mount his destrier. Nessa watched the worthy knight who suddenly seemed every hour of his age as he prepared to accompany the last of his line on the final journey home. Then a touch whose familiarity hadn't stolen its excitement restored a measure of warmth to her compassion-chilled heart. With his strong arm about her shoulders, Garrick turned her toward a tall stranger. For several long moments a narrowed gaze intently studied her. Though once her lack of confidence would have seen her cringing beneath so penetrating an examination, now she stood steady and returned it in good measure. By his graying fair hair and expanding waistline the man appeared at least a decade older than her dark tempter, but his face lacked lines of ill-humor, and he seemed not so much critical as merely curious.

"Nessa," Garrick announced with a proud smile. "This is the chancellor of England, Henry's son, and my friend, Geoffrey."

The unexpected meeting struck Nessa with sudden uncertainty. Did a countess curtsy to a chancellor or did he bow to her? Such niceties had not been deemed necessary knowledge for postulants. Before she had time to decide, the man lifted her hand and brushed a kiss across its back.

"Garrick's friend I am; and, I hope, yours as well." The broad smile accompanying his words was full of charm. "Clearly he is most fortunate to have won a protective angel for his own."

Nessa blushed. It was obvious that, in the time she'd spent with Sir Rufus, these two men had had an opportunity to share more than a few personal words.

"'Struth," Conal's ever amused voice broke into the silence between them. "He's been incredibly blessed."

The words not only deepened Nessa's embarrassment but also laid a tantalizing dimple at the corner of her lips.

"So, my unfairly blessed friend," the baron asked, "have you learned at last to trust a woman?"

"I've learned that my lady is an exceptional example. Honest, loyal, and trustworthy to perform any deed, she is a fiery angel, a dove of peace and purity—with the talons of a hawk—and mine always and forever." His dark velvet voice purred with satisfaction, and in the depths of gray eyes, silver flames flashed.

The entire company, including the one-time rebels who'd arrived with Lord William, returned to Castle Tarrant in time for an evening meal which became a victory feast. But first came another surprise, one awaiting within the impressive structure as Nessa, the only well-born lady amongst them, entered first. Even before she'd stepped from the entrance tunnel, her lips parted on an awed gasp. 'Twas as if some enchanted wizard had set to work in their absence, transforming the austere great hall into a thing of beauty. Intricate tapestries hung all about, their colors like jewels against whitewashed walls. Plain metal candlesticks and oil-fed lamps had been replaced with others intricately formed of silver and gold. Stunned hazel eyes moved to the dais where the high table was set with silver platters and goblets exchanged for ones inlaid with precious stones.

"Humor an old man, my dear," Lord William spoke softly in Nessa's ear. " 'Tis small payment for the life of my son."

Nessa numbly shook her head, feeling no more deserving of the beautiful ornaments now than she had when first she'd seen them in the locked chamber; but, with the whole company looking on, she could do little else but lay her hand upon the old earl's upraised arm and allow him to lead her to her seat.

As she settled on a now softly cushioned chair, William whispered, "The whole is rightfully yours for you are the true Countess of Tarrant and, like my Odlyn, as lovely within as without."

He reached for a chalice filled and waiting. Lifting the glittering vessel above his head, in his booming voice he called for the others' attention and when it was given solemnly spoke.

"Join me in a toast of gratitude to the one who has called us out from the cold darkness of earlier times." He paused and in the silence that followed let each man and woman mutely acknowledge what the sweet angel had done for them. From the serfs who'd found themselves in honorable service to one who cared up to their lords whose lives had been saved from their own chosen but destructive paths, they each had reason to praise her. "Drink to the honor of Lady Nessa, Countess of Tarrant."

Nessa blushed in pleasure, feeling as if her cup were in truth running over with the outpouring of love she could feel sweeping over her in waves. Every person within castle walls had risen to lift a drinking vessel high, and while those at tables on the dais and below held goblets, even the household serfs had been provided with crockery mugs to join in the deed.

After the toast had been drunk to and the meal was underway talk inevitably turned to the day's confrontation and all that had led to its being.

Light from the waxen candles clustered upon a silver platter in the center of the high table gleamed on black hair as Garrick slowly shook his head. "I still find it hard to believe that Henry loosed John's tether so far that the milky prince was allowed to visit the queen in Salisbury Tower."

Geoffrey gave a short bark of laughter. "He didn't. Only does he believe his son on a salutary hunting expedition where solitude and manly pursuits are meant to teach him right ways."

Dark brows rose and fell in a tiny shrug. Only love for an unworthy son could have led his wily sovereign to fall for so unlikely an excuse.

"Nessa warned me," Garrick admitted, giving Geoffrey a wry grimace. "But I couldn't accept its truth. And even Nessa thought John too craven to personally participate in dangerous games."

"And so he would have been," Conal interrupted, proud of his newfound ability to see treachery and turn its path. "But I knew Henry's youngest son was jealous of the oldest and so applied to Geoffrey. I knew your friend would work to see you safe from his little brother's treachery."

"And I," Geoffrey continued the story, "began a concerted campaign of teasing John that he'd never succeed in gaining lands or title except on the generosity of his father or brothers as he'd neither the cunning nor courage to claim

344

it for himself. Why, I said, even were he presented with such an opportunity, he'd be too cowardly to see to the deed done himself, sending instead another to earn it for him."

Garrick grinned. Both he and his foster brother knew the easily affronted prince all too well. "That, of course, assured John's presence at the final scene. But—" Garrick lifted his hands palm out. "—only after Sir Gilfrey had whipped the serfs to revolt so that they could be blamed for the deed." A renewed realization of how near he'd come to his end turned Garrick's amusement cold. Henry had sent him home to contain rebellion on his lands and would have found it easy to believe that he'd been killed by an unmarked arrow loosed by a mob of serfs.

"But they were fools, John and his accomplice," Geoffrey said, unaware of his friend's bleak thoughts. "Fools for expecting an army of serfs to perform at their call, then tamely wait to be dispatched into the eternal silence which prevents blackmail and betrayal. Fools, too, for believing the aid of their separate forces would hamper a hasty escape and increase the risk of blame later revealed—hence, their arrival at the Tor alone!"

Nessa had listened quietly yet still possessed more questions than answers. To distract her love whose cold tension she felt and wished to ease, she spoke. "John was there today and pointed the arrow at you, I know that for true. But what of other times? Who threw the first rock, shot the first arrow?"

Garrick looked down into the brown depths of hazel eyes wherein emerald flames burned, warming him again with love. He smiled, and with the tempter's power folded her near without a touch. When a small tongue flicked out to dampen suddenly dry lips, silver sparks ignited, and he found it difficult to concentrate on his explanation. "To meet their own spiteful ends Sir Gilfrey and his band of displaced men were responsible for both the flying rock and hunting mishap. But when, as you rightly warned, the knight met the prince, an unholy alliance was born. To cover his own greed and blacken the king in hopes of reward from the queen, Sir Gilfrey had been sowing the seeds of rebellion for years. Once joined with John, it became the perfect shield to hide the murder of an earl."

After his evening visits and morning ride with the common

men who Gilfrey and his prince had meant to see blamed for their deadly action, William felt more qualified than the others to give an account of the last participant and his part in the whole. "They hadn't counted on Erdel." Holding the attention of all on the dais, he went on. "Chafing beneath what he deemed an unfair lack of appreciation, he unexpectedly joined their cause. Still, the plotters thought they could use him to their own advantage, never expecting him to try to take the matter into his own hands by seeing the earl he resented dead himself while at the same time trying to win a prince's notice and displace Gilfrey. Hence, both the poison and the stone block from the parapet walkway."

William solemnly met his son's gaze and said, "With three men seeking your demise with all the resources they possessed, 'tis truly a miracle that you live."

Garrick's answering smile was grim until he looked into the soft eyes of his angel-dove. "A miracle whose source we know."

Nessa was thrilled by his approval but felt guilty for taking the credit when, her conscience insistently reminded her, never could she have done it alone. "As you once said, I've been so oft on my knees that I've accomplished little else. Nay, your safety 'twas not solely my, nor any other mortal's, doing but rather accomplished with a divine guidance which saw me ever in the right place, at the right time to prevent deadly success."

Garrick's words of apology for a wrongful accusation were forestalled by his father's quiet question.

"What do you intend for the murderous two? A knight you may punish, but a prince—beloved of his father—is quite another matter."

" 'Tis a knotty problem but one for which there is answer," Garrick replied. He motioned toward the two men sitting on his left, Reynard and Aleria having willingly made room for Conal and Geoffrey by sliding to the far end of the high table. On the journey home, while Lord William had ridden behind with the company he'd brought, the three friends had discussed this matter and come to a satisfactory conclusion. "The Chancellor of England, Baron of Wryborne, and Earl of Tarrant will witness and seal the confessions of the two men. Then Geoffrey will deliver both the culprits and their sworn statements to his father."

346

"And I am certain," Geoffrey added, "that within a fortnight they will both be far from English shores."

"Leaving for me only the responsibility of paying my debts." Garrick smiled as he rose to his feet, summoning the attention of the people lingering behind the much lightened tables below to enjoy a similar discussion of the day's events and happy end.

"Pray heed," he called out. "I've important announcements to make. First, and sorry I am to say it, a true friend who not only bided time caring for what needed special attention but worked with my lady to see foul deeds foiled, Conal, Baron of Wryborne, soon travels on to his own lands."

Like the wind through towering trees on a stormy day, a murmur of surprise and questions for the future swept through the hall.

"Thus, I must appoint a new castellan for Swinton." The words becalmed the room with a sudden cessation of sound. "My choice is a man who from its keep will be responsible for my wife's dower—and his own wife's as well. Sir Reynard de Gaise, my brother."

Overcoming a moment of surprise, Nessa leaned forward to stare down the high table's length to its farthest occupant. Reynard sat stunned with mouth open while Aleria threw her arms about his neck, her speechless state a demonstration of true joy.

"Thank you, my lord." Reynard squeaked out, then paused to clear his throat. "On my honor I'll pledge you my loyalty—if you'll accept it as binding."

"You've proven it already, and never again will I question your motives," Garrick seriously responded, then returned to visually search the room for another. At last spying his goal in a group of children at the very end of one line of tables, he issued a command. "Will, come to me."

The request raised a small commotion, but Will immediately obeyed. Once he stood before the high table, Garrick spoke again "You've proven yourself both brave and loyal—truly born of Tarrant blood—and proud I am to acknowledge you as kin. My father, your grandfather, asks that you be trained as knight. That I will see done. That and more. From this day onward will I see you recognized as my nephew and given the respect our shared heritage is due."

From the beaming boy Nessa glanced to Lord William's face where pleasure and relief mingled to produce suspiciously bright eyes. The risk she'd taken in bringing the boy to the castle had earned more than she dared hope.

In the commotion of a chair being placed at William's side for the boy, Garrick settled down beside Nessa and quietly murmured, "For you I've no reward of value, save a love and trust given and nevermore faltering."

A dimpled smile returned, under his influence becoming a common sight. "There is no greater gift than love and with love there is trust." She whispered, so aware of him that intimate memories wafted through her thoughts, bringing anticipation for the private world of shared nights. "Love is all I seek."

"Then let me provide you with proof of its depth and fire." Garrick softly growled, stealing her breath and invading her senses with the tempter's call to wicked pleasures.

Knowing just what he intended, she blushed but teased. " 'Tis early. We've yet to leave the evening table."

"Too early?" The smoldering heat in a gaze clearly able to burn as well as freeze fascinated Nessa, and she fell into charcoal depths where silver sparks flared. She slowly shook her head. "Never too early, nor too late."

Garrick stood so abruptly his chair rocked dangerously.

"Leaving?" questioned Geoffrey with a knowing grin. "When we've had so little time to talk. I thought we'd share the pleasures in a horn or two of ale and, until the night grows old, swap stories of past, yet glorious battles."

Garrick wrapped his arm about Nessa's shoulders as he looked down at his friend. "Ale is better aged and past battles are always available for discussion. Other pleasures are best savored without delay."

Oblivious to the cruel raillery behind, the earl and his countess crossed the hall and climbed the stairs to their chamber and shared pleasures both hot and wild.

❤❦ *Epilogue* ❦❤

In the weeks which had passed since the scene at Hydatha's Tor, life in Castle Tarrant had settled into a pattern of happily busy days, peaceful evenings with family and friends, and nights of fiery delights ending in a soft haze of warm content.

Thinking with gratitude of the wondrous gifts she'd been given in this home and this man, Nessa snuggled back against Garrick's strong form, appreciating his warmth from behind and the solar's blazing fire in front. Even summer nights within thick stone walls were cool. Aye, she'd offer her thanks to God and pray never to forget the wealth of good fortune He'd poured upon her—more even than any save she and Garrick had known—until now.

"I am truly pleased!" Lord William's hearty words were echoed by the hands he firmly clapped and rubbed together.

So involved with their news were those inside the small chamber that they'd failed to see either the door swing silently wide or the man who stood within its frame. Brows arched to meet tawny hair, Conal surveyed the joyous scene—Nessa blushing, Garrick grinning, and William thrilled. Never had he expected such juicy meat for his curious nature when he'd convinced the servants below to let him startle his friends by his arrival. He'd come with a surprise of his own but would hold it to himself until he'd learned the reason for their reactions.

"What is it that pleases you?" Conal asked of Lord William as he stepped boldly into the room.

The three already there turned in confusion toward the familiar if unexpected voice.

"We've received a letter from our king," Garrick quickly answered before the others could speak, suppressed laughter tugging at the corners of his lips. He knew his friend's curiosity well and meant to tease him in just retribution for arriving unannounced. "He apologized for John's 'boyish folly' and assures us that not only has he rescinded his hasty promise but, too, has put into the royal record that John can never become Earl of Tarrant. Moreover, as Geoffrey promised, John departed for the Continent in mid-June, taking Gilfrey with him as one of his traveling companions."

As Conal nodded, firelight glowed on hair more sun-streaked than when last they'd seen him. "Aye, I knew that the prince had been sent to put his talent for discord to good use in fomenting conflict with his brother Richard."

"The two deserve each other." Lord William's comment seemed to close the subject, and he eyed the visitor they'd known would stop by on his way between Swinton and his own home at Castle Dungeld. A trip and visit they'd expected quite some time earlier—but not tonight after the gates had been closed to day traffic.

"There must be more to please you all so well." Conal's quizzical brown gaze moved from one expression of repressed amusement to the other.

"We've heard also from the queen," Nessa responded innocently, restraining with effort the dimple beside her mouth which threatened to break free into a merry grin. "She reports having learned that Garrick had believed her behind the attempts on his life and swears by the Holy Cross that not only had she no part in such villainous deeds, but that—inasmuch as Garrick has given his care to two beloved foster daughters—so long as she lives neither she nor her sons will seek to ruffle the peace of either Tarrant or Swinton."

Garrick rubbed up and down Nessa's arms before wrapping his about her middle as he cynically added, "But note that she didn't claim to have had no part in spreading the

350

rumors once threatening to breed rebellion against her husband."

"Still, you do believe her oath to see us in peace so long as she lives?" Nessa tilted her head back against a broad shoulder and with full trust of a positive answer looked into silver eyes.

"Strangely enough, because of you, I do." Over the top of the luxurious mass of soft curls which Nessa had loosed in the privacy of their solar, Garrick grinned at his friend's surprise. "I know. You never thought to see me believe the word of any woman, Eleanor's least of all." At last he took pity on his friend's bewilderment. "Lest you think my wits have become completely deranged, 'tis only fair that I tell you we've another and surely more important block to such infamous plots as John's."

Conal took another step forward. Now they were coming close to providing an answer to the puzzle with which they'd teased his curiosity. He smiled in trusting anticipation.

Almost visibly swelling with pride, Garrick announced, "We're rejoicing in the prospect of a soon expected heir."

Nessa's dimple flashed and she beamed when Conal took her fingers, lightly squeezing them as he earnestly said, "You've my greatest good wishes for the health and happiness of both you and the small one you carry."

Conal looked at Garrick and offered congratulations to him as well before moving back, laughing merrily. "You kept me on tenterhooks long enough, but I thank you for sharing your secret, at last. Moreover, already have I had my own back. All this while I've kept one of my own." Tickled by their questioning expressions, he grinned. To the others' surprise he slipped out of the room leaving them staring at the empty door in confusion. Garrick had just stepped away from Nessa, intent on following when Conal returned—but not alone.

Dressed in secular garb of fine rose linen and white-blond hair gleaming like moonlight, Sybil moved immediately to stand before Nessa, eyes solemn. "Please, Agnes, be happy for me and not too disappointed by my choice."

Stunned, but quickly recovering, Nessa leaned forward and reached out to lift Sybil's tightly clasped hands. "I've come to know that love, whatever the form, is a gift from God; and by rejecting His gift, one rejects Him." She gave

351

the other woman a small, warm smile. Head tilted to one side, with quiet conviction she added. "Thus, there is no wrong in either your choice or mine."

Garrick found in Nessa's words the balm for a nagging discomfort which would not heal. A tiny hurt which like a small and seemingly inconsequential cut stung more fiercely than an open wound, the fear that he'd committed blasphemy by stealing Christ's bride.

Conal told Sybil the news of a baby; and, as Lord William called for wine to be brought so that they could toast the prospective heir and their friends' recent marriage, Nessa settled back into her tempter's loving embrace. She looked up, welcoming the gentle stroke of charcoal eyes, the banked silver fires in their depths. Silently they shared an awareness that they'd been blessed beyond measure.

Jude Deverayx

America's favorite historical romance author!

The James River Trilogy
____COUNTERFEIT LADY 67519/$4.50
____LOST LADY 67430/$4.50
____RIVER LADY 67297/$4.50

Enter the passionate world of the Chandler Twins
____TWIN OF ICE 50049/$3.95
____TWIN OF FIRE 50050/$3.95

The Montgomery Saga Continues
____THE TEMPTRESS 67452/$4.50
____THE RAIDER 67056/$4.50
____THE PRINCESS 67386/$4.50
____THE AWAKENING 64445/$4.50
____THE MAIDEN 62196/$4.50

POCKET
B O O K S

Simon & Schuster, Mail Order Dept. JRT
200 Old Tappan Rd., Old Tappan, N.J. 07675

Please send me the books I have checked above. I am enclosing $_____ (please add
75¢ to cover postage and handling for each order. N.Y.S. and N.Y.C. residents please add
appropriate sales tax). Send check or money order--no cash or C.O.D.'s please. Allow up
to six weeks for delivery. For purchases over $10.00 you may use VISA: card number,
expiration date and customer signature must be included.

Name_____

Address_____

City _____ State/Zip _____

VISA Card No. _____ Exp. Date _____

Signature_____ 388-05